McKensie Stewart

Deception

AN
EMILY GRAHAM
NOVEL

Tillman Publishing

Chapter 1

The family car follows the hearse along the peaceful tree-lined street of the cemetery. Emily extends her upper torso, positioning her nose to the cracked window. She closes her eyes as she inhales the familiar scent of fresh-cut grass; exhaling as she opens her eyes to the perfectly aligned tombstones. *All life ends.* Her eyes gradually move to the large green tent in the distance; her heart races, and beads of sweat form on her forehead. She tightly squeezes her eyes shut to close out the world. In and out, in and out, her breathing slowly regulates. She refuses to succumb to medication today. She wants a vivid memory of her mother, nothing clouding her mind. Emily's eyes pop open, surveying the passengers in the car, everyone preoccupied with their thoughts, not noticing her mild panic attack. She lowers her eyes. The stray piece of hair on her cheek she places behind her ear with her finger, the roots damp. Again, her eyes focus on the tent in the distance; the death of her mother so sudden.

Emily recalls her mother Doris's invitation for tea the day before her death. Emily knew it would include homemade pound cake or, as her mother called it, sweet bread. Emily skipped her morning breakfast, jumped into the car around eleven, and hurried to her childhood home. Doris did not disappoint—the moist cake, slightly sweet, melted in Emily's mouth; the hint of vanilla tingled her taste buds. Emily closed her eyes, savoring every bite, and sipped the Earl Grey tea to wash down the cake. She placed the teacup on the table. The plate, held chest high, gave Emily easy access to pick the crumbs with her fingers.

Doris sipped her tea, never looking up from her cup. "Why don't you go ahead and lick the plate? Surely you will get any crumbs your fingers leave behind." Her mother snorted with laughter. Emily smirked, lowered her head, and quickly placed the plate on the coffee table. She spotted one single crumb on the plate and used her index and thumb to garner it. "Would you like another piece of cake? There is plenty in the kitchen."

Emily laughed. "Maybe later, I will take a couple of slices for Madison and Connor." Who was Emily kidding? She would eat both pieces of cake before she made it home. Emily and Doris spent the rest of the afternoon laughing and talking about everything but nothing at the same time.

Tears form in the corners of Emily's eyes as she remembers the last time she spent with her mother. She opens her purse, pulls out her mother's starched white scalloped handkerchief, drapes it across her nose, and closes her eyes, breathing in the fresh scent of lilac, her mother's favorite perfume. Emily takes another deep breath, holding the fragrance in her nose a little longer, not wanting to let go of the memory. She folds the handkerchief into a square, places it back in her purse, but uses the tissue on her lap to blow her nose and dry her eyes. She searches the faces in the car. Everyone is still preoccupied with their thoughts; even the twins, Madison and Connor, are quiet.

Emily's thoughts take her to the last encounter she had with her mother, dissecting every interaction and conversation. *Did Mother know she would die the next day?* Emily raises her eyebrow, her back straight. Something did seem odd. Her mother had laid out on the bed the clothing she is wearing today. The handkerchief Emily is carrying today lay on top of her mother's favorite tan A-line dress, both pressed on the bed with Nana's pearl ring encased in diamonds. *That's right!*

Emily had carried a basket of folded towels to the linen closet in Doris's room when she caught a glimpse of Nana's ring lying on the bed. Emily placed the basket on the floor and slipped the ring on her finger, admiring Nana's exquisite taste in jewelry through the light shining in the window.

"Mama," she shouted.

"You don't have to yell. I am standing behind you."

"Can I wear Nana's ring to the Smithsonian fund-raiser next Saturday? The ring will pair well with the double strand of pearls Brendon gave me as an anniversary gift two years ago. You remember the ones?" Emily, engulfed in her admiration of the ring and imagining her outfit for the event, didn't notice tears streaming down her mother's face.

Doris sniffled quickly, wiping the tears from her eyes. "No, baby, I will need the ring this week."

Emily shrugged her shoulders. Placing the ring back on the bed, she picked up the basket, never questioning why her mother needed the ring. After all, Nana did give Doris the ring before she died.

Emily reflects on the ring conversation with her mother. *Mother always said she wanted Nana's ring on her finger when she died. Is that why she wouldn't let me borrow the ring—to have it laid out with her funeral clothes?* Doris had even placed her polished tan patent leather flat shoes on the floor next to the bed. *And why was Kyndall at Mother's house the day she died?* Why did the killer target the two of them? Did her mother know her killer?

Emily snaps her neck in Kyndall's direction; all the while Kyndall is staring back at her. *Why did Mother have to die and not Kyndall?* Emily gives Kyndall a shameful half smile, turns her head, and gazes out the window.

Brendon, Emily's husband, the senator for the State of Pennsylvania, caresses his wife's back. The two interlock fingers. Emily brings her soft lips to his hand, kisses the front and the back, resting his hand on her cheek. Emily's father died a tragic death years ago. Brendon and the twins are the only family she has left. Emily desperately needs a mother figure in her life. There is so much going on with the emergence of Julia, and she is trying to decide if she should leave Brendon for Julia or keep her mouth shut and live the life Kyndall wants her to live. *Can Kyndall be the person I can lean on for comfort? Can she be the mother figure I need?* She shakes her head from side to side. Warm tears slowly roll down both her cheeks; she dabs her face with the tissue. Brendon squeezes her hand.

<hr>

The corners of Kyndall's lips turn to a grin as she watches Brendon and Emily hold hands. She pokes her chest out, proud of keeping the family together. Doris's death is only a small hiccup in her dream of the White House for herself and Brendon. Kyndall closes her eyes, and her mind wanders to her new life in the White House. She and Brendon stroll from the Oval Office to the West Wing with the sun dancing on their faces. She stops, enjoying the fresh air; her white Tahari suit blends into the backdrop of the White House. Kyndall, conscious of all optics of her appearance, walks over to the rose garden. She inspects each bud until she finds the perfect rose. She takes in the sweet scent; she bends and twists the stem to loosen it from the bush and places the single rose on her lapel. She no longer blends in with the backdrop of the White House; she stands out. Kyndall adjusts her suit jacket and brushes her hair from her face, the television cameras snapping. She struts to the Oval Office to begin her day as Brendon hurries to catch up.

Kyndall's thoughts linger of her in the White House. She takes a deep breath, relishing her new life. Suddenly she arches her back; she strains her neck to peer around Brendon to examine Emily seated next to the window. *What am I going to do with Emily? I can convince Brendon of what he wants, but Emily is too independent. She is a hard one to crack, to control, just like her mother. Does Emily even want the White House?* Kyndall abruptly slams her back against the seat, places her hands on her lap. Her eyes wander from the back of the seat to the floor of the car to her outfit. She needs to gain control of her life once again. She spots a loose string on the right sleeve of her jacket. She twirls the string in between her fingers. Twirl, twirl, twirl. *Doris should have never meddled in finding Julia and the other baggage she brought along with her. Why Doris? Why?* Snap. She opens her hand; the string floats through the air and lands on the floor of the car. *I need to get rid of all loose strings in my life. Is Emily over Julia?* Kyndall's eyes inspect the left sleeve, searching for another string to take her mind off her crumbling empire. *What is the big deal? What woman didn't kiss a girl or have a relationship with one in college? I kissed many girls in college but didn't profess my love for any of them. Sex is sex no matter if you are with a man or woman; every woman explores their sexuality in college.* Kyndall scratches the itch on her leg, taking her mind off the rant in her head only for a moment.

Her eyes glimmer. What happened to her "friend" Amy from college? She remembers the night she and Amy did the thing where...Kyndall giggles. The eyes in the car divert toward Kyndall, the only person laughing in the funeral car.

"What?" asks Kyndall, shrugging her shoulders.

Everyone dismisses her and falls back into their thoughts.

Kyndall places her head on the headrest, her mind back on the issue at hand, the White House. If the news of a lesbian relationship between Emily and Julia surfaces, Emily will be subjected to a double standard. The American people will forgive Brendon for his indiscretions—maybe he will get high-fives in the locker room at the country club, but not Emily. Few people will offer support, and the whispers and negative public opinion will destroy her.

Kyndall promised Doris she would look after Emily and meant every word of it. She will not let Emily endure what she went through when the rumors at Temple surfaced about her. Kyndall clung on to Wellington immediately to debunk the speculations. She walked away from Amy and the future they planned together. Her heart isn't hardened; she knows what Emily will go through. Kyndall's fingertip examines the slightly faded scar on her right wrist. She still remembers when she tried to end her life. As strong as she is, it only took a moment of despair, the heavy burden of disappointing her family and the religious community. She took a knife to her wrist. Amy found her as she started to pierce the skin; the cut deepened as she moved the blade along her wrist. Blood drained in every direction from her veins. Amy rushed toward Kyndall after grabbing a dishtowel. She wrapped Kyndall's wrist and drove her to the hospital, pacing the waiting room floor while Kyndall was under the care of the doctor. After several hours of waiting, the doctor called Amy's name. She stood and walked toward the doctor. They took a seat in a quiet corner of the waiting room. Eager, Amy spoke first. "Is Kyndall okay?"

"Kyndall's wrist has been bandaged but she will need to be evaluated by a psychiatrist and held in the hospital for twenty-four hours to ensure she isn't a threat to herself."

"Can I see her?"

The doctor cleared his throat, rotated his neck side to side, relieving the tension, avoiding Amy's eyes.

"Can I see her?" asked Amy anxiously.

"She doesn't want any visitors."

"I brought her to the emergency room. I was the one who found her. Will you please ask her if I can go back?"

"Kyndall specifically requested you should not be allowed to go back and visit with her. I am sorry. She wanted me to let you know she is fine but doesn't want to see you."

Hot tears streamed down her face as Amy sprinted out of the hospital, never looking back.

Kyndall pretends she didn't care for Amy, but at times her heart aches for her. The weight of Kyndall's body is too heavy to support her she leans against the car door. She opens her purse and pulls out her compact to check her lipstick. Slowly she moves the mirror to her eyes, the crow's feet telling of the stress and secrets she carries. The dark circles under her eyes make her look hollow, almost ghostly. A chill travels from her head to her feet, and she shudders at the face staring back at her. Kyndall doesn't need to be reminded of all her evil deeds; she snaps the compact close and places it in her purse.

Kyndall diverts her attention to Brendon, one of the reasons it is so difficult getting to the White House. It should have been simpler. Intently Kyndall watches him. Brendon picks up his phone from his lap, smiling as he reads an incoming text. *Hi, I found your online profile intriguing. I would love to meet you, Andy. You are a cutie, xoxo Tiffany.* Brendon blushes as he responds. *I can't wait to meet you, too.* Kyndall watches him blush as he responds.

Here we go again. Who is he texting? He promised a month ago he would focus on his marriage and career. He would stay clean from all his toxic vices—alcohol, heroin, and escorts. I want to believe him, but he made the same promise many times over and look where that got us—dead bodies up and down the Northeast. Why can't he keep his penis in his pants? Gregory had rescued him from an apartment in New York with two escorts. Kyndall twists her lips, shakes her head in disgust. She shifts in her seat with her back now at an angle to the door and her stare pierces Brendon's skin. *What am I going to do with him? Is he capable of being President? He is getting increasingly reckless. Something must be done about Brendon's behavior and poor choices that jeopardize my dream of the White House.*

The heat of Kyndall's eyes on the side of Brendon's face burn his skin like fire. He quickly turns his head in his mother's direction, flipping his phone over. He gives her a weak smile.

Kyndall sharply lowers her eyes to avoid further eye contact with her son. He is a constant disappointment to her.

She squirms in her seat until she finds a comfortable position. Within minutes her head falls forward as she drifts off to sleep, and softly she snores. Sleeping only briefly, her phone vibrates.

One eye opens. Kyndall retrieves her cell phone out of her purse. The picture of the caller displays on the screen and her other eye flaps open, both eyes open wide. *Mitchell, great. The other ass that is destroying my life. What am I going to do with this bastard?* She ignores the call, shoving the phone back in her purse.

Chapter 2

The empty beer cans on the wooden nightstand rattle from the vibration of the repeated calls to Detective Oliver Hall's cell phone. He rolls onto his left side, slinging the pillow he once lay on over his head to shield him from the noise. *Ah, the phone no longer rings.* He slowly drifts back to sleep as his home phone rings. His right hand tightly secures the pillow over his head, and blindly with his left hand he searches for the ringing phone. He taps backward and forward; the back of his hand tips two of the empty beer cans over, and they crash to the hardwood floor one at a time, both landing on top of the empty liquor bottle. A reminder of how he spent so many nights, drowning himself in whiskey with his new best friend, Jack Daniel's No. 7. Jack, an encouraging friend, always urged Oliver he needed a little more even when Oliver knew he had enough. Last night was one of those nights. Oliver snatches the bottle from the coffee table, staggers to regain his balance. He closes his right eye to peer down the neck of the bottle to the lint-size drop in the inside corner. Oliver wraps his lips around the opening, tilts his head back, and the tiny drop of liquid travels the length of the bottle and lands on his tongue. Oliver smacks his lips together over and over; he barely tastes the minuscule drop of whiskey.

Jack snickers. "That drop ain't nothing, just enough to make you mad. You didn't have enough to taste my distinct flavors of caramel with added hints of spice, nuts, and a touch of smoke. That's how we distill liquor in Tennessee. Kentucky can kiss my ass."

Oliver giggles at his friend's language. "What time is it?" asks Oliver as he turns over his cell phone to look at the time.

"Why do you care? Time means nothing to me." Jack doesn't need a watch, nor does he care to own one. Drinks are poured in his honor throughout the day, every day of the week. "Man, the night is still young. You need another drink."

Oliver's eyes shift toward his car keys on the kitchen counter. Jack can only control Oliver's thoughts when he is drinking and says, "No, no, no, don't even think about it. You barely made it home from O'Malley's earlier tonight. Use the delivery app on your phone and get another bottle."

Oliver licks his lips. He can taste the Tennessee whiskey; his eyes barely open. Oliver slurs his words. "Shut up." Using the arms of the chair to steady himself, he methodically places one foot in front of another, finding his way to his bedroom. He tumbles onto the bed, adjusting his body slightly to place his head on the pillow, curling in a fetal position. Oliver falls into a deep slumber, softly snoring without movement.

Jack now stifled becomes bored; he leaves Oliver and moves on to the next empty soul who uses excessive drinking to get them through the stress of life.

The caller hangs up and calls back. This time Oliver, alert, answers the phone in a raspy voice. He licks his dry lips. "Hello."

Captain Adams screams in the phone, "You should've been at work over an hour ago!"

Oliver throws the pillow that once covered his head on the floor. He looks at his alarm clock: 9:45 a.m. *Where's Jack? He is usually dependable when the two of us drink. Why didn't he wake me for work?*

"I've been trying to call you for the last forty-five minutes! You're late for work!" screams the captain.

Oliver rolls to the far side of the bed and looks at his cell phone: eleven missed calls are displayed on the screen. Oliver begins to utter a word; the captain hangs the phone up before he has a chance to speak. Fully clothed Oliver sits on the edge of the bed, rubs his face for a minute as he gains his composure. He walks to the back of the bedroom door to retrieve his fedora. Oliver places the hat on his head and strolls to the kitchen and opens the refrigerator. He takes a gulp of bottled water, swishes it in his mouth to get rid of his beer breath, and swallows. Oliver opens the door to exit the house. His car is parked sideways on the grass, another indication of the night he and Jack had previously.

Chapter 3

Susan and Jim need a change. They have been in marriage counseling for the past year and have come to a crossroads: either they will end their marriage of fifteen years or start over fresh; move to another state. Jim calls their counselor, Maria Miller, to inform her of their decision.

"Hello."

"Hi, this is Jim. How are you?"

"I am well."

"The reason I'm calling is to inform you that Susan and I will no longer need therapy."

"Oh, why is that? There seems to be so much work that still needs to be discussed and…"

Abruptly Jim interrupts Maria in mid-sentence. "We have decided to save our marriage."

"Well, I am glad the therapy sessions are working for the two of you," says Maria, confused.

"With all due respect, the sessions didn't work at all. I am tired of putting your children through private school with these expensive session fees you charge." Jim chuckles. He has no idea if Maria has children; her office is clutter free with only her degrees on the wall.

"I don't understand. You said the two of you decided to stay together, which means you learned something about each other in therapy and wanted to fight for your marriage."

"I learned we need to leave this God-forsaken city and move someplace with a slower pace. Susan is a little hesitant about moving, but I convinced her the move is best for us. I went to the store, purchased a map of the United States, closed my eyes, raised my finger, and it landed in the state of North Carolina. It was settled that is where we will move."

Maria is silent as she intently listens to Jim trying to convince her the decision to move to North Carolina was random. He has apparently forgotten in his individual session with her he had confessed he met someone on one of those online dating sites. She lives in Charlotte, North Carolina.

Maria clears her throat before speaking. "Which city in North Carolina are the two of you planning to move?" She slides to the edge of her chair, elbows resting on the desk; the phone glued to her ear.

"Charlotte," replies Jim casually.

Maria exhales. *That smug son of a bitch!* "Are you sure Susan is on board with the decision to move?" Her voice rises one octave higher; she is still on the edge of her seat.

"Like I said she is a little hesitant about moving because she will be leaving her family and friends behind. I told her not to worry about it. I am the only person she needs."

Maria can hear the smirk in his voice.

"When do you plan to leave?"

"We should have everything wrapped up in New York by the end of next week. It is a blessing both of us have jobs where we can work remotely. We have the freedom to go wherever we want."

Yeah, just great. "It seems as though everything is so rushed. Do you even have a place to stay?" Maria asks with concern in her voice.

"No, the plan is to get the owner to sell and hopefully sign the paperwork on this trip."

"You are moving to North Carolina, and you don't have a place to stay?" *Jim, what are you up to? This doesn't seem well thought out at all.*

"The owner of the house hasn't lived there for years. It's vacant."

"If you want to move to Charlotte, why not find a vacant house? Where you don't have to persuade someone to sell if the house isn't on the market. That is a huge risk. What is so special about getting that particular house?"

"I have to have THAT house. It makes everything convenient for me." He corrects his last statement quickly. "Oh, I meant for Susan and me."

Maria intently listens to Jim, shakes her head. A moment goes by without a sound from the two of them. She focuses the conversation back to Susan, the innocent victim to whatever Jim is involved in. "Do you think Susan will want to talk to me before the two of you leave? The session will be on me," Maria pleads with Jim.

Occupied by his small win, he doesn't respond to Maria, so she takes a different approach. "I want to help her transition mentally, so she can be in a good place during and after the move. As you mentioned she will be leaving her family and friends to live in a city she never visited let alone lived in." Maria pauses for a moment. "Now I think about it, she has never lived any place outside of Brooklyn. She travels now and then for business but traveling and living someplace is different." Anxiously Maria waits on Jim to respond and uncrosses her legs at the thigh, only to cross them at the ankle, right foot over left.

"No, she's good," blurts Jim. It appears he didn't think about the option at all; he couldn't care less if Susan is comfortable with the move. This move is about him and his future.

Maria shakes her head. Jim's response saddens her; she isn't shocked but just sad that Jim is so selfish and self-absorbed. He had not grown from the therapy sessions at all.

"Well then, I hope this move goes well for the two of you. Please text me your address. I would love to send you a housewarming gift." Maria will send them a gift, but most importantly be there for Susan when Jim yanks the rug from underneath her. Maria doesn't know what Jim is up to but knows he is up to no good. She always thought Susan could do better; she has so much to offer, but Jim has always been emotionally unavailable to his wife.

"Thank you, Maria. Bye," Jim says in a hurry. He slings his tan overnight bag over his shoulders, runs to his gate. The gate agent is moving the doorstop as her final task. Jim runs toward the agent. "I can't miss this flight. Can I still board?" Jim doubles over, out of breath.

The agent secures the door and once again moves to her stand. "Do you have your ticket?"

"Yes." He shows the agent his e-ticket.

She scans the barcode. "Have a nice flight," says the agent with a smile.

Jim boards the plane and scans the seat numbers for his first-class seat. He places his bag in the overhead compartment and slides into his oversized seat. He takes his cell phone out of his pocket, searches his text messages from his lover for the address of the home in Charlotte to send to Maria as she requested. Jim hits send. All he has to do when he lands is to convince the property owner, Kyndall Graham, to sell him the house.

Jim moves in his seat to find a comfortable position. Once the deal goes through, he will have the best of both worlds, his wife Susan and his lover living next door. Jim closes the window shade, reclines his seat, and falls into a deep slumber thinking about his new life.

Chapter 4

Frederick parks the black Cadillac family car on the curb near the burial site. He jumps out of the car and buttons his black Brooks Brothers suit. He opens the rear passenger door for Kyndall, and the two exchange smiles as he assists her out of her seat to a standing position. Kyndall smooths the wrinkles in her skirt and tugs on her suit jacket, head held high. She projects the image the family hasn't fallen apart after the death of Doris. She is still in control; no one should doubt her ability to manage her family and the people in her inner circle.

The six pallbearers carefully carry the casket to the gravesite, resting the casket on the stand. They exit the tent and blend in with the crowd except for Gregory, one of the pallbearers. Gregory has a special place in the Graham family; he and Brendon were college roommates. After college, Gregory became useful to Kyndall with his advanced degree in Information Technology. Kyndall needed him to hack here and there, but when Brendon became a senator Kyndall needed Gregory increasingly due to Brendon's reckless behavior with escorts and drugs. Gregory waits for the family in the tent, rocking back and forth.

Frederick hustles to the far side of the car, opening the door for Emily. She steps out of the car wearing an elbow-sleeve black sheath dress. Her Coach black shoes match her handbag—simple, yet elegant. Brendon exits the car after his wife. Pearl, the housekeeper, and the twins, Madison and Connor, follow. The funeral director, a petite stout woman with auburn hair, escorts the family to the gravesite to their seat in the front row.

Emily, the first to approach the tent, greets Gregory with a hug and kiss on the cheek; she takes her seat. Brendon embraces his college roommate, Gregory, with a half hug and pat on the back.

Kyndall, following behind Brendon, kisses Gregory on the cheek and whispers in his ear, "Come, sit with the family." Gregory obeys his boss and follows her to the front row seats. He unbuttons his jacket and sits between Kyndall and Connor, his eyes vacantly fixed on the casket, not blinking, not focused on anyone or anything around him, just the casket. The words of the pastor ring in his ears, "For dust thou art, and unto dust shalt thou return."

Gregory thinks to himself, *Doris didn't have to die, but Kyndall wanted it.* Kyndall, sitting shoulder to shoulder with Gregory, feels his body tense, and she reaches for his hand. Slightly Gregory shifts his body and hand to avoid her touch. Gregory, a faithful employee, always cleans up Brendon's mess at Kyndall's request, day or night. *Everything I do is for Kyndall and her family; when will it be my turn to get what I want?* Kyndall reaches for his hand again, and this time he allows her to touch him.

Gregory, never taking his eyes off the casket, remembers the day Doris died. Kyndall called him for help.

"Hello?"

"Gregory, I need your help."

"You sound different. Is everything okay?"

"No, Doris stabbed me. The ambulance is on the way."

"Are you okay?"

"I am losing blood but should be okay."

"What? Doris who? Emily's mother?"

"Yes."

"Why did Doris stab you?"

"Doris interfered with my trying to get Brendon to the White House by reconciling Emily and Julia. That was not the deal she agreed to, so I went over to her house to make her pay. I shot her ass, and she's dead."

Gregory grinned. He knew Kyndall was a badass, but killing someone? He didn't think she had it in her. "What do you need from me? I am usually the clean-up man, but you have already done my job for me." The grin dissipated and his lips pressed together, making a single line. *Does this mean she no longer needs me to fix the family problems?* Gregory's survival in Kyndall's world only exists when he is useful to her. Knots formed in Gregory's stomach. He used his upper and lower teeth to pick at dry skin on his lower lip, anticipating his next move. Kyndall spoke, breaking his thoughts.

"I need you to act as a witness to the shooting by telling the police you saw the shooter run from the house."

She is thinking of it all, giving me direction on how to cover up a crime. Nothing left for me to do but follow orders.

"What is the address?" asked Gregory, anxiously entering the address in his phone's GPS, as he jumped into his SUV and backed out of the driveway. "I am leaving now." He hung up the phone.

Kyndall needs me more than she thinks. He beamed from ear to ear. Gregory wanted to obey the rules of the road for safety, so he put on his headset; connecting with the contact information for his adversary.

"Hello?"

"We need you at the home of Doris Massey."

"What happened this time?" Dennis sighed.

"Your girlfriend shot and killed someone."

"Is she okay?" Concern filled his heart. "Who did she kill?"

"Doris Massey, Emily's mother. Kyndall was stabbed by Doris but is okay. The ambulance is on the way to the house."

"Are you fucking kidding me?"

"Not at all. You know how she is about loyalty, Doris tried to get Emily and Julia back together. A reconciliation between Emily and Julia would ruin Kyndall's plan for Brendon's run for the White House."

"We always do her dirty work, but I didn't see this coming at all. I didn't think she had it in her."

"Yeah, you are right. Anyway, I will meet you at Doris's home. My job is to be a witness in the crowd. I need for you to do what you do on your end. You know, look pretty." Gregory chuckled.

Dennis ignored Gregory's comment. "What is the address?" He scribbled the address in his small blue notepad. "I know exactly where that is. I will see you shortly."

The two hung up the phone. Dennis sat in his car. The calm before the shitstorm that was about to come down over the death of Doris Massey, the mother-in-law of Brendon Graham, the senator for the State of Pennsylvania. And to add to the stink, Brendon's mother, Kyndall, was stabbed while at the house. Dennis shook his head while directing his police-issued Crown Victoria onto the highway in the direction of Doris's home.

Chapter 5

*G*regory pulled the baseball cap farther down on his head to shield his face as he approached the small crowd in front of Doris's house. Gregory was dressed in black from his T-shirt down to his black Chuck Taylor sneakers. If someone had to give a description of him, he would be an average guy who looked like someone but no one at the same time. Gregory's eyes moved from right to left scanning the crowd, and he made a mental note of the police car already on the scene. That was not his problem. Dennis would have to take care of the detective when he arrived. His job was to only act as a witness.

Dennis drove slowly down Doris's street, surveilling the environment. He frowned at the police car in the driveway, a small crowd in front of the house, the ambulance behind the patrol car. No available parking at the crime scene. He parked across the street from the victim's home. Dennis exited the car, slammed the door, and examined the mess across the street. A dead body, Gregory, a ruthless killer standing in the crowd, his pension already on the line for previous lies, not including what he had to do to get Kyndall out of this situation. Besides, how would he explain to the detective assigned to the case his presence on the scene? Lies and more lies he had to tell. He shook his head; the entire scenario made it impossible for him to fulfill Kyndall's wishes. He had two options: one, walk across the street and cover up whatever Kyndall had going on. Option two, get back in the car, drive to the precinct, give the captain his gun and badge, and walk away with his pension. He could live on the beach someplace. Dennis shook his head. He shuddered at the latter. Kyndall would never give him any peace. He would live on the run, never staying in one place for any length of time. Dennis took a deep breath, and his eyes found Gregory in the crowd; the two acknowledged each other with a nod. Proceeding with the mission, Dennis strutted toward the crime scene to the officer in charge, Detective Brown, his colleague and poker buddy.

"Hey, man, it's good to see you," said Detective Brown with a half hug and handshake. "Why are you here? I thought you were working another case."

"Yeah, I am working a case across town. I heard the call come over the radio and with this being such a high-profile case, I thought you might need help."

<hr />

Detective Brown carefully analyzed every word Dennis uttered. The emergency call was dispatched the same as any other call. It was only when Detective Brown arrived on the scene that he found out the senator's mother and his mother-in-law were involved.

"Yeah, okay. Thanks." Brown stared at Dennis. *Why is Dennis really here?*

"I will interview the crowd," said Dennis, not waiting on a response as he walked toward the crowd.

Dennis stopped, allowing the gurney carrying Kyndall to roll past him. The paramedic stopped, turned his back to open the door. Dennis reached for Kyndall's hand, their fingertips touching briefly. Then he drew back his hand and placed it in his pocket. He peered over his right shoulder and nodded his head toward Gregory. Gregory smiled.

Brown, skeptical of Dennis' story, continued to watch him. He didn't buy Dennis' story. Yes, he was an excellent detective, but who takes random calls when they are overburdened with their own caseload? And no one asked him to help with the case. *Who does that?* The hair on the back of his neck stood. The moment only brief, he caught Dennis touch the hand of the woman on the gurney. *Does he know the victim?* Brown pursed his lips together. His thoughts questioned Dennis' intentions. *You arrived quickly—did you have something to do with the murder?* Brown's eyes followed Dennis' movement, a slight nod toward someone in the crowd.

Brown scanned the crowd for something or someone that could be of interest to Dennis. His eyes stopped at a guy trying to be inconspicuous, the stranger in the black cap. He scribbled notes about his encounter with Dennis, along with what he just witnessed. Brown tapped his pen on his notepad, curious about what Dennis would include in the report. His eyes sparkled. This may be the first time he would be able to prove Dennis was on the take. For years he and his Brothers in Blue had suspicions but never shared their thoughts with one another. They all knew. For years Brown thought Dennis's detective salary could not afford him his lavish lifestyle and vacations—his house, located in one of the most exclusive neighborhoods in the Philadelphia. Poker night was always a treat when the guys met at Dennis' house. There were granite countertops and marble floors in the entryway. Brown knew he needed concrete evidence to raise questions about the integrity of a brother to Internal Affairs. His wife even dismissed his suspicions, saying he was jealous and should work extra hours so they could have the finer things in life.

Brown spit as he scowled in Dennis' direction, then turned to walk into the house.

————)(◍)(————

Dennis left Kyndall's side and walked to the crowd for the interview. "Hi, my name is Detective Dennis Jones. Did anyone see anything that will be useful to the investigation? Did you notice anything out of the ordinary?" No one in the crowd responded.

An elderly neighbor walked across the street toward the crowd using her cane to steady her steps. She approached the crowd and began using the end of the cane to push people out of the way, making a place to the right of Gregory. This position gave her the advantage of looking each person squarely in the face. As Eliza's eyes moved from person to person, she appeared to be matching each face with a house number and street—except the stranger standing beside her. Eliza with a piercing stare and bluntness asked, "Who are you? You don't live around here."

Gregory ignored the question and responded directly to Dennis. "Detective, I was visiting friends when I saw a Hispanic male, five-foot-nine, wearing a red T-shirt, bandana, and red sneakers, run from the house."

"Who were you visiting? I know everyone on this block," quizzed Eliza.

"I don't have to tell you who I know. Why do you care?"

"I care that you are lying, and I want to know why my dear friend died; I need to know who killed her."

Gregory grimaced at the small crowd as he turned in a small circle, his eyes observing the onlookers peering out of windows and standing on porches just to get a glimpse of the action. Most of the small crowd before him were using their phones as recording devices and videoing the scene live. Gregory's stomach churned. There was one body dead and another wounded. When would human kindness take precedence over the entertainment of posting on social media? They were cowards using the suffering of others to entertain themselves. Doris wasn't a coward; she faced her attacker head-on, even though she knew her fate was sealed when she disobeyed Kyndall. None of the onlookers were as brave as Doris, except maybe this nosy neighbor battling wits with him.

Eliza poked Gregory's foot with her cane; he broke away from his thoughts. "Who were you visiting?" Eliza stood her ground. Her neck craned toward Gregory as she gave him a sharp side-eye stare.

Dennis, needing to calm the feisty older woman, walked up to the two of them and chastised Eliza for doing his job. "Ma'am, I will do the interrogations. What is your name?"

"My name is Eliza Richards. I live across the street." She cut her eye toward Dennis. Beads of sweat formed on her upper lip as she told the story. She used her handkerchief to dab her lip dry. "I saw the lady who drives the fancy Mercedes visit Doris on numerous occasions. She was in the house for about twenty minutes, and that's when I heard the gunshot. *Bang.* I stopped my crocheting and immediately looked in the direction of the gunshot I heard. I picked up my cordless phone sitting on the table beside me and dialed 911. I waited on the porch until I saw the first squad car. No one ran out of the house, no one. I saw it with my own two eyes—that Kyndall is something else. I know she went over there to kill Doris."

"You can't throw around accusations." Dennis caught himself getting defensive and changed his tone. "Who is Kyndall?" asks Dennis agitated.

Gregory was silent, shaking his head at the fireball, Eliza, with disbelief. *Dennis has his work cut out for him with this lady.*

"The fancy Mercedes pulled in Doris's yard for the first time years ago. I had not seen the car before that day. Just as the car backed out of the driveway, I called Doris to ask who was driving such a fine car. She told me it was an acquaintance who offered her money, but she wasn't sure she should take it. I asked her if she needed the money; at the time I didn't know the amount. Doris said she needed the money. So, I told her blessings come in all shapes and forms and if she asked the Lord to intervene then he did." Eliza snapped her fingers. "Just like that out of nowhere her friend decides to visit and offer her money; that was a sign she should take the money." Eliza grew silent and shook her head. All eyes still on her, she began to speak slowly. "I felt bad after I told Doris to take the money. She was never the same."

Eliza dabbed the corners of her eyes with the starched hand-kerchief she kept in her apron pocket. After collecting herself she started to speak again. "I should have known something was wrong; Doris and I were friends for years, and we visited each other several times a week. I knew her like the back of my hand. When she talked about Kyndall, she became anxious; rocked back and forth shaking her head side to side. Like she wanted to erase something from her mind. You know me, when I want to know something I will ask, and I did just that. I was shocked when she told me she had second thoughts about taking $50,000 from Kyndall. My teeth almost fell out of my head. Doris didn't tell me why she needed that kind of money. You know she was a proud woman, so I respected her privacy and didn't ask. After that day Doris's spirit grew weary. She was quiet, withdrawn most of the time. You know I am a talker, but Doris rarely parted her lips when we had our tea. When she did speak, she talked about correcting a wrong she caused and needing to make it right. She said things would work out in the end." Eliza paused for a moment, gathering her thoughts, and swallowed hard to surpass the crackle in her voice.

Dennis and Gregory stole secret glances at one another. Gregory shook his head. *The small favor of acting like a witness just got complicated with this nosy neighbor, who is sharp, educated, and outspoken.*

Eliza picked up where she left off as though she never stopped talking, "I wonder if Doris was trying to make things right and that's why Kyndall killed her." Eliza chuckled. "The devil herself gets stabbed in the process of doing her evil." Eliza wiggled her arthritic finger in the air toward no one, but everyone followed it from side to side as she made her point about Kyndall. "God don't like ugly."

Impatiently, Dennis cleared his throat to gain the attention of the crowd. He was in charge. He dismissed Eliza's extremely long rant, avoiding eye contact with her. He directed the next question to Gregory. "Sir, I didn't get your name."

"My name is Sean Smith."

Eliza glared suspiciously at "Sean" from the top of his head to his feet. Passionate about not being ignored, she blurted, "He's lying. No one ran from the house. I know what I saw." She shook her index finger at *Sean*. "Kyndall killed Doris and somehow you both are in on it." She blinked several times, moving her head up and down, looking at Gregory and clenching her jaw.

Dennis had had enough of Eliza's accusations toward Kyndall and needed to get rid of her. "Eliza, I want to thank you for your statement. If I need any additional information, I will follow up with you."

Eliza didn't like to be put off and that's exactly what this detective was doing. She squinted at Dennis. "What's your name?"

"Detective Dennis Jones."

"Do you have a card?"

"Yes, I sure do." Dennis reached into his pocket, carefully slid a business card out of its holder, and flipped it in Eliza's direction, never taking his eyes off her. She snatched the card out of Dennis's hand. She turned to walk home and said under her breath loud enough for both Dennis and Gregory to hear, "I think you all are in on it." She shook her head. "I don't know why or how you pulled this off, but you all are crooks!"

Gregory, enthralled in Eliza's conversation, didn't notice the crowd had disappeared. "It looks like you got something on your hand. What are you going to do with her statement?"

"I will submit your statement as official and destroy her account. We need to keep an eye on her. She is the worst type of witness—boisterous and believable."

"What do you mean 'we'? I am only supposed to be a witness in the crowd. The old lady is your problem now." Gregory grinned wide at Dennis, used both hands to secure the ball cap on his head, and jogged back to his SUV two blocks over, leaving Dennis thinking about what to do with Eliza.

Chapter 6

O liver sits in his car staring at the front entrance of the precinct, officers scurrying in for roll call. *If I go in now no one will notice me.* He chews on his cuticle as he ponders his next move. Quickly he exits the car, rounding the corner to sneak in through the rear of the building. He swipes his badge, then takes two steps at a time to the floor of his department. He stops to catch his breath. Oliver hasn't been back to work since the death of his partner, Dakota Rose, and his wife, Sophia. Captain Zachary Adams issued him a mandatory month off with pay and counseling.

While on leave Oliver moves each day through the motions of a resemblance of a "normal" life; eating on cue, dressing when necessary when he leaves the house. Oliver hides his depression and excessive drinking from everyone, including his therapist, who recommended he go back to work. The thought of Jack lingers in his mind. Jack knows Oliver still needs him; Jack isn't ready to release his hold over Oliver, nor is Oliver ready to give him up either. Oliver licks his lips at the thought of a taste of Jack; he starts to sweat.

Oliver changes his mind of facing his troubles, reconciling his emotions, picking back up where he left off. He blames himself for not preventing the tragedy that killed his wife and partner. He places his hand on the metal door handle, ready to face his demons to start work. He takes a deep breath, but instead of walking through the door, he releases the handle, runs down one flight of stairs, stops on the landing, and doubles over to catch his breath. He paces in a circle. He can't face his colleagues; the last several months have been difficult. The last thing he wants to do is talk about his feelings; he did enough of that with his therapist. Even though he and the captain thought it would be a good idea for him to come back to work, Oliver is having second thoughts. He reaches in his pocket for his cell phone; he needs to let the captain know he can't return today. He isn't ready. The phone falls out of his hand on the floor, and he bends down to pick it up. As he stands, out of the corner of his eye, he sees Dakota, his deceased partner, motioning him to follow her. He places the phone back in his pocket, and she opens the door for him as he slowly climbs the stairs, hands on the rail guiding his steps toward the squad room. Dakota isn't dead. The image before him is real. She is wearing her favorite black Calvin Klein suit, black and white floral sleeveless blouse, and black wedge heels. The air is permeated with her signature scent, Dolce and Gabbana Light Blue. He knows Dakota is alive. He continues to walk up the steps purposefully. He and Dakota need to start their day. Dakota opens the door, and he walks through toward their office space, smiling. He will be working with his best friend. *Why did I waste so much time in therapy if Dakota is still alive?*

Oliver walks in the door with a swagger, fedora on his head, following Dakota to their desk. His colleagues stop him midway; he is a sight for sore eyes. They welcome him with pats on the back and friendly smiles. Oliver sits at the desk that faces his partner's, but no Dakota. *Where is she?* Oliver thinks back on his time in therapy;

seeing Dakota today was a coping mechanism to get him back to work, the place that gives him comfort. He would have never been able to step back into the office—the place he lost everything he ever loved—without her guidance. Dakota is his guardian angel, always looking out for him. He grins. She is something else.

———————— ((◉)) ————————

The captain, standing in the doorway, observes Oliver's crumpled appearance, his hair so oily you could fry a piece of chicken in it. Captain Adams shakes his head, walks back to his desk. He rests his reading glasses on the bridge of his nose, peering at Oliver over the top of his glasses. He scrutinizes his every interaction with the staff. *What kind of department does he think I run? He comes in late and doesn't uphold the integrity of the uniform, regardless if he is wearing street clothes. Look at him, clothes wrinkled. What a disgrace!* The captain throws his glasses on the pile of paperwork on his desk. *He better be glad I am in a bind and need his ass.* He shakes his head in disappointment, snatches his glasses off the desk, then places them back on his face.

———————— ((◉)) ————————

"Knock, knock," says Oliver at the same time he raps on the captain's door.

"Come in and have a seat, Oliver," says the captain, dismissing him by not making eye contact.

"Thank you, Captain. I just want to say…"

The captain sharply moves his eyes from the papers to look Oliver squarely in the eyes. "You don't deserve to say shit. You come in here looking like you haven't bathed in weeks. You reek of alcohol. And what…did you sleep in your clothes?"

Shamefully Oliver's eyes shift from Zachary to the floor, fixing on the mysterious stain on his left pant leg.

The captain yanks his glasses off, pointing them in Oliver's direction as he continues his rant. "You should be grateful I let your sorry ass come back to work looking like you slept on the street. I am telling you, you better get your shit together before I stop feeling sorry for your ass and fire you."

Ouch! The remark stings. *Does everyone feel sorry for me?* Oliver turns his head away from the captain to his colleagues milling around the office. The sound of the captain's voice brings him back to his pathetic reality.

"You need to look and act like you want your job. Go home, come back tomorrow."

Oliver sits completely still, waiting for the captain to cool down and change his mind; he wants his job, he needs his job, he wants to work today. His eyes gradually move from his pants up the front of the captain's desk to the frowning face glaring at him.

"Did you hear me? Take your ass home and come back tomorrow. I refuse to let you work hung over. Do you need someone to drive you home?"

Oliver shakes his head no, disappointed he let the captain down.

"Go. I don't want to see your face until tomorrow."

Oliver slowly stands, holding onto both arms of the chair as he balances the heavy burden of his pride that is weighing his body down. A tear creeps into the corner of his right eye; he clears his throat and wipes his entire face with his right hand.

"Captain, for what it's worth, I am sorry." The captain, engaged in writing on the document before him, never looks up at Oliver. Oliver slips out of the office and takes the stairs to not be seen by his colleagues.

Oliver sits in his car rehashing the conversation between him and Captain Adams. He isn't used to anyone talking to him in that manner. Oliver ignites the engine, places the car in reverse, and catches a glimpse of himself in the rearview mirror. He shakes his head at what he sees before him, a broken man. He has lost all respect for himself.

The ringing of his phone distracts him from the image of the hopeless man who stares back at him. He places the car in park and swallows hard to suppress the lump in his throat. "Hello."

"Hey, Dad, how are you?"

"Oh, hey, Angela, it's so nice to hear from you."

"Dad, have you gone back to work yet?"

Oliver reflects on the question his daughter is asking. He is too ashamed to recount the rebuke from his supervisor. Oliver's voice is a soft whisper. "No, no, I go back tomorrow."

Angela, a daddy's girl, knows her father's going through a difficult period with the death of his partner and her mother. "Dad, you know I respect you and what you do. You were the reason I decided to go into law enforcement."

Angela's encouraging words are what Oliver needs to raise his spirits. He feels the love his daughter has for him with every word. Oliver musters up the courage to divert his eyes back to the mirror, and the corners of his mouth curl on both sides, forming a resemblance of a smile. The light in his eyes twinkles, as his soul warms because of the love he feels from knowing his daughter appreciates the loving father and capable detective he is. The two end the call with Oliver knowing what he needs to do to make his daughter proud. He takes another glimpse of himself in the mirror, shakes his head, and drives slowly down the road toward the supermarket for cleaning supplies. He needs to get himself together.

Chapter 7

etective Hall's alarm clock buzzes at 6:30 a.m., and he hits snooze once. At 6:40 he turns the clock off and sits on the side of his bed collecting his thoughts. He scans the room, admiring the job he did the night before in cleaning. Oliver walks to the bathroom to take a shower. The hot water soothes his tired, achy muscles. He faces the shower, his head receiving the brunt of the water; with one hand on the shower wall, he lets the water drift down the entire length of his back. He shampoos his hair three times to remove the oily buildup from days without showering. Oliver, satisfied with the texture of his hair, exits the shower, dries his hair and body with a bath towel, and wraps it around his waist. Oliver reaches for the lotion and lathers his body.

Oliver dresses quickly in his black suit, starched white shirt, no tie. He adjusts his cuffs as he stares back at the image before him, proud, sober, a dedicated detective. Oliver quickly moves to the rack behind the door in his bedroom and picks up his fedora, brushing the top of the hat, removing any dust. He adjusts the brim as he places it on his head. He winks at himself in the mirror. On his way out of the door, he grabs a bottled water, locks the front door behind him, and walks to his car backed in the driveway. He pulls out of the driveway, looking both ways before he exits his driveway onto the street.

Detective Hall pulls in front of the precinct and turns the engine off. He takes a deep breath before opening and closing the car door behind him. He begins to walk toward the back entrance, stops, scratches his head, turns, and walks through the front entrance, taking the stairs to the third floor. Detective Hall opens the door to the squad room, strolls past Captain Adams office to his desk. The two make eye contact. Hall tips his fedora in the direction of the captain. Zachary smiles at the man he knows and respects, not only as a police officer but as his best friend.

Chapter 8

*T*he warm water rinses the soapy suds down the drain in a circular motion. Pearl insists on washing the dishes by hand, even though the Grahams have a perfectly good dishwasher. She holds the last glass to the light for inspection. Pearl shakes her head at the lipstick on the rim of the glass. "This will never do," says Pearl aloud for no one to hear but herself. She washes and rinses the lone glass again and holds it to the light for a final inspection. Her hand trembles; the glass shatters into tiny pieces as it hits the floor. Pearl's hands move to her mouth and she wails, her heart heavy from the death of her dear friend Doris. *Why, Lord, why did they have to kill Doris, a kind and gentle soul? Did the intruder want money or jewelry?* Pearl dries her hands and reaches into her pocket for her handkerchief; she dries her eyes and blows her nose. She folds the handkerchief and places it back in her floral apron pocket. Her arms stretch in front of her to support the weight of her body.

From the first day Pearl met Doris, they were inseparable.

Doris always treated Pearl like family and not the hired help as some of the Grahams' guests did.

Two days before Doris's death, Pearl on her day off visited Doris. They sat on the porch drinking sweet tea and eating home-made butter cookies Doris made earlier. In mid-sentence Doris pulled out her cell phone from the pocket of her gray sweater.

"Who are you calling?"

"I am calling Eliza to join us for tea."

"Child, don't waste your breath. You know Eliza is on her way over here. She sees everything from either the porch or from her recliner in the living room," said Pearl, pointing in the direction of Eliza's house.

Doris chuckled. "You are right but I'm going to call her any-way." Doris dialed Eliza's number and on the first ring she an-swered, "I'm on my way."

Doris laughed as she moved the phone from her ear to the side table.

"What did she say?"

"She is on her way."

"I told you." They both burst out laughing at the expense of their dear friend.

Pearl beams as she remembers the fond memories of Doris. She looks out the window, and her smile turns into a frown. Pearl, a religious woman, knows Doris's body lies in the casket, but her spirit is in Heaven, a better place. The thought dances in her head, *Why would someone kill someone so kind?*

The doorbell rings, distracting Pearl's memorializing thoughts of Doris. The crunch of the glass under her feet reminds her she never cleaned up the broken glass on the floor.

Kyndall, sitting in the living room reading a book, places it facedown and yells, "I'll get it."

Pearl hears Kyndall's response to the door and gathers the

broken glass into the dustpan and into the trash. Pearl enters the hallway and gasps at the sight before her: Kyndall passionately kissing the visitor at the door.

Pearl steps back into the doorway of the kitchen, peeking her head around the corner into the foyer. She has seen the pair around throughout the years but never put the two of them to-gether as lovers. *What else have I missed? Did Kyndall kill Doris?* Pearl stands in the doorway listening to the conversation between Kyndall and Dennis.

————)(◉)(————

"It's so good to see you."

"You too."

"What is going on with the investigation?"

"Nothing now. Gregory showed up at the crime scene and gave the statement you requested. He said he witnessed a male run from the house wearing gang colors. I suggested in my report it was a gang initiation."

"Good. How long will it take to close the investigation?"

"The captain just needs to sign off on the paperwork and the case will be closed by next week."

"What would I do without you?"

"Your little operation would not exist," says Dennis with a smile. He wraps his arms around Kyndall and gives her another kiss, but this time he twirls her around, placing her in a different position. Now Kyndall's back is to the door; she sees Pearl's reflec-tion in the mirror spying on her.

How long has Pearl been listening to my conversation? Pearl knows something, probably too much. I will have to deal with her later.

Dennis moves his hands from Kyndall's waist. "I probably should go. I just stopped by to update you on the case. Are you available for dinner tomorrow?"

"That sounds good." Kyndall gives Dennis a smooch on the lips. She opens the door and Dennis crosses the threshold, stops, and turns toward Kyndall.

"Oh, I almost forgot. We have a small problem with the neighbor who lives across the street from Doris. She is making accusations you killed Doris."

"What's her name—Lisa, Liz?" Kyndall stumbles trying to re-member the neighbor's name.

"Eliza, Eliza Richards."

"Yeah, that's right. She is friends with Pearl as well." Kyndall moves slightly to the left, discovering Pearl is still listening to her conversation. "Pearl, Doris, and Eliza were friends; they spent a great deal of time together. What did you do with her statement?"

"I never submitted it."

"Do you think she will be trouble?"

"I am not sure just yet. She went home in a huff thinking I didn't believe her, after getting into a shouting match with Gregory."

<hr />

I should have known Kyndall was up to no good. It sounds like she had Doris killed. But why, what is her motive? This is the mother of her daughter-in-law. The pot on the stove boils over onto the burner, catching Pearl's attention. She dashes to the stove, re-moves the pot, and turns the burner off. Pearl stands over the hot stove, head down and hands trembling. Her friend is dead, and she thinks she knows who killed her.

The ringing of the phone startles Pearl. She jumps. She turns and moves toward the cordless phone on the kitchen counter. "Hello."

"Pearl, this is Eliza."

"Liza, I was just thinking about you. Girl, you are going to live a long time."

"Well, I'm not going to live much longer. I am seventy-three years old." They both chuckle.

"You know what I mean. I was washing dishes and thinking about our afternoon tea, the three of us; you, me, and Doris."

"I miss her too. I can't believe the last time we had tea with Doris would be our last." The two of them grow silent, consumed in their own thoughts of Doris. Eliza is the first to speak. "I don't think Doris's death was an accident."

Pearl reflects on the conversation she overheard between Kyndall and Dennis. She knows her friend is right but can never tell her what she knows because Eliza will never let it go and end up on the wrong side of Kyndall. Maybe that's what happened to Doris; did she cross Kyndall? There is no telling with Kyndall and all her secrets and what she just overheard. Pearl sighs and turns her attention back to Eliza.

Pearl, playing along with Eliza, stirs her pot. "Why do you think Doris was killed? Who killed her?"

"She was killed by the lady in the fancy black Mercedes."

"Who would that be?" Pearl asks coyly.

"Kyndall, that's who," snaps Eliza. "I know you work for the family and know what side your bread is buttered on, but Doris was always unnerved after one of Kyndall's visits or even when she spoke of her."

"Go on with that kind of talk, you hear." Pearl moves to the kitchen door, looking up and down the hall, ensuring Kyndall isn't listening. Kyndall and the detective are still at the front door talking. After the coast is clear, Pearl proceeds with the conversation. "Kyndall gets on my nerves too, but I don't think she is going to kill me. That's who she is—a bitch."

"You're just sticking up for her. I called my daughter and told her Kyndall killed Doris."

"And what did she say?"

"Nothing. She grew quiet after I told her Kyndall murdered Doris. She is coming up here to check on me as she puts it."

Pearl laughs so hard her side aches. "You know that journalist daughter of yours will come up here and investigate you if you don't stop telling that ridiculous story and end up in a nursing home." Pearl's warning is in jest to her best friend. Pearl doesn't want either one of them to end up dead for what they know or think they know about Kyndall and her business. Pearl anxiously glances toward the kitchen door still watching for Kyndall.

"That's okay. You don't have to believe me. Doris deserves better. If it were you, she would not rest until your killer was caught." Pearl hears the hurt in Eliza's voice as she discusses their dear friend. She loves Liza too much and there isn't much she can do about Doris's death. Eliza weeps into the phone. "I have to go." Eliza ends the call in a rush without another word.

"Wait, Liza!" The phone line is dead. Pearl shakes her head. *Lord, I hope Liza don't do anything stupid to get herself killed.* She slowly places the phone on its cradle as Connor runs into the kitchen and wraps his arms around Pearl and buries his head in her midsection.

"What's wrong, Connor?"

"Mama yelled at me."

"Why did she yell at you? What did you do?" Pearl knows there are two sides to a story and never takes the side of the child. She raised too many foster children to fall for that ploy.

"For no reason. I didn't do nothing."

"You didn't do anything," Pearl corrects Connor. He may be upset but he is going to use proper grammar.

"It has to be something, Connor."

"I asked her why she is so sad all the time and she hurt my shoulder."

"Where, let me see?" Pearl inspects Connor's body, searching for bruises.

Emily drags her feet as she walks down the stairs and into the kitchen. Pearl steals a second glance at Emily as she opens the refrigerator for a bottle of water. *Did she not shower and change her pajamas from last night? It's almost time for dinner.*

———)(◦)(———

Kyndall closes the front door behind Dennis and makes her way to the kitchen. She stands in the doorway with her arms folded, observing Emily dragging her feet from the refrigerator to the table. She flops in the chair, draws her legs to her chest, wraps her arms around her legs, and rocks back and forth.

"Come here, Connor," says Kyndall. Connor moves toward his grandmother. She hugs him and kisses his forehead. "Go upstairs, baby. I will come get you for dinner in a minute. Let me talk to your mother."

"I want to stay with you." He hugs her tighter. She peels his arms from her waist. His head hanging down, he walks out of the kitchen and up the stairs to his bedroom.

Kyndall no longer bites her tongue. "Emily, I love you as a daughter. You need to go away for a while and heal. I don't take it personally when you snap at me; I know you are still mourning the death of your mother."

Kyndall walks to the kitchen table, where Emily is seated. "I know the death of your mother was sudden." Pearl sharply darts her eyes in Kyndall's direction. Knowing what she saw earlier between her and Dennis, Kyndall throw daggers with her eyes in Pearl's direction. The two of them fighting with their eyes, both refusing to blink. *Pearl doesn't know who she is up against. I am still in control of this house and everyone in it. Whatever you think you know; you better drop it if you know what's good for you.*

Pearl folds her arms, not taking her eyes off Kyndall. She can play this silly staring game all day. Pearl shifts her weight to her left foot.

Connor bursts into the kitchen. "Grandma, can I have a cookie?" Kyndall turns her attention to the sweet sound of her grandson, Connor.

"No, dinner is almost ready. Right, Pearl? You know that's why Emily hired you, to look after the family, which includes cooking." Kyndall wants Pearl to know her place, which is taking care of the family and not meddling in her affairs.

Pearl's smile disappears. Kyndall knows how to put Pearl in her place, an outsider and not part of the family. Pearl's shoulders slump as she walks toward the stove to obey Kyndall's orders. Connor brushes past Pearl as he runs out of the kitchen. Kyndall turns her attention to Emily. Pearl silent at the stove but within earshot quietly listens to Kyndall. "What if you took some time away to clear your head?"

"You mean go to a hospital for therapy?"

"No, this family doesn't air our personal business to strangers! You aren't yourself since the death of your mother. You should think about taking some time for yourself. You will need to be well rested to support Brendon's run for President. The media will scrutinize every inch of your lives and I need you to hold it together. You know to keep up appearances."

Emily is silent as she listens to Kyndall's proposition on taking time for herself. She sniffles.

Kyndall pushes a little harder. "I was thinking you could slow your pace and stay in a home I own in Charlotte, North Carolina, for a while. Clear your head so you can come back to be the best mother and wife you can be." Kyndall pats Emily's arm.

"What about the children? Who will take care of them while I am away?"

"Pearl and I will. We make a good team, don't we, Pearl?"

Pearl, who has heard enough, walked out of the kitchen

moments earlier; she couldn't stomach Kyndall's lies. Pearl didn't know what she was lying about but knew she was up to no good as usual.

The weight of the death of her mother overcomes Emily and she wails. Kyndall walks to the downstairs bathroom, picks up a box of tissue, and carries it to the kitchen table and places it in front of Emily. Emily, who has been crying the entire time feels guilty for yelling at her son, feels awful. This is not like her at all; she loves her children and would never intentionally hurt them.

In rapid succession Kyndall pulls three tissues out of the box, hands them to Emily with a flip of the wrist, not giving her eye contact. Emily takes the tissue, wipes her face, and blows her nose. She folds the tissue neatly over and uses the clean fold to blow her nose once more.

Kyndall checks the time on her Everose gold Rolex. *How long is this emotional drama going to last? I have better things to do and sitting here with this train wreck isn't one of them.* Kyndall stands and searches the room with her eyes for her car keys. She's had enough.

"I think it will be good for me to get away. I didn't know you owned property in North Carolina," says Emily.

"Chase, a friend from college, had a grand idea to start a housing community with walking trails, retail shops, food and entertainment on site. He called it Sweetbriar. I gave him seed money to get started and in return he built me a house and deeded it to me. I lived in Charlotte for about two years. I married Wellington, moved back to Philadelphia, and have been here ever since."

"Sweetbriar sounds beautiful. How many homes are in the community?"

"Well, Chase lost money during the economic downturn, homeowners didn't have the money to buy into a luxury development, so he stopped building." Kyndall's voice cracks as she talks about Chase. "I still have close friends who live there, Emma and

Harold; they live across the street from the house I own. I will ask them to keep an eye on you while you are there should you need anything."

"What about Chase? I would like to meet him. He seems progressive in how he planned the community all those years ago. I would love to talk to him."

"No!" snaps Kyndall.

"I am sorry if I was pushy, but…"

Kyndall cuts Emily off in mid-sentence.

"I am offering you a place to stay, not to ask twenty questions with me or anyone living there. Do you understand?"

Emily nods. She changes the subject. "Is the house empty?"

"Yes, there is furniture in storage near the community. Once you decide on a date, I can have the furniture delivered and they will set the house up for you as well."

Emily is silent as she reviews Kyndall's offer in her head. "Kyndall, I could use a vacation, like you said, to clear my head."

Kyndall, who has just spotted her keys, stops in her tracks. She didn't expect Emily to agree so quickly. *What is Emily going to do with the time away from her family and my watchful eye? Is she going to try to rekindle things with Julia?* Kyndall senses something is going on with Emily that she isn't sharing with her. Time will tell. Kyndall snatches her keys off the counter, adjusts her posture with her back to Emily, and says, "Be careful and discreet. You are a senator's wife and perhaps the first lady." She struts out of the kitchen, down the hall, and exits the house.

Chapter 9

The large oak desk swallows Chip's small athletic frame as he reviews bids for building contracts for Phase II of Sweetbriar. June, his wife, barges into the office.

"Honey."

No response from Chip as he continues to read over the contract, line by line with a ruler not to lose his place. Chip knows the trap he placed in the homeowner's association addendum which causes him to focus on every single line, word by word, of any contract he is considering. Once the residents were stunned by what they have gotten themselves into, they may have threatened him to get out of the contract; others saw the example he set and decided to play along until they fulfilled the ten-year contract. Chip hunches his shoulders to dismiss any dissatisfaction with his master plan.

"Honey, do you hear me?"

"What is it?" barks Chip, wanting to finish his review of the first contract bid by noon.

"I am going to leave in about an hour for Charleston. Mother called and she needs my help at the house. You know how she is when I haven't visited in a while; she makes up these stories to make me feel guilty for me to visit." June rolls her eyes.

Chip drops his pen on the stack of papers, leaving the ruler to secure his place, and stares at his wife; he can't believe the woman he loves is lying to his face. Did she forget she used the same story two weeks ago? June's words repeat in his head, *It's been a while. Who does she think I am, some fool?*

"Isn't Anita still working for your mother?" Chip knows the answer to his question. *Why does she need you? Anita cares for your mother and the daily chores.*

"If you don't want me to go, I won't." June fixes her eyes on her bare feet. She wiggles her toes.

"If she needs you, you must go, right?"

"Yeah, right." June walks over to her husband, kisses him on the lips, and turns to leave the room.

Chip reaches for her hand, and she stops, turning to look her husband in the face. Chip asks, "Are we okay?"

June steps closer to her husband, cradles his head in her hands, and gives him a passionate kiss. She pulls away, stares her husband in the eyes. "Yes, baby, we are solid."

June turns, and Chip watches his wife leave as she hurries to the door. *Where is she really going?* Over the last two months his wife has changed; she is often withdrawn at home, barely talking to him only when necessary. They both shared the same password for their phones, but June has changed hers; Chip can no longer check her phone. Even though she tells him they are solid, he knows June is hiding a secret.

Chip picks up his pen again and moves the ruler to the next line. He throws the pen on the desk, the ruler no longer holding his place. Chips places a call to Derrick, owner of You Can't Hide (YCH) Private Investigations. *Where is she really going?*

"Hello."

"Derrick, this is Chip. How are you?"

"Hey, man, I haven't heard from you in a while. What's going on?"

"I need a favor."

"Sure."

"I need you to follow June."

"Your wife, June?"

"Yes, if you are busy, I understand."

"No, I can take the case. Things have been a little slow lately. When do you want me to start?"

"Today actually. June says she is going to her mother's house in Charleston, but I don't believe her. I want you to follow her and tell me what she is up to. I will pay a thousand dollars for the day."

"You know that is more than my daily rate."

"I know. I just need answers quick. Thinking your spouse is unfaithful messes with your head. I obsess about this throughout the day and I can't concentrate."

"Man, I understand. That's how I felt when I lost my wife to the disease called infidelity. It seems everyone catches it every now and then. I am a private investigator; did she think I would not find out?" Derrick pauses for a minute and takes a deep breath. He caught his ex-wife in the bed they shared with another man after seven years of marriage. He is still mad about how his wife treated him. He was good to her. He wanted in his heart to take her back but couldn't uphold the ridicule from his friends that his wife stepped out on him.

Chip gives Derrick instructions. "June is home now. You can drive over here and follow her. She says she is leaving in about an hour to visit her mother in Charleston."

"I should be there in thirty minutes."

"Okay. Once you find out something, let me know."

"Will do."

Chapter 10

*E*mily walks into the bedroom. The floor-length mirror captures her image staring at her. The older she gets the more she looks like her mother. Warm tears stream down her face and she softly whimpers; slowly the whimpers turn into loud wailing. *Why, why did she have to leave me?* She flops on the floor, her legs drawn to her chest, her chin resting on her knees, rocking back and forth.

Emily suddenly springs to her feet, searching the room for her cell phone. Emily's chest is heavy, her breathing labored anticipating the voice on the other end of the phone. Emily flops on the bed, knowing the call will never be answered. "Hello, this is Doris. I can't answer your call at the moment. Please leave a message." Emily ends the call and dials the number again. The soothing sound of her mother's voice keeps her at peace. "Hello, this is Doris. I can't answer your call at the moment. Please leave a message."

Emily dials her mother's number until she tires. There is nothing like a mother's love. *Who will fill that void?* Restless, Emily stands, walking around the room biting her lower lip. She sits on the edge of the bed and twirls her hair. Quickly, she snatches the phone off the bed and makes another phone call. This time to someone who is living, someone who at one time gave her life when she doubted herself.

"Hello."

"Hi, this is Emily. How are you?"

Not wanting to miss a word, Julia places the call on speaker. "I'm good. Sorry to hear about your mother's death. I wanted to pay my respects but didn't think it was appropriate."

"Mother would have wanted you there, but I do understand why you decided not to attend the funeral." Emily moves the conversation in a different direction. "I don't want you to get the wrong idea or take what I am about to ask the wrong way, but... never mind."

"No, Emily, what did you want to ask me?"

Emily breathes deeply. "The death of Mother left a hole in my heart. I was thinking I could get to know Ian, spend time with him. I haven't stopped thinking about him since I found out he was my son."

"Dave and I adopted him, and we call him Stanley, not Ian."

"Sorry, I remember the name Brendon and I gave him at birth." Emily's voice trails off, leaving an awkward silence between the two. Emily runs her hand through her hair. She takes a deep breath and continues. "The death of Mother is causing so much confusion in my head. I know we gave Stanley up for adoption, but I want to get to know him."

"Your request is tough not only because of our past but Dave and I are raising him as our child. In a sense, we rescued him from the foster care system you put him in."

"Julia, this isn't about you; it's about me getting to know my son. And did you forget Dave raped me? Under the circumstances, I didn't know what to do, so I gave him up for adoption.

This decision to put Ian, I mean Stanley, up for adoption has all our lives in turmoil. Brendon was devastated; he turned to the comfort of escorts and drugs to fill the hole in his heart. Maybe Brendon and I can get to know Stanley and close the divide in our marriage. I'm not suggesting we take him out of your home but perhaps get to know him in a small way." Emily starts to cry, quietly wiping her nose with the back of her hand.

No matter how afraid Julia is of Stanley, she doesn't feel Emily has the right to see the son she gave up for adoption. "I don't think it is a good idea for you to have a relationship with Stanley."

"Will you reconsider my request?"

"No, my decision is firm."

——)((()))——

Stanley stands in the doorway intently listening to Julia's conversation. His name wasn't always Stanley. *I thought Julia and Dave were my parents.* His eyes blinking, his brow furrows as he recalls a time he didn't live with Julia and Dave. Stanley scratches the side of his face as he remembers both families, he lived with prior to being placed with Julia and Dave. He had another name, more of a nickname given to him when he lived with Ms. Gloria, his foster mother: MJ.

Stanley remembers Ms. Gloria, popular with the men. She had a boyfriend for just about every day of the week. Mr. Mason James Stevenson was the boyfriend who stayed over on Saturday nights, and he liked Ms. Gloria's other foster children but took a liking to Stanley, calling him MJ, short for Mr. Stevenson's first name. Mason couldn't have any children with his wife and looked to Stanley as the son he never had. Stanley beamed from ear to ear to know he was named after his idol. MJ, a young boy, couldn't tell time but knew the day and time Mr. Stevenson was supposed to visit Ms. Gloria. His favorite cartoon, *Tom and Jerry*, was on television. MJ moved from the far end of the sofa to be closer to the door, knowing Mr. Stevenson would turn the key in the lock. Today was no different. Ms. Gloria greeted Mr. Stevenson at the door with a kiss on the lips and a swat on the rear. He walked in the kitchen, placed his lunch pail on the kitchen table, and washed his hands in the sink. Ms. Gloria, knowing how to satisfy her man, had his dinner on the table waiting for him. The children huddled in the living room waiting for Mr. Stevenson to eat all he wanted before Ms. Gloria offered them dinner. All eyes on Mr. Stevenson as he sat at the table shoving steak, potatoes, and green beans in his mouth, coming up for air briefly to wash the food down with a gulp of beer. He let out a deep burp from the pit of his stomach. Ms. Gloria took it as a sign that he'd had enough, so she fixed plates for the children. "Come on, chaps, your food is on the table." MJ elbowed his way to the kitchen table to sit next to Mr. Stevenson. All of Ms. Gloria's suitors ate a well-balanced meal, but not the children; there wasn't enough food for them after she sold her food stamps for cash to purchase items like cigarettes and beer. Ms. Gloria placed a thick cube of cornbread and a tall glass of milk in front of the children. MJ's eyes sparkled as the food was placed on the table. Mr. Stevenson reared back, balancing the chair on its hind legs and picking the remaining meat out of his teeth with the toothpick Ms. Gloria handed him. Mr. Stevenson placed the chair on all four legs, stood, and walked toward the bedroom. He stopped, looked over his shoulder at Ms. Gloria. "Come on here, gal. Don't make me wait for your ass!"

"Stay in here and eat your supper. Mr. Stevenson and I have some business we need to discuss."

Ms. Gloria bounced toward the bedroom and within minutes the headboard knocked slowly on the wall, then rapidly within minutes stopped. The older children rolled their eyes at each other, knowing what was going on between Ms. Gloria and Mr.

Stevenson, but not MJ. His attention is on the cornbread on his plate. He savors every bite, swinging his feet underneath the table. The last time MJ had eaten was the day before at breakfast when Mr. Evans, Ms. Gloria's other friend, didn't eat all his food because of a toothache. MJ, the youngest but the quickest, snatched the homemade butter biscuit from Mr. Evans' plate within seconds of him leaving the kitchen table to examine his tooth in the bathroom mirror. MJ devoured the biscuit with three large bites; he was starved and couldn't think of the last meal he had prior to stealing the biscuit. MJ used the back of his hand to clean his mouth just as Mr. Evans came back to the table to finish his breakfast, chewing slowly on the left side of his mouth to avoid the bad tooth on the right. MJ sat on the floor beside Mr. Evans' chair, just in case he left the table again. Mr. Evans was nice, but MJ was fond of Mr. Stevenson, not because he gave him his name, but he would bring him gifts when it wasn't his birthday. On this Saturday, Mr. Stevenson brought MJ a coloring book and crayons. MJ used every color in the small crayon box, ensuring he was coloring inside the lines to impress Mr. Stevenson. He inspected his coloring, smiled, moved from a kneeling position on the floor to sitting on the edge of the tattered sofa with his colored picture anxiously waiting for Ms. Gloria and Mr. Stevenson to finish their conversation in the bedroom as they had every time he came over. MJ watched the bedroom door, the thick plastic chair cover crinkling under MJ as he squirmed in his seat. Finally, the bedroom door swung open, and MJ beamed. Mr. Stevenson walked out of the bedroom to the bathroom across the hall in his underwear and wife beater T-shirt and closed the door behind him.

Ms. Gloria left the bedroom in a floral satin robe. "Honey, I will bring you a slice of the red velvet cake I baked earlier." Obviously, a remark for Mr. Stevenson as the children barely got a meal, and dessert was out of the question.

"Okay, baby," shouted Mr. Stevenson as he left the bathroom and walked to the bedroom. On his tiptoes MJ snuck to the bedroom door, peering into the room. Mr. Stevenson, smoking one of Ms. Gloria's cigarettes, took a puff, blowing rings in the air. With admiration in his eyes, MJ opened his fingers, pretending to hold a cigarette, and motioned with his mouth, blowing imaginary smoke rings into the air. Mr. Stevenson caught MJ mimicking him; he smiled, and the shine of his gold tooth sparkled in the light. "Lil man, come here. You want me to teach you to be a man?" MJ nodded his head eagerly. Mr. Stevenson let the cigarette rest in between his lips, his hands free to grab the .38 pistol resting in his shoe, where he placed it when he took it out of his waistband before he made love to Ms. Gloria. He opened the barrel of the gun, removing the bullets. MJ ran over to Mr. Stevenson. "Let me hold it, let me hold it," said MJ as he jumped up and down. The metal was cold to the touch, heavy for a boy his age to hold on his own. MJ's arm stretched in front of him; Mr. Stevenson steadied the gun in front of MJ. MJ, wanting to be a man like Mr. Stevenson, yelled, "Let it go, I got it."

"Okay, little man. You got it, are you sure?"

"Yes, let go." MJ moved away from Mr. Stevenson to show him he could carry the weight of the gun in his tiny hands. MJ, holding the gun in front of him, turned his head toward Mr. Stevenson. "I told you I got it." As MJ turned his body around, his finger slipped on the trigger and the lone bullet in the chamber slowly and effortlessly traveled from the gun to Ms. Gloria as she walked through the door with Mr. Stevenson's large slice of red velvet cake.

The cake along with the plate tumbled out of Ms. Gloria's hand as she fell to her knees, holding the place where the bullet pierced her body, her stomach. It is funny how things work out with her starving MJ and the seven foster children often days at a time. The doctor reported she would live but would never be able to eat solid food again. After the incident, Ms. Gloria lost custody of all the foster children, including MJ. It was to MJ's benefit because Ms. Gloria couldn't stand the sight of him. All the foster children gone, Ms. Gloria no longer had income coming into the home and she went to live with her mother until she died from an infection she caught from the filthy conditions of her mother's home.

MJ couldn't get a break. The foster home where he was placed before Julia and Dave adopted him was worse than living with Ms. Gloria. When Julia and Dave expressed an interest in adopting MJ, the social worker decided not to disclose the horror MJ experienced growing up. She had just finished her master's degree and was seeking a promotion and needed a high family placement rate for the children assigned to her. She worked overtime getting MJ placed with Julia and Dave, changing Ian's name to Stanley, a request from Dave.

Out of the corner of his eyes, Stanley spots Dave walking down the hall toward him with a smirk on his face. Stanley, standing outside of Julia's door, starts to walk up the hall. Dave stops midway in the hall, waits for Stanley to meet him in the middle of the hallway.

"It's not nice to eavesdrop," says Dave.

Stanley gives Dave the evil eye as he continues to walk away past him.

Dave, curious, wanting to know why Stanley was eavesdropping, turns around to ensure Stanley is nowhere to be seen and then walks down the hall and takes the same position as his son.

He hears Julia say, "Okay, we can schedule some time for you to see Stanley."

Dave immediately rushes into the room, shouting, "Are you talking to Emily? Can I talk to her?"

"Yes, and no you can't speak with her."

Dave stands in front of Julia, pondering how he can convince Julia to give him the phone. "I want to talk to Emily about Stanley." Dave attempts to reach past Julia who is sitting in the chaise. She stands, snatching the phone off the end table. Dave moves to the left; Julia moves to the right. "I want to speak with Emily," says Dave impatiently.

Emily, hearing the commotion in the background, shouts Julia's name repeatedly. "Julia, Julia, is everything all right?" No response. "Hello, hello."

Julia, tired of fighting with her husband, gives in and hands her husband the phone. "Emily, this is Dave."

"Hello, Emily."

Emily hangs up the phone.

Dave stares at the phone confused. "Why did she hang up on me?"

"Really, Dave? She doesn't ever want to talk to you because you raped her."

Dave pauses for a moment, thinks about what Julia said. "No, it must have been a bad connection. She never would have hung up on me. I love her."

Julia rolls her eyes. "Whatever, Dave."

<hr />

Stanley, in the kitchen making himself a turkey sandwich, hears the commotion from his parents' bedroom. He takes a bite out of the sandwich while tiptoeing down the hall to resume the position he held outside his parents' door earlier, before the bastard Dave pissed him off. He leans against the wall, takes another bite of his sandwich as he alertly listens to the conversation between Julia and Dave. *Dave raped Emily? Why is Julia with him if she knows what he did to Emily? It seems as though Julia and Emily are friends.* He's learned Emily is his biological mother and now this; no wonder he can't stand Dave. Stanley fumes to himself, and his chest rises and falls. The reason he isn't with his mother is because Dave raped her. He spent so many years in foster care being mistreated. Stanley's mind drifts to the picture of Emily on Dave's side of the bed. She is pretty. He smiles to himself. *If Emily is my mother, maybe I can live with her.* The crash of the lamp on the floor turns his attention back to the fight between Julia and Dave. How can Dave disrespect Julia by saying he loves another woman? Julia doesn't deserve to be treated this way. She is a caring and loving person. Dave will pay for his actions; he will never touch Emily or Julia again. If it is the last thing he does, Dave will pay.

Chapter ii

The light of the lamp illuminates Eliza's bedroom as she reads *Death in the Afternoon*, by Ernest Hemingway. *Thump*. Her eyes leave the pages of the book, and she lays the book down with the spine upright. Her body rises from the pillows stacked behind her back. Her ears perk up. Silence. She pauses, intently listening for the sound again. Several minutes go by and nothing. Her back rests on the pillows; she flips the book over, scans the page. Her eyes pick up where she left off. It doesn't matter if Eliza finds her exact place. She has read the book many times over. *Thump*. Eliza places the book on the bed, throws the bedcovers back, swings her legs to the side of the bed. She slides her feet in her sheepskin bedroom slippers.

"Come on, Buddy, let's go!" Eliza says aloud. Eliza follows the noise to the bedroom her deceased husband, Emit, used before the tragedy that shattered their marriage. She enters the room without turning on the lights, walks to the window, stands to the left of the nightstand, and peers through the blinds with Buddy by her side patiently waiting. She looks over the view of the yard but doesn't see anyone. *Thump.* The thud of the ladder on the side of the house draws her attention below. A man climbing the ladder, rung by rung.

Eliza shouts, "If you know what is good for you, you will go and try to break in someone else's house. Me and Buddy only expect company through the front door, not the window, which means you are up to no good."

Eliza steps back from the window and places her right foot in front of the left to steady her balance. She snatches Buddy from the side of the nightstand, cocks the double-barrel shotgun, and points it in the direction of the window. The intruder, having used a shotgun a time or two, stops cold in his tracks, slowly descends the ladder, and runs through the yard to his SUV, the same place he parked it earlier in the week. He should have stayed out of it, but he needed a win in Kyndall's eyes more than sticking it to Dennis. He speeds off down the street toward his home.

Chapter 12

Eliza carries Buddy across her chest into the living room with both hands. She rests the gun on the side of the battered leather recliner. She uses her right hand twists the lamp on, and the low light illuminates the tiny room. She opens the drawer to the end table and finds the business card for Detective Dennis Jones. Eliza stares at the business card of the detective she met earlier in the week. *Something just doesn't sit right. Who was the person at my window?* With hesitation she calls the number.

"Hello?"

"Is this Dennis Jones?"

"No, ma'am, he left at five o'clock," says Sebastian as he glances at his watch. "I am the detective on duty. Sebastian Glover."

"I want to talk to Dennis Jones," demands Eliza.

"Ma'am, what is your name?"

Eliza dryly responds, "Eliza Richards."

"May I call you Eliza?"

"No. It's Mrs. Richards," snaps Eliza.

"I apologize, Mrs. Richards, for offending you. Dennis Jones works the day shift, and I work the night shift. I can help you if you like."

"What time does he come in tomorrow?" Eliza's voice cracks as she speaks.

"He comes in at nine o'clock. Is there anything I can do to help?"

Eliza wants to tell Sebastian about the visitor she and Buddy scared off but feels her problems are small compared to what Doris endured. She focuses the attention to her friend's death. "He is investigating the death of my friend Doris Massey. I am a witness."

"You saw someone kill your friend?"

"No, I reported the crime."

"So, you didn't witness someone killing your friend?"

"I saw the lady in the fancy Mercedes go over to Doris's house. She was visiting for a while and then I heard gunshots."

Sebastian picks up a blue pen from the desk and begins taking notes.

"Mrs. Richards, what is your friend's name again?"

"Her name is Doris Massey." Without asking Eliza spells the last name for him. He shakes the mouse several times, and the computer screen goes from black to the logo of the police department. His fingers go to work on the keyboard, entering his username and password. Now in the system he asks, "Mrs. Richards, what is the incident number?"

"Dennis didn't give me an incident report number."

"He didn't?" says Sebastian in an uncertain tone.

"No, why?"

"When someone gives a statement, a case or incident number is given to the person reporting the incident so they can follow up or add information. We can keep all the information in one place to streamline the process, and any police officer can go into the system to read the notes." *Why didn't Dennis give Mrs. Richards the incident report number?* Sebastian enters Doris Massey's name in the search box, careful to spell her last name correctly, glancing at his notes. He hits enter, and the report appears on the screen. Sebastian skims the report, but Eliza's name doesn't appear anywhere; the only witness name on the report is Sean Smith.

"Mrs. Richards, I did find the report, but there are a couple of details I would like to discuss with Dennis. Is it okay if I follow up with you on the murder of your friend tomorrow?"

"I suppose so," says Eliza without hesitation. "I waited this long for someone to take me seriously. I can wait a little longer."

"Mrs. Richards, is there anything else I can assist you with?"

"You can call me Eliza." Sebastian grins. "Someone tried to break into my house tonight and I know who it is."

"Are you okay?" Sebastian unlocks his gun in the lower desk drawer. He stands and places it in his holster.

"Yeah, Buddy and I were able to scare him off."

"Oh, that's good your dog scared off the intruder."

"Heck, no! I don't have time for animals. My daddy, a no-nonsense kind of guy, gave Buddy to me for my birthday. The girls in my class were all excited about their sixteenth birthday and what their parents were going to give them. Some had parties and others got jewelry. No, not my daddy. He said a young woman needed to be able to take care of herself. He gave me this very gun for my sixteenth birthday, showed me how to shoot that same day. He looked me in the eye and said, 'Child, this is your Buddy. He will always look after you when I am cold in the grave.' Sure enough, I made the intruder run off scared, chasing his tail." Eliza laughs.

Sebastian snickers to himself and his belly moves up and

down. *I like her. She is feisty just like Nana.* Sebastian turns on his serious demeanor. "Did anyone get hurt?"

"No, just his ego." Eliza is tickled again and begins to laugh.

Sebastian asks, "Eliza, what is your address?" He scribbles the address on his pad. "I will be there in twenty minutes to check the place out for you and to get your official statement."

"Okay. Well, let me go. I need to brew coffee, cook grits, turkey sausage, and toast before you get here. I need to get off the phone."

Sebastian's stomach rumbles at the sound of a home-cooked meal. He remembers the summers at his Nana's house. She would wake him and his sister at dawn to do chores. After the chores were complete Nana placed a bowl of creamy opaque grits with a piece of butter slowly melting in the center to a puddle. Sebastian licks his lips; he can taste Nana's grits dissolving in his mouth. He knows Eliza's breakfast will be just as good.

"I will see you in about fifteen minutes."

"Okay, I'm not going any place but in this kitchen."

Sebastian, needing the exercise, walks to the stairs; he pushes the door open and walks briskly to his car. Sebastian speeds out of the parking lot to Eliza's house. The drive is twenty minutes, but at the rate he is going he should be there in fifteen minutes. He hasn't had a home-cooked meal since the death of his wife.

Chapter 13

*S*tanley, knowing Emily is his mother, is determined to gain freedom from his adopted parents; he downloaded the documents he needs to change his name from Stanley back to Ian, the name Emily gave him before he was adopted. Stanley also has the name of an attorney who will process the paperwork for him. He walks into the living room, where both his parents are watching television. He ignores his father. "Mom, will you sign these papers for me?"

Julia takes the papers out of Stanley's hands. Reads the top of the document. "Son, I don't understand. You want to change your name? Why? Change it to what?"

"Horse's Ass," Dave interjects, never taking his eyes off his favorite cop show.

"What?" Julia turns her attention to Dave.

"He is going to change his name to Horse's Ass."

"No," shouts Stanley. "I want my legal name to be changed back to Ian." Both Julia and Dave turn their attention to Stanley, whose hands are trembling. He folds his arms to hide his nervousness.

"How do you know your name used to be Ian?"

"I overheard a conversation between you and Emily." Stanley sheepishly lowers his eyes. He should never have invaded Julia's privacy.

Julia chews on her upper lip for a few seconds. "Stanley, I am not pleased with this discussion, but I will sign the papers. If this is what you want. We can call you Ian."

"I do."

Dave snatches the document out of Julia's hand and tears it up into tiny pieces. He opens his hands and the shredded paper drifts from his hands onto the floor and sofa.

"Dave, why did you tear up the papers?" asks Julia, frustrated. She knows this is only going to grow the tension between the two of them.

"Stanley is my father's name and he will keep it until he dies."

"Dave, he is old enough to make up his own mind. If he wants to be called Ian, I will honor his request."

"If he is old enough to make up his mind, why does he need us to sign the document for the name change? So, he isn't old enough to know what the hell he wants," says Dave as he turns up the volume on the television.

Stanley shouts, "I don't care if you don't sign the documents to change my name. I will ask everyone to call me Ian, but you will pay for not honoring my request."

Dave rushes over to Ian, sticking his hand in his face. "You were a snotty ass boy who I rescued from a life of moving through the foster care system. You should be thanking me. I saved you."

"No, Julia saved me. All you want and talk about to her is how much you love and miss Emily. You disrespect Julia every time you bring up Emily's name and profess your love for her. How do you think I feel, Emily's my biological mother and you raped her?"

"Let me tell you something, you little twerp." Dave thrusts

Ian's body against the wall and grabs him by the throat. "Yes, I love Emily and we will be together eventually. I just need more time to convince her of my love. Once that happens, I will leave you and your mother to sit here and be miserable together. I will have the mother of my son, even though my son is a worthless piece of shit." Dave tightens his grip on Ian's throat.

"I can't breathe," says Ian, struggling to speak.

Dave positions his mouth next to Ian's ear and softly whispers, "You are weak if an old man like me can make you turn blue in the face. I should kill your ass for talking shit to me." Dave adds more pressure to Ian's throat. Ian gasps for air and his eyes bulge, trying to pry Dave's hands from around his throat. Dave stares at Ian with crazy eyes, determined he will win the fight. Julia dashes to Ian's rescue and tries to break up the fight between the two. Dave uses his elbow to guard his hands wrapped around his prey.

"Stop it, Dave; stop it!" The more Julia yells, the harder Dave squeezes.

Ian's body grows limp; his hands and legs stop fighting. Ian's bladder empties down the front of his pants to a puddle on the floor. Julia panics, draws back her arm, closes her fist, and uses all her power to punch Dave.

"Ouch." Dave doubles over, losing his grip on Ian's neck. Ian slides down the wall gasping for air. His neck is imprinted with Dave's hand, blue-black in color; his face red. Ian sits alone in the puddle of urine, desperately trying to suck in as much air as humanly possible at one time.

Julia, the wife and mother, is torn over who to comfort, her son or husband. Her eyes shift between the two of them and she quickly makes her decision. Ian carefully examines the scene before him, Dave within feet of him doubled over in pain, Julia at his side. *Why would she forsake me for him when he clearly messed with me first?* He sits on the floor for a minute longer until his legs can support the weight of his body; he inches up the wall to a standing position.

Ian staggers through the hall and up the stairs. He stops, leans against the wall as he enters the combination for the lock on his bedroom door; he manages to walk to the bathroom. The mirror on the wall magnifies his bruised neck. The tears in his eyes display the hurt to his ego; his eyeliner streaks as the tears roll down his cheeks. He unlaces his black boots, kicks them off, and they fall near the wall. Ian slowly unbuckles his black belt and peels his urine-stained black pants off his body and steps out of them; his Hanes underwear are soaked. Ian hasn't wet himself since he was four years old. He lifts his arms, pulls his black T-shirt off his body, and drops it on top of the pile of clothing on the floor. Ian turns the shower on and steps inside, closing the door behind him; he positions his face to the showerhead, and the tepid water flows on his face. Ian rubs his face harder and harder, remembering how his father humiliated him. He sobs; his tears blend into the beads of water on his face. Ian holds the wall and takes a step back; he doubles over and sits on the shower floor. His legs are drawn to his chest, arms wrapped around his legs. His head face down crying in his knees. He lifts his head and stares forward in a distant gaze. *Dave will pay for fucking with me.*

Chapter 14

Julia helps Dave off the floor. Once standing Dave snatches his arm from Julia's grip. "Why did you punch me?"

"You were going to kill Ian," shouts Julia.

"His name isn't Ian, it's Stanley," snaps Dave over his shoulders as he uses a turtle's pace to inch up the stairs to his man cave.

"If he wants to be called Ian, I will honor his request."

Dave ignores Julia's last statement and walks up the stairs one step at a time. Julia, watching her ornery husband struggle to make it up the stairs, scrabbles down the hall to the master bedroom and places a call.

"Hello."

Julia sniffles. "Emily, hi, this is Julia."

"What's wrong?"

"I need your help." She wipes her nose with the tissue she takes from the tissue box on the nightstand. "I am sorry for fighting with you earlier." She uses the other end of the tissue to dab the tears from her eyes. "I didn't know Dave raped you when we were in college. I would have never married him had I known. Please forgive me."

Emily can hear the hurt in Julia's voice, and she twirls her hair with her finger as she thinks. "Julia what is it, what do you need?"

"It's Dave and Ian. I broke up a physical fight between the two of them. If I hadn't been here, Dave would have hurt him."

"Is Ian okay?"

"He's fine. Just shaken up a bit. I will check on him when we hang up. I changed my mind from the conversation we had earlier; can Ian stay with you while Dave cools down? The two of them need space."

"Why are they fighting?"

"Stanley wants to change his name to Ian, and Dave isn't okay with the idea. Stanley is a family name, and Dave is set about not wanting the name changed."

"Why does Stanley want to change his name? Ian is the name Brendon and I gave him. What exactly does Ian know?"

"Apparently he overheard our conversation and discovered Dave raped you and you got pregnant with him. He knows you named him Ian and he wants to be called Ian. Tonight, he brought us the paperwork to change his name and asked us to sign it. If Dave didn't tear up the document, I would have signed the paperwork to change his name."

"You were going to sign the papers but didn't ask him why he wanted the name change?"

Julia breathes heavily. "There is something I didn't tell you earlier." Julia, embarrassed, hesitates before speaking. "I wasn't completely honest with you earlier." She begins to cry.

"Julia, what is it?"

"Emily, I was so mad because I thought you wanted to barge into our life and take Ian away from me that I didn't tell you I am afraid of Ian. I am ashamed of how I acted earlier."

"What does that mean you are afraid of him?"

"He has a lock on his bedroom door. I am not sure what or who he has up there."

"It sounds like he is wanting his privacy. All teenagers go through that phase."

"At first, I thought so too, but six months ago when the Goodwin's' Rottweiler, Daisy, went missing, I started to have my doubts about Ian. He had been taunting the dog for weeks, poking a stick wrapped with bacon through the chain link fence. Each time Daisy would get close enough to retrieve the bacon, Ian snatched the stick away from her. This went on every day for two weeks. I told Ian to leave the dog alone, but he wouldn't listen. One day Daisy had enough of Ian messing with her. She got out of the fenced yard and chased Ian for several blocks until he was able to jump on the roof of Mrs. Sadie's car not to be mauled by the dog. Mrs. Sadie called Ann, Daisy's owner, and she was able to calm the dog. Ann got her husband to reinforce the area in the fence where Daisy was able to squeeze through. Two days later, I found Ann screaming at the top of her lungs in her backyard where she found Daisy's collar on the back patio. The dog nowhere to be found. I comforted Ann for days because the disappearance of Daisy triggered the loss of her son, who asked Ann to watch Daisy when he went out of town for the weekend. On his way back, a drunk driver killed Mitch five years ago, and the death of Daisy reminds her of Mitch's death over and over.

"I comforted Ann for weeks, but it wasn't until I searched the garage for my gardening gloves that I found the shovel in front of my gardening cart. I picked up the shovel to hang it back on the utility hook when I noticed a large dried bloodstain on the back of the shovel. I haven't been able to look Ann in the face since I saw the shovel." Julia's voice trails to a soft whisper. "Emily, I think he killed the dog."

"Why would he do something so cruel?"

Julia sits on the chaise, bites her lower lip. "I don't know. I think living in foster care messed with his head. I don't know what he saw or experienced, but something is troubling him inside."

"Have you taken him to counseling?"

Julia is distracted by a car with a loud, noisy engine. She walks to the window, peers through the slats of the blinds at the muscle car in the driveway. The front door opens, and the young man in his twenties slams the door of his hot rod, greets Ian with a fist bump. The two talk for a few minutes, and the young man reaches in the car and hands Ian a crumpled brown paper bag. Ian glances inside the bag, rolls it several times, reaches in his front pocket, and hands the boy something. Julia, studying the exchange, assumes Ian gave the stranger money. The two talk for several minutes; the stranger gets back into his car, cranks the loud engine, speeds up the street and out of the community. Ian opens the bag once again, smiles, and walks back into the house.

Julia shakes her head at what she just witnessed. *Ian, what are you up to? This doesn't look good at all.* Julia, never answering Emily's question, changes the topic. "Emily, I need you to come and get Ian, let him stay with you for a while. I need to make sure he is safe."

There is definitely a difference in Julia's tone and position. She was set on Emily not getting to know Ian, but now suddenly, she changes her mind. Emily says curiously, "Is everything okay?"

"No, Emily, it's not. How soon can you get him?"

Emily is stunned, speechless.

"Emily, did you hear me? I need your help. Ian is in trouble, I know it. How soon can you pick him up?"

"The house Kyndall is letting us use isn't furnished, so I will have to fly to Charlotte and get the house set up and then drive down to pick him up. So, give me a few days."

Julia listens to Emily ramble about Kyndall, Sweetbriar; she doesn't hear any of it. Her thoughts are back on Ian. Abruptly

Julia responds, "I will let Ian know you will pick him up on Saturday. I will have his things packed and ready."

Emily's motherly instincts take over. "Julia, promise me you will keep my son safe until I get there."

Julia is quiet, not sure what she just witnessed between Ian and the stranger. Then there is Dave with his hot temper trying to show dominance over Ian every chance he gets. Julia, a mother too, knows she needs to step up, even if keeping him safe means protecting him from himself as well. "I will do what I need to do. You have my word."

"Thank you," says Emily.

As soon as Julia hangs up the phone, Dave hobbles into the bedroom, rubbing the side Julia punched.

"If Stanley visits Emily, I visit Emily." He walks to the floor-length mirror and pulls up his shirt to inspect his side: black and blue.

Julia's eyes are daggers as she stares in Dave's direction. He was snooping outside the door listening to her conversation again.

Dave turns his body to the side to get a different view of his bruises. "When is Stanley visiting Emily?"

"As soon as possible. I can't have the two of you fighting. What were you thinking? He is a child, for God's sake."

Dave lets go of his shirt, walks in Julia's direction, and looks her square in the eye. "Darling, you are right; he is a child. I will take my child to visit his mother."

"Why do you need to go with Ian?"

"First, let's get a couple things straight, DEAR. His name is Stanley and you need to stop referring to him by another name. Second, I am his biological father, and we don't need you to come if you were thinking about it."

"Why? I am his mother! If you are going, I should go too."

"Emily and I are his biological parents; you can stay behind. Keep the house up, do womanly things."

"Dave, let me ask you something. Is the reason you want to take Ian to visit Emily is because you still love her?"

"Damn it, his name is Stanley! If you want me to apologize for loving Emily, I won't. I love Emily then and now."

"Do you want to be with her more than you want to be with me?"

"Well, yes. I love Emily. If she just says the word, I will leave you for her."

Julia rises from the chaise. "So, you would give up our marriage to run towards something you never experienced except how you raped Emily to be with her."

"At least I had a sexual relationship with her. You only kissed her. But I had it all." Dave licks his lips.

The shocking comment takes the wind out of her, and she stumbles onto the chaise. *Where did this person come from who says those nasty, cold words?* She has never heard Dave speak in such a demeaning way. This Dave was not the kind person she grew to know throughout their marriage.

"You have to know I loved Emily before you."

<hr />

The loud arguing from his parents' bedroom sparks Ian's curiosity. He creeps down the hall and sits on the floor with his arms folded in front of him and his legs crossed at the ankle. He shakes his head in disgust. No wonder Emily put him up for adoption after Dave raped her. Ian remembers Emily from the hospital; she was concerned for him. Now sitting on the floor, he feels helpless. Julia is being demeaned by Dave daily, and Emily is being reminded of what Dave did to her over and over when she looks at him. When Emily calls, Dave taunts her, telling her he loves her—that must hurt. Ian raises himself off the floor and walks upstairs thinking how he can make up for all the hurt Dave has caused both Julia and Emily.

Chapter 15

Sebastian enters Eliza's neighborhood with one hand on the steering wheel and the other on his notepad. He flips to the last written page for Eliza's address. He looks in the rearview mirror—no one behind him. He stops the car, his attention diverted to the house with remnants of police yellow tape hanging from the bannister on the porch, another piece on top of a shrub. This must be Doris's home, the friend of Eliza, directly across the street from one another. The view from Eliza's house to Doris's is not obstructed. Eliza can see anyone entering and exiting the house through the front door. Sebastian checks his rearview mirror, pulls in front of Eliza's house. He shuts off the engine and sits in the car for a moment taking notes to not forget any of his observations. The front porch and the front window are well-lit areas; if Eliza were standing or seated in any of the areas, she'd have an excellent view.

Eliza, periodically checking for Sebastian, sees him from the front window in the living room, where she sees everyone and everything. The door opens, and she stands on the porch beaming with joy at her new guest. Sebastian sizes Eliza up as he unbuckles his seat belt. *She seems like an honest person and a good friend to want answers after the suspicious death of her friend.* He opens the car door, stands, and tries to button his jacket. The fabric stretches to reach the open hole, but the two don't meet. He decides to let the jacket hang open. He closes the car door, opens the fence, and walks up the driveway to the porch.

Eliza watches Sebastian's every move approvingly from her advantage point of the porch: she never liked scrawny men. She enthusiastically greets Sebastian with a wide grin. "Hey, Sebastian."

"Hi, Eliza. It is a pleasure to meet you." He extends his hand to shake.

"Oh, no need for a handshake. I am a hugger." She pushes his hand aside, stands on the tip of her toes, and wraps her arms around his neck.

Sebastian receives the embrace from the lady who reminds him of his grandmother, and the hug lingers a little longer than socially acceptable for two strangers. Sebastian rests his face on her shoulders. He misses his Nana. She died five years ago from complications associated with dementia. Sebastian holds back the tears, pushes back from the embrace, clears his throat. He isn't a man who cries. He regains his composure.

"I want to ask you a few questions about the incident this evening; look around outside for any evidence left by the intruder."

Eliza uses her hand in midair to dismiss Sebastian's suggestion. She is in control of what happens in her house. "Well, nobody got hurt or touched anything, so I don't see why you can't ask me questions at the kitchen table while you eat a hot meal. You can do your looking around later." She opens the screen door and walks inside. The smell of sausage trickles through the open door, and he closes his eyes and takes a deep breath. His mouth waters. He only had a Snickers bar for dinner, and that wore off hours ago. He misses his wife. She, too, could cook. She was a trained chef but in a deadly car accident off the PA Turnpike near the Norristown exit.

Eliza's questions go unanswered, so she stops and turns around, noticing Sebastian is still standing on the porch. She yells, "Are you coming or you just going to stand there?"

Sebastian, embarrassed, opens his eyes. "Yes, ma'am. I am coming." He enters the house, follows Eliza to the kitchen, and sits at the table. His eyes wander around the dark, dated kitchen. The gold appliances, the flooring brown laminate, the walls wood paneling. Sebastian shrugs his shoulders, not concerned with Eliza's seventies kitchen but how he will eat all the food piled high before him. Eliza blesses the food. "Amen," says Sebastian, never closing his eyes. He grabs his fork and digs in, savoring every bite as Eliza repeats the story, she told Dennis about the lady in the fancy Mercedes visiting Doris the day she died.

Sebastian wipes his mouth on the napkin beside his plate before speaking. "Did you see the intruder exit the house? The report mentions someone ran from the house dressed in gang colors."

"No one ran from the house, and the witness at the crime scene lied about knowing anything about the murder."

Sebastian shoves the food into his mouth as Eliza tells her truth about what she saw. With food in his mouth he asks, "Where were you when you witnessed or heard the gunshot?"

"I was in the living room in front of the picture window. If someone ran from the house, I would have seen it. Kyndall visited Doris earlier that day, and her car was still parked in the driveway when I heard the gunshot."

"Who do you think tried to break in your house tonight?"

Eliza takes a moment to ponder the question; she looks in the direction of Sebastian as if wondering if he can be trusted. "I think Sean, the guy at the crime scene, has something to do with it. He said he was visiting someone in the neighborhood but couldn't tell me whom."

Sebastian takes a deep breath. "Eliza, you don't know every-one in the neighborhood, so he could have been visiting a friend."

Eliza leans in from the waist and waves her index finger in Sebastian's direction. "I know everyone in the neighborhood. Why couldn't he tell me who he was visiting?"

"I don't know, maybe he was visiting a married woman and didn't want you to know." Sebastian chuckles.

Eliza cuts her eyes at Sebastian. "He doesn't belong in the neighborhood, not as a visitor, and he wasn't visiting a married woman."

Sebastian senses he hit a sore spot with Eliza. "I am sorry I misspoke about the witness visiting the married woman, but I want you to view things from my perspective. Every situation isn't cut and dry." Silence between the two of them as Sebastian closes his eyes and savors his last bite of sausage.

Eliza stands, clears the kitchen table, banging pots and pans in the sink. Sebastian, not wanting to disturb Eliza, eases from the table. He walks to the front porch and leans against the ban-nister. He stares at Doris Massey's house directly across the street. *Eliza could be right.* He pulls out his pocket notepad and flips to the page he scribbled Sean Smith's address. He taps the notepad against the porch rail, thinking.

Eliza finishes the dishes and joins Sebastian on the porch, wiping her hands on her apron. She, too, stares in the direction of Doris's house. "I miss her each day that passes. She was a good woman." Eliza wipes tears away from her cheek with her right hand. She sniffles. She reaches in her apron pocket for a wad of tissue and blows her nose.

Sebastian's body stiffens; he knows he must find the truth for his newfound friend. He looks at the notepad in his hand and clears his throat. "Eliza, I am going to head out. Thank you for a delicious meal." Sebastian rubs his belly.

"You be careful on that road," Eliza warns.

"I will," Sebastian reassures her; he reaches over and gives her a hug. He walks down the steps of the porch and out the gate. Sebastian settles in the driver's seat and cranks the car. He enters Sean Smith's address in his GPS. He waves to Eliza as he disappears down the street toward the highway.

Sebastian circles the block, searching for the address given in the police report. He double checks the address quickly, stops, and backs up. The address Sean Smith gave Dennis is an empty lot where a house once stood. The houses on either side of the lot are dilapidated, boarded up, grass and weeds waist high. *Why didn't Dennis check the address of the witness?* This seems to be sloppy detective work from his mentor. Sebastian shakes his head, takes the car out of park, and drives to the police station.

Chapter 16

*S*ebastian arrives back at the office, sits at his desk. He uses his right hand to maneuver around his buckled belt to unbutton his pants, tight after the huge breakfast with Eliza. Sebastian recalls the events of the night. Why didn't Dennis give her the case number? Sebastian has a nagging feeling he is missing something; he uses his credentials to log into his work computer, carefully typing the case number into the system. Sebastian lightly taps his fingers on the desk as he waits for the system to update. *Here we go.* Sebastian scans the document… Nothing. Eliza didn't get a case number because she wasn't listed as a witness; the only witness listed is Sean Smith. Why wouldn't Dennis include Eliza's account along with Sean's? They are two different accounts which would have sparked Dennis to investigate further. Did Dennis check out the witness story? If so, he would have discovered Sean's address is a vacant lot. *Is Dennis covering for the Sean guy? Does Dennis have something to do with the death of Doris? Why rush to close the case when there is still so much to uncover? Maybe there is some truth behind Eliza's speculations that someone killed her friend.*

He leans back in the chair with his hands interlocked behind his head. Sebastian, an excellent detective, concludes he won't make any rash decisions about his mentor until he has a conversation with him about the confusion surrounding the case. Sebastian knows himself well and he will not be able to rest until he talks to Dennis, so he decides to hang out for a few more minutes to confront him. The events of the night catching up with him, he yawns and checks his watch. Sharply at 8:30 a.m., Dennis struts out of the elevator with a box of Dunkin' Donuts and a tall cup of coffee, careful not to spill the drink and box of treats. Anxiously, Sebastian snatches his coffee mug from his desk as a ruse to follow Dennis into the breakroom.

"Good morning, my friend." Dennis greats Sebastian in a chipper tone as Sebastian walks into the kitchen.

"Hey, man, what's going on? How are you?"

"I can't complain. Nobody would listen if I did." Dennis chuckles.

Sebastian smiles. "Yeah, you are right, nobody would listen." Sebastian's belly moves up and down as he laughs. Quickly, he changes the tone of the conversation while Dennis is in a jolly mood. "Hey, I got a strange call last night."

"Yeah, Julia Roberts called wanting a date?" Dennis blurts out a hearty laugh.

"I wish." Sebastian pauses, thinking how he can ease into a different conversation without alarming Dennis. No way around it; he has to give him the facts. "No, an elderly lady, Eliza Richards, called wanting to follow up on a murder investigation of her friend, Doris Massey."

Dennis's body stiffens, the laugh lines around his mouth ease, and his smile disappears. Sebastian observes him out of the corner of his eyes as he pours himself a hot cup of coffee. Dennis notices Sebastian watching him, opens the top of the donut box, and carefully reviews each donut, looking up one row and down the next, deciding which he wants to consume. Finally, Dennis decides on the glazed donut with the mystery filling. He picks up the donut and reaches for a napkin on top of the microwave. He takes a large bite, and the strawberry glaze oozes from the donut to the corner of his lips. Dennis stretches his tongue to the outer corner of his mouth to clean up the mess. Dennis makes Sebastian wait before he responds, "What about it?" Acting as though the conversation doesn't interest him.

"She initially called to report an attempted burglary, but she and Buddy scared the intruder away."

"Who the hell is Buddy?" exclaims Dennis as he takes another bite of the donut.

Sebastian laughs. "Buddy is her shotgun."

"How is any of this relevant to the Doris Massey investigation?"

"There was an attempted burglary at the home of Eliza Richards, as she claims a witness to the murder of her friend Doris Massey. She told me she reported the incident to you, and I went into the system to find her account of the incident, but her account wasn't in the report. I asked her for her case number, but she indicated you didn't give her one. We give all witnesses case numbers so they can easily follow up." Sebastian's voice trails off. "I don't think it is a coincidence that she is a witness to a crime and the attempted burglary of her home."

"I see. Is she okay?" asks Dennis half-heartedly.

"Oh, yes, she is fine. But I am confused. The report says Brown is the lead on the case, but you were interviewing witnesses. What is that all about?"

"I was in the area and heard the radio call. You know I do what I can to help a fellow colleague," says Dennis as he picks at his cuticle.

Sebastian senses Dennis will not offer additional information unless he asks another set of questions. "Were you able to follow up on the eyewitness Sean Smith?"

"There was no need to. Follow up on what? He gave his statement and I tried to close the case."

"Well, that was the problem. Eliza gave a different account of what happened, and her statement wasn't in the case notes."

"The old lady seemed confused in her statement. Really not credible at all. There were times she couldn't recall details. So, I decided not to include her statement to close the case as quickly as possible. You know every open case costs the department. You get my drift—you are now working my case. Interviewing witnesses, I have already spoken to. Again, like I said, costing the department money by having two officers work the same case. Everyone has plenty of other work to do. Like yourself." Dennis looks Sebastian squarely in the eyes, letting him know he is on to his game.

Sebastian raises his hands as he takes a step backward. "Man, I don't want you to feel like I am stepping on your toes."

"Well, that's what it feels like." Dennis examines the remaining donut in his right hand with the red filling running down the side mixing with the cracked glaze. "If this interrogation is over, I am going to start my day. Again, the two of us standing here talking about a closed case is costing taxpayers." Dennis walks toward the breakroom door and tosses the half-eaten donut into the trash.

"Oh, one other thing." Dennis stops, his back toward Sebastian. "Did you know the address Sean Smith gave you is a vacant lot?" Dennis walks out of the breakroom never acknowledging Sebastian's request for an answer.

Sebastian walks over to the donut box and opens the lid. Immediately his eyes fix on the white powdered donut. *I wonder if the filling is lemon.* His mouth starts to water anticipating the sweet taste of the donut and the tartness of the creamy lemon filling. He looks around the room and picks up the donut and takes a bite. Speckles of the white powder fall on the front of his black suit. With his free hand, he wipes the powder off his suit, leaving white steaks. He wipes the jacket again. He takes another bite, this time leaning over the sink, letting the powder drift into the sink.

He finishes the remaining donut, turns the water on, and washes the residue off his hands. He dries his hands on a paper towel and exits the breakroom, checking his clothing for any traces of powder sugar. He glances up and stops. Sally, a rookie detective, is speaking to Dennis. Nothing would have been unusual about the exchange except for the schoolgirl smile on her face. In mid-sentence Dennis checks his watch, ends the conversation, and rushes to Captain Morrison's office, the door shut. Dennis leans against the wall with his back to the squad room. On Sally's walk to the elevator, her hand brushes Dennis's backside with little effort. Dennis, not expecting the touch of his friend, blushes; the coffee moves back and forth in the cup, not spilling. Sally with a straight face presses the button to go down.

Sebastian, still standing outside the kitchen, takes mental notes on what he is witnessing. Now curious, he walks to his desk instead of leaving to go home. He was off hours ago. Sebastian shuffles papers on his desk, keeping a watchful eye on Dennis.

The captain waves Dennis into his office. Dennis closes the door behind him and takes a seat. He takes a sip of his coffee, closes his eyes, inhales the euphoric smell of the coffee.

Dennis, only able to hear one side of the conversation, focuses his attention on relaxing with his coffee until the captain gets off the phone. He stretches his legs, crosses them at the ankle, leans his head against the wall.

"Do they have enough evidence for us to bring Brendon Graham in for questioning?" says the captain.

Dennis's ears perk up and he uncrosses his leg, his eyes staring at the black darts on the white tile, avoiding eye contact with his boss. He turns his body to hear the conversation out of his good ear.

Dennis doesn't have to wait for a response for the captain to know what the person on the other end says. He hears the yelling through the phone. "He is a senator, for Christ's sake! The last thing we need is negative fallout from an arrest if he isn't the guy. The New York detectives are pushing hard to interview Brendon."

Dennis knows the seriousness of the conversation because the person on the other end is Chief of Police Seth Gordan.

"Have you had the opportunity to review the report? What do you think?"

"Yeah, I read the report and think their evidence is flimsy, a thumbprint on a condom wrapper. The girl Samantha lived in New York in a luxury loft with a doorman. Her salary from the retail store could not afford her that lifestyle. Let's face it, she could have been a prostitute and the senator one of many clients. The other girl found in the apartment, Catherine, didn't live in the apartment; her only possessions were in a duffle bag. I think the entire NYPD is on a wild goose chase."

Rebecca, the captain's assistant, knocks on the door and enters, places the high-profile case in front of him. The name across the top is Doris Massey, scribbled on the tab in black Sharpie. Rebecca exits Morrison's office and goes back to her desk. Morrison glances over the file and puts his head in his hands. *Here we go again—the Graham family is involved in homicides.*

Dennis leans back in his chair, feeling more relaxed. He crosses his leg and takes a deep breath; he feels as though he is out of the web of lies. The captain doesn't want to move forward in the NYPD case Brendon is involved in from what he hears from the conversation. Dennis breathes in the aroma of the coffee, takes another sip. Dennis closes his eyes. He hears nothing from the captain; the chief isn't yelling, so he can't hear the raised voice on the other end of the phone. After all he is eavesdropping.

————)((O)) ————

Seth's chief assistant, Patty, forgets the formality of knocking and barges into the office with a note she hands to her boss. She stays in the office just in case her boss has questions or needs her. Patty knows the folder she gave him is information he needs for the call he is currently on. Seth reviews the file and shakes his head. "You now have to play nice with the New York detectives investigating their homicide into the death of Catherine and Samantha. Catherine's address is in Philadelphia and there were pictures of her and Brendon." The chief continues to read the information from the note. "The wife, Emily, may be a person of interest. Catherine sent Emily the photos of her and Brendon."

Patty glances at her watch, leaves the office and walks back to Seth's office with the files he needs for his next meeting across town.

"Morrison, I have to go. I have another meeting. We have to get this case right; there is too much at stake."

"Yes, sir. I certainly understand. I think that is best. The New York detectives can pay Brendon a visit along with his wife, Emily. If we have additional evidence, we will share with them as well." Morrison repeats what Seth told him. "Okay, they will be here on Wednesday. What are their names?" Captain Morrison repeats their names aloud: Makayla Moore and Levi Miller. "One last request—can you send me over what you have on the New York case? Any notes will be helpful."

"Yes, I will ask Patty to send over the case file." Patty hurries back to her desk to send the email to Captain Morrison.

"I will ensure we treat them as family. Have a good day, sir."

Captain Morrison hangs up the phone.

Dennis processes the parts of the conversation he heard and what he could extrapolate from the conversation. He and the Grahams are fucked. He shakes his head. "Is everything okay?" asks Dennis.

"Hell no! I was just given a file on Doris Massey." Morrison picks the file up only to throw it back on the desk. "Why am I just finding out the senator's mother is involved in a death at my back door? I was thinking New York was on a witch hunt, but now there may be truth behind what I'm being told. I will look over the file NYPD has on their case to be prepared when the two detectives get here on Wednesday."

Morrison opens the file, finds the lead detective's name. "Where is Brown?" he shouts.

"Remember? Brown is on leave; his father died two days ago. He flew to Puerto Rico to ship his father's remains back to the United States for burial."

Morrison, twisted about the case in New York, misses his opportunity to ask Dennis why he was interviewing witnesses when he has his own cases. "Good thing you are familiar with the case and can take the lead while Brown is away."

Dennis gives the captain a half smile. Every day he gets pulled further and further into Kyndall's world. When can he actually do the work, he was hired to do at the police department, to serve and protect? The only people he is serving and protecting are Kyndall and her family. *I need a way out.*

"Captain, I was thinking of retiring, you know, getting my pension and traveling, seeing the world."

"We can discuss retirement after this case, but I need you to help me with this mess." Morrison pauses. "Hey, I never thought of you as someone who would retire and travel the world. I figured

I would find you slumped over your desk, dead on the job." He chuckles.

Morrison begins to read over the case notes on Doris Massey's death. "It says here the circumstances surrounding the death of Doris Massey was gang initiation. The gang member entered Doris's home, shot her, and stabbed the senator's mother, Kyndall. Why did the intruder use two different weapons? Just shoot the both of them and get out of there."

Morrison waits for Dennis to respond. Dennis's thoughts are still on how he can get ahead of the story and leave town.

Dennis takes a deep breath. "I stand behind Brown's report, I just say…"

Morrison cuts Dennis off in mid-sentence. "Your ass will be on the line if this goes south. I don't care who you believe or stand behind. I want you to go back and ensure all I's are dotted and T's crossed before this file come back across my desk."

"Will do." Dennis stands to leave the office.

The captain begins to speak about the New York case, and Dennis sits back in his chair, crosses his legs, bouncing it every now and then. "The Doris Massey case has many links to two unsolved homicides in New York." The captain reviews the email Patty sent. "Samantha and Catherine are the names of the deceased. They were found in a luxury loft apartment neither one of them could afford."

Dennis doesn't care about anyone's financial situation but his own. He needs to get a handle on the situation because he could lose his pension and the extra cash Kyndall would give him under the table for taking care of odds and ends. He blurts, "What evidence do they have supporting Brendon could be involved?"

"A condom wrapper with his thumbprint."

"It seems strange that the senator left a condom wrapper out in the open. Single-handedly killed two women only to implicate himself because he was too stupid and left evidence behind."

"No, it could have been left behind by mistake. Maybe some-one else was cleaning the room on his behalf, or Brendon didn't take it with him. Or he was invited to the home of this prostitute and got caught up and killed her."

"Does Brendon have an alibi during the time of the young woman's death?"

The captain scrolls down the report. "Ahh, it says here Brendon met his wife for dinner to celebrate their anniversary."

"Is there surveillance footage from the restaurant?" Dennis already knows the answer to the question he is asking because Gregory ensured the recording would not be found regardless of the recording cycle.

Morrison advances the document to the next page. "Okay, the recording loops every twenty-four hours and was recorded over the original taping of events that night. The police information tech-nology team is working on what they can salvage on the tape."

Dennis already knows they will find nothing.

"Well, we just have to let this whole thing play out. The detec-tives will be here on Wednesday so the three of you can work out the details, compare notes. Emily, the senator's wife, is a person of interest and they definitely want to speak with her, and they have a witness, the concierge at the apartment building."

Dennis staring at the coffee cup in his hand. Just minutes ago, he cherished the aroma of the dark roast coffee; now the coffee smell churns his stomach. The contents of his stomach slowly creep up to his throat. He swallows hard.

"Are you okay?" says the captain, looking directly at Dennis.

Dennis, a shade of green, responds, "Yeah, yeah." To make his life even worse, the captain adds that Emily is a person of interest in the New York case. Dennis knows this news will not go over well with Kyndall when he gets up the nerve to tell her. Out of nowhere Dennis says, "Wait, wait, now they are jumping to a conclusion about Emily."

"Dennis, you know it's common to hear a jealous wife kills the husband's lover. Catherine had pictures of her and Brendon. Catherine sent the photos to Emily."

Dennis shakes his head; Emily is so innocent in all of Brendon's shenanigans. Emily deserves better. The time has come—he needs to call Kyndall and warn her. "Captain, I don't know about all the speculations surrounding the case. Let me review the notes to prepare for the visit on Wednesday."

"Okay, sounds good. If you need anything let me know."

Dennis stands and, on his way, out of the office, he throws the putrid coffee into the trash. He glances over his shoulders and dashes for the stairwell.

———— ((◊)) ————

Sebastian rushes to the door before it closes. His eyes search for Dennis. He stands there, not sure the direction he should go, up or down. While deciding he takes off his shoes. Sebastian follows the echo in the stairwell, his footsteps muffled by the softness of his black argyle socks. He carefully peers over the rail and sees Dennis is three flights down. He moves quickly and hears part of a phone conversation. The closer he gets to Dennis the better.

———— ((◊)) ————

"Hi, love."

"We have a problem."

"You sound like Brendon. Why does everyone call me with a problem? I do need answers sometimes."

Dennis ignores Kyndall's comment. "The New York Police Department found Brendon's fingerprint on a condom wrapper in a murder investigation in New York. Are you familiar with this situation?"

"I am. What information do they have besides the condom wrapper?"

"There is a witness, a concierge who works at the building. And they are looking to question Emily."

"Emily? Why?"

"The police will question both Brendon and Emily, but they want to rule Brendon out as a suspect. They think Emily killed the two women because she was jealous."

"We have to make sure Emily is shielded from Brendon's mess. I swear, sometimes…." Kyndall stops mid-sentence. "Doris is turning over in her grave. I told her I would take care of Emily. None of this mayhem would exist if Doris did what I asked. She made me a promise too."

Dennis's eyes narrow. *Why is Kyndall blaming Doris for Brendon's transgressions?* Dennis never voices his opinion; he doesn't want to further complicate the situation. Maybe he could ask Kyndall for a set amount of money to walk away for it all. He could get his pension, sell his house, and with the money from Kyndall he would be set. He needs to show Kyndall his worth in her inner circle to demand the money he wants.

"Gregory is getting sloppy, leaving evidence behind. He will straighten this mess out."

Dennis smiles and chimes in as well. This is his opportunity. "I told you he could not be trusted."

Kyndall, a woman who makes up her own mind, hangs the phone up on Dennis after his comment.

⸺ ⸙ ⸺

Kyndall calls Gregory. "Hello," says Gregory as he crunches a mouthful of Doritos.

"We have a problem. Remember when you went to New York and found Brendon with Julia's lover, what's her name?" Kyndall snaps her fingers in rapid succession, trying to recall the name. Gregory makes Kyndall wait before jumping in to give her the name. "Oh, you know, what's-her-name, the lesbian."

Gregory interjects, "Samantha."

"Yeah, yeah. The New York homicide department is investigating the death of Samantha and coming to Philadelphia to question Emily as the lead suspect. There is a witness, the concierge on duty that night."

Gregory throws the chip bag on the desk, and three chips spill on his paperwork for the other job he is working. He licks his fingers, reaches in the right drawer, and picks up a stack of driver's licenses bound together with a rubber band. He thumbs through them quickly, remembering each face, matching it to the crime he committed. He passes the concierge driver's license, stops, and reviews the last two and glares at Jake's picture.

"I have the address for the concierge. I will pay him a visit."

"The witness isn't the only problem. There is evidence of the condom wrapper with Brendon's fingerprint. How will you handle that situation?"

"Let's let the investigation play out. The detectives will interview Brendon. We will tell him to confess to having a one-night stand with Samantha hours before she was killed. Having an affair isn't a crime."

Kyndall thinks about the proposed alibi. "Okay, I will have a conversation with him about the matter. Give him some talking points." She changes the subject. "Gregory, I am concerned with the number of problems resurfacing. We have the problem in New York, not cleaning up the crime scene, and the failed situation with Eliza." Kyndall is careful not to give details of a crime on the phone. "I can't have loose ends among the new problems and the planning for the White House."

"Kyndall, I get it. The problem in New York, I made a split-second decision to get Brendon out of the apartment. I hit the concierge over the head with a vase and I had to deal with the security footage. I did know one condom wrapper was missing and I didn't check if the concierge was dead. My only concern was getting Brendon out of the apartment without being seen."

Gregory's phone beeps. He looks at the caller ID, rolling his eyes, the person behind his chastising. "Kyndall, hold on a minute. I need to take this call. Hello?"

"Hey, we need to talk, not over the phone."

"There is something I need to take care of that will take me out of town."

"When will you be back?"

Gregory thinks about the traffic coming across the George Washington Bridge. "It's going to be late—tonight around 11:00."

"Okay, meet me at my house at 11:00 tonight."

———— ‹‹◊›› ————

Dennis hangs up the phone, turns around, and starts to walk back up the stairs. Sebastian quickly turns and briskly walks up the stairs. In a split-second decision, he walks up a flight above the department's door he once exited. He doesn't want the door to be opened or to cause suspicion that someone was listening. He waits until he hears Dennis open the door to the department. Moments later the door closes. Sebastian breathes a sigh of relief. Not trusting Dennis, he decides to walk back down the stairs and exit the building. He doesn't want to tip Dennis off that he will be waiting for him outside his house at 11:00 p.m. when his visitor is scheduled to arrive. Right now, he needs to go home and get some rest.

Gregory clicks back over to his conversation with Kyndall, focusing his attention on the issue at hand—staying in Kyndall's fold. "I get it that I messed up, but I can assure you I am still a valuable member of your team." Gregory feels he needs to make the statement loud and clear, so she knows he is worth keeping. *I know too much for Kyndall to keep me alive after she feels she no longer has any use for me. If Kyndall is doubting my usefulness, it must be Dennis putting those thoughts in her head.* "I will call you when the problem in New York is handled.

"Okay, Gregory. Thanks for what you do for this family."

"Bye." They both exited the call.

Gregory eats the three chips on the desk and wipes the residue on his Levi's jeans. He finds a paper clip in the desk and gently folds the top of the bag over twice, clips the fold to keep his chips fresh. He walks to the closet and pulls out his fully packed overnight bag, unzips it, and places the bag of Doritos in the bag and zips it closed. He walks to the door of his office and up the stairs to the kitchen. His wife is preparing the vegetables for a salad. "Honey, what time do you want dinner?" she yells over her shoulder.

Gregory walks over to his wife and gives her a kiss on the cheek. "I just received a work call. I need to run out and will not be back until later tonight or tomorrow."

Gregory's wife knows not to ask any details of where he is going because he will never tell her. The only response from his wife is "I love you."

"I love you too."

Gregory walks out the kitchen door into the garage. He enters his SUV and plugs Jake's work address into the GPS; if he isn't there he will show up on his doorstep. Either way he will deal with Jake once and for all.

Chapter 17

Gregory surveilles Samantha's old building waiting for Jake, the concierge, to exit the building. Gregory, aware of the time Jake ended his shift, he called earlier that day. The young lady who answered the phone followed her scripted company response when non-employees asked about work schedules. Gregory in his most nonchalant demeanor informs Angelica the fresh fish delivery will spoil if not in the hands of the recipient today. Angelica will fully give Jake's schedule to the stranger on the phone.

Gregory circles the block once searching for parking on the street to ditch his SUV just in case Jake decides to walk. As luck would have it there aren't any empty spaces. Gregory pulls into a no-parking zone, sits, and watches Jake. Jake opens the door, stands outside of the building, and looks at his watch, then to his left. He locks his eyes with a beautiful young lady walking toward him. The girl's eyes beam at the sight of Jake standing in wait.

Gregory, a father himself, knows the young girl would not want to walk far; she looks as though she will have the baby, she is carrying any day. Gregory opens his phone and taps the Uber app to turn on his driving status. He does the same for his Lyft app. Gregory reaches in the console to find his jammer to block all drivers from receiving message alerts of a passenger needing to be picked up.

Jake walks toward his girlfriend and gives her a wet kiss on the lips. Gregory, not taking his eyes off the couple, reaches in his back pocket for his wallet and lowers his eyes briefly to search for his Metro card for the subway. He's ready for however his friend wants to travel. He puts his wallet back in his pocket but keeps the card handy.

Jake and the girl, hand in hand, take two steps, and she rubs her belly. She rests for a minute, proceeds down the street, taking small steps. The young girl stops again to rest. The two talking to one another. Jake shakes his head side to side, throws his hands in the air. Jake pulls out his phone and hits a few buttons. Gregory gets an alert on his phone; he has a fare. Gregory accepts the fare, gets out of his SUV, and jogs across the street and approaches the young couple. "Hey, I am Mike, your Uber driver. I am parked across the street."

"Hi Mike," says Jake. "My girlfriend and I were going to take the subway, but she is having cramps."

"When is the baby due?"

"Her due date is in two days."

"Yeah, I am a father and I know that look. She is going to have the baby today."

"You think so?" The proud father grins from ear to ear.

Gregory escorts the couple across the street to his illegally parked SUV. "Where are we going?"

Jake gives him the address to her doctor's office.

Gregory drives the couple in silence to the appointment. He pulls up in front of the doctor's office. Jake gives him cash for the fare. "Don't worry about it; put it in the kid's college fund. It's expensive raising a child."

"Man, thank you. You don't know how much this means to me."

"Not a problem."

The two exit the car and head into the doctor's office. Gregory, back to his old self, opens his glove compartment and picks up Jake's driver's license. He enters the address in his GPS. He figures he has a few hours to spare before the doctor sends the two home. Jake was right, the baby will be here in two days as the doctor instructed. Gregory has been an active father from the time his wife told him she was pregnant. He needed a ruse to get the couple into the car. He knows he was an active father and a part of the delivery of each of one of his girl's.

Gregory obediently slows when his GPS informs him, he has reached his destination. No parking on the street, he double parks his SUV with his emergency blinkers on. He watches the street for the house number. Gregory does a double-take when he sees a woman exit Jake's home with a garbage bag. She throws the trash in the receptacle. She closes the lid and walks back into the house and closes the door.

Huh, thinks Gregory. The woman who just exited the house could be Jake's sister or wife. If Gregory was a betting man, he would put his money all on wife.

No breaking and entering today. Gregory places his SUV in gear and parks two blocks over. He pops into the market on the corner and buys and wraps a bouquet of flowers into a fancy presentation. Gregory walks back to Jake's home, flowers in hand.

Gregory walks up the steps and rings the doorbell. The young lady opens the front door; the screen door is the barrier. She smiles at the stranger with the flowers.

"Hi, I have a delivery."

"Hi. The flowers are beautiful. Who are they from?"

Gregory stares down at the bouquet—no card. He smirks. "It looks like you have a secret admirer."

Tears fill her eyes. "I am too old to have a secret admirer." She touches her wrinkled neck, aged beyond her years because of overexposure to the sun. "I am sure they are from my husband, Jake." Jake's wife opens the screen door.

Gregory feels as though she is going to burst into a crying fit and shoves the flowers toward her. "Here you go. It seems Jake wants to turn over a new leaf," says Gregory as he reads her facial expression and body language.

Gregory takes a step forward, scans the living area from where he is standing—neat with a few toys on the floor. "How long have you and Jake been married?"

"Five years."

Gregory steps back, examines Jake's wife, and judges Jake in his mind. His wife is very attractive, a mature woman in her late thirties. *Why is he with the other woman? Maybe because she is young, but the lady before him is hot.* Gregory shakes his head in disgust for Jake cutting out on his wife.

"I'll tell you what," he says as he clasps his hands together. "Why don't I take a picture of you holding the flowers and you can post to social media? Brag to your friends that your husband did something nice for you."

"You know, that is a good idea. It's been a long time since he has done something so thoughtful. Come in."

Gregory enters the house, careful not to step on the plush toy on the floor. Jake's wife reaches for her phone, but Gregory has already snapped the picture. She turns to face Gregory for a better pose. "We can send the photo to your husband. What's his phone number?" She gives Gregory the phone number, and he sends the photo to Jake. It takes Jake a few minutes before he responds back to the text message.

"I am not familiar with the number. Who is this message from?"

"Would you like something to drink?"

"Yes, thank you."

"Oh, excuse me for being rude. My name is Nora." She extends her hand.

Gregory shakes her hand. "I am Gregory." He feels comfortable giving Nora his real name.

Nora walks to the kitchen, opens the refrigerator, which is bare. Jake didn't give her grocery money for the week. She yells, "Is water okay?"

"Yes. May I use your bathroom?"

"Sure, it is down the hall on the right."

Gregory maneuvers down the hall and into the bathroom, where he calls Jake's number.

"Hello."

"Hey, Jake, how are you?"

"Who is this?"

"Who I am is not a concern. I hear you gave a statement to the police about the last person who was in Samantha's apartment. I need you to recant your story. Tell them you don't remember who was in the apartment and the sketch was from someone in your dream."

"Why would I do that?"

"Because I know where you live. I am here with your wife. Do you want to see her again?"

"You are at my house?"

"Well, of course, silly; that's how I was able to take a picture of her holding the flowers you had me deliver to her."

"I didn't have flowers delivered."

"I know. You don't have time to have flowers delivered with the baby on the way with your girlfriend. You are going to be really busy trying to juggle two families."

"How do you know about Bethany?"

"Bethany can stay our secret if you give the police a call and change your story."

"Bethany is having the baby soon. I may not be able to speak with the police." Gregory opens the bathroom door to ensure Nora and Jake hear his comment.

Gregory responds to Nora loud enough for Jake to hear him. "Nora, thank you for your hospitality. I will be one more minute. My boss is giving information on another delivery."

"Sure, that's fine, take your time. I just like having someone to keep me company while Jake is at work."

"You really are at my house." Jake can hear Nora in the background.

Gregory ignores Jake's comment and responds with an odd comment to Nora. "Your husband wanted the flowers delivered before he got home from work. Where is he? You know what they say—when men send flowers, they are apologizing for something." Gregory laughs.

Jake breathes heavily into the phone.

Nora is puzzled by the change of heart of the delivery guy, who was trying to convince her that Jake was doing the right thing by her, but his new comment seems flip. She sits on the edge of her seat with Gregory's water in hand, and the water ripples in the glass. Her nerves are uneasy.

Through clenched teeth, "I am a professional hit man and I will kill you, your wife, girlfriend, and newborn and go home tonight and sleep like a baby. You need to make this go away. You have two days." Gregory hangs up the phone, walks out of the bathroom, turns his head in Nora's direction. "Thank you for your hospitality, Nora. Have a good day."

Gregory closes the front door behind him. He checks his watch. If he leaves now, he can make his meeting with Dennis. Gregory jogs to his SUV, pops an aspirin in his mouth, chugs the bottled water. The mess with Brendon gives him a headache, and now he has to deal with the traffic between New York and Philly during rush hour, which causes his head to ache even more.

Chapter 18

Sebastian's mouth flies open as he drives through Dennis's neighborhood. Large homes on both sides of the street, lawns immaculately mowed with straight lines in the grass. Dennis has to be on the take to be able to own a home in this area of town. *How can he afford to live in this neighborhood on his salary?* Sebastian parks his car across the street from Dennis's home and waits. He purposely arrived early to gather his Canon camera and binoculars to get a good view of the person Dennis will meet.

———— ▸(●)◂ ————

Gregory, punctual, arrives five minutes before the meeting time, pulls into the driveway, and exits the car. Sebastian snaps pictures of the mystery guy exiting the SUV. Sebastian's eyes follow Gregory to the door. Gregory rings the doorbell and waits only briefly before Dennis opens the door. Dennis steps out of the house onto the porch and closes the door behind him. Gregory cuts to the chase, no small talk. "What's so urgent?"

"Remember Eliza?"

"Who?"

"The lady who lives across the street from Doris, Eliza Richards."

"Oh, her." Gregory scratches his head. "What's going on?"

"Eliza called the precinct when you tried to break in her house and reported it. She started asking questions about Doris's case. Now Sebastian, another detective, is asking me questions about the case. He met with Eliza after she called the precinct, and her story sounds credible and your story doesn't fly right now."

"Don't blame this shit on me! I don't need this right now. I am tired and starved. And by the way I thought you said you were going to handle it, Mr. Top-Notch Detective. At least I tried to handle the situation."

"Yeah, I fucked up too."

"For once you admit you aren't all you pretend to be."

Dennis dismisses Gregory's rant. "What are we going to do?"

Gregory thinks for a minute. "What does the other detective know?"

"Not much but what he knows unravels your credibility as a witness. The address you gave turns up to be a vacant lot. Eliza is sharp, and he believes her version of the story."

"Okay, let's just let a day or two go by before we do anything. Play nice with the detective, agree to offer assistance so you will know what he knows when he knows it. If he has additional information, we will decide what to do, but just lie low." Gregory feels hunger pangs in his stomach, which growls.

Dennis scratches his head, thinks for a minute about the plan. "Okay. I will wait before I do anything."

Gregory walks down the steps of the porch. Dennis says, "Man, will we ever be free?" Gregory stops, not turning around and not asking what Dennis means because he knows. Every time the phone rings, the noose tightens around all their necks.

"No, we will never be free." Gregory proceeds to his car, turns to face Dennis. "There is only one way out."

"I know, that's why I am telling you. I want you to know you are the best man for the job before I start my journey."

Any other time Gregory would have gloated at the news, but he will be sad to see him go. "Good night, Dennis, take care."

——◦《◉》◦——

Sebastian takes a photo of Gregory's license plate with an older model Canon camera from his days of wedding photography on nights and weekends to make extra money. He had to work odd jobs to make ends meet, and Dennis lives in an upscale neighborhood. Jealousy overcomes Sebastian; he is no longer giving Dennis the benefit of the doubt. Dennis is a dirty police officer. Sebastian snaps away and captures both Dennis and Gregory talking on the porch and Gregory walking down the steps for a closer view of the stranger's face.

Sebastian takes a quick photo of Dennis standing in the doorway before he closes the door behind him. Gregory cranks his SUV, backs out of the driveway. Sebastian leans across the passenger side of the car not to be seen by Gregory as he speeds down the street. Sebastian hears the SUV pass his parked car. He leans slightly up to check Dennis's driveway. The driveway is empty, Dennis back in the house. Sebastian is motionless in the car.

Suddenly he gets a thought. He glances at his watch, the time 11:15 p.m. He contemplates whether he should call his new friend, and he takes his chances because she does keep late hours.

"Hello."

"Hi, Eliza, this is Sebastian."

"I know who this is. I know everybody's voice who place their feet underneath my table."

"I am sorry to call you at this hour, but I may have a break in the case. I want you to identify someone."

Eliza hesitates. "I don't drive well at night, so if you don't mind, I can come down to the station in the morning."

Sebastian shakes his head from side to side. "Oh no, I can drive over to your house for you to make the ID." He doesn't want Eliza coming to the station; he has a gut feeling Dennis is up to no good. He doesn't want to be seen with her at the station. She already had one scare and he doesn't want her to have another.

"I would love the company," exclaims Eliza. "I need to get off this phone so I can put some coffee on and fix a little something for you to eat."

"You don't have to go through all of that trouble for me." Sebastian rubs his belly, remembering what she cooked the last time he was over. He licks his lips; he can taste Eliza's home cooking.

"You don't tell me what to do in my house!" shouts Eliza.

Sebastian smiles. He rubs his stomach again. "Yes, ma'am. I am on the way." He doesn't put up much of a fight; he is hungry and needs to know what Dennis is hiding.

He starts his car and drives in the direction of Eliza's home, thinking of how much he misses his Nana.

Chapter 19

*S*ebastian walks through the fence with camera in hand up the steps to Eliza's front door. He rings the doorbell and rubs his belly as it growls. His mouth waters in anticipation of Eliza's home cooking. He uses his index and thumb to wipe his lips.

Eliza finishes the last of the dishes as the doorbell rings. Sebastian, knowing Eliza is elderly but unsure she heard the doorbell, rings it again. She wipes her hands on her apron while hurrying to the door and yells, "I'm coming." Eliza, winded, opens the door to greet her new friend. "Hey, I am glad you called. How are you?"

"I am fine."

"Come in." Eliza steps to the side. Sebastian squeezes between Eliza and the door. Eliza shuts the door behind him. She walks toward the kitchen, and Sebastian follows, taking in the smell of a home-cooked meal. "I know you liked my grits the last time you were here, so I fixed shrimp and grits. Then I wasn't sure if you were allergic to shellfish, so I smothered pork chops. I know you like pork because you devoured that sausage the last time you were here." Eliza chuckles.

Sebastian closes his eyes, breathes deeply, smiles, and pats his stomach. "No, I don't have any shellfish allergies. I can eat just about anything."

"Good, I am going to give you a little of both."

Sebastian's eyes open wide, his mouth waters, and he swallows as he watches Eliza carefully scoop the steaming hot food on the fine china. *I can get used to this.*

"Oh, Eliza, I almost forgot the reason I came here." Sebastian walks toward Eliza near the stove. He shows Eliza the camera with the photos he took of both Dennis and Gregory. "Does the person in the photo look familiar?"

Eliza places the pork chop on the plate next to the grits; the butter in a puddle on top of the grits runs down the side of the mound. She takes her serving spoon and scoops up a hefty portion of brown gravy with caramelized onions; she drowns the grits and the pork chop. Eliza, always doing things in her time, is ready to exchange the plate for the camera. Sebastian walks to the table, picks up his silverware, and cuts the pork chop and proceeds to place the piece of succulent meat in his mouth. He closes his eyes as the tender meat satisfies his palate. Eliza walks over and places the camera on the table next to Sebastian's plate. She hits Sebastian on the back of the head with the palm of her hand. "What do you think you are doing? You didn't bless your food. I am a praying woman and raised my children to do the same. I didn't birth you but when you put your feet under my table, you are my responsibility."

"Yes, ma'am" is Sebastian's only response. He knows better. He was taught to bless his food too. He lowers his head, the knife and fork to his plate.

"Go ahead, bless the food aloud. I want to hear you pray. Praying over your food is a different prayer than praying for a wife." Eliza grins. "Why aren't you married?"

"I was married once; my wife died in a car accident."

"Oh, now I get it. You haven't had a home-cooked meal in a while and dove straight in without thanking the Lord. Still no excuse, go ahead and pray before your food gets cold."

Sebastian complies with Eliza's request and blesses the food aloud. He opens his eyes, and Eliza nods letting him know it is okay to start eating. She watches Sebastian shove the food into his mouth, barely chewing. "Slow down. You are going to give yourself indigestion."

Sebastian's eyes slowly move from his plate to Eliza sitting across from him. Carefully he places his fork on the side of his plate and wipes his mouth with the cloth napkin before him. He chews his food in silence for a few minutes. Eliza smiles watching Sebastian enjoying his meal. Sebastian notices the camera back on the table.

"Did you recognize the two men in the photo?" Eliza is silent. Sebastian reaches across the table for the camera and hands it back to Eliza.

Eliza doesn't move. "I don't need to look at the photo again. The man to the left is Dennis, the detective; the other man is Sean, the guy who said someone with gang colors ran from Doris's house."

"Thanks, Eliza, the identification is helpful." Sebastian's exterior is stoic but inside he smiles knowing the walls are closing in on Dennis.

Eliza uses the table to support the weight of her body to a standing position, walks over to the counter, and packs up the leftovers for the wifeless detective. She glances over her shoulder at Sebastian. She will have to work on finding someone for him, perhaps her daughter, Scotty. She has been after Scotty to give her grandchildren. It is about time she settles down, and besides, Sebastian is a good man.

Chapter 20

$\mathcal{T}$he camera zooms in on critically acclaimed journalist Scotty Richards, the host of *Meeting of the Minds*. Scotty, holding a hand mirror to her face, dabs the corners of her lips to remove the excess lip gloss. Arnie, her assistant producer, yells, "Five, four, three, two, one." On the four Scotty gives up the mirror to her makeup artist. She turns her body in the direction of Camera 1. Scotty's eyes twinkle as she looks into the camera. "Thank you for watching *Meeting of the Minds*. Today, we have as our guest Brendon Graham, the senator for the State of Pennsylvania. Welcome, Senator."

"Thank you for having me."

"Brendon, let's get down to it. You are making your rounds with all the media outlets. What is this big announcement?"

Kyndall, once standing within eyeshot of Brendon, walks farther off the side of the set, still within view of Brendon but away from the rest of the crew. She has an idea. She might as well go for the gusto. She places the most important phone call of the day.

"Hello, this is Kyndall Graham. How are you, sir?"

"I am well, Mrs. Graham. How can I help you?"

"Please call me Kyndall. The reason I am calling you is to find out if you decided on your vice president nominee?"

"There are a few names I am considering."

"Well, do you have my son on the list of candidates?"

"Brendon, right?"

"Brendon Graham."

"There were a few people on the hill lobbying for him. We even vetted him but there were a few skeletons we uncovered. We decided to move in another direction. A candidate that speaks to more of family values."

"I am sorry you feel that way, Beau. I hope you change your mind."

"I won't but thank you for calling."

Kyndall ends the call without responding to Beau. On the other side of the room, Artie, the assistant production manager, walks toward her on his way to the control room. Kyndall, tapping the phone on the palm of her hand, stops and wiggles her index finger, motioning Arnie toward her. "Arnie, I have a tip from Beau's election campaign. Brendon is being considered as the vice president nominee."

"How can I validate your story?"

"Let me just give him a call back." Kyndall goes to her recent calls and hits Beau's number and puts him on speaker. "Hello, this is Beau."

"Hi Beau, I am sorry that I accidentally hung up on you earlier. Thank you for vetting Brendon through the vice president nominee process."

"You are so welcome."

"I will talk to you soon." They both end the call.

"Kyndall, thank you for the tip." Artie turns away from Kyndall and tells the control room to go to commercial. He's just learned breaking news concerning Beau Stanford's nominee for vice president, Brendon Graham.

Beau and his team are watching Brendon's interview and fuming at the rumor of his team considering Brendon for the VP nominee. Kyndall is the only person who could have leaked the information. Beau picks up his phone and calls Kyndall.

"Hello."

"What do you think you are doing?"

"What on earth are you asking?" asks Kyndall with a wide grin.

"Don't get cute with me!" shouts Beau. He heard rumors floating about Kyndall in Washington as well, and they weren't favorable.

"I know you leaked the information to the news media. Now we have to announce to the public we are considering Brendon a viable candidate. Candidates we are seriously considering are reported."

"Well, with the media outlets asking about Brendon as a candidate, you must put the information out to the public. With Brendon on your ticket, I will guarantee you will win the election."

"I don't know if I want to associate myself with the rumors."

"What rumors?" Kyndall snaps.

"Brendon is known on The Hill as a wildcat."

"A wildcat? What are you saying?"

"He indulges in extracurricular activities outside of his marriage—these are the whispers in Washington."

"You shouldn't believe everything you hear. There was a time or two he did stray in his marriage, but after he recommitted to his family Brendon has been on track. Every marriage goes through its difficulties. Wouldn't you agree?"

"Yes, but Brendon seems to be a liability. There's talk about him being associated with escorts."

"Who is Isabella, Beau? Do you know her? She says you like to be tied up as a submissive."

Beau uses his free hand to rub his tight chest. He cracks his neck from right to left. His damp shirt sticks to his body. "You bitch. What do you want?"

"I want you to formally announce Brendon on the ticket with you."

"The party will never agree to this."

"You need to convince them. You need to strongly convince them."

"Are you blackmailing me?"

"Of course not: however, once Brendon and I leave here, he has a radio interview and somehow the rumor of him being the VP nominee will a rise again. And perhaps question about you and Isabella will surface."

Beau breathes heavy in the phone without a word. Kyndall waits for a response. "Okay. I will ensure Brendon is the nominee."

"I am glad you were able to see it my way."

"Don't call me again." Beau hangs up without a response from Kyndall.

———— ◅◉▻ ————

"Yes, Scotty. I am passionate about our veterans. After they serve in the armed services, the transition to a civilian life is often difficult, not only for the service member but for their spouses as well. This program already exists but we are need ing more money to fund this program. I want all the viewers to contact their representative to encourage their vote when the Transition Assistance Program Overview bill is presented to Congress."

Scotty's assistant producer speaks to her through the earpiece. "Okay, we have a tip that Brendon is being considered on the Beau Stanford Harris ticket as the vice president nominee. I need you to change the subject; we want to be the first to get his reaction to the news."

"Senator, there have been rumors that you are being considered as the vice president nominee."

Brendon runs his right hand through his $200 haircut. He blinks, then again. "I never…" he stammers.

Out of nowhere Kyndall appears at the seven o'clock position. She makes eye contact with Brendon, shakes her head from side to side. She folds her arms and straightens her back.

"Scotty, I never respond to rumors."

"So, you aren't denying that you will be going to the convention as the vice president nominee."

"Again, I don't respond to rumors."

"Well, maybe you can answer this question, which isn't a rumor. You told me on this show your freshman year in Congress that the next presidential election you would run. Are you going to run for the presidency?"

"I don't recall making that statement."

"My assistant producer, Arnie, is prepared to cue up the video. Senator, are you going to run for the presidency?"

"No, I am thrilled to continue the work I'm doing in Congress."

"But as the President, you can touch so many lives and do good for the country."

"Scotty, I will support our party's nominee for President in any way that I can."

Scotty turns her body and speaks into the camera. "Folks, you heard it from Brendon Graham; he is not running for President. Thank you for being with us today."

Brendon nods his head and responds, "Thank you for having me."

"That's all the time we have. I will see you tomorrow on *Meeting of the Minds*."

Brendon removes the microphone, stands, and shakes Scotty's hand. "Thank you for having me on your show. You know you blindsided me with the question about the vice president nominee."

"You are a public figure; all questions are appropriate. By the way, how is your beautiful wife?"

"She is good."

"Scotty darling, it is so good to see you." Kyndall greets Scotty with an embrace, a kiss to the right and a kiss to the left side of her face. Brendon walks toward the men's room.

Scotty removes the microphone from her lapel and earpiece from her ear.

"It is good to see you too. There is word floating around Brendon is expected to run in the next Presidential election. We are in the next Presidential election, so is he running officially?"

"That we are approaching the next election cycle." Kyndall places her clutch handbag under her right arm and examines her well-manicured nails. "Well, the interview is over, but I can see the inquisition is at full throttle. You never know when to stop, do you?"

"I stop when I get the full story and I know you are hiding something."

"Scotty, what on earth could Brendon be hiding?"

"No, not Brendon, you."

"Me? I have never run for public office." She touches her chest with her left hand and chuckles.

"Let this be your warning, I will find out what you are hiding. You never make a promise that you didn't keep. I also know that you were the one who had me fired from the station in Philadelphia. And for the record I never slept with your husband."

"Maybe you did or didn't, but I needed to make a point to let you both know who was in control."

"You ruined my career. I had to move in with my parents. I did not have money; they could only offer me a place to stay. I went through all my savings. I finally caught a break and found a job in Wisconsin. I busted my butt and worked up to the morning show. I did that within two years, and I was hired at a station in Atlanta, and within a year CBN offered me a position in investigative reporting and I landed the spot I am in now."

"Like I said, I helped move your career forward."

"Are you serious?"

"Yes, look at you all grown up. Making difficult adult decisions."

Scotty grabs Kyndall's arm. "You destroyed my life and you will pay for it," she whispers in Kyndall's ear and briskly walks off set.

Kyndall turns to Brendon. "Are you ready to go?"

"Mother, what was that all about?"

"She and I were catching up. It has been years since I saw her last."

"It seems as though the conversation was heated."

"You know how it goes when someone's life doesn't go according to plan; they want someone to blame. She wants that someone to be me." Kyndall shakes her head, locks her arms with Brendon's, and they both exit the station.

Chapter 21

Scotty parks her Tesla S 90D at the airport and takes a flight to Philadelphia. She is concerned with her mother's mental health. The crazy rant about a lady with a fancy Mercedes killing her friend sounds so out of character for her mother. Maybe it is time to consider an assisted living facility. She reviews two brochures, preparing a speech in her head how to sell the facility to her mother. She wants her mother to live in a facility where she can get the care, she needs twenty-four/seven. Her mother has refused to live with her after numerous offers, so the next best place would be an assisted living facility. Eliza is a hard cookie to crumble but wants to continue to live by herself.

This instance of her neighbor being killed is worrying Scotty. Maybe her mother is going through dementia or perhaps Alzheimer's, Scotty doesn't know, but she needs to see her mother. She isn't close to her family, but her mother was the only one who believed in her when she was out of work. Her father, Emit, refused to allow Scotty to move back home after Kyndall got her fired. He strongly believed once children turned eighteen, they either went to college or got a job. Scotty didn't feel as though she fell into that mold because she went to college and had a successful career but hit a bump and needed a place to stay until she got back on her feet.

Her grandfather kicked Emit out of the house at eighteen to fend for himself, and he worked two jobs to provide for his family. If he could find a job and take care of his family, his children should be able to provide for themselves. Scotty thought her situation should have been different. She lived the young adult dream, earned her degree, landed a prestigious anchor job. Scotty didn't stay with her family long after her dismissal. The arguments between her father and mother became more frequent, and her father knew that the more he showed disrespect to her mother, the sooner her mother would have a conversation with Scotty to leave.

Her father would pick a fight with Scotty, and Eliza would step in to defend her. Scotty left the room and slammed her bedroom door and the arguing between her mother and father would start. She never knew when they stopped shouting; she would cry herself to sleep. Eliza, a young woman at the time, body worn, eyes never meeting Scotty's as they passed in the hallway or at the kitchen table. Scotty knew she needed to devise a plan to leave because her mother would soon have a conversation for her to leave her family home. Luckily within days of her mother's distant stare, Scotty found a job out West; she left Philadelphia and never looked back.

Chapter 22

*E*liza sits on the edge of the leather recliner pretending to watch television. Every few minutes she shifts to the window in anticipation of her daughter. Scotty called an hour ago when she landed; she should have been here by now. Eliza flips her wrist to glance at her watch. Eliza's faced forward toward the television when the yellow taxi pulls up in the front of the house. The glare of the car in her peripheral vision, Eliza jumps up from her chair and races to the door. In no time Eliza is on the front porch, smiling from ear to ear to greet her daughter who she hasn't seen since last Christmas. Eliza shakes her head. Her baby is too thin, just skin and bones. She will have to do something about that before she leaves, says Eliza through her eyes and shake of her head.

Heather, the taxi driver, retrieves the Louis Vuitton luggage from the trunk and places the two high-end pieces on the sidewalk. Scotty pays the driver in cash. "Keep the change."

"Thank you, ma'am."

"Goodness, call me Scotty. When I hear ma'am, I think of my mother. I'm not that old."

Heather steals a secret glance at Scotty and licks her lips. Eliza, standing on the porch with an overview of the yard, witnesses the taxi driver flirting with her daughter and clears her throat to show her disgust with Heather's behavior. Heather jumps, not realizing her actions were being examined by an onlooker. Heather turns her head to the porch. "Hello, ma'am, how are you?"

Eliza, arms folded, taps her foot. "I am well. I am sure you have a busy day."

Heather turns her attention to Scotty. "If you need a ride to the airport, you call me directly. My phone number is on the bottom of the receipt."

Scotty, oblivious to Heather's flirting, folds the receipt and places it in her purse. She extends the handle of her luggage and pushes it through the fence and collapses the handle to carry the heavy bags up the steps to the porch.

"Hi Mom." Scotty hugs her mother's fragile body, careful not to break any bones.

Eliza rises to the tip of her toes to reciprocate a hug from her daughter, who is wearing heels that are just too high for her liking. Eliza steps back from the warm embrace and puts her hands on her hips. "Why are you here? You only visit during the holidays."

Scotty smiles. She knows her mother like the back of her hand and is prepared for the question. She wants to disguise the real reason for the trip. "Oh, I thought I should spend more time with you. The visits during the holidays aren't long enough."

"You don't say." Eliza looks suspiciously at her daughter. "Come inside. You need help with that fancy luggage of yours?"

"Oh, Mama, I got it."

Eliza opens the screen door, her back to the door propping it open.

Scotty lifts the luggage across the threshold, rolls it down the hall to her childhood bedroom. She stops in the doorway; her eyes move from wall to wall. The faces of Oprah Winfrey, Jane

Pauley, and Barbara Walters adorn the light pink walls. Scotty's eyes slowly move from the wall to the white bookshelf. Scotty grins at the sight of her tape recorder. She clicks play. The tape starts to play her recording. In her best Barbara Walters imitation, she is interviewing two of her best friends who are running for student council president and vice president. Scotty bursts out laughing. At a young age she planned her career; she would major in journalism, intern at the number one network, work hard to sit in the anchor chair.

Each year she checks her journal, where she outlines her career goals; she is on track to getting a seat at a major network, and she is a general assignment reporter in the Philadelphia market searching for "the big story" to get her noticed within her station, but she has her sights on New York. Scotty smiles. She is proud of her fifteen-minute crime segment during the 7:00 p.m. news, where she helps residents get justice. Scotty remembers the day Bessie called her after her segment to report being swindled out of her life's savings.

Bessie hadn't gone in the basement in a week to do laundry and found the basement floor covered with water. She immediately called Oscar, her son-in-law, to replace the water heater. Oscar wet vacuumed the basement, stood back, admired his handiwork, turned off the video on how to fix water heaters, kissed his mother-in-law on the cheek, and drove across town to his lovely wife. Oscar, who knew nothing about water leaks, didn't check the hose, and a tiny pinhole sprayed the back wall. The moisture grew mold. Bessie saw the black mold expand the length of the wall, her asthma getting worse every day. She was aware she needed to do something, and she thought she'd met her savior when Kerry, the contractor, knocked on her door to help with miscellaneous chores around the house. Bessie invited Kerry in and showed him the mold, and he said he could take care of the problem in one day. He walked the length of the basement and gave Bessie a list of other problems that didn't need to be fixed but he added them to the list. Kerry told her she needed to write him a check today so he could get a crew to start the work the next day. Bessie wrote him a check for $10,000, her life savings. Kerry told her he would be back first thing the next morning.

The next morning Bessie woke at 6:00, dressed, ate her breakfast, and sat at the kitchen table waiting for Kerry. She walked to the living room and paced in front of the window, looking at her watch. Bessie looked out the window every hour on the hour for two weeks as her laundry spilled on the floor from the packed hamper. Her asthma wouldn't allow her to continue to go up and down the stairs.

Exhausted at the end of the second week, she decided to take her mind off her troubles and turn on the local news. There Scotty was on television asking viewers who were defrauded to give her a call—she could help. Bessie called Scotty and within a week Scotty had located the scammer. He was arrested. He didn't have all the $10,000 but gave her back $5,000 and made a deal with law enforcement to pay Bessie $250 over the next twenty months. Several honest contractors pitched in and renovated the basement for free. Scotty was proud of the positive impact she was making in the community where she worked and lived.

Scotty's shoulders slumps. She blinks fast to suppress the tears, and her bottom lip quivers. She sits on the twin bed. Tears flow down Scotty's cheeks as she remembers the hurt, she felt all those years ago as though it happened that morning. Kyndall Graham got her fired from the job she loved. If that wasn't bad enough, Kyndall hit deep by getting her blackballed from the profession she loves the most.

Chapter 23

Scotty, never a saver, spent the small salary she earned on her appearance to glow while on air. She had chemical peels, teeth whitening, and a personal trainer. The list goes on to the extent she wanted to look better than the next journalist to get some kind of edge to the anchor chair. So, when she got fired, she went through her savings within three months. Once her savings were depleted, she called her mother, crying, incoherent; she had no place else to go but back home. Eliza wanted her daughter home to be safe, but her father made it very uncomfortable for her. He asked her every day when she was moving out. Scotty decided to expand her job search to smaller markets even though it would set her career back years. She had to do what she needed to get out of her parents' house. She turned to drinking to take the edge off. One day, she received a call from a small station in Wisconsin. Scotty borrowed money from her mother for the ticket with a promise to pay her back.

Scotty whimpers. She should have never taken the flight to Wisconsin.

She remembers the night before the interview when she visited the local tavern…

—◦《◎》◦—

Scotty sips a drink at the bar. A handsome man walks into the bar, skin a touch of olive, hair wavy. His eyes roam the room and stop at the stranger. A slick smile on his face, he walks toward the bar with a swagger to sit next to the beautiful woman. Peter, the bartender, pours the regular his drink of choice and places it in front of him. Donovan nods, acknowledging Peter's excellent customer service. Peter nods in return and walks to the other end of the bar to talk to his brother, keeping a sharp eye on Donovan.

Donovan, not the shy type, introduces himself to Scotty. "Hi, my name is Donovan. What's yours?"

"It's nice to meet you, Donovan. I'm Scotty."

"What brings you to town?" Donovan stops by the bar every night after work for a drink or two and is quite familiar with the locals, but Scotty sticks out like a rose in a bed of weeds.

"What makes you think I am from out of town?"

Donovan shakes his head. "You look like the type who lives in a big city and is slumming it in our little town. Tasting your way through the city on twenty dollars per day. Am I right?"

She laughs at the thought. "No, I am here for a job interview with the local television station."

"Which station?"

"WDYP."

"Oh yes, I hear the station owner is a prick." Donovan chuckles.

"Prick or not, I really need this job. This is my last opportunity to get back in the industry before everyone forgets about me and the great stories I reported."

"What happened at your last job?"

"I interviewed a powerful man, and his wife accused me of sleeping with him. She convinced the station manager to fire me."

"How can this woman get you fired? She has that much control or power?"

"You don't know the half of it with this woman. I can't wait for the day to get even with Kyndall Graham. She destroyed my life." Scotty motions to the bartender for another drink. She sips on the fresh drink, thinking of the many ways to get revenge on Kyndall.

Donovan breaks her thoughts with an absurd question.

"Did you sleep with her husband?"

"Absolutely not! I am a professional and would never lower my values to have sex with someone's husband."

Donovan wrinkles his brow and plays with his wedding band. He didn't expect to get this type of response from Scotty. He was hoping the two could go back to her hotel, but that is out of the question. He exclaims, "Well, good! Let's make a toast to new beginnings."

"To new beginnings." Scotty echoes Donovan's sentiment, clinking their glasses together. Both tip their heads back to gulp the entire drink. The liquor burns as it coats their throats and settles in their stomachs.

Donovan jumps off the barstool and extends his hand to Scotty to shake. "It has been a pleasure meeting you. I hope everything works out for you tomorrow. Maybe our paths will cross again." Scotty shakes Donovan's extended hand. Donovan walks toward the door with his hands in his pocket and disappears on the other side. Scotty motions to the bartender for another drink; a glass of wine this time. She needs to be sober for her interview tomorrow.

The next day Scotty arrives at the radio station fifteen minutes early. She sits in the lobby eyeing the other candidates interviewing for her last chance job before she has to be a greeter at Walmart. Her phone chirps, and she looks down. She has a bank alert—her balance is negative $220.00. Scotty takes a deep breath as a tear rolls down her cheek. She uses her index finger to wipe the tear away; she looks around the room to ensure no one saw her moment of weakness. The room is filled with sharks smelling the blood called weakness. She is desperate. She needs to pull herself together to land this job. She reaches in her purse and checks her makeup. There is a little smudge on the outside corner of her left eye. She uses her index finger to fix the smudge. There, good as new. She drops the mirror into her purse, closes it, and looks at her watch. Sharply at 11:00 the secretary, Linda calls Scotty's name. Scotty stands and follows her to the station manager's office. Linda opens the door and introduces Scotty to her manager, Donovan Walsh. Donovan stands and smiles slyly at Scotty. *Why didn't he tell me he was the station manager?* The two of them exchange pleasantries in front of Linda. Linda moves back toward the door and closes it behind her.

"Please have a seat."

Scotty, originally nervous about the interview, starts to feel at ease with Donovan; they had a pleasant evening last night getting to know one another. Her shoulders relax, and she crosses her legs at the ankle with both her hands resting on her portfolio on her lap. "You and I met last evening and talked a lot about your previous work history. Now the million-dollar question is, why should I hire you? I have twenty candidates to interview—the entire lobby of candidates you just saw. They are just as talented as you or more so. Again, why should I hire you?"

Scotty begins to speak. "I have several critically acclaimed documentaries and news pieces, but I am most proud of the Peabody award."

Donovan interrupts her before she continues giving him all her accolades. "I know all this. I need to know about the other skills you can offer me that no other candidate or employee can contribute to this office; to me."

Scotty smiles, flattered. She begins making future career plans in her head. She will land this job and be taken seriously. *I will stay at the station for a few years and move to a station in a larger city but not forgetting Donovan and how he kicked started my career.* She is going to climb the ladder to get her career back on track. The anchor desk is calling her name in her mind's eye; she is wearing a coral short-sleeve dress with a gold zipper. Her matching jewelry—gold earrings, necklace, and bracelet—sparkle along with her pearly white teeth shining bright in the camera. She will have to make an appointment to get her teeth bleached before she starts. Perhaps Donovan will give her moving expenses and an advance to get herself ready for the job. Oh, she needs highlights too. Many things she needs to do to prepare to get back on the air. Scotty smiles as she thinks about sitting in the anchor chair at her new job. She is distracted when Donovan starts to speak.

"Congratulations, I want to offer you the job."

"Really? Thank you so much," says Scotty as she clasps both her hands together in front of her.

Donovan stands and walks to the front of his desk, unzips his trousers, finding the opening to his boxers, and pulls his penis through the opening. Looking directly at Scotty he strokes his penis to be hard as a brick and says, "Once you bring me your medical records, the job is yours. I don't like to use condoms; I wouldn't want my wife to find out I was having sex with someone." He closes his eyes, pleasuring himself. "Today, you need to satisfy me orally. You know to seal the deal."

Scotty briskly runs out of Donovan's office past the receptionist desk, down two flights of stairs into the parking lot. She vomits once outside, releasing what he made her swallow. Inside her car she screams while violently beating the steering wheel with the palms of both hands; no one is around so her tantum goes unnoticed. She stops and closes her eyes to control her breathing. In and out her breathing controls her rage and she starts to calm down. *Ding.* An email alert on her phone distracts her meditation. Scotty searches her purse for her phone and views the email alert from her bank. Her checking account is now overdrawn by 480 dollars, which means the check she wrote for her car payment will bounce. Scotty starts to cry. The phone suddenly becomes heavy, her heart breaking as she composes the email with her medical records attached to Donovan. She is financially ruined, and this job is what she needs to get back on track. *Kyndall and Donovan will pay for humiliating me.*

After two years and one abortion, Scotty leaves Donovan's control. She calls one of her guy friends who told her if she ever wanted to do something about the situation, he knew someone who had a friend who would have a conversation with Donovan. Scotty does just that. She calls the friend of her friend to get him to "talk" to Donovan. She hangs up the phone and thinks about what she just did. Her mother didn't raise her to be so cruel.

The whistle of the kettle reminds Scotty she is in the comfort of her mother's home waiting for a cup of tea. She wipes the single tear that streaks her light beige foundation.

"Honey, our tea is ready."

"Yes, Mother. I will be right there," says Scotty as she dries her hand on her pants.

Scotty makes her way to the living room, where her mother has poured her hot water and submerged a teabag. The cubed sugar reminded Scotty of her childhood tea parties where she placed her two dolls around her play table and her mother sat on the end of the table, sipping tea with her pinky in the air. Scotty mimicked her mother; she too stuck her pinky in the air. The two giggled. They thought they were royalty. It was always difficult for her to make sure the feathers from the boa did not land in her tea.

Scotty focuses on her mother sitting in front of her enjoying her tea and biscuit. Her mother was strong then, very sharp she still is, but Scotty worries about her mother's accusations that her neighbor was killed by the lady driving the fancy Mercedes.

Scotty leans over, picks up her teacup, dances the teabag up, down, and around. The color of the hot water turns a deep brown, increasing the strength of the tea, just the way she likes it. She leaves the teabag in the cup while taking the tiny tongs and picks up one piece of cubed sugar; she stares into the cup watching it dissolve. She stirs her tea. The tea now ready for her to sip, Scotty leans back in her chair, crosses her leg, right over left. "Mama, who is the lady that drives the fancy Mercedes?"

Eliza takes a sip of tea and places the floral teacup on its matching saucer. "The lady who killed my friend, Doris."

"What friend Doris? I don't recall your mentioning a friend Doris."

"You know, Doris Massey, who lived across the street."

"The name sounds familiar, but I can't place her face."

"She's been over there for years. Remember she was married to Steve Massey? He used to fix your car after your father died." Eliza cuts her eye at Scotty at the thought of her deceased husband. Scotty, knowing not to touch the topic of her father, comments only on knowing Doris.

"I vaguely remember her."

"If you came home more often to visit, you would know my friends." Eliza raises her brow while rolling her eyes toward her daughter.

"Mother, you know I work and try to get home when I can." Scotty pauses and stares into her teacup. "I have a confession. The real reason I came to visit is because I am worried about you."

"No need to worry about me." Eliza picks invisible lint off her apron. "I'm fine. Just fine."

"Then who is this made-up lady who drives a fancy Mercedes and killed your friend Doris?"

Eliza sharply cuts her eyes toward her daughter. "Well, she is something. What I'm not going to do is let her get away with murder. Pearl wants me to back down and stop talking about Doris's death and who I think killed her. I refuse to back down. Pearl can but I won't. We all know where her loyalty lies. No, not me. I seek the truth. That's right, I am a truth seeker," Eliza rambles.

Scotty taps her fingernail on the side of the teacup as she listens to her mother's story. She sighs, places the teacup directly on the coffee table.

"Scotty!" shouts Eliza. "I'm not that upset to notice you placed the teacup on my table and not the saucer. I taught you better etiquette than that."

With a smirk on her face, Scotty obeys her mother; she leans over, moves the teacup, and places it on the saucer. Scotty pauses for a moment thinking of the best way to present to her mother the information on the assisted living facility near her in Atlanta. Before Scotty can begin to speak, Eliza starts her rant once again. "I was sitting on the porch and the lady drove up in that fancy black Mercedes. You know, the one your father had before he died."

Here we go again on both, the lady with the fancy Mercedes and my deceased father. I will appease her but not for long. Scotty glances at her watch for the time.

"The E-class?"

"No, the other one."

"The CLS?"

"Yes, that one! Kyndall pulled into Doris's driveway and it took her a minute to get out of the car. I was sitting on the porch. You know my spot. I see any and everybody walking up and down this street. I told you about the Jefferson's toddler, who unlatched

the fence and was walking down the street. I dropped my crocheting and scooped that baby up and returned him to his young
mother before she knew Elijah was out of the yard."

"Yes, ma'am, I remember. Now, who did you say drove the
fancy Mercedes, the one that Daddy drove before he *died*?" Scotty
blankly stares at her teacup. Her father isn't dead. He lives across
town with the person he left his wife for.

———◄((◊))►———

When Emit grabbed his hat and suitcase and turned the handle to walk out, Eliza told him, "Once you step on the other side
of the door, don't look back because you aren't welcome here any
longer."

With his back to his wife, Emit paused for a moment to think
about the choice he was about to make. He closed his eyes, took
a deep breath, turned the knob, and crossed the threshold. Emit
turned around, and Eliza slammed the door in his face. Emit rested his forehead on the door. Hot tears streamed down his face;
he couldn't tell his wife the real reason he was leaving. He found
love and comfort in someone else, but he still loved his wife and
would marry her all over again. She was his prize, his forever after,
but he desired a new love—Damien. Damien was half his age and
made him feel in touch with his identity, his true self. Emit wait
ed anxiously for the touch and the kiss of his lover. Emit's eyes
sparkled as he remembered Damien's touch. Damien made him
feel young again, and he was alive for once in his life. Damien's
kind heart and spirit forced Emit's body to take the steps to move
from the porch.

Eliza, standing with her hands and ear pressed against the
door, could hear Emit's footsteps as they descended away from
the door and down the steps. The last words Eliza uttered still
tore him up at night. "You are dead to me. I don't ever want to

see you again. Even though you have retired, you are still a man of the cloth."

Emit was torn by the vows he professed before God and the lustful feelings he had for Damien. The satisfaction and fulfillment of the flesh took over his body. Emit knew the church would not approve of his lifestyle, so he never returned to the pulpit or walked through the doors of a church again. He was now an outcast, a person his friends would turn their backs on if they knew about his new life; his free life.

—————)(◉)(⚊—————

Scotty, standing in her bedroom, heard the exchange between her mother and father, not knowing why her mother was so cruel to him. Scotty, being a daddy's girl, didn't want her father to leave. Truth be told if anyone should leave, she thought it should have been her mother. Scotty cried. She wanted her daddy, but her mother drove him away.

Then she learned the real reason her father left. Tammy's mother on the phone with her sister Addison explained which friend of Tammy's was spending the night. "You know, Scotty—her father left his family for a man." Scotty, on the other side of the door, gasped. She placed her hands to her mouth not to scream. She backed into the wall, closed her eyes, and the pit of her stomach dropped. She was embarrassed, she held a grudge toward her mother for years. Scotty wept not because her father was across town living with a man but because she was mean to the only person who ever cared for her. If it made her mother feel good to say her father was dead, she would refer to him as dead too.

—————)(◉)(⚊—————

"Kyndall, Kyndall Graham."

Scotty jumps up from the chair. The cloth napkin once on her lap falls to the floor. "Kyndall!" shouts Scotty. "Why would Kyndall kill your friend Doris? What is the connection between the two of them?"

"What do you mean the connection? Kyndall's son, Brendon, married Doris's daughter, Emily," says Eliza innocently.

"Emily's mother is your friend who died?"

Scotty thinks back on Emily growing up; the two of them went their separate ways after high school. Emily stayed close to home, and Scotty moved as far away as she could from her family; her father ruled the house with a steel fist. "Wait, Mother, there was a rumor that Emily was a lesbian."

"Well, there was some talk." Eliza shakes her head, remembering the day Doris ran across the street to tell her the news. "Doris's heart was broken when she found out. Emily was home on break and invited Julia over for a few days, but Doris could see the lust Julia had for Emily in her eyes. Emily was innocent, but Julia seemed worldly...you know the type; loose."

"Mother..."

"You know me. I went on about my business trying not to judge because of what happened with your father, but I still couldn't understand Emily wanting that girl over a man." Eliza shakes her head in disgust.

Eliza knew her husband desired someone else, she wasn't quite sure who, but eventually she figured out that it was a "what" according to her. Eliza found the pornography of boys Emit had left in his special hiding place; the bottom of his sock drawer. Then it was the way Emit would stare at men when they were in public. It was a stare of a lion licking his lips waiting on his prey.

The day they were at Green Eggs & Ham, the waiter named Damien flirted with Emit and Emit blushed. Eliza could sense Emit was attracted to him by the way his body reacted to

Damien's smile. Emit, erect, rubbed the front of his pants casually not to draw attention to himself. Eliza went to the bathroom and when she returned, she saw Damien pass Emit a piece of paper. Emit slid the paper in his pants pocket. The late-night phone calls and last-minute trips to the store told a story of a man cheating and stealing time trying to keep up with his lover. One day Eliza overheard a conversation between Emit and Damien, where Emit told his lover he couldn't leave his wife. He described her as fragile and couldn't take care of herself if he left, but he still wanted to be with him. The two hung up the phone as Eliza cleared her throat standing in the doorway; Emit jumped. "I'm not as fragile as you think. You don't owe me anything. You can go if you want."

Emit sat on the edge of the bed, his heart racing, excited that he would be free to live the life he always wanted, especially now that he found the type of love he needed. The beating of his heart slowed to a normal pace as he thought about the seventeen year marriage he would be leaving behind, the other love of his life. It was settled in his mind; he would honor the commitment he made with Eliza all those years ago.

Eliza noticed the look in his eye. She wasn't going to continue to be anyone's sloppy seconds. Eliza rushed toward the dresser drawers, haphazardly emptying the contents into a black Samsonite suitcase. Without a word, Eliza handed him the suitcase and her hand brushed the top of his as he reached for the handle. Quickly, she released the handle, letting the suitcase fall to the floor. Emit picked up the suitcase and, conflicted, he paused. He wanted to stay with Eliza but had a new life awaiting him across town. Something he was never able to explore because of his calling as a minister and strong family values. As a child he learned that men marry women, not men marrying men. His father would just die if he wasn't already dead that his son left his wife for a man. He shivered at the thought of his father being disappointed with him. Emit walked to the coat closet with suit-case in hand and grabbed his hat and placed it on his head.

———— ⚫ ————

Bingo, Kyndall, Scotty thinks. *I got your scandal.* "Mother, what did you say Emily's girlfriend's name was, the one she dated in college."

"Her name is Julia."

"Right, you mentioned that; do you remember her last name?"

Eliza thinks for a moment in silence. "No, I don't remember her name. Boy, Doris was mad about the news, but she came around, eventually. She even apologized to Julia before she died." Eliza pauses for another moment thinking about the conversation she had with Doris. Out of nowhere, she shouts, "Sutton."

"What?" asks Scotty. She lost track of the conversation when her mother said she did not remember Julia's last name.

"Julia's last name is Sutton. Doris used her first and last name to find her on one of those social media sites."

Scotty smiles admiring her savvy mother. She wants to be like her when she reaches her age. "Mama, you had me thinking you were losing your mind with all this crazy talk about a lady driv-ing a fancy Mercedes killing your friend. You never mentioned a name and I thought you were going senile."

"Child, please. I have all my wits about me, and I know what I saw."

"Mama, before you tell me what happened, let me grab my phone. I need to place a call."

"Okay, go ahead. I will be right here enjoying my tea." She takes another sip of the lukewarm beverage.

Scotty races down the hall to her tiny childhood bedroom.

Eliza yells, "Stop running, you would have thought I raised a pack of wolves."

Scotty slows her pace to a speed walk. She enters the bedroom and picks up her phone. She puts in her passcode and, too lazy to go through her contacts, she hits the recent call icon. She scrolls down until she finds Artie's phone number. The phone goes straight to voicemail. "Hey, Artie, it's me. You won't believe what just fell into my lap. Kyndall Graham killed her daughter-in-law's mother. My mother is the witness. Give me a call back." Scotty retrieves a pen out of her purse and a notepad from the bookshelf. She races back to the living room, where her mother is pouring herself another cup of tea. Scotty sits and drapes the cloth napkin across her lap.

"Would you like another cup of tea?"

"Yes, Mother, please." Eliza moves to the end of her chair, leans over the coffee table, and pours Scotty tea. "Mother, tell me the story about what you saw and heard the day Doris died."

Scotty waits with pad and paper.

Eliza slides back in her chair, looks at her fingernails, and is quiet. She is having to relive the death of her friend with Scotty, hopefully for the last time.

Scotty, careful not to rush her mother, patiently waits; she knows her mother likes to take her time with everything she does, even her conversations. This was a hard lesson Scotty learned growing up.

One Friday night, Scotty and Karen agreed to hang out at the mall. Karen pulled her mother's Toyota Corolla in front of the house and honked the horn. Scotty glanced out the window, rushed over to her mother, and gave her a kiss on the cheek. "Bye, Mama, Karen is outside waiting for me. After we leave the mall, we are going to grab something from the burger joint across the street."

"Oh, it just reminds me, Carolyn wants you to babysit tomorrow night. She and her husband are going out…."

"Okay, Mama, I got to go." Scotty reached over her mother to grab her house key on the end table. As Scotty reached over Eliza, her mother pinched her on the cheek, stopping her where she stood.

"Ouch!" squealed Scotty. "What did you do that for?"

"I am talking to you. I don't care anything about Karen waiting for you. Don't be rude and never rush me."

"Yes, ma'am." Scotty sat in the same chair she is sitting in today and never interrupted her mother again. Karen, having had a run-in or two with Eliza, patiently waited for Scotty in the car.

Scotty laughs at her childhood memory. Her mother is something else.

Eliza tells Scotty the exact story she told the police of Kyndall pulling into the yard and Doris inviting her in and hearing the gunshots. She also describes how condescending Detective Dennis Jones was and the stranger she knew was lying about his account of the story. Eliza stands and walks into the kitchen and removes the magnet that holds the detective's card onto the refrigerator. Eliza walks back to the living room, hands the business card to Scotty. The more she talks to her mother, the more the story sounds credible. "Mama, I want to apologize. I…."

Eliza bends down and kisses her daughter on the cheek and places both hands to her daughter's cheeks and then to her shoulders. She sighs heavily and looks Scotty square in the eyes. "I know everybody thinks I am crazy." Eliza pulls out a handkerchief and dabs both eyes. "Please do one thing for me."

"Yes, Mother, anything." Scotty reaches for her mother's hand and looks up at her.

"Expose Kyndall for killing my friend."

"Mother, I tell you what, I will seek the truth and report what I find."

"Deal! The truth is all I want. But I know what I saw."

Even though Scotty wants the facts to speak for themselves, secretly she wants Kyndall to be found guilty. Kyndall will get what's coming to her if it's the last thing she does.

Chapter 24

Alicia Keys' "Girl on Fire" blares from Scotty's iPhone; she hits snooze, needing a few more minutes to sleep. She can't sleep, the events of the day before consuming her thoughts. Did her mother tell her Kyndall killed Doris? Is this a dream? Scotty pinches her arm. "Ouch." No, this isn't a dream. Her mother told her Kyndall killed Doris.

Scotty snatches her phone from the nightstand, and reviews the phone, searching for a missed call from Artie. "Hum," she says aloud. Scotty hits Artie's name to redial his number. The phone goes straight to voicemail. "Hey, Artie, this is me, Scotty. I haven't heard back from you. Give me a call. I plan to drive to DC today to speak with Brendon. I plan to press him for the truth about his mother." Scotty whispers the next part of the message. "I believe Kyndall killed Doris Massey, my mother's friend who lived across the street from her. Give me a call back."

Scotty furrows her brow. *Why hasn't Artie called me back?* The smell of bacon distracts her from the mystery of Artie's unresponsiveness. Her nostrils flare; her stomach gives way to a loud rumble. Scotty throws the covers back, swings her legs over the side of the bed, and stands. No need to stay in bed any longer. Her mother will be in soon to tell her breakfast is ready. Scotty steps out of her room wrapped in her plush pink robe with matching slippers heading in the direction of the bathroom. The hearty laughter of a man stops Scotty in her tracks. Her eyes dart from right to left; neither the voice nor the laughter sounds familiar. Who is the stranger in the kitchen with her mother? Scotty carefully takes steps toward the kitchen and stops. Eliza doesn't allow anyone to put their feet under her table without being fully dressed—no pajamas—it doesn't matter the hour of the day or night. Scotty takes a shower in record time, curious to know who the stranger is in the kitchen.

"Good morning," says Scotty. She walks over to her mother and kisses her on the cheek.

Eliza and Sebastian in unison respond, "Good morning."

"Scotty, I want you to meet Sebastian Glover; he is the detective helping me solve Doris' murder."

Sebastian chuckles, and his belly bounces up and down.

Scotty extends her hand in Sebastian's direction. Sebastian gazes in Scotty's eyes. "Nice to meet you," says Scotty.

"You as well. I have heard all about you from your mother. She is very proud of you and your accomplishments."

"Thank you." Scotty smiles in her mother's direction, and Eliza beams. Scotty knows her mother is proud of her, but underneath that smile is a woman playing matchmaker.

Scotty turns her attention back to Sebastian, who hasn't loosened his grip. She wiggles her hand free. Sebastian blushes.

"Come on, have a seat. I will fix your plates for you."

Eliza hums as she piles the grits on the plate. Sebastian sits at one end of the table, Scotty on the other. Eliza places their plates in front of them and she sits in the middle.

Sebastian, wanting to impress Scotty, says, "May we pray."

He reaches for Eliza's hand. He blesses the food. Sebastian turns his head to Eliza for approval, and she gives him a wink. Scotty is oblivious to the exchange between Sebastian and Eliza.

Scotty chews her turkey bacon. "Sebastian, where are you on the Doris Massey case?"

"Well, I can't really say much because it is an active investigation."

Eliza cuts her eye in Sebastian's direction. Sebastian looks up from his food long enough to nod at Eliza, giving her the okay to tell Scotty what she knows. Eliza rehashes the events until that very moment. By the time Eliza tells her story, everyone is finished with breakfast.

Scotty knows Sebastian gave Eliza permission to give her the update about his investigation, so she decides to share what she knows about the Graham family. They talk for about an hour. Sebastian asks detailed questions just as a cop would do, but there is something different about him. Scotty scrutinizes him as he takes in the information. *He has kind eyes,* she thinks. Scotty's back straightens, her mind races. If she slips and tells Sebastian about the crime she committed, she could go to jail. She looks at her mother. Who would take care of her mother if she went to jail? She senses Sebastian is a good detective and knows if he wasn't taking notes, he would have noticed she was hiding something. Scotty puts on a forced smile.

Scotty's account of what she knows about the Graham family absolutely suggests Dennis is a dirty cop and Kyndall killed Doris.

Eliza muddles around the kitchen cleaning while the two talk. She hums to herself.

"Is there anyone else I should know about?"

"No, I can't think of anything."

Sebastian chews on the end of his pen.

Scotty chimes in, "Well, my plan today is to take a trip to DC to speak with Brendon. He is the weakest link. He is a mama's boy. She tells him what to do, I swear she even tells him what to think." Eliza, who is tending to the dishes, has to chuckle at Scotty's statement. Scotty shakes her head remembering an occasion when Brendon was asked his position on a policy, and he gave the reporter his statement. Kyndall said, "That's not what we discussed." At that very moment, he changed his opinion.

"Do you think he will talk to you?"

"I have interviewed him on my show, and he is comfortable with me. I don't know if he will give me useful information, but it sure is worth a try."

Eliza smiles. With both Scotty and Sebastian investigating, Kyndall will surely be in jail soon.

Chapter 25

*A*rtie glances at the caller ID and ignores Scotty's call. The voicemail shows on his end complete, and he listens. He picks up his glass and slowly sips his vodka with a splash of Sprite and a twist of lemon through a cocktail straw. He wants to savor the taste of the warm vodka coating his throat as he swallows the liquid joy. Artie stopped drinking after the incident but started again when the network reneged on their promise of giving him another opportunity to sit in the anchor chair if he went to counseling. They hired Scotty to host the segment *Meeting of the Minds,* forgetting the promise they made to him. This show would have been his comeback.

The day it all happened he was sitting in the anchor chair getting the last touches from hair and makeup as he sipped vodka out of his coffee mug. He already had two drinks in his dressing room and one on his commute to work, so he was saucy. Artie, bold when he drank, went into Belinda's, his co-anchor's dressing room to discuss the breaking news of the day. He stood at her open dressing room door and squinted at Belinda with disdain in his eyes; he never cared for her after she denied his sexual advances. Instead of discussing the news he barged into her dressing room shouting. He scolded her for everything from A to Z. She smiled because his rambling had nothing to do with her. Artie grew angrier, Belinda was trying to handle him with a sly smile, so he went deep and told her she was too old to sit beside him as a co-anchor. The viewers wanted someone to complement him, not turn the channel from the hag that sat next to him.

Belinda's confidence was low, and she was getting older, wondering when the network would replace her with a younger face. She started to weep. Belinda knew Artie had the ear of the station owner and she would be out of a job soon, nowhere to go at her age. Artie, satisfied with the great job of making Belinda's life hell, stumbled to the set and waited for airtime.

Belinda pulled herself together, asking the makeup artist to add more concealer to the dark circles under her eyes. Belinda waited in the dressing room within minutes of airtime; she did not want to sit beside Artie any longer than she had to. They were in position to go on air, the producer of the show counting down to showtime. Belinda couldn't stand it any further and said under her breath, "You smell like a distillery." She smiled for the camera. They were on air.

Artie blurted, "Mind your business, bitch." Belinda's eyes grew wide, stunned Artie would disrespect her not only in public but on air. However, Artie on the other hand didn't miss a beat. He was a functioning alcoholic. He went into the news story as though nothing happened. When it was Belinda's turn to read the teleprompter, she was frozen. Artie, unscathed from his comment, reads her part of the news. The producer was astonished by Artie's outburst and immediately went to a commercial break. Belinda raced off the set down the hall to her dressing room and slammed the door. Artie, oblivious to his actions, asked Thomas the producer, "What's wrong with her? Is she sick or something?"

"Sick of you. Did you realize what you said to her?"

"No. What?"

"You told her to mind her business, bitch. Everyone in the control room plus millions of viewers heard what you said." Thomas shoved a mug of piping hot coffee in his face. "Here, the real coffee is in this mug instead of your cocktail you are nursing in the other mug. You need to sober up before the executives' pay you a visit for your comment on air. Heads will roll, and your friends in high places will no longer be an asset in this case…"

Artie obeyed Thomas and took a sip of the black coffee, frowning at the bitter taste.

"You will be on the air in twenty seconds."

Artie took another sip of the coffee and moved from side to side in his chair, straining his neck searching for Belinda in the studio.

"You are going on the air in five four, three, two, one."

Artie completed the newscast without another incident. The executives all hovered in one corner of the stage; arms folded. waiting in the wings for the show to end. Artie peeled out of his seat and walked toward his supervisor and his bosses. That was the last day Artie sat in the anchor chair in an official capacity.

Now he spends his days working behind the scenes as executive producer of *Meeting of the Minds* in spite of the agreement his supervisor made with him of going to rehab for eight weeks. After he was released, he went to his AA meetings to demonstrate goodwill of overcoming his demons. He was only back at work one week before the announcement was made of the new show and an external hire.

Artie isn't happy about the broken promises and betrayal from the station owner. He will even the score any way he can; he has no loyalty, only to himself and his goal of getting back in front of the camera. He just needs to wait until the time is right.

Artie takes another sip of his drink, the straw constricting the amount of the cocktail he consumes at a time. He removes the straw, throws it on the table. He turns the drink up to empty the contents in two large gulps. He wipes his mouth with the back of this hand, stands, walks to the kitchen, and pours himself another drink.

He picks up his cell phone to place a call. "Kyndall."

"Hi, Artie. Your calling indicates you have something to share."

"Scotty has some information on you in the death of Doris Massey."

"What information?"

"I didn't speak with her; she left me a voicemail."

"So, you don't have information for me. Why are you calling?"

The vodka gives Artie courage he never had with Kyndall, and he goes bold with his demands. "I think we need a revised deal. I want my old job back plus $10,000 for the information I give you from Scotty."

"This is a road you don't want to go down. I will pretend you aren't blackmailing me."

"No, you heard me right. I want to renegotiate our deal."

"Okay, we can play this game with the new rules, but I guarantee you will not like how this ends. Get me the information and we will discuss your new terms."

"I will reach out to you when I have additional information." He hangs up.

Chapter 26

*J*une scampers out of Chip's office, up the stairs to a hot shower in the master bathroom. The warm water of the shower dances on her face as she tilts her head back, closes her eyes, and uses her hands to rub her entire body, her muscles relaxing under the pellets of small pools of water on her body. She opens the Dove body wash and saturates her white mesh sponge and scrubs her body to rid the lingering scent of sex after the lovemaking marathon between her and her husband earlier that morning. Slowing, she walks in a circle, letting the water rid her body of all the suds from the body wash. She turns off the water, reaches for a towel, and completely dries her body before she steps on the gray mat outside the shower door. She wraps the towel under her arms and around her body and tucks the end to secure it. Gravity pulls the towel to the floor; she steps over it and starts drying her hair. She looks at her reflection with the short, sassy haircut. She runs her hand through her hair. At first, she struggled with the decision to cut her hair short, but her lover thought it would make her sexier. He was right.

Now fully dressed she admires her appearance and choice of outfit; she wears a tight black pencil skirt with a sheer black blouse covering a black tank top. The tank top is so fitted her cleavage pours out the top. She looks at her body from the side. The stilettos make her legs look long. She smiles at her appearance. June moves to the bed and grabs her Gucci overnight bag by the handle and trots down the stairs. She enters Chip's office and walks over to him and gives him a kiss on the lips. "Bye, honey. I will see you tomorrow."

"Bye, June, see you later," says Chip with a dry tone, wiping the lipstick off his lips with the back of his hand.

June exits the room and uses the garage opener on the wall to open the garage door. As she sits in the sleek black Jaguar, she glances at the clock on the car's dashboard; she is late. She doesn't want her lover to wait too long. His plane landed twenty minutes ago, according to the text he sent from the tarmac.

June backs out of the driveway and follows the circle out of the cul-de-sac. She drives to the end of the street and stops at the stop sign. She looks to the left, then to the right. At the end of the street she sees a car parked but doesn't think anything is out of the ordinary. She turns the car to the left and drives toward Charlotte Douglas Airport.

Chapter 27

Jim deplanes and heads toward transportation. Oh, how he misses his new love interest, June. This is their third rendez-vous since they met online. Jim loves everything about her from the smell of her skin to her intelligence. Jim wanted to move to Charlotte to be close to her, he couldn't live without her, and she confided in him about the master plan for the Sweetbriar Community; the plan was so clever, and he wanted in. *Homebuyers are so stupid.*

He exits the building and stands on the sidewalk looking up and down at all the strangers hurrying to get to their destination. Jim, standing in the median, looks up and down the street for June. June spots Jim looking for her, so she puts the car in park and opens the door. She stands and waves her arms in the air to get his attention. Immediately Jim sees this beautiful woman he loves.

Off in the distance Derrick observes the interaction between Jim and June. The two embrace, kissing passionately for what seems like hours, but the kiss lasts only seconds. Derrick takes pictures with his Canon EOS 5DS R camera. The resolution is high definition and he could see a pimple on either one of their faces if they had any. Derrick switches from the Canon to the camera on his phone. *Snap, snap.* It will take a while to develop the film, but he can send the pictures on his phone to Chip right away. Not now—he has more spying to do.

June signals left, pulls her Jaguar F-TYPE Convertible away from the curb, and eases onto the flow of traffic toward the Ritz-Carlton to satisfy both of their desires.

June pulls into the circular driveway of the Ritz-Carlton, and the valet rushes to her car. "Welcome to the Ritz-Carlton. My name is Larry. Will you be staying overnight?"

"Yes," says June as she steps out of the car, leaving the engine running. She reaches for her claim ticket from Larry and places it in her purse. Jim extends his hand to June; their fingers interlock. He brings their hands to his lips and kisses the back of June's hand. They walk into the hotel lobby swinging hands.

"Hi, welcome to the Ritz-Carlton. My name is Jennifer."

"Hi, Jennifer. You have a reservation for June Carter."

Jennifer reviews her computer screen. "Do you need one or two cards?" The question is directed toward June, but Jim quickly answers. "We only need one. We won't leave each other's side." Jim leans toward June and nibbles on her neck. She giggles.

Jennifer, who just broke up with her boyfriend, tightens her eyes at the loving couple. June and Jim are too into themselves to notice the envy on Jennifer's face.

Derrick valets his car, moving in and out of the shadows of the patrons entering and exiting the hotel not to be recognized by June. He walks toward the entrance of the hotel and places a call to Chip, keeping a safe distance with his back toward the door.

"Hello."

"Are you ready for my news? You aren't going to like what I found out."

"Just tell me," snaps Chip.

"June met a man at the airport, picked him up, and the two of them are at the Ritz. She just picked up the room key and is heading upstairs with him."

"I need you to get her room number. I am on the way."

"Will do."

Derrick walks into the hotel and toward the beautiful lady who just assigned June's room.

"Hello. How are you? Welcome to the Ritz-Carlton!" says Jennifer.

"Hi, I am well. My name is Derrick. You just assigned my wife a room. The beautiful lady with short hair." He uses his hands to mark the side of his face to show Jennifer the length of June's hair.

"Oh yeah. I remember her. How can I help you?"

"I was valeting the car and couldn't catch up with her; she was entering the elevator as I was walking into the lobby. Can you tell me our room number?"

"Derrick is your name?"

Derrick moves his head up and down, agreeing with Jennifer.

"Mr. Derrick, we can't give that kind of information out. Perhaps you can call her, and she can tell you the room number."

"Well, that's the other problem. My phone is in her purse."

Jennifer hesitates for a moment. "Hum. Mr. Derrick, I would love to help but I can't give out that kind of information."

Derrick reaches in his pocket, pulls out his money clip, takes a crisp $100 bill from the top, folds it in half, then a second time. He covers the money with his right hand and slides it in Jennifer's direction, opening his hand enough for her to see the C-note. Jennifer tilts her head, raises her eyebrows, and her lips twist into a frown. Derrick, with a smirk on his face, shakes his head. This is going to be harder than he expected. Derrick repeats the same steps as before but this time he is concealing two $100 bills under his hand. Jennifer surveys the room for her manager, who is nowhere in sight. Expeditiously, Jennifer snatches the money from under Derrick's hand. She slides the money in her left pants pocket. Carefully she prints the number 1429 on a sticky note and hands it to Derrick.

"Can I have a key too, please?" Derrick bats his eyes at Jennifer. Before he receives another disappointing stare, he gives her another $100 bill from his money clip. This time he hands her the money across the counter. She pounces on it just as before. Jennifer smiles and reaches for a blank key card and duplicates a key for room 1429.

"Good day, Mr. Derrick."

"Thank you, Jennifer. Have a nice day." Instead of walking toward the elevator, Derrick walks out of the hotel.

Jennifer's eyes narrow as Derrick leaves the hotel, her hands on her curvy hips.

Chip arrives at the hotel in record time, speeding through traffic. He finds Derrick waiting on the outside of the hotel leaning against the building, texting his new love interest as Chip approaches him. Derrick puts his phone in his back pocket.

"Hey, man. I got the room number you requested; it's 1429. I have pictures if you want to see those as well."

Chip shakes his head yes.

Derrick shows his friend the pictures he took earlier on his phone. Chip sighs and snatches Derrick's phone out of his hands.

He scrolls through the photos of his wife and another man in silence. His back grows stiff, eyes glazed and fixed on the pictures. He places his hand to his cheek and rubs the stubble on his face. "I will take it from here."

Derrick hands Chip the sticky note with the room number along with the key card in silence as the exchange takes place.

Chip extends the envelope with the ten hundred-dollar bills, opens his wallet, and places his valet ticket inside to ensure he will find it later.

"Thanks. Be careful," warns Derrick as he strolls toward the valet attendant to retrieve his car.

Without another word, Chip enters the hotel and heads straight to June's room.

Chapter 28

Chip stands outside the door to the room of June and her lover. He places both hands on the frame of the door, his upper body carrying much of his body weight, his left leg steadying himself. He takes a deep breath, his chest expands, and he blows air out through his mouth. His upper and lower lips tremble. *Am I ready to face the reality of June making love with another man?* Slowly with trembling hands Chip inserts the key card into the door and with reservation walks into the room, gently closing the door behind him. He scans the spacious living area: empty. He walks in the direction of the bedroom. He folds his arm at what he witnesses, Jim on his stomach while June straddles him, giving him a massage. Jim moans with pleasure. Suddenly June turns her head toward the door to find her husband staring at her. June smiles and gives her loving husband a wink. She likes when her husband finds her. She is aroused now. "Jim, honey. I have a surprise for you."

"Baby, you can surprise me all you want." He turns his head from the far wall to the door, never opening his eyes.

June looks down at Jim. "Open your eyes, baby. I have someone I want you to meet."

Jim, startled at the sight of the stranger standing before him, quickly raises his upper torso. June falls off his back onto the edge of the bed holding the mattress to steady herself.

"Who the hell are you?" shouts Jim.

"I am June's husband. I am sure she told you about me." Chip smiles.

"Why are you here?"

"I came to watch," says Chip, matter-of-fact.

"Watch your wife and I have sex?" Jim retorts.

"Well, of course, Jim." Chip leans against the dresser, arms folded, and legs crossed.

"June informed me she shared with you the details of my master plan community, which by the way is too much information for you to possess, but nonetheless you now know our secret." Chip reviews June, the love of his life, from head to toe with disdain. He will have to deal with her later. June lowers her head in shame.

"If you are going to live in the community, you need to understand who I am. That's why I am here today."

"By understanding who you are, you want to watch your wife and I have sex? What kind of freaks are you?"

"Why the sudden change? You told June that you wanted 'in.'" Chip uses air quotes. "I thought you understood what 'in' means."

"I do but I want to be on the management side of things."

"Oh, no! This is my plan. There were many who tried to stop me, but they were surprised by my determination and savviness." Chip chuckles.

Jim gets off the bed still wearing his boxers, finds his pants on the floor next to the bed. "June told me Sweetbriar is her idea. There are many people who want to live among others like themselves. Their spirit is restless; they want to live their life free, including their sexual prowess."

"It sounds like she is the real brains of the operation. You are just along for the ride."

Checkmate.

Chip's beady eyes are angry.

June had refused to marry Chip unless he shared their bedroom with another couple or a unicorn, another woman. June further warned Chip of the strict rules. First, they would never have sex without the other present. Second, there shall always be consent of the sexual partner, and protection is always used. Finally, no kissing. Kissing is personal, and the idea of an outside partner is to add spice and is for the sex.

Chip hesitated at the thought initially but studied Hedonism and learned to practice the principles of pleasure and pain. Chip even took his neighbor Harold's anthropology class at the local university on cultures that even today explore this practice.

Chip and June discuss the arrangement while sitting on the front porch overlooking the undeveloped community. June asks, "What if we complete the development of the community with only lifestyle partners?" Chip knows not to say the word *Swingers* as it is a dated term. They now like to refer to themselves as a Lifestyle Group. He thinks for a moment. "How will we pull this off?" June thinks a moment and sips her class of chardonnay. She bursts out laughing at the thought. "Here's how we do it. People never read closing paperwork, nor do they read the Homeowners Association Addendum, except when they need to upgrade or perform work around their home. By the time they read the HOA document, they would have already closed on their home and locked into the deal. We can place in the contract in fine detail that they have to stay in the community for at least ten years. If they leave before that time, they will have to turn their home over to us while they still cover the cost of the mortgage."

Chip thinks for a moment. June the lawyer could be right. He pipes up, "What happens if they read the document? We will be exposed as a fraud, go to jail."

June gives her husband a stern look. "That will never happen." Chip stares blankly at his wife, missing key details.

"Chip, listen, I will offer to waive my fees as the closing attorney. We will hire our own hand-picked Realtor that will work in house. Give her a bonus above her closing percent; she will not ask questions with all the cash in her pocket."

Chip snaps at Jim, "You don't seem to know when enough is enough, do you?"

Jim must pay for his comments, he thinks. His secret is exposed along with June's dominance in the relationship. Jim will not disrespect him in his town and in front of his wife.

While Chip is thinking about the past, Jim dresses and slips on his Brooks Brothers brown American Alligator loafers and struts to the bedroom door.

"Jim, where do you think you are going?" snaps Chip as he grabs Jim by the arm.

"I am leaving here," says Jim as he tries to wiggle out of Chip's firm grip.

"No, you are going to have sex with my wife, and I am going to watch."

"The hell you say!" He continues to try to shake Chip's grip on his arm. But Chip squeezes harder, snatches Jim's arm, and places it behind his back with the left half of his face pressed against the wall.

"Jim, that's not how this works. You signed the agreement you would consent to our 'play time,'" says Chip through clenched teeth.

"What 'play time' and what agreement?"

"You told June how dumb homeowners are and yet you didn't read over the closing documents. Now, now look who's the fool."

"I haven't signed the closing documents yet. Kyndall, the

owner, hasn't gotten back to me whether she will sell the house, so I am not obligated to do anything I don't want to do. Again, I am leaving—you can't stop me." Chip scolds June with his eyes; he was supposed to sign the contract if not on Kyndall's house, a future development.

"Okay, if you want to go, I will take you to the airport." Chip releases Jim's arm. Chip walks back to his original spot, leans against the dresser, and starts inspecting his well-manicured nails.

Jim uses his hands to slowly peel his face off the wall. He turns and looks at June and then focuses his attention on Chip. Jim seems untrusting of the pair. "No, I can get my own ride to the airport," responds Jim in a pitiful, strained voice.

"No, it's the least that we can do. June, call downstairs and have them bring our cars around. Look, if it makes you feel more comfortable, June can take you to the airport in her car and I can follow." Chip extends his hand to Jim as a peace offering.

Jim looks him in the eye and extends his hand to shake on a gentleman's promise.

"Hello, this is June from room 1429. Can you bring my car around? Ticket #5216. Honey, what's your ticket number?"

Chip reaches in his left front pants pocket—no ticket. He then searches in the right pocket—no ticket. Chip remembers that he placed the ticket in his wallet when he paid Derrick. The number is #5225. June repeats the number to the attendant over the phone.

The three of them leave the room, Jim in front of June and Chip. Chip needs to keep an eye on Jim just in case he tries to make a run for the exit. While walking down the hall, Chip grabs June by the elbow and shoves her body toward him and whispers in her ear. "We need to talk when we get home. You disobeyed me by telling this knucklehead conversations between husband and wife. Does it matter whose idea it was to start the community?"

June keeps her eyes forward not looking at her husband; she knows she is in big trouble.

Chapter 29

*C*hip glides through the hotel with June's overnight bag thrown over his shoulder as he squeezes June's left hand so hard her fingers stick together. He refuses to show the outside world his frustration with his wife and her loudmouth. She should have never told Jim the secrets of their community. Chip makes eye contact with the guest and hotel staff as he struts through the lobby. June, keeping pace and appearances with her husband, flashes her smile to the onlookers as heads turn in their direction.

Jim, dumbfounded, shuffles behind Chip and June barely holding his head high enough to detect where he is walking, so he focuses on the heels of the happy couple. *Why did I think someone as beautiful as June would want to leave her husband for me?* His cell phone vibrates on the screen and the beautiful smile of the woman he treated poorly appears. He ran around on his wife for years, ignoring her needs. How could he have treated his high school sweetheart so badly? Jim says a silent prayer. *When I get out of this mess, I will be faithful to my wife. I will be willing to start over in a new city other than Charlotte, a place where neither of us knows anyone.* The spirit that overcomes Jim after the prayer leads him to believe he will not get out of this situation alive no matter how hard he tries. He is certain his fate is sealed with this pair, and out of despair he sends his wife a simple text. Something he should have told her every day of their marriage: "I love you." He places the phone back in his pocket.

———◆———

Jennifer, desk clerk, acknowledges the couple with a nod. Their once-a-month meeting funds her shoe fetish. She always earns enough money from Derrick to splurge on new shoes. She has already picked out three pairs of Nine West shoes that will make her girlfriends green with envy.

———◆———

Outside the revolving door Jim, standing with his hands in his pockets trying to figure out how he can talk his way out of this situation or escape, gives his surroundings a reconnaissance scan up and down the street.

Chip kisses June on the cheek, another ploy for the observers to think they are happy at this moment. June rushes to the driver's side of her car held open by the valet; she tips him forty dollars. Chip gives Jim a solid nudge toward June's car. Chip opens the door for Jim; he sits in the passenger seat. He hasn't said a word until now. In rapid fire Jim asks, "Where are you really taking me? I know you aren't taking me to the airport!"

"You said you wanted to live in the masterplan community. I am going to show you the community."

Maybe Jim's fate isn't sealed even though he refused the disgusting offer to have sex with June in front of her husband. "Oh," he says in a much cheerier voice than earlier. His shoulders relax, he takes a deep breath. *I may get out of this mess after all and still get the girl of my dreams.* He smiles to himself. Jim forgets about his earlier prayer and starts to plan in his head the conversation he will have with Kyndall to convince her to sell. This should be easy.

June and Jim ride in silence as she drives to the masterplan community called Sweetbriar off I-485.

Chapter 30

June and Chip park their cars in the driveway, forgoing the garage with their guest, Jim. June walks into the house to start dinner, anticipating their guest will be staying.

Jim stands in the driveway and scans the beautiful partially developed community. The bones to a strong community are there but only the houses on Sweetbriar Lane are fully developed and occupied. He knows he made the right decision to leave Brooklyn for Charlotte all within a month of meeting June. Jim closes his eyes, sucks in the clear air; he can hear birds chirping in a tree nearby—peaceful. He wipes the beads of sweat on his upper lip. He will have to get used to the extension of summer; by now the air would have been crisp in New York.

<hr />

"Let's take a walk. I want to show you the house you want to purchase," Chip says.

"Yeah, sure. Let me ask you something," Jim says. "Since the house isn't actually for sale, how should I approach the home-owner to sell? She hasn't lived in the house for years, right?"

"Correct. Kyndall Graham owns the house; because she hasn't lived here, maybe she will be motivated to sell. All I know is she and my father go way back; they went to college together. Throughout the years they stayed in contact. My father, a real es-tate developer, found this property at an amazing deal. He needed a few investors in order to purchase the land, so he asked my grandfather and Kyndall to put up some money. Kyndall wrote him a check for her portion, and they agreed he didn't need to pay her back—just build her a home in the community. When my father started the community, there were only three houses on the block, which are the houses in the cul-de-sac, Kyndall's house, my father's, which is the home where June and I live, and the home of Emma and Harold."

Chip points to the house to his right. Jim intently listens.

"My father died before he could complete the community, so when I finished college June's mother gave us a nice monetary wedding gift, and with bank loans, we finished the houses on Sweetbriar."

Chip swallows hard to make the lump in his throat go away as he talks about his father, Chase. Chip, a young boy when his father died, witnessed the murder of his father. His childhood therapist is still working with him to remember the murderer, who stood feet from the boy and never harmed him. Ever since that night he experienced night terrors as a young boy, but as an adult, he experiences bouts of rage stemming from an incident small or petty to resentment from years that encourage him to fight to the death of his opponent. His therapist says he is lash-ing out to avenge the murder of his father. On the night of the murder, he stood motionless and did nothing to protect his father from his death. Chip has flashes of the person who killed his fa-ther, but his mother, Megan, told him a different account of the story. She insisted his father killed himself when a family member embezzled money from the company. Chase could no longer pay the bills, and creditors hounded him night and day. Chase, a proud man, didn't want his friends and family to view him as a failure and he pointed his Smith and Wesson Model 10 revolver toward his temple. This is the story Megan told him all those years; she repeated it enough that he believed it even though his subconscious wanted to reveal a different story to him.

Chip scratches his head. "You know…" His voice trails off. He starts up again. "You will have a difficult time getting Kyndall to sell. She and my father were tight, and with his death this is the only connection she has with him. And Kyndall lived here a few years before she met her husband."

"Well, I plan to make her a generous offer."

"It is up to Kyndall; it is her home."

They both walk next door.

Chip breaks the awkward silence. "You are very determined to live in Sweetbriar. Why are you so fascinated in our little community?" Chip laughs as he puts "little" in air quotes.

"I met June online a few weeks ago. She told me about the swinging community. People who live here are free; they aren't confined to the rules or scrutiny of society. The community is exclusive. Not everyone knows what you do."

"No one uses the word *swinging* anymore. The term dates back to the 1970s and is not used or recognized by our community."

"Oh, okay. If you aren't swingers, then what are you? Couples switching or sharing partners is what swingers do. Am I right or am I right?" says Jim, feeling himself.

"We consider ourselves a lifestyle community. In some cases, this alternative lifestyle has been accredited to saving marriages."

Jim chuckles. "Saves marriages? You can't believe the shit you are shoveling."

"Yes, I do. This lifestyle gives couples variety, more spice to their marriage. Just because you haven't been exposed to our way of living, don't knock it if you haven't tried it." Chip grins.

"Well, I only want to live in the community to be with June."

"You aren't curious what we do?"

"No, I told you before I want to be a part of management. Don't take this the wrong way, but I am going to take June from you. June and I will run the community." Jim winks at Chip. "June and I will start a life together," he says in a dreamy tone.

"Jim, just humor me. How are you going to take my wife from me?" Chip feels his temperature rising, his shirt damp.

"Well, she has already fallen for my charm. On my second trip to the city, June took me to the eclectic area NoDa. I remember the day as if it were yesterday. June and I strolled down the street holding hands, sneaking kisses as we popped in and out of the shops and bars. The electricity that ran through our bodies when we kissed… I knew it was love."

Chip folds his arms, and his smile dissipates; he locks his mind on something Jim said in his rambling. Chip thought the encounter at the Ritz was their second meeting; the first encounter was only brief as described by June. They have met a total of three times. *Why is June lying to me? First, she betrays my trust by sharing with Jim the secret of the community. Now this? Having sex without the partner approval!* The only reason she told Chip about Jim was to cover her trail of secret meetings. *Is June falling for Jim? She is telling him too many secrets.* Chip's face turns red as he grows angrier and angrier just looking at Jim's pathetic face. Chip's mind now takes him to a state of confusion: on one hand he is mad at his wife and on the other feeling vulnerable. Is June going to leave him for Jim? Chip recalls the conversation he had with Derrick earlier in the day. Derrick wife cheated on him, *and he was a detective. Is June cheating on me with this prick?*

Chip, staring past Jim, unconsciously rubs his outer right thigh vigorously, up and down with his fingers creating heat and friction. The soothing strokes regulate his breathing just as it did when he was younger. The therapist explained to Megan this was a coping mechanism to deal with the night terrors and memory flashes of the person who killed his father. His conscious and unconscious memory were in conflict, one trying to suppress to protect him and the other wanting to expose the killer.

"Chip, are you okay?" Jim waves his hand in front of Chip's face to get his attention.

Chip refocuses on the man he despises, Jim. "Let's go and look at the house you want to buy. It is right here at 7478, and I have the keys; you can do a walk-through with me." The two of them walk down the driveway to the house next door. Chip reaches into his pocket and pulls out a huge key ring.

"You sure have a lot of keys on your ring. Afraid you are going to get locked out?" says Jim jokingly.

Chip boasts, "I have all the keys to the houses on the block." Chip needs to show Jim he has power over all the residents in the community, including him if Kyndall decides to sell him the house.

"I know this is my first home purchase, but you should not have keys to everyone's home. You can give me the key to my house."

Chip continues to unlock the door to the empty house, ignoring Jim's request. The two walk through the threshold into the foyer. Chip closes the door. "This is the living room," he says dryly. He cuts his eyes at Jim. He loathes this guy.

"Chip, I can take the key for my house from you." Jim extends his hand.

Chip opens and closes his hands to a fist, pumping them open, closed, open, closed. Chip's eyes glaze and his stare fixes on Jim, in his mind the enemy. He rubs his thigh up and down, faster and faster. Chip, now confused, the room swirling—his mind goes back to the night his father was killed. His father's killer in his dream when he was a child appears wearing white, the face blurry. He struggles to make out the facial features, the blood crimson in color all over the front of the killer. "No, no," shouts Chip. Just as quick as the image appears, it vanishes. Chip uses the palms of his hands and rubs his eyes. His consciousness suppresses the image of the woman.

Jim, standing before him, shouts, "Yes, yes. Give me the key!" his hand still extended.

Chip, unsteady, braces himself against the wall, needing more support to carry the weight of his body.

"Man, what is your problem." Jim walks over to Chip and snatches the keys out of his hands.

Chip wants to prove Jim is not going to win this fight. He bounces from the wall and grabs Jim by the shoulders from behind. Chip snatches the key ring back from Jim's grip. "Jim, you will get a key once you close on *your* house."

Jim slams Chip into the wall next to the fireplace, his hands around the collar of Chip's shirt. "You walk around thinking you are better than me. You don't know who you are messing with. No wonder June loves me. You are a bump on a log. You are just like your daddy—worthless." Jim walks away from Chip and murmurs, "I will move to another neighborhood. I can't deal with you."

"What did you say about my daddy?" Chip's reflexes get the best of him; instantly, with the fireplace poker in his hand, he races toward Jim and whacks him over the head. Jim's body crashes to the floor face first upon impact; his front teeth loosen. Ruby red blood oozes from the back of his head. Chip hits Jim over and over on the head, his back, his arm, repeating the words in variation. "How dare you call my daddy names?" Chip rants aloud as he hits the body over and over with the poker.

June walks through the door to tell Chip and Jim dinner will be ready in fifteen minutes, but to her surprise she finds Chip hovered over Jim's lifeless body with a poker in his hand.

Standing in the foyer, she screams at the top of her lungs. She races to her lover's body, "No, no, no," shaking her head at what she is witnessing.

"Stop it, Chip; stop it!"

The sound of his wife's voice stops Chip's swing midair. The poker still in hand Chip turns to his wife, pointing in her direction.

"Jim crossed the line with all this talk about taking you from me. The insults about my father." June slowly backs up as Chip walks toward her with the poker. "You told me the two of you met twice, but today was your third meeting. Why are you lying to me? Jim said you want to leave me. Is this true?"

June stands still, clears her throat before speaking. "Yes, that is true, this was our third encounter. I didn't mean to lie to you. I followed the script but there was something about him I liked. I wanted him all to myself. The more I talked to him the more I wanted to be around him. I didn't want to bring him back to the community to share with the others." June doesn't hold back; her life is on the line. Chip slaps his wife. The slap stings. June screams, "Ouch!" She sobs loudly, holding her face.

"Not only did you lie; you told him about community business. I can't trust you. You know what happens when I can't trust someone." Chip moves in closer to June with the poker directed at her face. June backs up slowly with her hands in the air; palms out pleading with her husband.

"Please, Chip, don't!"

———— ⊰((•))⊱ ————

Emma, driving down the street, notices the lights on at Kyndall's vacant home. She slowly pulls into her driveway, parks the car, and looks in her rearview mirror at Kyndall's house across the street, where she sees shadows. She glances at her phone, looking for missed calls or messages—none from Kyndall. She opens the door of the car, reaches for her purse, steps outside the car, and hears a scream coming from the direction of Kyndall's home. Emma hobbles as quickly as she can to Kyndall's house; the closer she gets to the house, the louder the voices become. Emma slings the door open to find Chip holding the fireplace poker at his wife's neck. "What is going on here?"

Chip stands motionless, but June knows this is her sign to get out of his direct line of fire. She huddles behind Emma to shield her from her husband.

"Chip, put down the poker!" shouts Emma.

Chip stares past both Emma and June.

Emma walks closer to Chip and calls his name again. "Chip, Chip, snap out of it." Emma shakes his shoulders with both hands. Chips focuses on the petite lady smiling in front of him. "It's going to be okay. Give me the poker." She slowly maneuvers it out of Chip's hand.

While Chip and Emma are preoccupied, June walks over to Jim's body, stoops, and takes the watch she gave him off his left wrist. She slides it into her pants pocket.

Emma, who has been in the room for minutes that seem like hours, out of the corner of her eye notices for the first time the bloody body on the floor where June is squatting. Her hand flaps to her mouth in disbelief. Emma surveilles the room for more bodies, not caring about the poor dead guy on the floor—just protecting Chip and June from the mess they have gotten themselves into. She begins to take control of the situation and barks orders.

"June, go home and bring some cleaning supplies and a trash bag. We need a bucket as well and a mop." June moves toward the front door. "No, you have to leave through the back door."

A cell phone rings, everyone jumps, and the three of them individually search for their phones. Nothing, no missed calls. The phone rings again. "It's his." Chip points in the direction of Jim's dead body. Emma walks over to Jim's body and finds the phone. The screen displays two missed calls. "Do either of you know someone by the name of Susan?"

Chip points in June's direction. "Ask her. She seems to know more about him than she's letting on."

"He has a wife by the name of Susan. I am sure it's her."

"Are the two of you going to tell me what's going on?"

The pair start to speak at the same time, interrupting each other. Emma tunes them both out. Staring at Chip she folds her arms in front of her, her right hand up to her mouth. Jim's dead body stares up at her. Where is Chip's deep-seated anger coming from? Emma shifts her position and places her left hand on her hip and uses her right hand to touch her lips; she paces the floor in the living room. Tears of disappointment fill the corners of her eyes. *What happened to the innocent young boy Chase and Megan raised?* Emma starts to cry; she knows what happened and why. She made a horrible mistake.

Chapter 31

Emma and her husband, Harold, were the first couple to move into Sweetbriar. They moved next to Chase and Megan. Emma, a pharmacist in one of the popular pharmacy chains, and Harold, an anthropologist, were clearly chasing separate dreams. The couple had been in their new home for two years when Harold was promoted to an archeology dig in Giza, Egypt. The assignment was to figure out how the three monuments during the Fourth Dynasty Old Kingdom were constructed 4,500 years ago. Harold, knowing how important his work was, spent months answering the questions his employers had but very little attention nurturing the needs of his new wife and their relationship back home. He visited every three months but found each visit she was more withdrawn and not affectionate toward him after all the months he was away. Harold's last visit was revealing of how depressed Emma had become. They argued about him leaving his job and them starting a family. Harold, torn with the success of his career, told Emma he didn't want any children at the moment, and they should wait.

"What are we waiting for? I am here lonely and wanting a child that you don't want to give me. How do you think that makes me feel?"

"Damn, just give me some time to breathe. I will finish in Egypt and I will come home for a while and we can concentrate on us and our relationship."

"I don't think you love me anymore; if you did you would have chosen another career or taken an assignment closer to home."

"I resent your looking down on me when I am helping put food on the table."

"Get out," screamed Emma.

Harold threw his overnight bag over his shoulder and walked out of the house. He opened the door to the rental and headed back to the airport to fly back to Egypt. At the airport, he called Chase.

"Hey, Harold, man, what's going on?"

"I need a favor. Emma and I just had an argument and I need you to check on her from time to time. She seems as though she gets depressed when I'm gone. Not answering the phone, not going to work, not living her life. I understand I am in Egypt, but I want her to have a social life with friends and family."

"Okay, you know you are my best friend and I will do anything for you."

"Give her a call within the next several days and check in with me on what she is doing. I am concerned with her mental state."

"Okay, will do."

"Thanks. Talk to you later."

Immediately, when Harold landed in Egypt, he called Emma. She sounded distracted. Her voice faint and scratchy.

"Are you okay?"

"Yes, I am fine. I took the day off from work to rest. I just seem to be tired all the time."

"Do you want me to come home? I can if you want."

"No, I know your work is important. You just started this assignment. You are only there for ten more months."

"Okay. I asked Chase to check on you."

"That's fine."

"I'll talk to you tomorrow."

That afternoon Chase rang the doorbell. *Ding Dong.* Emma raised her head from the throw pillow on the sofa. This was day two that she called out of work. She barely had enough energy to place the phone call to her boss. "Who is it?" Emma yelled from the sofa, laying her head back on the pillow.

"It's Chase," he yelled from outside the door.

"Come in, the door is open." Emma didn't move off the sofa. She pulled the blanket up to her chin to cover her sheer blue gown.

Chase opened the door and called, "Hello," wanting to get a response so he would know the direction he should be heading toward.

Emma raised her head. "Hi. I am in the den watching television."

Chase made his way to the back of the house. He knew where every room was located because he built the house with his bare hands with the help of a small crew.

Chase always admired Emma from afar. Her smooth milk chocolate skin and voluptuous breasts. He loved his wife but fantasied about making love to Emma. Now wasn't the time to let those thoughts creep into his head. Emma needed a caring friend now.

Dishes were piled high in the sink and on the counter, trash overflowing onto the floor. Chase stopped by the kitchen first and washed the dishes. He swept and mopped the floor. Chase made his way to the living room, where Emma lay on the sofa. "Emma, are you okay?"

"I am fine."

"You have been lying here it seems over the past couple of days. Have you eaten?"

Chase walked back to the kitchen and peered into the refrigerator and cabinets, deciding what was available to cook for her. He banged kitchen cabinets looking for a frying pan and a bowl, then added basil, pepper, and salt to the bowl with three eggs. While the eggs scrambled, he spread margarine on two slices of bread and broiled them in the oven and placed both pieces of toast next to the eggs on the plate. On top of the refrigerator he found bamboo trays. He placed a plate, fork, knife, and cup of cranberry juice on it. Chase carefully balanced the tray and placed it beside Emma on the coffee table. "Emma, I fixed you something to eat. Are you hungry?"

"I don't want anything to eat."

"You have to build up your strength. Let me help you up." Chase gently moved Emma's body in the upright position.

How many days had she been lying here? he wondered. A strong aroma caused Chase to gag. He moved the tray from the coffee table to Emma's lap. She stared off into the distance, hands lifeless resting on her thighs. Chase picked up the fork and cut the egg mixture on the plate. He poked the egg with the folk and directed it to Emma's mouth with his left hand cupped below her chin to catch any excess from falling on Emma's lap. "Come on, Emma, open wide."

"No." She shook her head like a child.

"Come on, Emma, take a bite."

Emma looked over at Chase for the first time and ate the food on the fork in front of her. She didn't realize how hungry she was, as she took the fork from Chase and shoved the scrambled eggs in her mouth, then drank a sip of cranberry juice and ate a bite of the toast.

"Now that's more like it. Since you are eating on your own, I am going to run you a hot bath." Chase walked upstairs to the master bathroom and beside the bathtub he found bubble bath. He poured the floral sweet scent liquid into the bathtub running his hands the length of the tub, the bubbles expand. With the bath all set he found Emma's lingerie drawer and pulled out a baby doll pink outfit with a pleaded front outlined with a satin black bow. He laid the gown on the bed.

Imagining Emma wearing the sexy outfit, he got excited and the bulge in his pants expanded. The breaking of glass downstairs distracted him. Chase ran out of the bedroom forgetting he laid the nightgown on the bed. He turned around and threw the lingerie back into the dresser drawer, slamming the drawer as he raced down the stairs to see about Emma.

Emma was on her hands and knees.

"Emma don't worry about it. I will get the broken glass."

"No, I got it." Emma raised her arm, releasing herself from Chase's grip.

"Emma, I drew you a bath. Let me help you up." Chase led Emma upstairs to the bathroom so she could soak in the tub. He helped Emma into the tub, exposing her naked body. Chase admired Emma's body, but he shut the door behind him and took Emma's soiled clothing to the washroom. He placed her clothing into the wash and threw one of those detergent pods into the cycle, closed the lid, and turned to the appropriate cycle. He used the quiet time to clean the living room and wash the remaining dishes. He walked back into the living room, turned, and smiled. He inspected his work and was proud of the job he did. No rest for the weary, he thought and climbed the stairs once again; he needed to check on Emma.

Chase knocked on the door—nothing, no sound. "Hello, Emma. This is Chase. Are you okay?" Still no sound from the other end of the door. Chase stood behind the door, not sure if he should open it or just try to talk to her from outside the bathroom. He wanted to see Emma's milk chocolate skin, but this was his friend's wife. Torn no more, he turned the knob and announced himself.

"Emma, I am coming in," he warned as he entered the bathroom. "How is your bath?"

No response. The washcloth lay on top of the towel, dry. Chase shook his head; she was in worse shape than he thought. He knelt near the tub and placed the washcloth in the water. He wrung the cloth and gripped the Dove bath bar with the washcloth and slathered the cloth with soap. He gently rubbed the soapy cloth on her body, holding her arm and wiping the cloth back and forth, cleaning Emma's body. The warm water running across Emma's body transformed her spirit, and she blinked. She snapped out of the sadness, smiled up at Chase, and he smiled back at her. "I know I have been a big mess.

Chase laughed. "No, just a small mess." He used his index and thumb to measure the smallness of the mess she is. They both laughed in unison. "What happened?"

"I go through bouts of depression when Harold is away so often. I just feel my world is closing in around me. I want children but he's away so often."

"I'll tell you what, after your bath we will take a stroll in the park and have a nice dinner with fancy tablecloths." Emma blushed at the thought of a man other than her husband taking interest in her even though it was Chase, Harold's dear friend.

Chapter 32

*C*hase increased his visits to "check on" Emma. The more they saw each other, the more they wanted to see each other. Their relationship moved from a friendly one to one of a sexual nature. Their fling lasted for years. One night Emma was preparing for dinner for her and Chase.

"Hey, Emma." Chase entered the house with a bottle of pinot noir.

"Thanks." Emma kissed him on the lips, took the wine into the kitchen, and reappeared with a glass of wine for Chase. Chase took the glass from Emma and spun her around playfully.

"Aren't you going to have a glass with me?"

"No, I have some exciting news for you."

"You do?" Chase touched Emma's nose with his index finger. Emma ran upstairs to the master bedroom and grabbed her surprise. She ran down the stairs with excitement.

"What's going on with you?"

"Guess what?"

"Okay, what?"

Emma brought her hands around to the front and exposed the pregnancy test. "I am pregnant. Aren't you excited?"

"No, I'm not, Emma. How did this happen?"

The smile on her face vanished and turned to a frown. "We were having so much fun together and you knew I wanted a baby."

"Yes, but with your husband, not his best friend."

Tears of disappointment streamed down her face. She stormed into the kitchen and threw the pregnancy test into the trash. She walked to the kitchen sink, looking out the window with her arms folded. Chase followed her into the kitchen. He came up behind her and used both his hands to caress her arms. He gently whispered in her ear, "You know I love you, but we can't have this baby."

Emma turned to Chase. "I am not going to abort this baby. I will raise our baby."

"Tell me how you are going to tell Harold that we had an affair and a child was conceived. He is my best friend who asked me to look in on you while he was away. You don't just tell a man that you slept with his wife and now the two of you are expecting a baby.

"This doesn't end well for either one of us. I can leave Harold and you can leave Megan so we can be together."

"I don't want to leave my wife. Yes, we have been going through a rough patch, but I'm not going to leave her. We are on the right track. I don't want to lose her or you. But if you keep up this nonsense of keeping the baby and telling Harold, then I can't have any part of this." Chase took several steps backwards, creating a distance between him and Emma. Chase turned and walked out the door.

"Chase, no!" Both of Emma's arms were extended with her hands opening and closing, wanting him to come back to her. She sobbed loudly. Emma screamed at the top of her lungs, "Chase, no, don't leave me. I love you." The door closed behind him.

Emma got more hysterical. She screamed his name one last time. "Chase, no, come back. Our baby needs us."

Emma left the kitchen and walked by the dining room, where she had already plated their dinner. She glanced over at the meal she took such pride and care to prepare. She continued to walk up the stairs and into the bedroom. Emma lay across the bed and cried herself to sleep.

Chapter 33

Only back to work for several weeks, Harold asked his supervisor for a leave of absence. He felt guilty the way he left things between him and his wife. He had been neglecting his wife and needed to hold her in his arms and touch her soft skin. As he sped through traffic from Charlotte Douglas Airport, he prayed it wasn't too late to save his marriage. Harold, wanting to surprise his wife, parked several houses up the street. While he was home the two could start the family she desired. He jogged down the street to his home with his olive duffle bag thrown over his shoulders. Once on the porch of the house, Harold placed his bag on the white rocking chair and reached in his pocket to find his keys. His hand trembling in anticipation of his surprise to his wife, he dropped the keys in the shrubs. Harold sighed. He moved from the porch to the shrubs, slowly moving between the bold colors of the double knockout roses. He found the key ring. Startled by the loud shouting from inside the house, he dropped his keys again. He stood and through the window he witnessed Chase and Emma in an intense argument. He left the bushes and walked up the steps to validate what he thought he heard. The two were yelling so he heard enough but he wanted to make sure he consumed all the details.

"Get rid of the baby if you want us to be together." *That bastard,* thought Harold. *I trusted him to look after my wife and he is having sex with her and they conceived a child together.* Harold backed away from the window, stumbling off the porch. He grabbed his ankle.

"Harold, is that you? Why are you at the window?" said Megan, enjoying her evening stroll.

Harold picked himself off the ground and wiped the tears of disappointment from his face.

"Harold, what's wrong? Are you hurt?"

He limped toward her. Feeling alone in the world—his wife, the love of his life, having an affair with his best friend—Harold confided in Megan. "I came home to surprise Emma and found Chase and Emma arguing about a baby they conceived. Emma is pregnant with Chase's child."

"What? How could he be so reckless? Emma is pregnant!" Megan, childless, rubbed her belly where the child she conceived never grew. She wept.

"Did you know Chase and Emma were having an affair?"

Megan regained her composure and wiped her face. She cleared her throat.

Harold's eyes turned into beads. "Megan, did you know about the affair between your husband and my wife?" Harold lunged toward Megan and began shaking her shoulders. "Did you know?" The only reason Harold heard Megan's response was because he was within inches of her lips.

"I knew."

"Did you know she is pregnant?" Harold released his grip on her shoulders and took a few steps back.

Megan closed her eyes and shook her head, no. "If I told

Chase I knew, he would have left me for her. I saw how he lusted after her when she worked in the yard or saw her at the grocery store. I know the look. Chase used to share the same look for me years ago. He was happy when you gave him the green light to check on Emma when you were away, and the affair started then. I am not sure exactly when but that was the time frame. A woman always knows when her husband is cheating."

Harold screamed, "You knew this whole time and didn't tell me my best friend and your husband are having sex? And what's wrong with you that you accept your husband is cheating on you?"

Megan stared Harold in the eyes, emotionless.

"Megan, you are a beautiful young lady inside and out and you don't need to take this kind of treatment from Chase."

"Stop it, Harold, I don't want to hear this nonsense. He is my husband and I am not going to do anything to mess up my marriage. What do you want me to do?"

"If I had it my way, I would kill that SOB."

"Well, Harold, that is ridiculous. You can't go around threatening to kill someone."

Suddenly, the door to the house opened. Harold darted on the other side of Emma's car not to be seen by Chase as he slammed the front door.

Megan was still standing on the curb. "Hi honey."

"What are you doing out here?"

"I was taking a walk, stretching my legs. You look flushed. Are you okay?"

"Oh, yes, I am fine."

"How is Emma tonight?"

"Oh, she is doing well. You know the only reason I visit her is to check on her for Harold's benefit."

"You mention this to me every time you visit her." Megan

rolled her eyes as she walked toward the home she shared with her husband, careful not to look in Harold's direction. Chase followed his wife, his heart heavy; he always wanted a child but not this way. He ran to catch up with his wife. He reached for her hand to hold, but Megan avoided his touch.

Once the front door closed at Chase's house, Harold found his keys in the shrubs. He walked to the front porch, grabbed his duffle bag, and watched his wife through the front window crying. His heart broke because she was hurting but his world was destroyed, and he chose to take care of himself. He couldn't talk to her now. Harold probably sprained his ankle when he fell off the porch; he limped to his car and drove back to the airport away from the heartache. Not one to let something rest, Harold figured out how he could get even with Chase. He would not let him get away with having sex with his wife. He knew Emma would do right by him and not have the child, but this would not end well for Chase.

Chapter 34

*H*arold was furious about the affair between his wife and Chase but had no reason to be upset. Harold was not innocent himself. He had been carrying a secret for years. He fathered a child with Tara, an intern, while working in Egypt. Once pregnant Tara went back to the States and settled in Philadelphia, where she raised their son, Gregory. Harold continued to work in Egypt until Gregory was born, and he too moved back to the States. He took a teaching job in Philadelphia to live with his lover full time. Harold never told Emma his secret; he kept up the façade for years, telling his wife he was still working in Egypt.

Eighteen years earlier

Today Harold has to put his lies behind him and spend more time with Emma.

Tara gives Harold a kiss on the lips; a tear travels down her cheek and seeps to the corner of her lip. She wipes her face with the back of her hand. Tara is sad Harold is leaving and she will miss him dearly, but she is sad because she knows what's in store for her when Harold leaves. Tara is embarrassed that her only son Gregory would physically and verbally abuse her. She's never told her sister, but Zoe is smart; she could figure it out. Tara slowly walks into the house, leaving Harold loading the car. She is thinking this time will be different.

———————

Gregory watches Harold from his bedroom window loading his luggage in the car. He stands to the left side of the window, the long drapes covering his body and face; his left eye is the only body part exposed to track Harold's moves. Gregory holds the baseball bat at his side, tip tapping the hardwood floor in his bedroom, the sound echoing throughout his room.

———————

Tara walks from the dining room to the kitchen and stops. She hears the signal, the tapping of the bat, which means he's ready to play his cat-and-mouse game. Tara glances out of the kitchen window; she has only seconds to hide. Harold is walking from the trunk of the car to the driver's side. Tara takes her shoes off to run faster up the stairs. The engine of Harold's car ignites. This is her last opportunity for safety. She runs up the stairs, taking them two at a time. She reaches midway but is blocked by Gregory at the top of the stairs with the bat angled across his chest, his left hand holding the top, his right hand holding the handle.

"Mother, where do you think you are going?"

"Hi honey," says Tara in a shaky voice.

Gregory extends the bat in front of him, the tip touching his mother chest. "I thought he would never leave."

"Why do you say that about your father? Don't you like having him around?"

"He may be my father, but you are a worthless whore."

"You can't talk to me that way. I am your mother!" shouts Tara.

"So, you're not a whore."

"No."

"Where is DADDY going?"

"He is visiting a friend."

"You mean his wife."

Tara gives Gregory a puzzled look. She didn't realize Gregory knew Harold was married.

"Oh, Mother, you didn't think that I knew." Gregory reads her mind. Shamefully Tara's shoulders drop, and she lowers her head. She isn't proud of her living arrangement with a married man.

"Silly mother." He pokes the bat into his mother's chest, causing her to lose her balance, and she moves her right foot to the next step down to keep her balance. She then moves her left foot to rest on the same step to secure her position on the stairs. Gregory moves one step down again to regain distance to poke his mother with the bat once again. *Poke, poke.*

Tara moves to the right to slide past Gregory, so he moves the position of the bat across his body with his elbows out to prevent his mother from passing him. He smirks as he shoves her. Tara loses her balance and falls backward grabbing the railing to steady herself.

"Mother you need to be careful, wouldn't want you to have an accident."

Meanwhile, Tara's cell phone rings from her bedroom. "Come on, come on, pick up," her sister on the other end of the phone says. "I don't like it when you are in the house alone with that monster." Zoe anxiously looks at her watch. Harold is leaving for Charlotte today. Zoe has had numerous conversations through the years with her sister for dating a married man, but when Tara ended up pregnant, Zoe didn't speak with Tara throughout her pregnancy. Zoe remembers when she received the phone call from Tara letting her know that she had delivered a boy and she named him Gregory. Zoe shed a tear. Here she was a Christian woman and refused to speak with her only sister because of her sin. She felt embarrassed that she did not pray with her sister for her sin and ask the Lord for forgiveness, but she gave her the silent treatment. "What kind of sister am I?" Zoe remembers the day as if it was yesterday. She went to the hospital that day and never left her sister's side. Anything that she wanted or needed, Zoe was there for her.

Last year Tara started to change, and the closeness they experienced when Zoe visited her sister in the hospital was gone. The two went shopping and Zoe helped Tara zip the dress she was trying on. Her left arm exposed a fresh bruise, her back and leg older bruises. Zoe, furious, asked if Harold was abusing her but immediately stopped mid-sentence. Harold hadn't been home in months. Zoe asked the hard question no sister wants to. "Is Gregory abusing you?"

In a huff Tara demanded Zoe unzip the dress; she was ready to go. After that day Tara never wore shorts or short-sleeve shirts. Zoe never mentioned it again but increased her visits when Harold was out of town.

Tara and Zoe were having lunch the other day and she could sense Tara's spirit was restless. "Is everything okay? You seem tense."

Tara *was* tense. Harold would be leaving for Charlotte, and she would be all alone with Gregory. "I know that we have had our differences in the past, but I have a favor I would like to ask you."

"Sure, anything."

"If something ever happens to me, will you promise me, you will take care of Gregory? I want him to go to college. Will you make sure he does?"

"I promise, I will ensure he goes to college. I will drop him off myself."

Zoe turns her attention back to the ringing phone, which goes straight to voicemail. Zoe dials the number once again; the phone goes to voicemail again. She panics, runs out the door, and drives to her sister's house. The car barely parked, she jumps out and uses her spare key to open the door to find Tara lying at the bottom of the stairs, Gregory standing over her with a smirk on his face. The sound of the door opening causes Gregory to jump. Zoe dashes toward her sister lying on the floor.

"Have you called the ambulance?"

Gregory shakes his head from side to side.

Zoe pulls out her cell phone to call for help.

"You can if you want, but I think she is dead." He sings the word *dead*, throwing the bat back and forth in his hand.

Her sister strains her neck in the direction of Gregory. "What did you do to her?"

"Nothing and that's what I will tell the police."

———— ((●)) ————

Gregory places the bat in the corner of the dining room, walks into the kitchen, opens the pantry, and pulls out a bag of Doritos. He opens the junk drawer and uses a pair of scissors to cut open the top of the bag and pours his favorite chips on a paper towel.

He goes to the drawer and finds the bag chip clip to secure the Doritos, so they don't go stale. He places the bag in the cabinet, walks through the kitchen to the dining room, grabs his bat with one hand, the other hand securely holding the paper towel that wraps his chips. He steps over his mother's body as he makes his way to his bedroom. Gregory enters his bedroom, closes the door, and places the bat in his closet. He sits on the bed and opens the paper towel, revealing the orange nacho chip. He opens his mouth wide, tries to place the entire chip in his mouth without touching the corner, his eyes closed. He chews the delightful chip, licking his finger after each chip is placed in his mouth. *Crunch, lick, crunch, lick.* He places the last chip in his mouth as the police car abruptly parks in front of the house. He cleans his index and thumb of the residue from the chip by licking his fingers. He uses the napkin to wipe his mouth while walking into the bathroom, where he washes any of the remaining orange paste from his hands. Gregory stoops and reaches in the cabinet in his bathroom sink. He pulls his aerosol hairspray out, pries open the top, and sprays it directly in his eyes. The aerosol in his eyes burn, and they water; he continues to rub them round and round. His eyes now red from the irritation, he turns to walk to the bathroom door, halfway in, halfway out. He grabs the handle of the door, moves closer to the door frame, and slams the door on his shoulder over and over. Tears stream down his face to set his plan in motion to look as though he is torn up that his mother is cold and dead lying on the floor. He knows she is dead. He pushed her the rest of the way down the stairs.

Chapter 35

$\mathcal{T}$he timing of Tara's death and Emma going to the hospital
force Harold to decide on a life back in Charlotte. Tara's
Last Will and Testament gives strict instructions that Gregory will
live with Zoe until he is old enough to go off to college. Zoe
does just that; she drops him off at Temple and never looks back.
Harold has nothing to do with his son after the death of Tara.

Harold, an absent husband for years, has to keep his lies
straight and tell Emma the job in Egypt has ended. Keeping his
composure, he calls Emma. She tells him she can't talk because
she is on her way to the hospital. Harold doesn't press her for answers because she seems to be in pain. His next call is to Chase,
to be his eyes and ears on Emma's condition until he can fly to
Charlotte.

Chase's ears perk up at Harold's request to check on Emma.
This is his opportunity to speak to Emma; she cut off all com-
munication with him when he refused to leave his wife for her.
It is tough not talking. The situation is even more complicated
because Chase and his wife Megan live next door to Emma and

Harold. Chase continues to listen to Harold talk but never reveals to Harold his speculation on why Emma is in the hospital. Chase, eager to accept Harold's offer to check on Emma, rushes Harold off the phone to be by her side.

Emma is lying in a hospital bed watching television.

"Hi, Emma."

Emma, knowing Chase's voice without turning her head in his direction, smiles. "I missed you all these months."

Chase, now standing beside her bed, rubs her arm. The hair behind her neck stands tall, and a chill follows down her arm to her toes.

"You know I love you. I would never have let you deliver the baby by yourself. You weren't speaking with me after you told me you were pregnant, so I didn't know your delivery date." Emma, not sure of what to say, decides to stay quiet. "Are you putting the baby up for adoption?"

Emma quickly shifts the position of her arm away from Chase's touch. "I can't believe the only reason you came to the hospital is to find out if I plan to put our baby up for adoption. To answer your question, no, I am not giving our baby up for adoption. You know I can't tell Harold about the baby; about us. My mother is on the way to the hospital; she will raise our baby. I will be close to him and I can look in on him. If that was the only reason you came to the hospital, you can go."

Chase stares at Emma. The two of them stare at each other in silence. Chase drops his head, shoulder hunched over, and exits the hospital room with his hands in his pockets. He takes the stairs to avoid Emma's family seeing him leave the hospital.

Bertha, Emma's mother, misses Chase by seconds; she charges into Emma's room, one hand on her chest, the other flapping in the air. "Baby, are you okay? I got your message you were in the hospital. Where's Harold?" Bertha blurts it all out in just one sentence.

"Mama, Mama, calm down. Harold is away on one of his digs. He's not here. Have a seat. I have something to tell you."

"What, baby? Spit it out. Oh, are you on death's door? Let me get the reverend down here to pray with you."

"Mama, the reason I am in the hospital is I am having a baby."

For the first time Bertha's eyes move to Emma's midsection. "Oh, sugar, I am so happy for you and Harold." Bertha slides the chair close to Emma and sits. She opens her purse, pulls out her handkerchief, and dabs her forehead and cheeks, drying the perspiration.

"Mama, you know I don't ask much from you. As a matter of fact, I haven't asked you for anything since I graduated from high school."

Bertha, losing her patience, blurts, "Child, just tell me what you have gotten yourself into and what Mama can do to help."

"The baby's not Harold's. The baby's father is Chase."

"Chase, the white man from next door? Harold's best friend. The one with the petite wife. Is he still married? Does Harold know?"

"No, Harold doesn't know." Emma only answers one of the many questions thrown out at her to soften the blow to her dignity.

"You mean you spread your legs to a man who's married and to top it off Chase is Harold's best friend. What will the ladies at the church say about your sinful ways?" Bertha shakes her head in disgrace while picking a piece of invisible lint off her polyester floral dress.

"Mama, I know you are disappointed with me, but I need a favor. Once I deliver the baby, will you raise my son?"

"You know people are going to ask me questions about where I got this half-white-looking child from."

Emma starts to weep. "Mama, I am begging you. I need you to raise this child. Harold can't know what I did. You can tell the people in the church you are a foster parent. I don't know what else to do. I have never asked you for anything. Can you just do this one thing for me, please, Mama?" she whispers. "I beg you to do this for me." Emma wipes the tears with the back of her hands.

Bertha opens the clasp of her patent leather white purse and pulls out a perfectly ironed handkerchief. She extends it to Emma. Emma reaches over and grabs the handkerchief, touching her mother's aged, wrinkled hand. Emma knows this is too much to ask a woman her mother's age, but she doesn't have anyone else she can ask.

Bertha stares in the eyes of her baby girl and changes her demeanor. She whispers, "You said you are having a boy? What's his name?"

"I want to name him Christopher, but Chip for short."

"You know Christopher was your father's middle name."

"That's why I settled on such a strong name for my boy."

Bertha, not leaving her daughter's side, scrubs in to help Emma deliver her baby.

Chapter 36

Two years after the birth of Chip, Bertha, Emma's mother, was rushed to the hospital with chest pains and never returned home. By this time, Harold was living in Charlotte, working at Queens College as an associate professor in humanities. He enjoyed his new job, but life in Sweetbriar had changed his wife; she was often timid around him, and his best friend barely parted his lips to him. Harold often wondered if Chase was jealous he was home or if there was something more serious going on between Chase and his wife.

Emma loved the fact that her husband was home but suspicious of her husband's motives. She was unsure if he suspected the affair between her and Chase or their secret. Now with her mother dead, what would she do with Chip? Emma burst out in tears, crying uncontrollably. Harold walked over to his wife and engulfed her in his strong arms. She buried her head in his chest, softly weeping. "I know you will dearly miss your mother. It will take time, but you have the good memories that can comfort you and bring you peace."

It was true Emma would miss her mother and mourn her death, but the secret and shame caused the tears. Emma thought about her loving mother and her poor health. It was only a matter of time Bertha would die of a heart attack. She was one plate of mac and cheese away from a heart attack; fried chicken, cornbread, all foods dripping in butter or margarine. Her doctor told her to lose the weight and watch her cholesterol, and she watched it all right; she watched it every time she ate what the doctor told her not to. Emma took a deep breath as she remembered the countless conversations, she had with her about following the doctors' orders. *Why didn't I try harder to get her to eat better? If I had I wouldn't be in this situation.* She looked up at Harold with tear-filled eyes and kissed him on the lips.

"I'll be right back. I need some fresh air."

"Okay." The two of them released their embrace and Emma walked out of the room and exited the hospital. She walked to the far end of the parking lot and pulled out her cell phone and placed a call.

"Hello."

"Hey, it's me, Emma."

"I know who this is," Chase said with a hearty chuckle. "I miss you."

Emma ignored the comment. "I am at the hospital…"

Before Emma could complete her sentence, Chase interrupted. "Are you okay?"

In a dismissive tone Emma said, "Yes, yes, I am fine." Tears welled up in her eyes. "My mother died this afternoon."

"Oh, Emma, I am sorry to hear about this."

Emma ignored Chase again; this time she was all about business, and she didn't have time for idle chitchat. "The reason I am calling is I need you to take Chip. You know my mother was raising him, and now with her death he has no place to go."

"Why can't you and Harold take him?"

"I can't. He is already suspicious. I don't know what he knows, but he has been acting strange lately. He is leaving his dream job to work at the local college and teach. You know that's not him. He likes the action of doing the work, not reporting what someone else has done." Emma paused for a moment and sat on the curb. "I think this is an opportunity for Harold and me to get our relationship back on track. We have been two ships passing in the night. I want the man I married back, and this is the second chance we need. I don't need the black cloud hanging over my head that Chip is my child from a relationship where I cheated with his best friend while he was gone."

Through clenched teeth, "What do you want me to do? Megan suspects a relationship between the two of us as well. Now you want me to take Chip and have a black cloud over my marriage?"

"Let me put this another way to help you understand. If you don't take Chip. I will tell Megan about our affair and the child. And I will tell your best friend that you forced yourself on me. Do you want that kind of black cloud over your marriage and friendship? Is that what you want?"

Chase considered the alternatives Emma just gave him and in a soft whisper said, "No."

"Here's what you will do. You will drive to my aunt Vivian's house who is watching Chip. Tell her I sent you. Aunt Vivian is the only other person besides my mother who knows the situation, and she is taking the secret to her grave. You will take him and all his belongings with you and never look back."

"What do I tell Megan? I am sure you have thought that through too?"

"Don't get cute with me!" shouted Emma. "No, I haven't figured out what you should tell her. For all I care tell her you picked the baby up at the park. Chip needs his father; he needs *you* right now. Do you have the address?"

Chapter 37

*H*arold, an anthropologist not afraid of the dead, waited in Bertha's room until her body was carried away to the morgue. Harold walked to the hospital window, saw his wife below on her cell phone pacing up and down the sidewalk, hands flying in the air. *Who is she talking to? She seems angry.*

Harold continued to watch her from above, hands in pockets, bouncing from the heel of his foot to his toes. A strange feeling overcame him. *Where is Vivian, Bertha's sister? Why isn't she by her side comforting her? Where is the child Bertha is caring for?* The hairs on the back of his neck were on alert. Could the child Bertha was raising be Emma and Chase's baby boy? He was gone long enough for Emma to have a baby; the child should be… Harold counted the years and months in his head. *Who are the parents of Chip? And why was Bertha keeping the toddler?* Both Bertha and Emma were very protective of the boy, and whenever he visited, the child was never around long enough for Harold to take a good look at his features. Harold asked the same questions over and over in his head. He wanted to know for sure if the boy

Bertha was raising was the son of Chase and Emma. He left the hospital in a huff, and drove over to Vivian's house, where the boy was staying while Bertha was in the hospital. He drove up the dirt road to the trailer, the dust from the car whirling in the rearview mirror of his car. Harold parked next to the stranger's vehicle. He rapped on the door.

"Come in, it's open," yelled Vivian.

Harold turned the knob and stepped into the trailer and closed the door behind him. He jerked his head back in astonishment—face-to-face with Chase, his best friend, holding the hand of the boy. The boy was squirming, not wanting the strange man to hold his hand. "It's okay," Chase reassured the boy.

"Chase, I am surprised you are here. How do you know Emma's aunt?"

"Well, you know, I, you know…"

"What?" Harold stepped toward Chase.

Vivian lived next to Bertha, both double-wide trailers identical. *Why would Chase know where either Bertha or Vivian live?* Harold's eyes took him to the young boy, searching his face for a semblance of Emma in his facial features.

Vivian snapped her fingers and directed his attention to her. "Harold, why are you here?"

"Chase, I can ask you the same question. Why are you here? You aren't family."

Vivian, knowing a pissing contest when she saw one, decided to pipe up and shut it down. "I had a birthday party for Chip, and Emma invited Chase and Megan. That's how Chase knows where I live."

"Yeah, what she said."

Vivian cut her eyes at Chip to shut up. "Since Bertha has passed, little Chip here is going to be adopted by Chase and Megan." Vivian took a puff of her Virginia Slims menthol cigarette and blew the smoke in Harold's face.

"What?"

"Chase and his wife couldn't have any children of their own and want to raise Chip."

"Is that right," replied Harold, not believing Vivian was helping Chase out of this mess. The biracial child was the spitting image of Emma and Chase.

Vivian took another puff of her cigarette, stepped within inches of Harold, and blew the smoke directly in his face. "That's right. You got a problem with it?"

Chase, not wanting the wrath of Vivian, remarked, "Well, I better go," in a hurried speech. Chase picked up Chip, snatched his duffle bag off the sofa, placed the strap over his left shoulder and picked up Chip's small suitcase with his left. He ran down the wooden steps and placed the luggage in the trunk and the baby in the car seat. Harold walked to the door watching Chip speed up the dirt road to the main highway.

Harold turned toward Vivian. "Thank you for your hospitality," he said bitterly.

"Where are you going?"

Harold was not playing games with Vivian any longer. "I needed to find the answer to a question that has plagued me for the last two years. Is Chip the child of Emma and Chase? Don't give me the song and dance you gave me just a few minutes ago."

Vivian sat on the worn floral sofa. "Have a seat. I will tell you everything you want to know." Vivian used the ashtray to put out her cigarette and within minutes she fired up another. Her legs crossed, her arms stretch the length of the back of the sofa, cigarette in her right hand. Harold sat in the wingback chair to Vivian's left. Vivian closed her right eye as she took a puff of the cigarette and twisted her lips, so the smoke flowed away from Harold.

"I'll tell you what. I will tell you all you want to know if you answer one question for me."

Harold bobbed his head up and down; he had nothing to hide. "Okay."

Vivian slid to the edge of the sofa, directing the hand holding the cigarette in Harold's direction. "Who the fuck is Tara?"

Harold's mouth flew open.

"That's what I thought. I knew your kind when Emma brought her prize possession home for her mother to meet all those years ago. You weren't ready to get married; you jumped on the first opportunity to get from under the roof of your wife. What newlywed goes all around the world to work?"

Vivian slid back on the sofa and took a long drag of the cigarette, tilted her head back, and blew the smoke in the air above her head. "How long were you in Egypt? Not long, right before you moved to Philadelphia?"

"How…?"

Vivian cut him off. "How what? How trailer trash like myself knew what the fuck you were up to? Is that your question? I have a PhD in spotting bullshit and knew what you were telling Emma smelled. You don't need to know about me and what I do. I make an honest living uncovering bullshitters like yourself."

Harold's appearance changed. He was silent. Vivian was smarter than he thought. He imagined the conversation between the two of them going differently. *Did Vivian tell Emma what she knows?*

Vivian stared intently at Harold as she enjoyed her cigarette. She put the butt of the cigarette out on the ashtray. There was at least a pack of butts in the ashtray, Harold observed. Vivian reached for her glass of vodka, took a sip, not offering her guest a drink.

"No, I haven't told Emma if that's what you are thinking. I couldn't bear to hurt her. She believed in you all these years."

Harold felt bold. "Is the boy Emma's?"

Vivian took another sip of the vodka. Fired up another

menthol cigarette, inhaled the euphoric drug, her body relaxing, her eye squinting slightly. She held the smoke in as long as she could to satisfy her addiction, and exhaled, blowing the smoke in the air away from Harold. "Is Gregory your son?" Vivian took another long drag of the cigarette and blew the smoke in Harold's direction.

Harold stood. "Thank you for your time."

"That's what I thought. Get the fuck out of here." Vivian understood the secret code. Family business was kept among family; you didn't reveal secrets to others even though they may be family through marriage; and blood was thicker than water. You could divorce a spouse but not your mother or brother; they were who they were…family.

Vivian stood and pushed Harold out the door. "Go on, get!"

Chapter 38

*H*arold sped out of Vivian's driveway, tires skidding as he turned the corner to the main road leading out of town. The inside of his hand white, his grip on the steering wheel slowed the circulation of blood. He slowed his speed and pulled into an abandoned gas station. The engine running, Harold sat in the car with his head hung down, both hands gripping the steering wheel as though it would fall off if it were not for his steady hand holding it in place.

His cell phone rang, and he jumped. *Why is Chase's wife calling me?* He ignored the call. She called repeatedly. Harold answered the phone without pleasantries. "Megan, I am in the middle of something. Can I call you back?"

"You aren't going to believe what Chase just told me."

"No, what, Megan—what did your husband tell you?" Harold said sarcastically.

"Chase just told me he adopted a two-year-old child and is bringing the boy home with him. You know he's lying. He didn't adopt a two-year-old. He is bringing the child he conceived with that whore. I can't believe he would throw his affair in my face again. If it wasn't hard dealing with the affair, now he wants me to care for this love child. He and his whore can go to hell."

Harold snapped, "Don't call my wife out of her name."

Megan forgot Emma birthed the child Chase was bringing home. "Oh Harold, I am sorry. I forgot. I am so mad at him. What are we going to do? I can't have him bringing another woman's son into my home. How are we going to fix this problem?"

Harold, a manly man, never cried, only when his true love broke his heart back in college and now what he suspected of Emma. The tears streamed down his face, and the anger boiled in his head and pit of his stomach. His response to Megan was shocking. "Leave the back door open tonight." He hung up the phone, not waiting for a response from Megan. He would keep his promise he made years ago. He would take care of the man who betrayed him once and for all.

Chapter 39

*H*arold's chest tightened as he sped through traffic toward home, his eyes bloodshot. After leaving Vivian's house Harold decided not to return to the hospital. He didn't care what anyone said or hid from him; in this case he was convinced the biracial child Chase carried from Vivian's house was conceived by his wife and best friend.

Harold took secondary roads to thwart police scanners and traffic lights, just the open road to clear his head or in his case to ponder the lies Chase told him throughout the years. *Emma is fine, he said. Was that after he had sex with my wife? Emma is getting out of the house and going to work. Did he help her get dressed after hours of lovemaking? Megan and I took Emma out to dinner to celebrate her birthday. Or was it just Chase and did he sex her up afterwards?* With each thought Harold's foot increased his speed, and he rounded the curves without braking—a man reckless, not caring about his own life. How could he be such a fool?

Harold made a sharp right and slowed his speed to follow the rules of the road on the highway toward Sweetbriar. He pulled in the driveway, the car still running, and stared at his best friend's house right next door. How convenient for him to take advantage of his wife. Chase would not have another opportunity to betray him again. He turned off the engine and used the garage opener affixed to the visor in his car. He gathered tools needed for his mission later. He shoved the supplies in his olive-green duffle bag with gray patches of duct tape protecting the worn snags and gashes. He thinks how much Gregory admired this old bag so much. He would have to check on him.

Harold finished packing his bag and went upstairs to change into his black Adidas windbreaker, pants, and matching sneakers. He made his way to the attic, where he used binoculars to spy on Chase and Megan's home. The porch light went on, then the light leading up the stairs went out, then the master bedroom light. The house dark, one streetlamp illuminated the driveway and the cul-de-sac. Harold slipped out of his house, walked through the trees and shrubs that separated his home from his enemy. He made his way to the backyard, reached over the wooden fence, unlatched the security bolt, and stepped inside the yard, careful to latch the fence back. Harold took one step at a time up the deck, turned the knob to the back door, and with a gentle push the door opened. The small flashlight illuminated his path in a house he hadn't visited in years. As he moved through the kitchen, he heard laughter. He stopped and took several steps to the left. Nothing. He walked back to his original position and heard the laughter again, so he decided to walk to the right. The noise was louder. He wanders toward the living room, where he found Megan with her back toward him. Harold, within earshot, called out to her, "Megan, are you okay?"

Megan stopped laughing. "Harold, is that you?" She turned toward Harold, wearing an ankle-length white cotton spaghetti strap gown. The gown was stained in red blood, a knife in her right hand with bits of flesh stuck to it.

"Megan, what happened?"

"He thought I was a stupid bitch, but I showed him. I knew he was sleeping around with Emma but no, he denied it each time I asked. For years I ignored the cheating but this last time when he got Emma pregnant, I became bitter toward him but again over time I forgave him…today was a different story altogether. He called me under false pretense that he wanted us to start a family and brought this love child into our home like I am stupid. But I had the last laugh tonight." Megan, tickled with her comment, chuckled. She didn't care she was carrying on a one-sided conversation. Harold, stunned, still standing in the same place he found Megan.

"Megan, what have you done?" Harold said calmly while his eyes searched the room for Chase. After moments of no luck, he turned and took the stairs one at a time expecting the unexpected. Once in the master bedroom he found Chase's lifeless body in the bed, the white sheets soaked in crimson blood. Harold's gag reflex suppressed the contents of his stomach from moving past his throat. He concentrated hard not to vomit and swallowed hard. The laughter from downstairs stopped, and he heard footsteps ascend the carpeted stairs. Harold turned. Megan's small frame seemed dwarflike in the doorway, hand still gripping the knife, ready to strike if Chase wasn't dead. In a little girl's whisper, she said, "What are we going to? I need to know what to do. Please tell me." Harold, still disoriented, stared at the body, not blinking, engrossed in the death of his enemy. Megan tugged on the sleeve of his windbreaker. "Tell me what to do."

Without taking his eyes off the dead body, he said, "Do you have a wheelbarrow?"

"A wheelbarrow?"

"I am just thinking of how I can get his body downstairs."

"I know I am petite, but I can help you."

"I can carry the weight, but I will need you to guide his body as much as you can." Harold threw back the bloody sheet from Chase's body, and grabbed his upper torso while Megan grabbed his feet. Chase's lifeless body was heavy, dead weight. They eased the body off the bed and the weight of Chase's legs pushed Megan backwards; she fell on the floor, head hitting the windowsill and her slipper falling off her foot. "Ouch," remarked Megan, rubbing her head. She rose off the floor and resumed her position of holding Chase's feet. They took two steps at a time not to overwhelm Megan. They moved the body from the bedroom down the stairs and into the backyard of Kyndall's vacant house next door. Harold ran through the bushes back to his house, grabbed a shovel, dug a hole. On the count of three Megan and Harold dumped Chase's body in the ground as though it was trash. Harold covered the hole with the excess dirt until the hole was filled.

Harold turned to Megan. "Go home and take care of Chip; we will never speak of this again."

Megan obeyed Harold and ran home and entered through the unlocked back door. No longer in a fog, she was hit with the reality she killed her husband. She raced up the stairs, stripped the bedding, and placed it in the washer with bleach; she flipped the mattress over for now until the morning when she could purchase another. She took a hot shower and threw her nightgown and the knife in a trash bag. Megan took a step back and inspected the room—good as new. She walked down the hall to Chip's room. His covers were thrown back, the middle of the bed wet. Chip was sitting on the floor rocking back and forth. A thought crossed Megan's mind: Did he witness the murder? Even if he did, he was too young to remember. Megan cleaned the boy up and the two of them fell to sleep in the bed where she killed his father.

Chapter 40

*E*mma uses her fingertips to massage her temple, the shouting between June and Chip giving her a headache. The thoughts of giving her son up doesn't help the matter either. Emma screams, "I can only hear one of you at a time! Shut up!" Immediately June and Chip stop talking and stare at Emma, waiting for further instructions. "June, go home and get the cleaning supplies I asked you to get." June does not move. "Go now," shouts Emma. June turns and runs out of the back to her home, not to be seen, especially by her nosy neighbor Kelsey, who is her own neighborhood watch.

Once in the house June foregoes the cleaning supplies and takes the stairs to the bedroom two at a time to secure the watch, she took off the arm of her lover. She slings open the door to the walk-in closet, unfolds the stepstool, and carefully climbs the two-rung small ladder. On her tiptoes she retrieves the gray box, steadying herself not to fall. She backs down the stepstool, places the box on the floor. June reaches for her treasure in her back pocket and runs her hand across the face of the watch. She weeps for Jim. She wipes her tear-stained cheek with the sleeve of her pricey long-sleeve sweater now with bloody residue from Jim's watch. June plops on the floor of the closet remembering the day she purchased the watch for her lover; it was an impulsive gift.

June just left the salon, where she had her long locks cut after her lover told how sexy she be with shorter hair. June hung up the phone with him and pranced into the salon and told her stylist to cut it all off. Andre did exactly as his client of sixteen years told him; he cut her hair the length she insisted. June, feeling free, strutted out of the salon toward her car. She dropped her keys on the sidewalk, picked them up, and was standing directly in front of the gorgeous Tag Heuer Link Calibre 17 Automatic. June handed the sales associate the credit card her husband didn't know about. As June waited for the sales associate to run her card, she ran her hand through her sassy hair. *What the hell*, she thought. "Excuse me, Tim. I would like to get the watch engraved."

"Sure, what would you like the watch to say?" Tim handed June her receipt along with pen and paper to ensure the engraving said exactly what she wanted it to say. June scribbled on the paper, gave it back to Tim.

Tim read the note aloud. "Jim, the love of my life, June. Is this correct?"

"Yes," said June with a wide grin as she fluttered her eyelashes.

June threw caution to the wind by giving a gift to her lover and having it engraved. She didn't care—she wanted to express her love to Jim.

June is distracted by the email alert on her phone. She places the watch on top on the box, finds her phone, unlocks it. She has an email from an online dating site, The One. She clicks on the link to the website. Once on the site she opens her message. "Wow!" she expresses out loud to no one in the room but for her benefit of this gorgeous man smiling back at her. Forgetting about Jim, she has a new conquest. His name is displayed on the screen on top of his picture, Andy. June responds to his message, "Hey, how are you? I would love to meet you too." She hits send. June places the phone back in her pocket and turns her attention to the situation at hand, hiding Jim's watch from her husband.

She picks up the watch and opens the lid of the box; her eyes glisten at her collection of treasures. She places Jim's watch in the box next to the three-carat antique platinum Emerald ring she gave Lily for her birthday on May 15th, the last day she saw her. June pauses for a moment; Lily was her love interest before Jim. *Right, right, right...*June has to get the order straight in her mind. Lily, a real estate agent, worked for Chip and June to sell the remaining houses on Sweetbriar, which is considered Phase I. Both June and Chip were impressed with Lily's work and planned to ask her to stay to help sell homes in Phase II, but before they could make her the offer, Lily disappeared, and no one heard from her after her birthday.

Chip had a smooth deal with Kyndall. Since her house was vacant, Lily could use the house as a model to show potential owners the craftsmanship of the custom home. This was a win/win for both Kyndall and Chip; her house was vacant and available to show, and if someone wanted to purchase in the community, Chip would get a loan from the bank to start construction. The more houses in the community, the more Kyndall's home would increase in value.

<hr />

Over the year of Lily working for Chip and June, June grew fond of Lily. They shared an intimate relationship, one in which June was the aggressor, chasing Lily. Lily, not sure what to make of the relationship, was conflicted. June was married and the two of them could not pursue a relationship in the open. June even insisted she keep their relationship secret from her family, with whom she shared everything. It was eating at her that she couldn't tell her best friend and brother, Khan, she was in love. Her highly religious Muslim family would be disappointed by her intimate relationship with June, and June was pressuring her to keep secrets.

Lily was further conflicted by language she found in the HOA addendum. Homeowners weren't aware they would be living in a swinging community for a minimum of ten years. Lily was so consumed with her love for June, she felt as though she misled all the homeowners in the community. She was so detailed oriented and would have brought this to Chip and June's attention sooner. Was June trying to distract her? Lily, lost in her thoughts, didn't hear June when she entered the model home.

"Hi, how are you?" June walked over and gave Lily a kiss on the lips.

"Hi, I am good."

"I have a surprise for you."

"I love surprises." Lily rubbed her hands together, forgetting the doubt she had about June's true intentions for her.

"Happy birthday!"

June pulled out a beautifully wrapped box from her purse. Lily, eyeing the box, jumped up and down, clapping her hands in front of her. "What is it?"

"Open it up." June extended the box to Lily, who within seconds snatched the box out of June's hand and pulled—the ribbon cascaded to the floor. She opened the box, exposing the ring.

"Do you like it?"

Lily's eyes grew wide and her mouth gaped open. "I love it!"

"Happy birthday."

"Thank you."

Lily took the ring out of the box and placed it on her right ring finger. She stretched her arm in front of her, admiring the ring from a distance. "You are so thoughtful. This is so beautiful. Thank you so much."

Lily leaned over and gave June a kiss on the lips.

Chip walked up the driveway to the model. Lily backed away from June quickly. In the middle of the driveway Chip stopped, intensely looking at his phone.

"Is something wrong?" June was curious why she only got a quick peck on the lips for the expensive ring she gave her lover. "What are you staring at?"

"I am looking out the window at Chip. I called him earlier with a concern about the Homeowners Association addendum."

June knew all too well the language in the addendum; she was the lawyer who embedded the views of the swinging community in the document. The master plan around the Sweetbriar Community was to help residents explore sexual pleasure outside their marriage with people of the community without confined societal thoughts about how they live. June patiently waited for Lily to share what she knew about the secrets of the community.

—————— ⚬《◊》⚬ ——————

Chip entered the house. "Hey, Lily." He cut his eyes sharply in June's direction.

"Hey, Chip. I called you earlier to discuss a concern I have about the HOA document."

"I know. I need to speak with June about an alert from our bank; there was a purchase that exceeded the daily limit on the debit card."

"I am going to let the two of you have some privacy." Lily unfolded her arms, giving Chip an opportunity to catch a glimpse of the emerald ring on her finger. When Chip received the alert, he called the jewelry store that he and June used on many occasions to buy each other gifts. He knew Mr. Saul personally and spoke with him. He told Chip about the ring. As Lily dropped her arm, Chip grabbed her right hand for a better view. "What a beautiful ring. Is it new? I've never seen you wear it before."

Panic in her eyes, Lily searched June's face for an idea of what to do. June nodded to signal Lily to tell the truth.

"It was a gift," responded Lily, pulling her hand out of Chip's tight grip; she placed her arms behind her away from his view. "June gave the ring to me as a birthday gift."

"She did." The word *did* rang in the air. June lowered her eyes to the floor to avoid direct eye contact with Chip. *This ring is a gift of love. Does June love Lily? Why won't she abide by the rules of the community—no sex outside of the marriage unless the other person is present?* Chip started to perspire, his armpits hot, shirt sticking to his back; his head starts to hurt. There were flashes of light, so he closed his eyes. Quickly the image of the person in white dashed before him. The room spinning. He took a deep breath and started to rub his leg, back and forth. Now calm, he opened his eyes. Chip turned toward Lily, focusing his attention on her. "You called me earlier. You mentioned you had a concern about the contract."

"Oh, yes. A homeowner had a question and as I was reviewing the document to research the answer, I uncovered troubling information that this community is a swinging community and all residents have to participate. I never thought to review this document because they are all standard. If you want to add a permanent structure, you need to get approval, not force people to participate in sex parties.

"You had to have known that this was included. Right?" Still no comment from Chip. "I don't know if I will be able to sell homes in this community knowing that you aren't giving homeowners the opportunity to opt out."

June and Chip, who were at odds with each other earlier

through the secret, stared and glances united. No one would accuse the other without the other coming to their rescue. Chip just stared at Lily with no comment.

"I feel so passionately about my stance. I will disclose to clients this is a swinging community. Chip let me ask you a question. What happens after the homeowner closes the loan, moves into their residence, and finds out they are living in a swinging community?"

"They can leave anytime they want."

"No, they can't. According to the document they must live in the community a minimum of ten years or they will be penalized. What is the penalty?"

Chip, still feeling bold, responded, "They have to sign their home over to me, the builder, and they can walk away free and clear."

"Walk away with what? Nothing, that's what. You are holding these people hostage. The more I think about my role in all of this, the more guilty I feel."

"All of the homeowners in this community love being here, and we haven't had any problems."

"I started poking around and there is a young lady who used to live in this house who is now missing." Lily's last statement was to get a rise out of Chip.

"Who told you that?" snapped Chip. *Is there a traitor among my flock?*

"So, you aren't denying it? You know what, I quit! I am going to the police because what you are doing is unethical and I am sure illegal. I refuse to be a part of this any longer," Lily screamed. Lily turned and briskly walked toward her desk. She yanked the lower drawer open, snatched her purse, and threw it over her shoulders.

"Where do you think you are going?" asked Chip.

"I told you. I am going to the police. It's not right you have these people under your thumb, holding them hostage because they can't get out of their contract. They are all sex slaves to you."

June chimed in, "Wait, Lily. Going to the police will destroy Chip and me." June walked over to Lily and gently brushed her straight black hair over her left shoulder away from her face and kissed her soft lips gently. "Going to the police will destroy all of us." June caressed her arm. "Please, you know I love you."

Chip, looking in both June and Lily's direction, already had a head start. He snatched the poker and smashed it on Lily's head with a swing that would make any golfer proud. The blow to her left side knocked Lily to her knees. The second swing to her head was the fatal blow. The strike to the head splattered blood on the front of June's white silk blouse and on her face. She yelled, *Ugh*. June looked around the room. Her lover was dead, and blood covered the area where they were standing and splattered on the walls. "Why did you kill her?"

"June, you are testing my patience with you. You know the rules. I need you to take that ring back to the store. The ring is now tied to us and Lily's murder, and we can't have any loose ends. Now help me bury the body in Kyndall's backyard."

June grudgingly helped her husband drag the body out of the house to the grave Chip dug for Lily.

Paige, standing in the upstairs window, watched the body being discarded. She turned away from the window, wondering who was next.

The next day, June could not bear giving up the only memory

she had left of Lily. She called the jewelry store to return the purchase on one card, only to buy it back on her new personal charge card.

———— »«◊»« ————

June brings the ring to her lips, kisses the memory of her love, and places it next to the tennis bracelet that once belonged to Poppy.

June jumps when her phone alerts her of another email, excited. It may be from Andy. She drops the tennis bracelet back in the box. She pulls the phone out of her back pocket and smiles as she reads the message from Andy. "I would like you to visit me in DC." June, who is known on the site as Tiffany, responds. "I would love to meet you. Send me the details and I will be there. Here is my phone number." She hits send. Within twenty minutes June receives a detailed text message with her flight information and hotel accommodation.

She turns her attention back to the box and picks up the tennis bracelet.

———— »«◊»« ————

June met Poppy at a sorority mixer where she was a guest speaker. The theme of the event was Positive Woman Positive Results. June had finished her speech and was packing her briefcase when a preppy, beautiful young lady approached.

"Excuse me, Mrs. Carter."

"You can call me June. It is nice to meet you." June extended her hand to Poppy.

Poppy blushed. "I'm Poppy. It is such a pleasure meeting you."

"You as well. Poppy, let's get out of here and go to the bar for a drink. You do drink?"

"Oh, yeah, yeah."

The two made small talk as they walked toward the bar on the other side of the conference room. "You know what, I don't want to carry this briefcase to the bar. I am going to go upstairs to my room, change into something more comfortable, and leave this briefcase. You can get us a table or take the elevator upstairs with me; that way you have more time to ask me all the questions you have written on that notepad of yours."

Poppy blushed. June liked that Poppy was smart and detailed. Pleasantly, she smiled at Poppy as she pushed the button to call for the elevator. The doors opened, and June stepped inside, not waiting for Poppy to reply. Poppy, outside, searched June's eyes for any danger warning signs. Then she threw caution to the wind and entered the elevator to spend more time with her mentor. June pushed the number fourteen on the panel and kept her eyes forward. A mischievous smile crept across June's lips; her plan was set in motion when Poppy stepped into the elevator. The elevator door opened and the two exited without a word. June used her key card, opened the door, walked over to the desk, and placed her briefcase on the floor. She stepped out of her heels and cracked her toes by stretching them wide and closing them tightly over and over. "Oh, that feels so much better." Concentrating on how much better her feet felt, she turned and was startled by the sight of Poppy standing near the door. "Poppy, you scared me. I forgot you were even here. Let me put on a pair of flats and we can get that drink and talk as long as you want."

"Okay, that sounds great," said Poppy, still standing near the door. June slipped on a pair of flat shoes and picked up her purse and key card. "Ready."

"Yes," said Poppy.

Poppy, an astute student, did her homework on June and knew what she could possibly be getting herself into when she accepted the drink offer, which turned into a bait and switch. She'd heard the tall tales that were told throughout the years about alumni in sorority houses who challenged the system, and June was one of them. She held wild sex parties where there was a cover charge to enter. The rumor said she got the idea to charge for sex because her mother was a madame. Poppy was glad that June didn't force herself on her because she wasn't into paying for sex or a homosexual relationship. Poppy felt a sense of relief. June was a good person, not the horrible monster everyone made her out to be.

———

June opened the door for Poppy to exit in front of her. She knew Poppy approved of her; she didn't dare try anything with her today. Poppy would be more useful to her long term. The Sweetbriar Community was missing a unicorn, a single female to participate in a threesome. She knew she and Chip needed one every now and then.

The two went downstairs for the drink June promised.

Chapter 41

The following year Poppy graduated from college, and she and June kept in contact. She wanted to purchase a home in the Sweetbriar Community after her parents gave her the first check from her inheritance of $50,000 to do what she wanted, but Poppy, being the disciplined person, she was, decided to use the money as a down payment on her first home. June, being the loyal friend, she became over the year, used her persuasive skills to steer Poppy to purchase in Sweetbriar. June walked her through the community, imagining what Phase II would look like. She even introduced her to many of the neighbors, except Paige, who wanted out. She was another story altogether. Poppy, excited about the community, wanted the paperwork to look over, so June gave her a copy of the Homeowners Association document and loan packet to start reviewing.

June underestimated Poppy's attention to detail. She took the document home, highlighter in hand, and went through the entire document finding all the language of the swinging community.

The rumors of June being a swinger came to mind. Poppy threw the highlighter on the desk and called several of her sorority sisters seeking more information on June. Most of the information she'd heard before, but the majority were speculations around June and her husband having an open relationship; that's all any of her sources would give. Poppy had a restless night; she watched the clock all night. At 9:00 a.m., she jumped up and called June. They agreed to meet to discuss the details of the contract. Poppy kept the details of the meeting vague not to alert her of what she discovered.

Poppy arrived at Sweetbriar still fuming, thoughts swirling in her head as she walked through the door of the model with the documents rolled into a tube in her hand. Chip and June sat waiting for the meeting with Poppy, prepared for her to sign the closing documents with the loan officer's information. They were even willing to sweeten the pot by offering to pay the closing costs on the loan.

No greeting—Poppy got straight to the point. "Did you think I would not read the document to find out what you wanted me to do?"

June was the first to speak. "Calm down."

"Who are you to tell me to calm down? You wanted me to be the third person in sex whenever the neighbors wanted— what do you call it?" Poppy flipped through the pages of the highlighted document to find the word "unicorn" underlined. "June, I heard the rumors, but I refused to believe them after I met you. You were kind and wanted to mentor my career. I thought you were sincere but all you wanted to do was to use me for sex."

"Don't get overly dramatic," said Chip. He stood and moved close to Poppy. Chip reached for her hand, but she snatched her hand from his grip.

"How many people living in the community signed documents

to participate without knowing? I am going to go door to door to let them know what they have gotten themselves into and take the names to the police."

June jumped into the conversation. "Don't, Poppy! Let's talk. It's not what you think."

Poppy, passionate about her position, started shouting at June.

—————— ((O)) ——————

Chip closed his eyes, dizzy as the room swirled around. The lady in the white cotton gown ran through the room and disappeared. Chip searched for her, moving around in a small circle, around and around. The shouting made it hard for him to concentrate. He grabbed the edge of the desk to gain his balance. He stopped long enough to hear Poppy exclaiming that she was going to start polling the neighbors. Chip turned and ran toward Poppy's voice, but the head on her body was of his father's killer. He wrapped his hand around her neck. Poppy struggled to breathe, his grip tighter around her neck. "Why did you kill my father, why?" Poppy's limp body fell to the floor when Chip lost his grip and stumbled backward.

June witnessed the entire event, cried at the loss of a special friend. "Chip, what do we do?"

Chip was wet in perspiration, his shirt soaked, forehead and upper lip beaded with sweat. "Do the same for her as you did for Lily; bury her in the backyard."

"Okay, I will get the shovel. Are you okay?"

"I am finally okay. I know who killed my father."

—————— ((O)) ——————

June jerks when the phone rings. *Another dead body to cover up*. Before she can say a word, Chip barks, "What's taking you so long?"

"I'm coming."

"Well, hurry up."

"Okay." June slides the lid back onto the box she climbs up the stepstool and places the box back in its hiding place in plain sight.

June runs through the house and picks up everything Emma told her to get. She decides on adding latex gloves; she has buried a body or two and is familiar with what she needs. June changes into something more practical, jeans, a T-shirt, and sneakers. Before leaving the house, she detours to the garage to pick up the shovel. They will have to dig a grave for Jim, the same place where they did for the other bodies. With shovel in hand June scurries through the backyard to Kyndall's house and burial plot of so many: Lily, Poppy, and now Jim. June loved them all. June slips back into the house through the rear to find Emma and Chip still standing in the same place she left them, hovering over Jim's dead body.

Chapter 42

Oliver hasn't had an encounter with Jack ever since his first day back to work. He had too many people counting on him—his deceased wife, partner, and Alina Ivanovich; he needed to find out who killed them. Alina, the escort found in the hotel dead. He started eating healthy and running in the morning and at night to escape his demons.

He has just come back from a run. After a shower he sits on the edge of the tub as he dries in between his toes. The television in the other room loud, the broadcaster reports on Putin in Russia. Oliver stands quickly; he knows the first death he will start to solve, Alina. His gut tells him there is a single murderer. Dakota's death was a warning to back off the investigation of Alina, which is pointing directly to Brendon Graham, senator for the State of Pennsylvania. He dresses, putting on a pair of slacks, a dress shirt with tie. He stares at himself in the bathroom mirror. He will never embarrass the captain again with his unkempt appearance. He walks to the bedroom closet, slips his feet into his loafers, walks to the table in the hall, snatches his keys, and drives to the station. Oliver parks his car in the front of the building; there aren't many cars in the lot at this hour, so he has a front spot. He grabs his briefcase and enters the precinct. Once upstairs he sits at his desk and clicks the end of a pen rapidly as he thinks where to start. He looks across his desk to where his partner Dakota used to sit. What would she do in a situation like this? He sits for several minutes as he thinks. He smiles. He knows exactly where he needs to start. He takes the elevator to the basement to the evidence storage department.

"Hey, Marty, how are you?"

"I am good. Glad you are back. You look good."

"You know I am." Reflecting on his progress, sobriety, he adds, "Not quite back to my old self but one day at a time."

"Good, that's all we can do is take it one day at a time. What can I do you for?"

"I need to sign out an evidence box; the name is Alina Ivanovich."

Marty checks in the system and finds the file number associated with the box. He writes it on the form and turns the notebook toward Oliver to print and sign his name along with the date, time. Oliver knows the drill. He can only examine the contents on the counter to the right of the night watchman, ensuring no one takes any evidence out of the box. Marty, an excellent officer, carefully watches without hovering at a distance from his desk. Oliver reviews the evidence list and takes the items out of the box one piece at a time. He spends at least two hours examining and re-examining the contents. Oliver puts the contents back in the box, closes the lid, and hands the box back to Marty.

"Did you find what you were looking for?"

Oliver sighs. "No." Staring blankly at the box, he begins to speak again. "You know how you have a nagging feeling that something isn't quite right with a case, but you don't have evidence to support your gut feeling? I have checked all the databases and the victim is clean. Don't get me wrong, she isn't a saint. It seems as though she was a high-class escort. I can't place her with the public official, but he was staying at the hotel the same night she was found dead, separate rooms. He could have done it or had someone do it for him because the room the girl was found in wasn't assigned to a guest. A fire alarm was pulled and with the guests evacuating the building, the body was dumped."

"Well, if she is a high-class call girl in this town, she has to be one of Stella's girls."

"Stella who?"

Marty laughs. "You know madams don't have last names, and I am not sure Stella *is* her real name. She runs a tight inner circle of Johns, from lawyers and diplomats to senators—all high-powered people. The ones who could risk it all if the public knew they used Stella's service; family, career, you name it."

"It seems like Stella is someone I need to talk to. Where can I find her?"

"You don't. Her business is built on trust and word of mouth. You don't just roll up on her." Marty knows Oliver isn't the judgmental type, pulls out his cell phone, and goes through his contacts, where he finds Stella's contact along with phone number. He opens his desk drawer and writes the information on a bright pink sticky note.

Marty stands and squarely looks Oliver in the eye. "I am in your corner. I know how hard it was for you to lose it all; come back to work only to be humiliated upon your return." Marty hands the note over to Oliver, both their hands on the note. "I am doing you a solid; don't tell Stella how you got her number."

Sincerely Oliver says, "I won't reveal my source. Thank you for supporting me." Oliver gratefully takes the sticky note and walks to the elevator to return to his desk. Oliver makes a phone call to a colleague in the IT department, hoping Joseph is still hanging around the office at this time of night. Joseph answers on the first ring in a distracted voice. "Hello."

"Joseph, this is Oliver, Oliver Hall."

"Hey, man, I heard you were back at work." Joseph has heard the rumors of Oliver's first day back and they aren't positive. There was an office pool that Oliver would not come back to work. When he was asked to contribute, Joseph shook his head and went back to the one place in the precinct that calmed him, the IT department. His office in the back right corner, no personal effects, just his computer and pen holder.

"Yeah, I have been back for a few weeks. I was wondering if you would do me a favor."

Joseph stops typing, removes his hands from the keyboard, and his hands fall in his lap. He reclines in his chair, curious. "I'm listening."

"I need a phone trace."

"Done. When do you want to do it?"

"You aren't going to ask me who and why."

"No, I believe in you and trust your judgment." Joseph will never forget when Oliver came to his rescue when a boy in his neighborhood played a prank on Joseph because he was withdrawn, not very social and told his parents Joseph touched one of his nerdy friends. The mother called the police and arrested Joseph and brought him to the precinct for questioning. The office had a field day with that news; his colleagues said he had to be into something. He never talked about women or was ever married. Joseph was released after Oliver investigated the boy's story to find it was untrue. Oliver, a homicide detective, worked around the clock to clear Joseph and his name. So, no, he would do anything to show everyone Oliver was and is a good detective.

"Okay, I will make the call from your office. I will be there in a few minutes." Oliver stands and sprints to the elevator to head to the IT Department.

Once downstairs Joseph sets up the equipment to trace the phone call. Joseph nods, indicating to Oliver he is ready to start the trace whenever he is. Once seated Oliver picks up Joseph's desk phone and dials Stella's number.

Stella's phone rings and she stares at the caller ID displaying the police station's number. She answers on the first ring thinking one of her girls is in trouble. "Hello."

"Stella?"

"This is she. Who's calling?"

"I am Homicide Detective Oliver Hall with DC Metro Police Department." Stella is silent, waiting for the reason Mr. Hall is calling.

"I am investigating the death of Alina Ivanovich. I was wondering if the two of us could meet."

Stella gasps, places her hand over her mouth. Poor Alina, Stella knew something was wrong when she didn't check in after the date with Andy, but she couldn't risk her reputation looking for her. Alina called her mother in Russia every day and when her mother didn't hear from her, she called Stella. Alina had given her mother Stella's number as a point of contact. Alina's mother started to cry, which in turn made Stella cry, both crying for different reasons. Alina's mother worried that her daughter was in trouble. Stella knew Alina was dead when she didn't check in. Stella called Andy, and he didn't come out and specifically say she died nor how; the only statement he did give was that "it was an accident." Stella gave Alina's mother the phone number to the coroner's office to ensure her body could be laid to rest back home where her mother could mourn her daughter's death at peace.

"Detective, I am not sure how you got my number or why you would think I would know…what's her name again?"

"Alina."

"I don't know anyone by the name of Alina, and no, we can't meet. Is that all?"

"Stella, I have one more question."

"Yes, Detective."

"Do you run an escort service?"

"No, I provide a matching service for high-ranking officials who need eye candy when they attend events. Married men or men with a gorgeous woman on their arm get the business deals. No one want to have dinner with the odd man out. I provide a single man a date for the night. What adults do after that point is up to them."

"Do your clients pay for the service?"

"What are you asking me? They don't pay for sex if that is what you are asking."

"I would like to speak with you in the morning if you don't mind."

"I don't think that is necessary; as I mentioned I don't know anyone by the name of Alina."

"Thank you for your time."

Stella disconnects the call, not knowing that she and Oliver stayed on the phone long enough for Joseph to trace her location.

———— ((◉)) ————

Stella dials Kyndall's number, and the call goes directly to voicemail. Stella leaves a message. "Kyndall, this is Stella. We have a problem. Detective Oliver Hall is asking questions about Alina, the escort who overdosed at the Loews Hotel. He wanted to meet with me and of course I declined. I don't know how he got my number, and you know Alina was the last person with Brendon that night. I am worried all this is coming back to me. Do you know how many clients can be exposed? I must protect my reputation, which includes you and Brendon. What are we going to do? Give me a call."

Stella hustles to the guest closet and reaches for her luggage on the top shelf. She rolls it across the hardwood and throw rugs to her bedroom and places it on the luggage rack. She haphazardly packs, placing miscellaneous items in the suitcase all the while thinking she can buy what she needs if she forgets something. She just needs to get out of DC as soon as possible. Stella places two additional calls, one to her daughter June to tell her she is on her way to visit for a few days. The second call to her friend Rose asking her to watch her house while she visits her daughter in North Carolina.

Stella carries the luggage to her black Mercedes convertible. Jude, walking home from a math study group, sees Stella struggling with her luggage and races over to help her put the luggage in the trunk. Jude likes Stella. When his mother had problems with her immigration status, Stella gave her money for a pricey immigration attorney who took care of getting her another visa issued and she is now in good standing with the U.S. and Haitian governments.

"Thank you, Jude."

"No problem, Ms. Stella."

Stella opens the door to the car. "Tell your mother I left her a message. I am going out of town to spend a few days with my daughter. I need her to water my plants."

"Yes, ma'am. I will tell her to check her voicemail."

"Be careful going home."

"I will."

Stella jumps in her car and enters the highway toward I-95 South to visit with her daughter June and husband Chip.

━━●《◉》●━━

The next morning Detective Hall wakes and dresses; he drives over to Stella's home in Georgetown and rings the doorbell. No one answers. He rings the doorbell again, still no answer. He walks down the steps backward. *Where did she go? Another lead disappeared.* Is this the control of the Graham clan? Or Stella running a prostitution ring.

An older white woman walking her dog carefully studies Detective Hall standing on Stella's porch. Detective Hall's instincts tell him to survey his surrounding, and he sees the petite blonde lady staring at him. As their eyes meet, she turns her attention to Brandy, her terrier, taking care of business. She stoops down with the doggie waste bag and cleans up the mess. She stands, ties the bag in a knot, and throws it in the pet waste receptacle. With a sideways glance she keeps an eye on Detective Hall's activity while cleaning her hands with sanitizer from her fanny pack, slathering the gel over the front and back of her hands.

A young boy walking toward the city bus stops and notices the stranger on Stella's stoop. Oliver rings the doorbell again. "She's not home," the boy says from the sidewalk.

"Do you know her?"

Jude looks around and sees Ms. Ruby staring at him. "I'm not telling you. Who are you, the police?"

"Actually, I am. My name is Oliver Hall. What's your name?" Detective Hall flips his badge toward the boy.

Jude, feeling more comfortable with the conversation, responds, "Jude."

After Oliver pulls out his badge Ruby and Brandy scurry down the sidewalk to their home. She has seen enough. The stranger's profession is to keep the streets safe.

"Okay, cool," says Jude. "You like being a detective?"

"As they say when you are doing something you love, it doesn't feel like work."

"I'm thinking about becoming a police officer when I gradu-
ate college."

"Really? How old are you?"

"I'm fifteen."

"I tell you what, take my card and I will let you shadow me.
You seem like a smart kid."

"For real! Oh snap!" Jude's eyes get large, his grin wide, the
corners of his mouth almost reaching his ears. He carefully places
Oliver's business card in his wallet not wanting to lose it.

"Stella and my mother are friends. I saw her last night packing
her car. She said she was going to visit her daughter."

"Where does her daughter live?"

"Her daughter June lives in Charlotte, North Carolina. My
mom and I visited last year for Thanksgiving. They live about
thirty minutes from Uptown. My mom and I explored the city
riding the light rail. Cool city, a little country for me, but cool."

Oliver laughs. Most people have the same reaction after having lived in a larger city. He shakes his head. Jude is a city boy
through and through.

Jude moves closer to Oliver, looks up and down the street,
starts to speak in a soft whisper, even though no one else is around.
Oliver leans in to hear his new friend. "Stella and her daughter
are different, if you know what I mean." With more emphasis on
"you know what I mean."

"No, I don't." Oliver shakes his head.

Jude, not wanting to come straight out and tell Oliver Stella's
business, hints, "They like to have fun."

Oliver squints his eyes, shakes his head back and forth. "What
does that mean? Lots of people like to have fun. I like to have
fun."

Jude has been raised not to discuss other people's business, but
he seems to trust Oliver to keep this secret.

"Last Thanksgiving when my mom and I visited, I overheard

my mother and Stella talking." Jude looks up and down the street again and moves much closer to Oliver to tell him the secret of the community. "They are swingers."

"Oh," says Oliver in a surprised tone. He clears his throat and looks at Jude. Does Jude know what it means to be a swinger? "Thank you for the information; if you think of anything else, let me know."

Jude smiles at Oliver. "Yeah, man, I will."

Oliver thanks Jude for the information and drives to the precinct. He analyzes his notes on the death of Dakota, Sophia and Alina until well after the end of his shift. He checks the time and decides he will stop by the Loews Hotel first thing in the morning. This is the last place Alina stayed before she died.

Chapter 43

June, pretending to be Tiffany, prances through the airport wearing all-black attire, and heads turn as this stunning woman passes them. Some wonder if she is someone famous. She follows the airport exit sign to the taxi waiting area. As the escalator descends, she sees the chauffeur holding a sign with her name, Tiffany. At least that is the name she is using for the online dating site. Tiffany sizes up the chauffeur, holding the sigh. *Eye candy.* "Hi, I'm Tiffany." The smile she gives him makes him blush.

"Hi, I'm Owen. Welcome to DC!"

"Thank you." June peers over the top of her sunglasses to get a full view of Owen's ass. If she wasn't here to meet Andy, she would hook up with Owen regardless of the wedding band on his ring finger. June obediently follows him out of the airport. Once strapped into the backseat June sends Andy, her new lover, a text message. "Hi, I am here. Heading to the hotel." She hits send. She glances at her phone—nothing; there isn't a response for several minutes. She looks at her phone again—three gray bubbles floating on the screen. The bubbles disappear and magically the message pops up with a ding: "Hi there. I am glad you made it safely. Will see you soon." Tiffany smiles at the thought of her new love interest. She can't wait to meet him. She stares out the window enjoying the peacefulness of the ride to the hotel; she closes her eyes and nods off.

The black Cadillac CTS stops in front of the Loews Hotel. The doorman, Theodore, opens Tiffany's door while Owen grabs her overnight bag from the trunk. Owen gives the bag to Theodore. Tiffany extends two twenty-dollar bills to Michael, but he pushes her hand away from him, refusing the tip. "The trip has been taken care of, along with a generous tip. Have a nice day." Owen gets back in the car and drives away.

Tiffany follows Theodore into the building and gives the doorman the money she previously offered Owen. Theodore gladly accepts the money and places it in his right breast pocket. He escorts Tiffany to the reception area.

"Welcome to the Loews Hotel. My name is Brook. How may I assist you?"

"Hi, I need to check in. My name is Tiffany Daniels."

"Yes, ma'am. We have you down for a one-night stay in the penthouse suite. Your room is taken care of, but I will need your credit card for incidentals."

Tiffany pulls out her wallet and hands Brook her Black American Express. Brook swipes the card, taking note the name on the front is different than the name Tiffany just gave her. Brook examines the card, then Tiffany's body language. Tiffany, realizing her mistake, needs to get the card back.

"Tiffany, you gave me a credit card with the name June on it."

"Oh, I am sorry." Tiffany's hand slaps the counter. "I gave you my mother's credit card I use to pay her expenses."

Tiffany, wearing heels, leans over the counter; snatches her card out of Brook's hand, and grabs her overnight bag. She races through the lobby in a huff, not aware of her surroundings, and bumps into a handsome man. The two exchange stares look into each other's eyes.

"I am sorry, ma'am."

"No, please forgive me."

"Good day."

Detective Hall tips his fedora in the beautiful woman's direction. Her striking facial features are etched in his mind's eye. He takes a second glance at the beautiful woman as she walks away from him toward the revolving door. The voice in Oliver's head says, *Follow your heart.* Oliver turns on a dime and dashes after the beautiful woman. He catches her on the outside of the building standing beside Theodore and a taxi driver.

"Excuse me!"

Theodore, the taxi driver, and Tiffany all turn their head in the direction of the voice, startled.

The taxi driver is scared he's been caught using his brother's taxi without a driver's license or permission to use the car. He took the car when his brother lay down for a nap.

Theodore is stealing overtime; he should have clocked out an hour ago but needs the extra money to buy his girlfriend an engagement ring.

Tiffany is looking for some excitement since her evening was ruined.

Oliver, now standing in the midst of the group, speaks only to Tiffany, forgetting the others are watching. "Hi," he says, blushing.

"Hi."

"I know this may seem a little forward, but I wanted to know if I can take you out to dinner sometime."

Tiffany blushes and doesn't respond, which leaves Oliver doubting himself.

"Oh, I am sorry I never asked if you were married or had a boyfriend. I am sorry. A woman as beautiful as yourself, I am sure you are spoken for."

Tiffany smiles. "I would love to have dinner with you, but I am heading back home to Charlotte."

"Beautiful city. My daughter lives there."

"Here's my number. If you are ever in the Queen City, let me know."

The two exchange phone numbers. Oliver steps away from the taxi, watches his new friend Tiffany disappear in the streets of DC. He had a thought he would call his daughter Angela and schedule a visit. But for now, he needs to question the house-keeper whose cart was used to dump Alina's body and transfer it to one of the rooms she was assigned to clean. Did she kill Alina? It was her cart that was used to transport the body. *I won't jump to conclusions yet until I hear her story.*

<hr/>

Tiffany, sitting in the back of the car, receives a text from Andy asking if her room is okay. Tiffany texts back informing him she was unable to get the room because her card was declined. The real reason she couldn't get the room is because she didn't get a prepaid card she could use for incidentals.

"No problem," says Andy. "I will call the hotel and tell them to use my card for the incidentals and the room."

"Would you do that for me? Thanks. I was headed back to the airport."

"Oh, no. No problem."

She addresses the taxi driver. "I need you to turn around and take me back to the Loews."

"Will do."

By the time Tiffany arrives back to the hotel, Andy has spoken to the manager and the problem with the incidentals gone. She is well on her way to her room to freshen up for dinner.

Chapter 44

Scotty and Sebastian are both stuffed after the breakfast fit for a king and queen Eliza served them. Somewhere after Scotty told Sebastian all she knew, they both decided to work together to solve the murder of Doris Massey.

Scotty and Sebastian leave Eliza's house with brown paper bags with a sandwich and an apple for later to accompany them on the road to DC.

Sebastian, conducting official police work, still remembers chivalry isn't dead even though he hasn't been on a date in a while. He hustles to the passenger door, Scotty slides into her seat, and he closes the door. He waves to Eliza standing on the porch admiring her matchmaking. She waves back. "Be careful," she shouts to the two of them. Scotty waves good-bye as Sebastian makes a three-point turn to exit in the direction he came.

"Before we go to DC, I need to swing by the department to submit paperwork to take a few days off. Officially I can't investigate a case outside of my jurisdiction, so a little vacation time will allow me to do so." Sebastian winks at Scotty.

Scotty turns her head to look out the passenger window. She reaches in her purse—no call from Artie. She sighs.

Sebastian, not receiving a comment from Scotty, takes his eye off the road briefly. "Is everything okay?"

"Yeah, yeah. It makes sense for you to take time off to investigate. I probably need to do the same. This visit was only supposed to be a few days, but I am unsure when I will make it back to Atlanta."

Scotty puts the thoughts of Artie out of her mind and enjoys getting to know Sebastian. She turns in her seat to get a better glimpse of him. Her eyes move from his face to his left hand, searching for an indication of his marital status. Sebastian, eyes on the road, doesn't notice Scotty checking him out.

He pulls into the parking space. "Do you want to come in?"

"No, I will wait in the car; it shouldn't take long, right?"

"Oh, no, no. I just need to fill out the form and hand it to the captain." Sebastian sits in the car awkwardly wanting Scotty to change her mind. He would be honored to walk into the station with a woman as beautiful as Scotty. The two smile at each other. Sebastian takes his cue, opens the door, and walks toward the station, looking back at Scotty sitting in the car. He shakes his head and murmurs to himself, "Who am I kidding? I am out of my league."

With the thought of impressing Scotty, Sebastian takes the stairs to his department. He opens the door, winded, stops, and uses the back of his hand to wipe the sweat off his forehead. While catching his breath, he realizes he doesn't remember the new process the department last put in place eight months ago; he never takes vacation or sick time. Billy opens the door, Sebastian blocking his path. "Excuse me," says Billy, not realizing it is Sebastian in front of him. Sebastian turns around and steps to the side to let the person behind by.

"Hi Sebastian. How's it going?"

"Good." Billy walks past Sebastian.

"Billy." Billy stops and turns toward Sebastian. "I need to request time off work; how do I do that."

Billy smiles, no stranger to being off work. Every time he earns four hours, he is taking time off to be with his girl.

As Billy and Sebastian walk to Sebastian's desk, Billy explains the department no longer uses the paper form to request time off. He explains how to find the electronic version of the form. "Are you good? I have a meeting in five minutes."

"Yeah, I'm good. Thanks for your help."

"All right, man, I will see you later."

Sebastian stares at the top of the form. All requests need to be made two weeks in advance unless it is a documented emergency. Sebastian immediately submits and prints the form. He signs off his computer, picks up his request form from the printer, and heads to the captain's office. He deserves time off; he never requests time. "Knock, knock," says Sebastian as he enters the captain's office without prior notice or meeting request.

"Come in," says the distracted captain. "What can I do for you?" Sebastian hands Morrison his time off request form. The captain reads the document. "What is this?"

"I thought I would burn some of my vacation time. I always have so much time at the end of the year, I end up losing most of it."

Morrison remembers last year when he demanded Sebastian take time off so he wouldn't lose two weeks of vacation. The captain did get approval for Sebastian to carry time over to the current year, so he has even more time to take this year. The captain sighs heavily. "Sebastian, I believe all my officers need to take time off for work, but now isn't a good time."

Sebastian wrinkles his brow. "Oh, why is that? I thought we were free to take time off when we need to take it. I will never take time in the middle of an official investigation."

Morrison drops his glasses on the desk, rubs his tired eyes. "Brown is out taking care of his father's affairs, and Dennis is working the case of Doris Massey full time. I have the chief calling informing me the Doris Massey case has links to the death of two call girls in New York. One call girl is from Philly originally. Senator Brendan Graham is linked to both cases."

Sebastian interrupts the captain. "What do you mean Brendon is linked to both cases?" He needs to know what the captain knows. The captain has a great deal of trust in Sebastian and begins to tell him the situation.

"His mother-in-law is Doris Massey, and a condom wrapper with his fingerprints were found in the apartment of the call girls in New York."

Sebastian's stomach turns into knots. He feels bad for sort of lying to his boss about the reason he wants time off work. He wants to start an unofficial investigation. He walks to the captain's office door and closes it. The captain cautiously watches. "Captain, there is something I need to disclose to you. I have been unofficially investigating Dennis."

"You have been doing what!" The captain's face turns crimson.

"Before you blow a gasket, let me explain. I can fill in the missing pieces of the case for you." Sebastian starts from the first time he spoke to Eliza on the phone to meeting the reporter daughter to the real reason he is requesting time off work.

The captain is now reared back in his chair, chewing on the end of his glasses, thinking about Dennis's behavior earlier. The captain always wants to believe and trust all his people, but Sebastian is presenting him a compelling story of why Dennis cannot be trusted. "This is what I want you to do. Continue to investigate Dennis, but you won't be doing on your own time. I will tell everyone you are on vacation. I want you to check in with me at least once a day or more if you can. I want more concrete evidence before I officially file paperwork with internal affairs."

The two sit in silence until the captain begins to speak again. "Does Dennis know you are investigating him?"

Sebastian thinks for a minute. "I confronted him about the omission of Eliza's witness statement from the police report."

"Have I created an atmosphere where you didn't feel comfortable talking to me about what you learned about Dennis?"

"Oh, no, Captain, not at all. I wanted to be sure I had all the facts before I accused a fellow officer of a crime. I didn't want to believe what I was hearing. He is my mentor. At the time I only had a vibrant lady who professes she knows what she saw and heard. I visited her on several occasions, and she seems credible. Each time she gave me more information I needed to prove what she shared was true."

The captain stares at the documents on his desk, still silent.

"Oh, yeah!"

The captain jumps, the comment coming out of nowhere.

"When Dennis interviewed the witness, Sean Smith, he gave a conflicting story of what happened. The address recorded for Sean was a vacant lot. Dennis was in charge of witness statements—why didn't he verify the address and why he didn't record Eliza's statement?" Sebastian rambles on. "The other day when you met with Dennis, he left your office and I followed him and overheard a conversation; he was going to meet someone that night. I waited across the street from Dennis's house and took pictures of Dennis and the mystery person. Guess who it was."

The captain, wrapped up in the story, says, "Who? Who did he meet?" as he leans forward, enthralled.

"Sean Smith. Eliza, for some reason, doesn't believe that's his real name." Sebastian shows Morrison the picture on his phone of Sean.

The captain chuckles. "Maybe we should hire Eliza as a detective."

They both laugh. Sebastian scrolls through all the photos showing Sean and Dennis knows each other.

———————— ⋙•◉•⋘ ————————

Meanwhile, the elevator opens, nine o'clock on the dot. Dennis struts out of the elevator. He looks in the direction of the captain's desk, but the door is closed, and Sebastian is huddled over the captain's shoulders looking at a phone. Maybe it belongs to Sebastian. Dennis squints at the interaction, trying to figure out what's going on. *Is Sebastian snitching on me?* Dennis continues to carefully watch the two as he walks to his desk, stumbling on the legs of his chair.

The captain raises his eyes long enough to see Dennis staring directly in his direction; he nods, just as they do every morning. Dennis exhales a sigh of relief. Sebastian quickly places his phone in his pocket as though he is hiding a secret from Dennis. Sebastian nods and moves back to his seat in front of the captain's desk.

Dennis stares at the back of Sebastian's head. Sebastian slowly moves his head to the left, glances over his shoulder to meet Dennis's eyes glaring back at him. Sebastian snaps his head back and focuses on the captain. Dennis is more suspicious now of what's going on in the captain's office.

———————— ⋙•◉•⋘ ————————

Sebastian patiently waits for the captain's lips to stop moving. "I have a bad feeling Dennis is caught up in a web of lies and unethical conduct or he is a killer. I am not sure which scenario is worse."

He stands, leans over the captain's desk, and picks up his

request for time off. He rips it in half and tosses it in the trash on his way out the door.

Dennis immediately rushes to grab Sebastian as he walks to the elevator. "Hey, Sebastian, wait up."

Sebastian stops and rolls his eyes and slowly turns to face Dennis.

"Where are you going? You normally brief me on the events the night before."

"I am officially on vacation, taking some time off."

————))(())((————

Dennis reviews Sebastian from head to toe, skeptical of this sudden vacation. In his peripheral vision he sees the captain leave his office headed for the men's room. Dennis decides to leave the vacation issue alone with Sebastian; his attention is needed to solve another mystery. "Okay, have a good vacation." The elevator door opens, and Sebastian dashes through the open doors, pressing the close door button, preventing anyone else from entering. Dennis searches the department with his eyes. Everyone is working, head down, not paying much attention to him. He enters the captain's office to find what Sebastian tore in half and placed in the trash. Just as he thought. *Vacation, my ass.*

Chapter 45

*S*ebastian walks toward the car with a purpose. After speaking to the captain, he has another idea. He opens the car door and sits behind the wheel.

"Sorry it took so long. The captain and I had a long conversation. I ended up telling him about my plan to investigate Dennis."

Sebastian tells Scotty about the conversation, and her eyes grow wide in anticipation of each word.

"I knew something was up. I have been waiting for you for about an hour."

"I think we can find out more if we split up. Originally you were going to DC. Now I think I should pay Kyndall Graham a visit."

"Okay, I am fine with the new plan, but I need a car."

Sebastian thinks for a moment, takes the key to his personal car off the ring, and hands it to Scotty. "You take my car and we can meet back later tonight or tomorrow."

"Okay, that works." Scotty presses the button to unlock

the car; the headlights flash and she knows exactly which car belongs to Sebastian. She walks over, fires up the engine, and exits the police station. So does Sebastian but he goes toward Society Hill.

Chapter 46

*S*cotty drives in silence from Philly to DC—no radio just the sound of the tires beating the highway. She needs to clear her head before she ambushes Brendon about the death of his mother-in-law. Scotty parks Sebastian's Toyota Camry in the parking deck near Brendon's office. She uses her press credentials to badger her way through the building to Brendon's office. Outside the closed door Scotty takes a deep breath, tugs on her suit jacket, and opens the large door. It's showtime. She grins from ear to ear as she approaches the senator's assistant, Amelia.

"Hello. I am Scotty Richards here to see Senator Graham."

Amelia's eyes move from the computer screen in the direction of the young lady in front of her; she jumps from her seat to a standing position. Her idol, Scotty Richards, is standing before her. Amelia is an avid fan of *Meeting of the Minds* and watches her idol each weeknight. She reaches for Scotty's hand and shakes it uncontrollably. Scotty blushes, flattered she has a fan of the show, but at this point her visit isn't official business, not yet. Scotty peels her hand out of Amelia's grip, and Amelia's cheek turns red, hot to the touch as her hand brushes her cheek and she tucks a piece of hair behind her ear.

"I will tell Mr. Graham you are here. Usually I don't allow anyone to see the senator without an appointment." Amelia smirks and leans toward Scotty from across her large oak desk. "I will see what I can do to get you in front of the senator. He does have a full schedule today. You may have to wait a while, but I will get you in to see him as quickly as I can." Amelia gives Scotty a wink of assurance.

"Sure, I will wait."

Amelia, embarrassed from her encounter, dashes toward Brendon's office to announce the celebrity here to see him, at least in her mind. Brendon has never been fond of the reporter by the side comments he makes when she is on air giving her opinion of political news of the day.

Scotty takes a seat and browses through magazine after magazine, watching Brendon's appointments come and go. Scotty glances at her watch. It is late in the day and she has been sitting there for hours. Scotty extends her arms upward and legs downward in an elongated stretch. She moves her body to the left side of the chair; she closes her eyes for what seems like a minute but when she wakes, Amelia has already gone for the day. Brendon shakes her shoulders. Scotty stares into Brendon's gorgeous brown eyes. "I am sorry I kept you waiting so long. Please come to my office so we can talk." Scotty stands, walks into Brendon's open office door as Brendon follows. Scotty takes the seat in front of the desk as Brendon walks behind the desk and has a seat. "What brings you all the way from Atlanta to DC? I thought we covered everything during my interview with you."

"We did. I am not here on official business."

Brendon's shoulders relax and he sits back in his ergonomic chair and crosses his legs, hands in a position of a temple. He glances at his watch.

"I learned recently your mother-in-law passed away. Please let me give you my condolences."

"Yes, we were all shocked. She was killed in a home invasion."

Scotty studies Brendon's facial expression to figure out if he is lying. She is a good read but nothing.

Brendon continues, "Emily is devastated and is spending time in North Carolina; my mother has a home there."

"What part of North Carolina?"

"Charlotte."

"Why Charlotte? I would have thought she would have visited one of your family's vacation homes."

"You know Emily is modest. She prefers no frills and detests staying at one of Mother's vacation homes. Charlotte is quiet, plus Mother has a friend, Emma, who can look after her until I can get away from work. You know Mother. She is so caring."

"Yes, I do know your mother," says Scotty dryly.

Brendon glances at his watch once again. Scotty notices Brendon's preoccupation of time. *Where is he going after he leaves the office tonight?* Scotty decides to capture his attention back to the conversation. "Did you know my mother lives across the street from Emily's mother?"

Brendon's eyes move from the desk to Scotty's smiling face. "Really? I didn't realize that. I have visited Doris on several occasions. Maybe I met your mother. What's her name?"

Scotty reviews his body language and mannerisms—still nothing. Maybe he is telling the truth. "Eliza, Eliza Richards." Scotty takes a deep breath. "On the day Doris died, Mother said she saw Kyndall go into the house, and moments later she heard the gunshots. She didn't see anyone run from the house or anyone enter other than Kyndall."

Brendon drops his hands and uncrosses his leg; his body stiffens. "Are you suggesting my mother killed Doris? Mother would never do anything like that. She loved Doris, always had. You hear about the stories of in-laws fighting…nothing like that ever happened between the two of them. Mother adored Doris. Maybe your mother is mistaken?"

Scotty is stoic in her response. "No, my mother is very sharp. She indicated she saw Kyndall pull into the driveway."

Brandon's attention is drawn to his fingers intertwined and resting on his desk. Scotty scrutinizes Brendon's change in body language. His confidence seems to leave his body, as he no longer looks at her but the desk. Brendon runs his hand through his $200 haircut; his right hand rests on the back of his neck, where he massages the stiff muscles.

Scotty pushes harder. "Did Kyndall kill Doris?"

Brendon's phone dings, indicating he has a text message. Distracted from Scotty's conversation he picks up his phone, reads the message, and responds with a text. Brendon excuses himself from his conversation with Scotty; he calls the hotel and gives them his credit card to take care of the room for his new love interest, Tiffany. Brendon steps back into the office, sits behind his desk.

Scotty, determined for answers, asks her question once again. "Did your mother kill Doris?"

Under the pressure of getting his new lover to stay at the hotel, he snaps, not thinking of his response or implications, "I don't know! No, she didn't kill Doris!"

Bingo, thinks Scotty; *Brendon isn't sure.* One thing she does know: Brendon has no idea what happened to Doris, but he knows who does. Scotty has more questions but decides to hold the other information to herself for the time being until she can conduct more research. "Brendon, I am sorry to have upset you with this type of questioning. My mother is old and senile. She is upset her best friend died and I told her I would find answers to her questions." Brendon relaxes his posture. "You know how it is when you promise your mother you will check on something for them."

Brendon again checks his watch.

Scotty notices his cue. "I have taken up too much of your time. Thank you for seeing me without an appointment." Scotty stands and places her purse on her shoulder. She extends her hand to Brendon. "Have a nice evening. Are you going back to Atlanta tonight?"

"No, I will enjoy the city and have a quiet dinner."

"Sounds good. Bye Brendon." Scotty leaves Brendon's office. The conversation swirls in her head. She has an idea. It appears Brendon has some place he needs to go because of the frequent checking of his watch. Scotty sprints to Sebastian's car; she has a hunch Brendon will go straight to his mother to confront her with Scotty's accusations. Scotty previously dated a senator and knows where Brendon's driver is parked.

Brendon exits the building and enters the black SUV with the open door waiting for his arrival. The SUV moves through the parking garage and Scotty follows. Scotty thought Brendon took the train to Philadelphia, but the car is moving through the city's evening traffic. *Maybe Kyndall is staying in town,* thinks Scotty. *I wonder if Sebastian is having any luck.* They pull in front of the Loews Hotel. Scotty smiles. *A tick mark for me.* She is right, Kyndall is staying at the hotel. The driver gets out of the car and opens the door for Brendon, who enters the hotel. One of the valets comes over to Brendon and shakes his hand. "Good evening, Senator. It's so good to see you again." *Huh, he must be a regular here,* thinks Scotty. Brendon continues into the hotel and approaches the woman at the reception area. He checks in.

"Hi, Senator, how are you?"

"I am fine, Chloe. How's your day?"

"Good."

Brendon clears his throat, waiting on Chloe to give him his

key. She blinks and looks embarrassed to have been caught drooling over him.

Brendon walks away from the desk. Chloe's eyes follow his backside until he disappears around the corner.

Scotty walks to the right toward the bar. She finds a seat on an empty barstool with her back toward the street to give her a full view of the entire lobby area. She looks for Brendon and doesn't notice him. She decides to order a James Bond martini—shaken not stirred.

The bartender places the drink in front of her. "Would you like to start a tab?"

"No." Scotty reaches in her purse and gives him her debit card. She signs the receipt and licks her lips; she hasn't had a martini in months. She removes the pick, securing the two olives, and places it on her napkin. She eyes the drink and glances toward the reception area, where Brendon rounds the corner with a beautiful woman on his arm. They are laughing and talking as they walk toward the restaurant. Brendon pulls out the chair for the lady and she sits; he helps her in getting her chair closer to the table. He leans in and gently kisses her on the lips. He walks over to the chair across from her.

So, Emily and Brendon aren't the happy couple after all.

Scotty texts Sebastian. No response.

——◦((◦))◦——

Oliver approaches Brendon and his guest. "Good evening, Brendon." June, using the name Tiffany, blushes. This is the gentleman who approached her earlier. She snaps her neck in Brendon's direction. *I thought he said his name was Andy.* Tiffany takes a sip of water. *Who is Andy really?*

"Hi, Tiffany, how are you?"

"It's nice seeing you again," says Tiffany.

———«O»———

"I have a few questions. Is now a good time?" says Detective Hall to Brendon.

"Tiffany, excuse me." Brendon places his napkin on the table and slides his chair back with the calves of his legs and stands. Detective Hall motions with his right hand for Brendon to lead the way. They exit the hotel through a side door to the parking garage next door.

"Detective, what can I help you with?" says Brendon through clenched teeth.

"I want to follow up on an open case, a young lady by the name of Alina or Candy as she goes by in her line of business. She was found dead in the hotel. It was the first time I met you. You were staying here on the day she was found. I am following up on everyone that was here that night."

"That must be an exhaustive search to interview everyone. Why are you talking to me?"

"There was a conflicting story of events. Dakota and I checked the alibi Emily gave that she had an interview with Savannah with the *Today Show*." Brendon runs his hands through his hair, his back to the door, and moves to where he is facing the door. He glances over to the table and walks in a small circle until he is facing the hotel, the place Tiffany once sat empty. Brendon sighs. He thought she would be someone he could see on a regular basis and not use escorts. Brendon turns his attention back to Detective Hall. "I don't know what to say other than it was another news show." He chuckles. "They are all the same."

"No, Brendon, they are not! Especially when you are trying to establish an alibi. Either Emily had an interview with the *Today Show* or she didn't."

"Emily had the interview, not me."

"You don't know with whom?"

"I thought the interview was for the *Today Show* with Savannah but according to you it was not."

"Who scheduled the interview?"

"My mother. She thought it was a great way to get Emily in front of the news media to discuss her interests other than being the wife of a senator."

Oliver takes notes. "Why were you at the hotel the night of Alina's death?"

"I was tired, it was a long day at work. I decided to stay in town instead of going back home to Philadelphia, plus Emily had the interview the next day."

"Why didn't she meet you the night before instead of having to drive from Pennsylvania the day of the interview? The timing of the interview with Savannah seems odd. Probably because it didn't exist and a lie for you to cover something up, like killing an escort."

"No, not at all. Detective, are we finished here because I have left my companion long enough?" Brendon already knows his date is long gone, probably the minute he turned his back to leave the table.

Detective Hall glances in the direction of the table that once occupied Brendon's guest. "It looks as though she left. Maybe I kept you too long. By the way, how is your wife?" Oliver beams with his last statement.

"She is fine," Brendon says flatly. "Are we done?"

"One other question. Tiffany, the young lady you were with tonight, is she an escort?"

"I am not going to answer that question."

Detective Hall uses his right hand and tips his fedora. "Good day. We will talk soon." He turns and disappears out of the garage.

Brendon walks back into the hotel and straight to the elevator. There isn't any need for him to search for Tiffany; he knows she left. Detective Hall blew his cover and used his real name. He knows he will never see her again.

The ding of the elevator pulls his mind back to the task at hand. Once in his room he places a phone call to report the events of the evening.

"Hello."

"We have a problem."

"What is it now, Brendon?"

"I had two troubling conversations today. One with Scotty and the other with Detective Hall. I am headed back to Philadelphia tonight."

His mother is silent on the other end of the phone.

"Hello," says Brendon when his mother doesn't respond. "Are you busy? I can call you back."

"I am always busy securing your run for the White House. Gregory and I are in a strategy session."

"Please put the phone on speaker. He will need to hear this, and I don't want to have to repeat this story."

Kyndall complies with the request. "You are on speaker; can you hear me?"

"Yes, Mother."

"Okay, go ahead, what have you gotten yourself into this time!"

"I had a run-in with Scotty Richards at the office this afternoon. I thought she came to visit me on official business when she showed up, but that wasn't the case."

"What did she want?"

"Did you know her mother Eliza lived across the street from Doris?"

Kyndall pauses.

"No."

"Scotty came to the office and told me her mother saw you at Doris' house the day of the shooting and she heard the gunshot."

"No one is denying that I was there."

"Mother, she said that no one ran out of the house. You were the only one there."

"How old is she?"

"I don't know. I didn't ask."

"We can claim she is senile." Kyndall laughs.

"Not quite," Gregory speaks up. "I met her, and she is very sharp. I would say she is in her late sixties, early seventies."

"Was that the day I asked you to be a witness in the crowd?"

"Yes, Eliza was not backing down from her story. Dennis took her statement but never submitted it."

"So, there isn't a written statement anywhere. We should be okay, right?" says Brendon naively.

"Don't be stupid! There may not be a written statement but now her nosy daughter is snooping around. Gregory, you and I can continue to work on our strategy, but someone has to take care of Eliza and now Scotty." She pauses for a moment. "Artie." Kyndall lets out a huge sigh. "I will ask Dennis to work on this new problem."

"Remember, Dennis has the detectives from New York he has to babysit when they come to town."

In a bold tone Gregory responds, "No, I will take care of the situation with Eliza, Scotty, and Artie."

"Okay, fine, you can do it. We will fall behind on our other plans." Kyndall can't wait any longer on the White House and miss the election year coming up. She can't wait another four years. She changes her mind. "Do you know anyone that is available to do some freelance work? Just some of the 'light' work we have from time to time."

"No, you know I work alone, and no one knows what I do for a living, not even my wife."

"This isn't negotiable. Find someone."

"Brendon, is there anything else we can do to make your life more pleasurable?" says Gregory in the most sarcastic tone he can garner.

"Don't be an ass."

"Okay, that's it then."

"No," says Brendon cowardly. "The other problem is Detective Hall. He's been asking questions again about Alina's death. I saw him at the Loews Hotel."

"Why were you at the hotel?"

"I was meeting someone."

"Stop playing games and tell us everything," barks Gregory.

"I met someone online and we were on a date."

Both Kyndall and Gregory are speechless.

Gregory is the first to speak. "Why would you meet someone at the Loews Hotel? It's the scene of a crime. And on top of that you were with an escort."

In a whisper Brendan says, "She wasn't an escort."

Disgusted with Brendon's stupidity Kyndall joins the conversation. "Who is she?"

"I met her on an online dating site. I was too ashamed to call Stella after what happened to Alina."

"How stupid is that!" yells Gregory. "The senator for the State of Pennsylvania is meeting a strange woman online! Man, what's with you? I don't get it for the life of me. Emily is the woman of any man's dreams, but you step out on her every chance you get. You can't keep it in your pants, man. Kyndall, you are right; I need someone to help me keep up with Brendon and his shenanigans."

Brendon thinks for a minute and comes at Gregory strong with accusations. "I knew you always wanted Emily. I saw how you lusted after her, always lurking around watching her in college even now!"

"Boys, cut it out. I can't hear myself think."

The air on either side of the phone thick, Brendon's nostrils flare as he breathes hard.

All three are silent until Kyndall gets the group back on track. "What did you tell Detective Hall?"

"He called the network to verify Emily's statement. Savannah's assistant confirmed Emily was never scheduled for an interview with Savannah. I have a feeling the detective is going to speak with you."

"Why do you think the detective wants to speak with me?"

Brendon pauses for a moment. "I told Detective Hall you told Emily about the interview."

"You have got to be kidding me!" yells Gregory.

"Calm down, Gregory. There's nothing we can do right now until I hear from Detective Hall."

"Is there anything else I need to know?" asks Kyndall.

Brendon thinks for a moment. "No."

"Brendon, can I ask a favor," asks Gregory.

"Shoot."

"I need you to get out of town for a few days while I clean up your shit."

Scotty observes the man with a fedora who was speaking with the staff abruptly leave his conversation to rush toward Brendon like he is an old friend he needs to catch before he disappears from his life again. Scotty pulls out her phone, casually takes a picture of the three of them. She takes several pictures and sends them to Derrick through text with the caption "Hey, can you tell me who the people are in the photo?"

Derrick had a crush on Scotty during college. He made the big mistake of marrying his cheating wife but should have married Scotty instead. They found each other on social media. She hired him a few times to investigate guests before their appearance on the show.

Derrick texts back. "I see you are still playing detective."

"Ha ha. What have you been up to?" Scotty frowns, the pop-up on her phone low battery. She clicks okay to continue to text Derrick.

"You know me, keeping a low profile, doing my thang. What about you? How is Hot Atlanta?"

Scotty receives an incoming call from Sebastian and hits ignore; she can call him back later. She digs around in her purse, no phone charger. Scotty's shoulders droop. She will have to deal with the phone charger later. She has to get this real-time information from Derrick.

"Atlanta is good, but I flew to Pennsylvania to visit Mother and started to work on a story she is involved in. That's why I asked you about the people in the photo."

"I will have to dig a little, but the woman's name is June Carter. Not sure about the other two."

"How do you know her?"

"She is the wife of one of my clients. She lives in Charlotte. The guy sitting across from June looks like the senator from Pennsylvania."

Scotty responds, "Yes, Brendon Graham."

"Yeah, you are right, that's him. I remember that expensive haircut. Once I find out who the guy in the hat is, I will hit you back."

"Okay… One more question."

Before she can type the next response, Derrick types "Yes."

"Yes, what? You don't know the question."

"Yes, I will marry you whenever you are ready." Derrick sends an emoji blowing a kiss.

"Lol." Scotty is not sure of what to say back to Derrick. Is he serious? Scotty decides to ask her original question. "Will you give me the address of the friend's wife?"

"Why? You know this could compromise my relationship between me and my client."

"I am not interested in your client. His wife was with a high-ranking government official that I am following. If I can find but anything about her, I can nail him. I am not interested in your client."

"If you don't go after her husband Chip, then I will give you the address."

"You know me. I will never reveal my source. I pledge on my profession."

Derick texts the address to his college crush.

"Thanks, Derrick!"

Scotty flips her phone over, reaches for it again, remembers the conversation with Brendon earlier, and starts to search the Internet for counties in Charlotte. The largest she finds is Mecklenburg County; she can't see Kyndall living any other place. She finds the county tax assessor's website; she plays around with Kyndall's name and the county where she thinks her house may be and finds Kyndall's name on the deed. Bingo! Scotty screenshots the information to start a record of her informal investigation. She reviews the text from Derrick, and the address she found online with the state for Kyndall is next door to Kyndall's address. Scotty's eyes narrow at the link between the two.

Scotty is concerned about Artie not returning her phone calls. She's heard rumors he has a drinking problem. She calls and leaves another message, not giving up on him. "Artie, I know from time to time life gets hard and we make some choices we shouldn't. Our lives aren't defined by the choices but the actions we decide to take to change the direction of our lives. I want you to get in on the action. I am at the Loews Hotel watching Brendan meet with this mysterious man wearing a fedora. Give me a call and I can catch you up on my unofficial investigation. I am following a lead to Charlotte, North Carolina, where Kyndall owns a home next to Brendon's lover. What are the odds." Scotty hangs up the phone; the voicemail shows complete. Scotty leaves the bar and her drink untouched. She calls the airlines to book a flight to Charlotte as she walks to valet.

———)((0))(———

Artie listens. He is sad he resorted to using Scotty and black-mailing Kyndall to get back at the network.

Artie is concerned about his actions, but his problems started long before this incident. He isn't at the place to understand how his own actions got him here. He continues to make poor choices. He texts Kyndall. "The information I have is worth so much more than $10,000. I want you to pay me $40,000."

Kyndall immediately responds, "What information do you have?"

"Scotty is at the Loews Hotel witnessing Brendon speaking with a guy in a fedora. I personally don't know who this person is, but I know within the hour Scotty will know his name. She has connections. As I move forward you will find my information valuable."

Kyndall will keep him close to get whatever information she can and pay him within reason. She texts back, "Thank you. I will wire you the money. Please send me your banking information."

Artie's eyes glistens with the thought Kyndall will give him the money he requests. He takes another swig of the drink. He gets bolder and sends another message requesting an additional $10,000; now he wants $50,000. The vodka controlling his thoughts adds an emoji smiling after his request.

"I will give you half now and the additional money I can give you later."

"Okay, but I want cash. I have already given you the information, so I need to get paid."

"Where do you want to meet? And when?"

Kyndall turns to Gregory. "Do we have $25,000 in cash?"

"Why?"

Kyndall gives Gregory her phone and he reads the messages. "You are kidding me! You aren't going to pay this prick. After Brendon talks to the detective, he's going to call you and tell you everything, so the information this Artie is giving you is useless."

"Do we have the money or not?"

"We do but we shouldn't pay him. What happens when he wants more money? Originally, he wanted $10,000, now $40,000, and now an additional $10,000. If you want me to pay I will, but he is only going to ask for more, and the information is useless."

"Gregory, I am tired. Artie wouldn't be asking for money if Brendon wasn't wherever the Hell he is and not home with his wife. I know you are right, but Brendon is sucking the life out of me. I don't know if I have it in me to keep fighting for this dream." Kyndall sounds defeated.

Gregory reaches for Kyndall's hand. "You know I always have your back. So, I won't allow you to pay this prick off."

Kyndall smiles. "You are right. What are we going to do with Artie?"

"Just be honest with him. The information he is giving you is useless. Brendon will call you with the same information."

Kyndall texts Artie exactly what Gregory told her to say. Immediately Artie calls Kyndall. "Don't answer the phone," says Gregory. Artie calls thirteen times; both Gregory and Kyndall stare at the phone.

Artie gives up and paces the floor. He pours himself another drink and fumes. Kyndall is ignoring him; she will not ignore him. She should have given him the money.

He goes online and books a flight to Philadelphia, then stumbles to the bedroom to pack a bag. He has to hurry. His flight leaves in four hours.

Chapter 47

Sebastian verifies the address he needs to drive two houses down. Just his luck, a parking space in front of the house. Sebastian enters the black wrought-iron fence and uses the lion knocker to announce his presence at the door. A few seconds go by before a Hispanic woman opens the door, casually dressed. "Hi, may I help you?"

"I am Sebastian. Is Kyndall Graham home?"

"No, she is at her son's home a few houses down the block." She gives him the address.

No need to get back in his car; the houses are within walking distance and anyway he needs the exercise. He uses the doorbell to announce his visit this time.

The door opens. "Hello, how can I help you?"

"My name is Sebastian, homicide detective with the Philadelphia Police Department. I am here to see Kyndall Graham."

"I am Kyndall, please come in." She was expecting a follow-up; no one involved in a murder and no one asks questions but why him. Dennis is supposed to handle this case. Gregory, standing in the doorway cutting the apple with a knife in his hand, hears everything. He too thought Dennis was handling the situation. "Please have a seat." Kyndall escorts Sebastian to the living room. Sebastian's eyes never leave Gregory as he walks past; he is the guy in the photo who met with Dennis. Gregory is still standing in the door, not expecting to move anytime soon.

"What can I help you with, Detective?"

"I want to follow up on the death of Doris Massey. You were at the home when Doris was shot."

"Right, I was stabbed as well."

"I am glad you mentioned that. Why were you stabbed, and Doris shot and killed?"

"The doorbell rang while Doris and I were having tea. She opened the door and the hoodlum rushed in. I had gone to the bathroom. I heard a gunshot, ran out of the bathroom, and the guy placed the gun in his waistband. He must have known Doris lived alone and when I came out the bathroom it startled him. I saw him standing over Doris. I moved toward him and he pulled out the knife and stabbed me."

"So why not shoot you too? Not being disrespectful."

"I don't know—you will have to ask him. Have you found the killer?"

———— ✦ ————

Gregory walks outside. He calls Dennis.

"Hello."

"Guess what I'm doing?"

"Gregory, I don't have time for games today. I am on the way to a crime scene." Dennis is still tense about the ruse Sebastian gave for taking time off work. His gut tells him Sebastian is up to no good.

"Well, let me tell you. I am witnessing a detective by the name of Sebastian Glover interviewing your girlfriend."

Dennis' car drifts over to the next lane, barely missing the Fiat driving alongside him. He quickly maneuvers his car back into his lane. Dennis tightly squeezes the steering wheel. "Why is he there?" He knew Sebastian was telling a lie but wanted Gregory to think he had everything under control.

"Oh, I am sorry. Now you have time to listen to what I have to say."

"I don't have time for your sarcasm; just tell me what's going on!"

Gregory doesn't let up. "I thought you were in charge of the investigation. Sebastian shows up asking Kyndall about what she witnessed and why she didn't get shot, just stabbed."

"What did she say?"

"You know Kyndall, she sidestepped the questions as best she could." He asks valid questions. "Why is Sebastian investigating the case and not you? We are back to this question you didn't answer earlier." Gregory needs to rub Dennis's nose in his mess.

Dennis responds pitifully. "I am compromised. Sebastian told me he was going on vacation and I found out later he's not on vacation. I think the captain gave him his blessing to investigate me. If they don't have enough evidence, they will continue to search. I am sure that's the reason he is questioning Kyndall. The Doris Massey case isn't assigned to him."

"I need to go but I will take care of our little problem." Gregory hangs up the phone. Kyndall is standing at the window watching the interaction between Gregory and Sebastian. Sebastian standing in front of Gregory asks, "I didn't get your name earlier." Gregory keeps his cool. "I didn't tell you my name. You came to visit Kyndall. I don't live here."

"Who are you?"

"I am the guy who delivers groceries."

"Let me guess, apples."

"Yeah, apples." Gregory turns his back to the detective, walks back to the house, and closes the door.

Chapter 48

*S*usan stands in the TSA checkpoint waiting her turn to walk through the invasive body scanner. She dressed down for her trip, less complicated articles of clothing to have to remove; jeans, Michael Kors black ballet shoes, white long-sleeve T-shirt, and Michael Kors black belt.

"Please move forward into the scanner," says the older TSA agent. He uses his right latex gloved hand to wave her through. Susan stands, still gazing at the white speckled tile. There are twenty specks per tile or is it twenty-five. Susan starts to recount when a young man dressed in a sleek gray business suit brushes her arm as he rushes past her to take her turn in the scanner. As he walks by her, he huffs, "You act like no one has anything to do today." He walks into the scanner and places both feet on the designated footprint on the floor and raises his hands. The machine performs a full rotation of around his body, and he exits. He turns to the right, waiting for his belongings to slowly make their way down the conveyor belt.

In a louder voice than previously, the TSA agent says in Susan's direction, "Ma'am, we are ready for you."

The stranger behind Susan gently taps her on the shoulder and Susan jumps. She turns toward the stranger. "It's your turn," says the woman. Susan blushes, now aware she was holding up the line. She steps into the scanner, places her feet on the mark below, and raises her hands just as many have done previously. She exits the machine, gathers her belongings, and puts on the clothing she had to take off for the sanctioned inspection by the government. She walks to the gate and finds a chair isolated from the gathering crowd. She pulls out her phone and calls Jim one last time, hoping he picks up. The phone call goes directly to voicemail. She shoves the phone in her pocket and stares out the window at the planes landing. She pulls her phone back out and calls her therapist.

———◦《◉》◦———

"Hello?"

"Maria, this is Susan."

"Hi, Susan. I was hoping I would hear from you. How's the move going?" Susan is silent. "Hello, Susan. Are you still there?" Susan doesn't speak; she sobs into the phone. Maria knows that it is therapeutic for her patients to cry to alleviate whatever is troubling them. After several minutes, Susan breaks the silence.

"I don't know what to do."

"What happened, Susan?"

"Jim flew to Charlotte to sign the deal on the house, but I haven't spoken with him since."

That weasel. "How long has he been missing?"

"I haven't spoken with him in about a week."

"Hum," says Maria.

"I know you are my therapist and not my friend, but what should I do? I don't know where in Charlotte the house is located. I feel so all alone." Jim may be a jerk, but he takes care of her—from buying all her clothes to paying the bills. She is barely functioning without him. She wanted to purchase the airfare with her debit card but didn't know the password on their online bank account to check the balance.

Maria shakes her head and pouts her lips. She knew Jim was up to something no good. She still isn't convinced that Jim's not in trouble, which makes it difficult to tell Susan she can't help her. She takes a deep breath and blows air out of her mouth, making her lips tremble while tapping her pen on her notepad.

"Maria, what should I do?"

"Susan, I..." Maria stops mid-sentence. She remembers the text Jim sent her with the new Charlotte address.

"What, Maria, what?"

"I do have the address of the house in Charlotte. I told Jim I wanted to send the two of you a housewarming gift and he sent me a text. Let me send it to you via text."

"Thank you so much for your help."

"You are welcome. Let me know how things work out."

"I will."

They both hang up the phone. Maria sits at her desk staring at her phone, thinking about Jim. *What kind of mess have you gotten yourself into?*

Chapter 49

Susan's plane lands at Charlotte Douglas International Airport and she pushes her luggage to the taxi waiting area. She makes her way to the front of the line and a yellow taxi approaches her. The driver stops and pulls the lever for the trunk. He walks over and greets his customer.

"Good day, ma'am."

"Hi, how are you?"

"Great. Did you have a good flight?"

"Uneventful."

"Those are the best kind. Please may I." The driver takes Susan's luggage and places it in the trunk. Susan settles in the backseat and uses her hand to fan her face. The weather down South is warmer than expected.

The driver cranks the car and turns on the air- conditioning. Susan feels the cool air on her damp face give her chills on her arms. Feeling appreciative she says, "Thank you so much for turning on the air. My name is Susan."

"No problem. My name is Khan. Where are you going today?"

Susan, unfamiliar with the address, opens the text message Maria gave her. "I'm going to 7478 Sweetbriar Lane."

Khan's eyes pierce through the rearview mirror carefully watching Susan. He thought she was not the "type," but you never know. He frowns. *I thought she was normal like the rest of the world. She doesn't look like the type that would visit a place like Sweetbriar.* Susan's eyes meet Khan's through the mirror. Susan smiles. Khan never takes his eyes off her and shakes his head. To each his own. Khan focuses on the road and pulls off from the curb and heads to the interstate to Sweetbriar Lane.

Chapter 50

The cab pulls up in front of 7478 Sweetbriar Lane. The house is deserted, no lights or car in the yard. Susan sits in the car not moving.

Anxiously Khan leans forward and scans the neighborhood, looking to the right then to the left. "This is it," he says, wanting his fare to exit the car. He didn't want any part of the neighborhood.

Susan bites the inside of her cheek. "I don't know. The house seems empty; it is so dark. My husband is supposed to be here."

Emma, out on an evening stroll, waves at Khan and Susan. Susan presses the button and rolls down the window. "Hello, excuse me." Emma stops short of her house and walks over to the cab. Khan, distrusting of everyone who lives in and visits Sweetbriar, clicks the door lock button to reassure himself no one else from this lifestyle group enters his car. He can fight off one crazy but can't take the chance on two.

"Hi, my name is Susan. My husband Jim and I purchased the

house across the street. He flew down just a few days ago to sign the paperwork and I haven't seen him since."

Khan turns sideways in his seat to look at her. His heart flutters listening to Susan's story; his sister worked in Sweetbriar and was never seen again. The pit of his stomach burns. He doesn't think he will see her alive again.

Susan starts to weep. Khan reaches over the seat and gives her a handful of napkins that he had in his armrest. Susan accepts the napkins and dabs her eyes. Susan looks at the crumpled napkins in her hand and sheepishly stares at the stranger staring into the car.

Emma reassures Susan, "I'm sure there's nothing to worry about."

"Have you seen him?" asks Susan, remembering Emma never answered her question the first time.

"No, I haven't seen anyone or anything out of the ordinary," Emma lies.

"Can I show you a picture of him?"

"Sure."

Emma walks closer to the car. Susan opens her phone and shows Emma the picture on the display screen. Emma purses her lips together and shakes her head. "No, I haven't seen him. Actually, the owner of the home Kyndall Graham didn't put the house on the market."

"Okay. Thank you for your time."

"Have a nice night."

<hr>

Emma hurries to her house dials Chip's cell phone.

"Aha," Chip moans, closing his eyes as he receives pleasure from Kelsey as her husband takes her from behind, slapping her buttocks.

"Hello, Chip, hello."

"Emma, what's up," he says, distracted.

"We have a problem. Susan, Jim's wife, is looking for him."

"What did you tell her?"

"I didn't know who he was, and I didn't see him."

"That was good. Problem solved. Let me get back to one of the perks of my community."

"Cut it out. Do you think she is going to stop? No, she will probably go to the police," says Emma in a rant.

Chip moves Kelsey's head upwards and rolls to the side of the bed. "Okay, you have my undivided attention. What do you think we should do?"

"Nothing now but the police will probably come around snooping. We need to have a community meeting to encourage everyone to be on their best behavior, including you."

"Okay, I will have everyone over tomorrow night for an emergency meeting."

<hr />

Meanwhile Susan and Khan are still parked in front of 7478 Sweetbriar Lane. "Susan, I don't mean to pry but my sister went missing and she worked in this neighborhood selling homes. So, you need to be worried about your husband."

"Why do you say that?"

"My sister has been missing for six months and we haven't heard from her."

"When did you talk to her last?"

"She left for work that morning and she was supposed to come over to our parents' house for dinner and game night. Every Thursday night we would come together no matter how busy our lives for dinner and a game of charades. Lily loved that game; she was an introvert but when she got in front of the crowd, she knew her stuff. She was competitive and would win every time. I always wanted to be on her team." Khan clears his throat as he thinks about his sister. She was so beautiful. He grows silent. He remembers Susan is in the backseat when she shifts her position. He resumes his story. "We waited for her for an hour before we started dinner. We ate and cleaned up the dishes. Instead of playing charades we all came here where she worked looking for her. This house where you were directed was the model home, they used to show prospective customers. It was locked with no lights like it is today. Her car was nowhere to be found. We then drove to her apartment off Seventh Street. I had a spare key and access to the building and her car wasn't on any of the levels in the parking garage or outside the building. I went back to my house thinking she may have gone there, but with no luck. She wasn't there. My parents went home, and we agreed if she had not contacted us by the morning, we would go to the police. None of us heard from her and we went to the police to report her missing."

"What did the police do? Did they find her?"

"No, the police did not take us seriously because we are Muslim."

"What should I do?"

A tear falls down Khan's cheek. He thinks of his sister and puts aside his thoughts about society. "Maybe we both should go to the police, me to retell the story of my missing sister and you letting them know your husband is missing. Maybe now they will take me seriously about this place." He looks around the neighborhood with disdain in his eyes. He cranks the car and leaves the community toward the police department.

Chapter 51

*S*usan and Khan enter the police station. The woman at the desk asks, "How can I help you?"

"I would like to report my husband missing."

"Ma'am, how long has your husband been missing?"

"He has been missing for a week." This is a half-truth. She hasn't seen her husband in a week but has only been in town for several hours to verify he isn't where he said he would be, which isn't actually the police definition of missing.

Angela Hall and Cheyanne Winters are partners. They left work both too tired to cook dinner and decided to have dinner together and then figure out tomorrow's dinner arrangement when they were forced to make a decision. Cheyanne pulls the car into the parking space and they both get out and walk toward the precinct instead of jumping in their cars to go home. Angela forgot her phone charger and Cheyanne her running shoes; she wants to go on a long run in the morning to burn the extra calories consumed from the beer and nachos she had at her favorite

Mexican restaurant, Los Lupe's. The two enter the precinct laughing about a horrible date story by Angela.

Susan turns around, the badge resting on Cheyanne's hip telling her all she needs to know. Someone will talk to her tonight.

"Excuse me, my friend and I are waiting to speak with a detective."

"Ma'am, have you checked in at the front desk?" asks Cheyanne.

"We did but my husband is missing, and I need to find him."

"My name is Angela, and this is Cheyanne. What is going on with your husband?"

"He's missing."

Cheyanne and Angela usher Susan and Khan to a quiet section of the lobby. "Please have a seat," says Angela.

"My husband and I planned to move here from New York. Jim, my husband, came down a week ago to purchase the home. I haven't heard from him since he left. I flew down today and went to the address and the house is vacant but there is no sign of him. I was told by one of the neighbors she never saw him, and she told me the house Jim said he wanted to purchase wasn't for sale."

"Do you have reason to believe this is some type of real estate scam? Did you ever speak with the person selling the home? Do you have any information?"

"No, I didn't have any information before today. I called my therapist and she gave me the address." Susan wants to give the officers all the information she knows to get her husband back.

"Your therapist? Why would your therapist have the information?"

"Maria spoke to Jim before he headed to Charlotte and gave her the address." Cheyanne and Angela both steal glances at one another. Susan, hearing aloud how ridiculous her story sounds, defends herself. "I know you don't believe me, but my husband is missing."

The two detectives turn their attention to the man with Susan. "Sir, who are you and what is your connection to the situation?"

Khan pipes up and tells the two detectives what happened to Lily. "There isn't much for me to discuss. My family and I have come to this police station on numerous occasions to report my sister missing and nothing. We have to wait for hours and we are told that a detective will get back with us and no one ever does. We are being discriminated against because we are Muslim. We get the dirty stares like we are coming in here to blow up the place, and you don't want us sitting in the lobby for too long because you would not be able to explain how a bomb went off in the police station under your nose." Khan takes a breath after his rant and crosses his right leg over his left and locks his fingers at his chin, moving his right leg up and down. He is controlling his anger.

"Khan, I can assure you that no one here was discriminating against you or your family. Who was the detective that took your statement?"

Khan, who keeps every scrap of paper in his wallet, pulls out a business card for Benjamin Murray. He hands it to Angela. "I documented the dates and time of when I came in to speak with the detective."

Angela reaches for the card and flips the card over and sees the dates and times as Khan indicated. Angela hands the card over to Cheyanne and they both shake their heads. It was unfortunate that Khan and his family spoke to Benjamin Murray. He was fired over a year ago for making racial slurs on social media. He justified his rant because an African-American was promoted to supervisor over him. The video went viral and the mayor received it. There wasn't anything anyone could do at that point—the mayor was hard on the commissioner because of their high crime and low arrest rate, and the video was one more indication that the priorities of the department were covering up and not holding its officers accountable. Benjamin was an example and many on the force decided to close their social media accounts, not because they would say something disparaging about another group of individuals; they were worried about others posting to their timeline who may say something inappropriate.

"Khan, I am sorry to inform you that Benjamin Murray no longer works for the police department, but I will speak with my captain about your case and ask him if Cheyanne and I can personally find answers for you and your family. Is that okay with you?"

"Did he get fired?"

"Khan, all we can tell you is Benjamin Murray is no longer working for the department. As I stated before Cheyanne and I are more than happy to help you with your sister's case, if you are interested."

"That will be fine, but I know he got fired. He treated us poorly."

Susan jumps into the conversation, even though no one cares about what she must say.

"The lady, Emma, who lives across the street says that the house belongs to Kyndall Graham."

Khan's story is sounding credible; however, Angela still has reservations about Susan. "Now that we have Khan's situation settled. Tell us about your husband."

Cheyanne and Angela take notes.

"What is the name of the community?"

"Sweetbriar."

Angela's phone rings; she looks at the caller ID and it reads "Dad." "Excuse me," says Angela as she answers her phone and goes outside for privacy.

"Hello, Dad."

"Hey, baby, how are you? Are you busy?"

"I was just sitting with Cheyanne while she took a statement from a lady who said her husband was missing."

"How long has he been missing?"

"Well, she said about a week, but she just flew to Charlotte today because he had not been answering his phone. They were supposed to move into the house today. But you know the weird part? She told me her neighbor across the street said that the house wasn't for sale."

"What? How could they purchase a house not on the market?"

"That's the same question I asked."

"Why is that particular house so important to them? Maybe a celebrity owns the house," says Oliver, sounding bored.

Angela, curious, flips through her notebook. "Somebody by the name of Kyndall Graham." She hears Oliver cough and then it sounds like he is choking. He coughs again, clearing his throat, and coughs for a third time. "Daddy, are you okay?"

"Yes. Just choked on my coffee." He clears his throat again. "There may be some truth behind the story the wife is giving you. If the owner of the house is the same Kyndall Graham, the wife of the attorney general for the state of Pennsylvania and the mother of Brendon Graham, the senator of the State of Pennsylvania, there may be more to the story than you have on the surface. As random as the story seems, you want to check into it. I was working a case and I couldn't connect the Grahams, but they were close to the investigation in some way."

"Really? You never mentioned a case with a senator involved."

"I didn't want to go into a lot of details with the death of your mother and all." Oliver holding back tears. "This was the case I never solved, the death of your mother. I believe to my inner core the Graham clan had something to do with it. It was revenge for me asking too many questions and getting close to finding the answers."

Angela's teeth rest on the inside of her cheek as she ponders how to move forward with what could potentially be a high-profile case.

Oliver gives his daughter a stern warning. "Angela, this family is dangerous. Be careful. If you need me, I am a phone call away."

"Thanks, Daddy." The two end the call, Angela wondering why she agreed to help Susan and Khan.

Chapter 52

*G*regory is quite familiar with the Darknet; he needs to find an assistant from time to time. He browses the site looking for new opportunities but never takes the leap to leave Kyndall's enterprise. Kyndall fills the void in his life, being a mother figure after his mother's death.

Gregory opens the junk drawer, pulls out a pair of scissors, and cuts the top of the unopened bag of Doritos. He discards the top and places the scissors back in the right drawer where he found them. Gregory is a stickler for order; just because his job is messy doesn't mean he has to be. He puts his hand in the bag and grabs a large chip. *Crunch, crunch.*

Gregory focuses his attention back to the Darknet, seeking an assassin to work with him. *Okay, here we go.* Gregory reads the profile of someone who might fit the bill of a "helper." He says he is twenty-five with one assignment completed. Gregory knows what "assignment completed" means.

He focuses his attention back on finding an assassin. He never wants to think of himself as that type of a person; in his mind he is a helper. He helps those in need solve problems. He continues to scroll through the profiles on the site. He knows the one criteria for the job that will stick out more than any other skill; he wants someone who can follow orders but also someone he can train. An extensive list of skills or traits he isn't interested in. He mindlessly continues his search as he remembers his first kill just as if it was yesterday.

He picks up two more chips, *crunch, crunch*, and licks his index finger and thumb, enjoying scraping the orange paste off his fingers just as he did when he was a child. Gregory starts a chat with the stranger. On paper Gregory likes the stranger, who calls himself MJ, well enough to meet him. He doesn't need a James Bond—just someone who can do an odd job here and there for a couple of bucks to line his pocket. Gregory in the message area leaves MJ his burner number; by the time Gregory exits the site his phone rings.

"Hello."

"Hey, you told me to call if I was interested in a job. My name is MJ."

"I am not interested in your name. Where can we meet?" Gregory is careful not to say his name because he isn't sure who is on the other end of the phone. After all, he is looking for a contract killer. "What's a good place? I can travel to you."

The stranger thought about where they could meet. He wanted to sound clever but knew his travel would be scrutinized so he decided to ask his potential employer to meet him in the city he lived. He suggests the local Starbucks, within walking distance from his house.

Chapter 53

*G*regory walks into Starbucks and spots his potential employee. He walks over to the table of the young man who looks out of place. First, he doesn't look old enough to drink coffee. Gregory approaches the table.

"Hey, are you MJ?"

"Yeah, who are you?"

"Your contact."

"Do you have a name?"

Gregory looks this MJ up and down. "Doesn't matter, my name, because I can assure you, MJ isn't yours."

MJ smiles in admiration. "So, what do you want me to call you?"

Gregory takes a seat and looks at MJ or whatever his name is. "I don't give a fuck what you call me. Let's get down to business or do you want to braid each other's hair and talk about nail polish colors?"

MJ stops smiling. His mood seems more serious—back straight, shoulders back.

Gregory pushes the clasps together on the manila envelope and pulls out a piece of paper with ten typed names.

"Who are these people?"

Gregory stares directly at MJ, reaches across the table, and snatches the paper from him. Gregory opens the envelope and pushes the paper in the opening.

"What are you doing? I want this job."

"It is obvious that you don't understand how this works. You don't ask me questions. I give you the information on a need-to-know basis until I can trust you. You do as I say and stop with all the questions."

"Okay, man, you need to chill. I just want to know who these people are and how I can help. Didn't mean to get your panties in a wad. Give me the list again."

Gregory takes the paper out of the envelope and hands it back to MJ. "I need you to find out everything about these people on the list. From where they live to where they attend church and purchase groceries. Once you conduct your research you will find out how all the people on the list are connected."

"What do you want me to do once I find them and make the connection?"

Gregory rolls his eyes at MJ. "If you have to ask you aren't ready for this type of work."

"No, I can handle it. You will see. The next time you hear from me, I will have completed the job."

Gregory smiles. He doesn't want to be rude to the boy, but he does want to groom him into a team member he can trust and rely on. *I will see if he lives up to my standards.* Gregory hands MJ the empty envelope with a large x across the front, and he stands.

MJ places the piece of paper in the envelope. He stands and extends his hand to Gregory to shake. "Thanks, boss man."

Gregory shakes his head at the kid. Leaving MJ's hand in

midair, he walks out of the coffee shop and disappears around the corner.

MJ places his hands in his pocket, walks up to the counter, and places an order for a large coffee. As he waits for his coffee, he devises a plan on how to tackle the list. MJ pays for his coffee and goes back to his table to start his work. He is determined to find the connection between the people on the list. MJ opens his computer and starts to search using his favorite search engine. By the time MJ reaches the seventh name on the list, he knows the connection. He smiles. He scans the crowd in the coffee shop, peers out the window, turns around in his chair to ensure he isn't being watched. What he discovers is huge. His contact wants to influence the highest position in the United States, the presidency. The people on the list are from the states with the most votes to cast from the electoral college. The last name on the list is Stanford Beau Harris. MJ knows the name sounds familiar but isn't sure why. He isn't a news-watching fella; he is more interested in video games. He finds a news clip of Scotty Richards, an anchor interviewing Stanford. MJ inserts his earbuds and watches the video. His eyes grow wide, not because Stanford prefers to be called Beau, but who would want the good ole boy from South Carolina to win the election.? No, wait. The contact wants him dead if he is on the list. He lets that thought drift as he continues to go through previous interviews conducted by Scotty. He finds an interview of Brendon Graham and, curious, hits play.

Is this plan for Brendon to run for the presidency against Beau? But in the interview, he said he wasn't going to run. He taps his index finger on the computer, not searching, just thinking. *What is the angle?* That isn't for him to figure out. He needs to find the information on the people on the list, and he has done that. MJ sends his boss a message letting him know he knows the connection and how to find the people on the list. In return Gregory responds to MJ, "Welcome to the team. Hold off on moving forward. I will contact you with additional instructions." MJ smiles, closes his computer, and places it in his backpack. He slips the strap over his shoulders, picks up his coffee, and walks out of the coffee shop toward his house.

Chapter 54

M J, eager to please his contact, made mistakes during their initial meeting, but he isn't new to the Darknet or killing. MJ found his first job to kill a businessman who lived in Wisconsin. MJ found the client through the Darknet and was given the details of the job with the picture of the target. The client didn't give him a deadline other than to call once the deed was done. MJ used the weekend his parents were out of town to fly to Wisconsin and used the money wired to his savings account to purchase government identification from the Darknet, including the gun and knife. When MJ was in need of something local, Freddy, a high school dropout, became his source: guns, knives, drugs, you name it, he could get it for you. MJ booked his flight and rented a car using the identification with the name Mason James, which isn't his real name; he likes the name Mr. Stevenson gave him so many years ago. He wonders what happened to him.

><((●))><

The noise of the GPS distracts MJ from his thoughts. He pulls up outside the target's place of employment and waits for two hours. The target walks to his car and uses the keyless remote to unlock it. He backs out of the parking space and pulls the car onto the street. MJ cranks his rental and follows his target, careful not to be detected. MJ has an idea where the target is headed because of the detailed information the client gave him of where he likes to hang out after work. MJ watches the target enter the bar. He gets out of his car and pulls out his knife and stabs it into the right rear tire of the target's car. He pulls the knife out and puts it back in the leather case around his ankle. MJ enters the bar and locates his target but sits on the opposite end of the bar near the restroom sign.

"What can I get you?"

"A Heineken."

"Do you have ID?"

MJ pulls out his wallet and flips it open and pulls out the ID he purchased. Peter, scans the driver's license and looks at MJ. He gives MJ back his license and turns to the refrigerator and grabs the beer. He uses the bottle opener and opens the beer for his customer. He places the beer on a coaster. MJ takes a long swig of the beer and burps. He eyes his victim as he grabs a handful of peanuts. His prey downs his drink in one gulp and places it on the counter stands and throws his hand up.

"See you, Peter."

"All right, man, later."

MJ takes another long swig of the beer and places it on the counter, stands, and goes to the bathroom. He assembles the silencer on the gun and places it in the back of his pants hidden by his leather jacket. He finds his victim on the side of the building hovering over the trunk of his car.

"Hey, man, do you need some help?" says MJ.

The man turns toward the voice and smiles. "Yeah, that would be great. I had one too many drinks, and an extra pair of hands would be helpful to change this tire."

MJ, standing beside his victim, reaches for the gun and shoots him in his right leg. The victim leans on the car to take the pressure off his leg. The jack in his hand falls to the ground, hitting the pavement. The victim's eyes widen with surprise. "Don't even think about screaming."

"Why did you shoot me? Here, take my wallet."

"I'm not a thief."

"What do you want."

"I don't want anything. I have a message for you."

"A message; a message from who?"

"I have a message from my client. Not quite sure of her name but she did say you humiliated her during her interview and sexually harassed her throughout her employment at the station."

Donovan's eyes are wide and his mouth open. He knows the client, Scotty Richards. After steady income she was able to catch her bills up and find another job in Atlanta. When Scotty quit, she told him he would get what's coming to him. Donovan knew forcing himself on Scotty was wrong, but his wife was into their two children more than tending to his needs. She forgot he had needs too. After Scotty left the station, Donovan and his wife divorced; she knew he was cheating, and he no longer wanted to pretend he loved her. He spent most of his nights at the bar nursing a Johnnie Walker neat. He didn't bother with a splash of anything; he wanted to taste the liquor as it coated his throat.

"This is the last time you will fuck with me."

"What?"

"The message from my client. Man, you must have done something really bad to piss her off because she wants you dead."

"Don't kill me. Please don't kill me." Donovan begs for his life. "I will give you money. How much is she paying you? I will double it."

"Taking your deal is bad for business." MJ stands still as patrons enter and exit the bar. He gets nervous but then without a second thought he places the gun to the business owner's temple and pulls the trigger. Donovan falls into the trunk of the car. MJ places the gun back in the waist of his pants and swings the victim's legs into the trunk with his gloved hands. He throws the tire jack on top of Donovan's body. He gets into his rental and drives to the nearest rest area and sends a text to his client. "Done." MJ uses the app on his phone and logs into his online banking. The $25,000 has been successfully sent to his account as promised.

He reclines the seat and pulls his ball cap over his eyes and goes to sleep. He has an early flight in the morning.

Chapter 55

Gregory drives by the modest home, slows down, and surveilles the area for people outside in the yard, porch, or walking dogs. He parks one block over on the street behind the house. He makes his way to the back porch and uses his lock picking tool to unlock the door. He slowly enters the house with his gloved hand and closes the door behind him. Gregory walks through the house downstairs, then takes two stairs at a time to enter the second floor. Gregory had seen enough. He goes downstairs to the kitchen and looks in the refrigerator—not much in there: half a container of orange juice, two bottled waters, milk, a six-pack of beer, and Chinese take-out still in the large box.

He takes the Chinese take-out out of the refrigerator, opens the lid, and sprinkles "gray death" on the fried rice, then opens several drawers looking for a utensil. He finds a plastic knife. Gregory stirs the fried rice, blending the drug in the food. He places the food back in the refrigerator.

Gregory sprinkles more of the drug in the orange juice. He throws the knife in the trash and shakes the orange juice container to dissolve the lethal combination of heroin and fentanyl. He exits the house the same way he entered at the same time as Sebastian parks on the street in front of his house.

Sebastian walks up the walkway to his home and enters the house through the front door with a Philly cheesesteak sandwich, fries, and a diet drink. He sits down and inhales the fast-food. The last time he ate was earlier that morning with Eliza and Scotty. He decides to wait for Scotty to return his call. He hunches his shoulders and continues to eat his sandwich. Sebastian slurps the remaining diet drink from his cup, burps, stands, throws the empty drink in the trash. He opens the refrigerator, his backside keeping the door open. He reaches into the refrigerator, grabs a beer, twists the cap off, and tosses it in the trash, not moving from his position. Sebastian scans the items in the refrigerator, taking a mental note of its contents to remember the items to pick up on his next trip to the store. Sebastian sighs. He might as well clean the refrigerator. He throws out the Chinese food from three days ago. Checks the expiration date on the orange juice and leaves it in the refrigerator—still good a few more days. The heaviness of the food drains his energy and he crawls up the stairs to the bedroom and falls into a deep slumber.

Gregory, sitting in his car one block over from Sebastian's home, answers his phone.

"Hey, Kyndall, what's up?"

"I have a problem sitting in my living room. I need you over here now!"

"Okay, I am on the way."

Chapter 56

Gregory parks on the street in front of Kyndall's house, enters the gate, and walks into the house. Kyndall jumps to her feet at the sound of the door opening and closing. "Gregory, we are in the living room." Gregory strolls into the living room, not sure who has Kyndall rattled. He furrows his brow toward Kyndall, not recognizing her guest. Kyndall sharply uses her head to motion toward Gregory, communicating with body language. Gregory shrugs his shoulders; he has no clue who the guy is sitting in the chair. "Gregory, I would like you to meet Artie. He came all this way to get his money. Artie now says I owe him $75,000 and he wants it all tonight. I told him you have access to the money."

"Hey, man, what's up?" says Gregory.

Artie stands and his phone falls out of his back pocket onto the floor. The plush carpet protects the phone from damage. "Sorry we have to meet under these terms." Artie extends his hand to shake. Gregory leans in to shake Artie's hand, smells the booze oozing from Artie's pores. Artie is sweating profusely. Gregory

walks between Kyndall to sit beside her on the sofa. He steps on
the corner of the phone, stoops, and picks the phone up. Just as
the phone is in Gregory's hands, it rings, and the caller ID displays the name Scotty Richards. Gregory hands Artie the phone,
flipping it over as he extends it to him. Artie flips the phone over,
looks at the caller ID, and smiles to validate the reason he is asking for more money. Artie enters his passcode, listens to Scotty's
voicemail. He smirks as he cuts his eye at Gregory then Kyndall.
He has access to Scotty feeding him information on her unofficial
investigation about Brendon. Artie places the phone in his back-
pant pocket.

"Artie, do you need privacy to return the call."

"No, I'm good."

"I'm going to fix myself a drink. Do you care for something?"

Artie licks his lip at the thought of a drink. "No, I shouldn't."
He receives an incoming text from Scotty, who is now leaving the
hotel to follow a lead to Charlotte where Kyndall has a home. He
smirks at the message, sits back in the chair, crosses his legs. He
can demand more money for the information he holds.

"Okay, do you mind if I indulge?" Gregory asks. "I've had a
long day and will pour myself a glass of wine. Kyndall, do you
want a glass?"

Kyndall cuts her eyes in Gregory's direction; this isn't a social
call. "No, no." Kyndall shakes her head, smooths her eyebrow
with her right hand. Gregory walks into the kitchen and pours
himself a glass of red wine, walks back in the living room. He sits,
deliberately makes the drinking of the wine an event. He smells
the wine, swirls it in the glass, takes a sip. All the while Artie,
an alcoholic, sits on the edge of his seat engulfed in Gregory's
wine tasting. Artie's shirt sticks to his back, the collar agitating his

neck. He rolls his head back and forth, uncomfortable. Gregory, the wineglass still in his hand, takes two gulps, the wine gone.

"You must have been thirsty," says Artie.

"I am. Let me get another." Gregory jumps up and walks toward the kitchen. Kyndall rubs the back of her neck and stares blankly at Gregory, his back to her as he walks to the kitchen. Artie turns in his seat. "I changed my mind. I will share a glass of wine with you as we talk about my money."

"No problem." Gregory walks back into the room with two glasses, careful to give Artie the drink laced with the empty contents of his vial he used earlier at Sebastian's house. Gregory bends down, places the wineglass on the coffee table. Artie snatches the glass from the table and takes a gulp of wine. He closes his eyes, the alcohol satisfying his palate. Gregory could have offered him something stronger, but he won't complain since he is a guest.

"Artie, how much money do you want?"

"I think the information I am giving Kyndall is worth at least $75,000 to start."

"What do you mean to start?"

"Every couple of hours Scotty calls me with information on her investigation and all roads lead to Brendon. Actually, Scotty is leaving DC and heading to Charlotte, North Carolina, to follow Brendon's date." He uses air quotes when he uses the word "date." "Kyndall I hear you have a home there as well."

Kyndall slides forward on the couch, her hands balled in fists. Gregory stretches his right arm in Kyndall's direction, and she stops herself from punching Artie in the face.

Artie takes another gulp of his drink and smacks his lips. "This is a tasty selection, probably expensive."

"Artie, we are common folk around here, no lavish lifestyle," says Gregory.

Artie looks around the furnishings of the room. "You could have fooled me." He turns up the remaining contents of his glass.

"Can I have another?" He points to the glass and smiles. His drink of choice isn't wine, but this will do just the same.

This time Kyndall offers to get refills. She comes back into the room with the bottle and empties the contents in Artie's glass; as soon as she places the wineglass on the table, Artie snatches it up and takes a sip of the wine.

"Artie, how do you want the $75,000? You flew from Atlanta, so you can't carry a suitcase full of money back home." Gregory gives a hardy laugh.

Artie pounders the thought. "You can wire half of the $100,000 and give me the other half in cash. I don't trust the two of you will give me my money."

Gregory slides to the edge of his seat. "Oh, you went from $75,000 to $100,000!" Impatiently, he glances at his watch. *The drug is taking too long.* He jumps up, snatches the empty wine bottle from the coffee table, and smacks Artie over the head. Artie literally doesn't know what hit him. Artie slumps to the right of the chair, the wineglass he is holding slipping from his hand and onto the plush carpet, leaving a red stain. Blood trickles from the deep gash on Artie's head, down his face; his shirt soaks it up.

"About time. I thought you were going to take him out for dinner."

"I had it under control."

"What was with all the drinks and making him feel comfortable?"

"I put a drug in his drink."

"How did you know he drank? He could have said no."

"He was sweating profusely when he came in the house. I could smell the alcohol coming out of his pores."

Kyndall and Gregory stand over Artie's body. Gregory pulls his black gloves out of his back pocket and checks Artie's pulse—none. He pats Artie's body down, searching for his phone, and with little effort gains access to Artie's phone. Gregory looked directly at Artie's phone earlier and remembered his passcode. While Artie's body temperature slowly cools, Gregory plays all of Scotty's voicemails. Now Kyndall and Gregory know everything Artie knew about Scotty and her mother's knowledge about the case. Gregory places Artie's phone back in his pocket, then proceeds to search Artie's body again. He finds the keys to his rental.

"Kyndall, follow me in your car." Kyndall doesn't ask questions as Gregory lifts Artie's body to a limp standing position, places Artie's arm around his neck, and slowly walks the body to the rental just as he would a drunken friend. He balances Artie against the car, opens the door, and places Artie in the passenger side.

Gregory pulls into the older neighborhood, stops, and rolls down the window to motion for Kyndall to pull around him. She does, stops, rolls down the passenger window of her car. Gregory instructs her where to park. Kyndall pulls off and finds her spot. She keeps the engine running, on the lookout for Gregory.

Gregory parks Artie's rental in front of the familiar house, the front window covered with the dark curtains. Gregory exits the car, careful not to make a sound. He doesn't want to draw any attention to himself. Gregory jogs to his familiar parking spot now occupied by Kyndall and opens the door. "Let's go."

Kyndall turns to Gregory. "You are playing a dangerous game."

Gregory grins, and the two drive back to Kyndall's house in silence.

Chapter 51

*T*he barking of the dogs in the neighborhood wakes Eliza. She slides her feet in her bedroom slippers. She grabs Buddy and the two of them make it to the front of the house. Eliza peeks her head out the window in the living room at a mysterious car parked in front of her house. She turns on the light, looks at the clock—an odd hour for a visitor. Eliza goes back to her bedroom, retrieves her housecoat from across the foot of her bed, and puts it on, tying a strong knot not to reveal her nightgown. She grabs Buddy once again but this time the two of them cross the threshold of the front door and onto the porch. Eliza cranes her neck to inspect the person slumped over in the car parked outside her fence, no one in the driver's seat. Eliza walks from one end of the small porch to the other looking for someone on foot, the street empty. Eliza grabs the rail as she takes careful steps not to lose her balance and walks outside the fence. She walks over to the passenger side of the car and taps Buddy on the window. The stranger doesn't move. Eliza places Buddy at her side, walks closer, and peers into the car. Eliza gasps, takes a step back, places her wrinkled hand to her mouth at the sight of dried blood on the stranger's face. She scurries back into the house to call the only person she trusts besides her daughter.

———— ⇒((●))⇐ ————

"Hello," says a drowsy Sebastian.

"There's a dead body in front of my house."

"Dead body? What's going on?" Sebastian climbs out of the bed and dresses while waiting for the answers to his questions.

"There is dead body in a car parked in front of my house."

"How do you know the person is dead?" Sebastian walks to the bathroom, mutes the phone and brushes his teeth. Runs a warm washcloth on his face. Sebastian knows if Eliza says the body is dead, the body is dead. He hurries around the house getting what he needs to get on the road.

"He looks dead, that's how I know."

Sebastian pours himself a tall glass of orange juice and searches for his keys.

"Sebastian, you still there?"

Sebastian unmutes the phone, "yes, yes, I will be right over. Don't touch anything."

"I know I know. I am back in the house. I'll be here waiting on you."

"I'm on the way." Sebastian cranks his engine and speeds to Eliza's house.

Chapter 58

Sebastian shakes his head at the sight before him, Eliza standing on the porch with Buddy by her side. Sebastian parks behind the mystery car. His eyes move in the direction of the slumped body in the passenger seat. He carefully walks over to the compact car and unsnaps the safety on his holster, ready to draw if needed. He uses the flashlight on his phone to scan the slumped body. From where he is standing, the body looks dead to him. Sebastian calls dispatch for backup and an ambulance, walks back to his car, opens the trunk, and pulls out a pair of latex gloves. He walks back to the stranger's car and opens the passenger side back door. Sebastian looks around the car; the keys are still in the ignition. He slams the door, walks around to the driver's side, and pulls the latch to open the trunk. He reviews the identification tag, a business card with the name of Artie Stone and address of the television station. Sebastian rummages through Artie's luggage—nothing unusual, just clothes and toiletries. He walks back to the driver's side and placing his knee on the seat, he reaches across the armrest to search Artie's pockets. He finds his phone and wallet. Artie's work identification is behind a few dollar bills. Sebastian's mind races and he takes a deep breath. This is no accident. The body was left in front of Eliza's home. This is a message from Doris's killer. His eyes shift to the porch—empty. Eliza must have gone back inside. He calls Scotty to warn her, but the call goes straight to voicemail.

The ambulance and police arrive at the same time. The police block the street. Sebastian tells them all he knows about the deceased; he doesn't tell anyone who he suspects killed Artie, just sticks to the facts. The police officers pair up and canvas the neighborhood, while several start taking witness statements from the few residents gathered.

Malcolm, the lead EMT, takes Artie's pulse and announces to the group, "He's dead, no pulse." Sebastian makes the call to the coroner's office. Malcolm retrieves a sheet out of the back of the truck and hands it to Sebastian to cover the body after they search the victim. Malcolm directs his response to Sebastian. "Do you need anything else? We have another call."

"No, thank you for your help."

"That's what we are here for."

Two officers follow Sebastian up the steps of Eliza's house. Randy reaches for the doorbell just as Sebastian opens the door and enters Eliza's home. The two officers give each other side stares and follow Sebastian into the house. Sebastian walks into the kitchen, where Eliza is over the stove stirring a big pot of grits. "Eliza, we want to ask you a few questions about what you saw."

"Okay, have a seat while I fix you a plate."

Sebastian knows what he is dealing with, so he takes his place at the table, folds his napkin, and places it on his lap.

Randy speaks up first. "No, ma'am, we don't have time to eat."

"Why not? The body is dead. He ain't going no place."

Sebastian blurts out a hearty laugh.

Eliza places Sebastian's plate in front of him, the grits steaming, the bacon crispy, just like he likes it. Eliza walks back to the stove and fixes two plates for the officers. Eliza sits down at the table with her plate in front of her, the officers still standing.

Sebastian turns around. "Fellows, she's not going to answer any questions until you sit down and eat. That's just how this works."

The officers slowly walk to the table, take a seat, and carefully watch Sebastian to find out what to do next. Sebastian blesses the food and begins to eat. The officers pick up their forks and begin eating as well. The officers clean their plates. Sebastian rubs his stomach up and down, pats it twice, and uses his napkin to wipe his mouth. He throws the napkin on the empty plate. "Eliza, what happened tonight?" he asks.

Eliza places her wrinkled hand on the table as she recalls the events of the night. Slowly she fills the officers in on the details. "I woke up to the noise of my neighbors' dogs barking. Buddy and I went to the window and saw the car parked in front of the house. Sebastian, you know the window in the front of the house where I can see everything."

Sebastian nods his head as he continues to take notes. Randy asks, "Who is Buddy?"

Eliza says matter-of-fact, "My shotgun." Titus, the other officer, cracks up laughing at Eliza. Eliza continues her story without hesitation. "I saw the car parked in front of the house and I went out to investigate."

Of course, you did. Sebastian dares not speak his thoughts aloud to Eliza.

"I called you when I saw the body."

"You did the right thing."

"Do you know the victim?" asks Randy.

"No, I've never seen him before. Who is he?"

Sebastian avoids Eliza's question, and his eyes dart to his notepad to avoid her piercing stare. Eliza sits back in her chair and folds her arms. "You know who the dead guy is, don't you?"

Sebastian turns another page in his pad, not looking at Eliza. Eliza squints and Sebastian's heart sinks. He takes a deep breath. "Can I have the room?" The two officers, not sure what is going on, gladly stand and drop their napkins on their plates.

"Thank you for your hospitality," says Titus.

"Yes, thank you." The two scurry out of the kitchen toward the front door.

In a soft whisper Sebastian says, "He works with Scotty."

"What?"

Sebastian cracks his neck from side to side. "The person found in your yard is Artie Stone; he works with Scotty at the television station." Sebastian lowers his eyes. "I think the body was placed in front of the house as a message. We are getting too close to the Grahams. I visited Kyndall when Scotty went to DC to pay Brendon a visit. While I was at the house, I met Sean. He wasn't a nice guy. If I were a betting man, I would place all my chips on Sean killing Artie." Sebastian picks at a hangnail on his left thumb.

"Whatever his name is, I told you I think he was lying about his name. He didn't look like a Sean."

Sebastian scribbles notes on his pad. *What is Sean's real name?*

Eliza is calm. "Scotty can take care of herself. I am not worried about her. She gets her spunk from me." She smiles and shakes her head from side to side, then focuses on Sebastian seated in front of her. "Where do we go from here?"

Sebastian ponders Eliza's question. "I am waiting to hear back from Scotty. I need to find out what she uncovered speaking with Brendon."

"Okay, give her another call."

Sebastian dials but the call goes straight to voicemail. "Eliza, there is no answer from Scotty. I will continue the official investigation and let you know what I uncover. The officers are speaking with people in the neighborhood."

Eliza stands, discards the scraps on the plate in the trash, places the plate in the sink. She turns to face Sebastian. "Even if someone knew what happened to this Artie character, they won't talk against the senator or his mother."

Sebastian opens his mouth, says nothing. He shakes his head and walks out of the house.

Chapter 59

*S*cotty races to find the nearest parking space in long-term parking ahead of the shuttle bus. The bus turns into her row, and she dashes out of the car, turns around, points the car alarm in the direction of the loaner Sebastian gave her. *Beep, beep*, the doors lock. She runs alongside the stopped airport transportation bus and up the stairs to find a seat in the back of the bus. Scotty braces herself as the bus makes its way to her airline's departure area, where she tries to find an unoccupied kiosk. She taps her right foot waiting for her turn. After printing her ticket, she proceeds to security checkpoint, then runs to her gate with a few minutes to spare. The gate personnel are calling first class customers.

She pulls her phone out of her purse. The battery is drained, and the phone won't power on. She scans the room for someone with a friendly face and willingness to loan her their charger and moves from area to area. She gives up on the kindness of society and dashes to the nearest bookstand for a charger. She cuts her thumb tearing open the packaging. Scotty sucks the blood oozing from the torn skin. She charges her phone on the charging station. The gate agent calls zone. She starts to unplug her phone but thinks twice; she doesn't have any luggage to check. She checks her phone every thirty seconds for an increase in battery life. Scotty closes her eyes, takes a deep breath. She needs more juice to check in with Sebastian, as she has much to update him on. The gate agent calls the final boarding. Scotty scratches the charger base out of the outlet and listens to her missed voicemails. She sits in her coach seat as Sebastian informs her Artie is dead and he needs her to be careful, Artie's death suspicious. If Scotty wasn't already seated, she would have lost her balance and fallen down. Her eyes are glazed.

"Excuse me, ma'am, you will have to place your phone in airplane mode."

Scotty complies with the flight attendant, wondering who's been reading her text messages to Artie; she has been getting "read receipt" notifications. A cold chill goes up her spine, and her body trembles. She has an uneasy feeling that something bad has happened but unsure what because she can't use her phone to call anyone. This is the first time in her career she is afraid for her life. Scotty rests her head on the window, closing her eyes tight as tears creep in the inner corner of her eyes. She swallows hard to get the lump out of her throat. She looks out the window until her tired body refuses to give in, and she falls asleep.

Chapter 60

In Charlotte, Scotty decides to get a taxi instead of renting a car; it's late and she doesn't want to navigate the new city in the dark. Plus, she is emotionally drained by the news of Artie. Scotty uses the Marriott app to secure a room close to the address for both Kyndall and June. Once behind the secure walls of her hotel, Scotty locks the door to her room, including the security bolt. She searches the room top to bottom looking for anyone hiding to grab her when she lets her guard down. The room spins. Is someone after her? Who killed Artie? Scotty plugs her phone into the outlet and sends Sebastian a text message.

"I'm torn up by the news of Artie. Who could have killed him? I've been texting him over the last several days even in the timeframe you said he was dead. Somebody wants me to think he's still alive. I'm safe right now. I'm in Charlotte, following June Carter, Brendon's lover. Kyndall has a house here as well. Who knows what I will find under that rock?" She hits send.

Scotty throws the phone beside her on the bed. Her mind draws back to Artie. Scotty snatches the phone and enters the address of the hotel and Kyndall's North Carolina address. She plugs her phone into the charger, undresses down to her under-garments, turns the lights off, and falls into a deep slumber within minutes of her head touching the firm pillow.

Chapter 61

*E*mma's call spoiled Chip's sexual appetite. He dresses quickly, kisses Kelsey on the lips. "Is everything okay?" asks Kelsey. Her husband cuts his eyes at Chip, walks to the bathroom, and slams the door. Kelsey didn't like the mess they were in after they closed on the house but soon fell in love with Chip. She is glad she has two men she loves; her husband, on the other hand, wants out. He doesn't like the fact that Chip had a key to their house and can come and go as he pleases.

"We have a slight problem but it's nothing I can't handle. I'll see you later." Chip dashes out the door and down the street to his house in the cul-de-sac, the Nest, the neighbors call it. The place where the parties happen. Chip invites other swings to celebrate their freedom, openness to life.

Chip opens the door to the house, opens the garage, no June. He calls her phone, which goes straight to voicemail. Chip runs up the stairs taking them two at a time. He calls June again, still no answer; he throws the phone on the bed. He searches the bedroom for something to tell him where his wife is. The room is spotless, nothing out of place. Chip's rage gets the best of him and he picks up the mattress, drags his hand from the top to the bottom; nothing. He opens every drawer in the room haphazardly throwing clothing. He sighs. Where is she? Chip moves to the walk-in closet and stands, not sure where to look first. June's side of the is closet neat, the hangers an inch apart, everything in place. Chip's shoulders slump and he tilts his head back, his eyes closed. He slowly counts backward in his head from ten to one. His breathing is slow and steady. Chip opens his eyes, and this is when he sees the gray sweater box slightly ajar. He opens the lid to discover June has been hiding valuable items belonging to the victims he killed. These items could implicate him in any formal investigation. Is this her way of framing him for a murder investigation? The chime of the doorbell startles Chip, and the contents of the box fall on the floor. He stoops, throws the stolen items back in the box, runs in the small circle of the closet to find a place to store the box. The doorbell rings again. Chip runs out of the closet still with box in hand, stops, catches his breath, and decides to slide the box of stolen merchandise under the bed. The doorbell chimes again. Now with the box hidden and Chip's emotions under control, he runs down the stairs ready to ask the police for a warrant.

"Who is it?" Chip asks, looking through the peephole, not recognizing the person at the door.

"I am Vincent with Secure Me Security company."

Chip opens the door, the screen door a barrier between them. "What can I do for you?"

Vincent begins to ramble. Chip pretends to listen to the long-rehearsed sales pitch. His eyes dart up and down the street, anticipating the police coming to arrest him.

"Sir, did you hear me?"

"What? Listen, I am not interested in a security system." Chip begins to close the door.

"Sir, can you tell me if someone lives over there." says Vincent, pointing to Kyndall's house.

"No, the house is vacant." Chip slams the door in Vincent's face. So, used to Kyndall's house being vacant, he notices the car backing out of the driveway.

Chip walks upstairs to retrieve the box. He has an idea of where to hide the box. He secures the box from under the bed and places it in a cloth reusable bag. He grabs the keys to the community and walks next door to Kyndall's house.

Vincent, standing on Emma's porch, watches Chip unlock the door to the house he told him was vacant. He pulls out his phone and takes pictures of the ass who slammed the door in his face. *He seems up to no good*, thinks Vincent.

"Hello, can I help you," says Emma. Vincent forgot he rang the doorbell; the owner caught him off guard. Emma's eyes follow who Vincent is watching. Chip is letting himself in Kyndall's house.

Emma has rushed Vincent off her porch without a sale. He stands in Emma's driveway and spots the rude guy who slammed the door in his face leaving the neighbor's house, locking the door behind him. Vincent knows this dude is up to no good.

Chapter 62

After hearing the statements from both Susan and Khan, Angela and Cheyanne decide to knock on a couple of doors to find answers to the disappearance of Lily and Jim. Angela signals left and her police-issued Crown Victoria slowly enters the Sweetbriar Community. "This is a very impressive community."

"Yes, there is a wooded area between each home. There is privacy between the homes you don't find in many communities."

"Look over there—the common area is well manicured. There isn't much to the community; the only street fully developed is Sweetbriar Lane."

"You know, you are right," says Cheyanne, looking around.

"It looks as though the developer ran out of money and could not afford to continue to build."

"It looks like the community ends here." Angela stops at the end of the paved street, turns the Crown Victoria around, and makes a left to turn down Sweetbriar Lane. They park behind Jorge's Ford F-150 truck parked in front of the address Susan gave them for what was going to be her new home.

Jorge watches the black Crown Victoria as it pulls behind his truck. He turns his body sideways to see the direction the two officers are going. Jorge knows an unmarked police car; he has seen enough of them in his lifetime. When he lived in Phoenix, he was harassed by police officers wanting to see his papers. They thought all Hispanics in that area were undocumented. Jorge spits at the thought.

He watches the two detectives get out of the car with sunglasses and ring Emma's doorbell. No one answers.

Jorge, a stickler for time, sits in his white Raptor, waiting for the clock on his phone to display eight o'clock on the dot. The clock changes from 7:59 to 8:00 a.m. and Jorge walks around to the passenger side and opens the door for Ace, his golden retriever. Jorge never leaves home without Ace at his side. He reaches down on the floorboard on the passenger side and picks up the tattered briefcase his father left him before he died. Jorge has eight siblings and his father didn't leave them much except for the business he started when he migrated to the United States. Jorge's siblings thought that it was best for Jorge to run the business because he was the oldest and his father showed him the business. Because he was *el hombre a cargo*. Jorge smiles as he remembers how his brothers and sisters tease him whenever they are together. He runs his hand across the briefcase, says a silent prayer, and uses his right hand to make an invisible cross on his chest. He closes the truck door behind him. Ace walks with Jorge up the steps to the front porch. Jorge rings the doorbell and Ace sits at his feet.

Emily opens the door. "Hi, how are you? You must be Jorge. Please come in. I'm Emily." Emily bends down and speaks to Jorge but is looking down at Ace. "Who is this handsome fellow here?" Emily scratches behind Ace's ears. Ace moves his head in the direction of Emily's hands. He pants heavily, dropping his head in Emily's hands. Both Jorge and Emily laugh. Emily stops rubbing Ace's head. Ace uses the tip of his nose to flip Emily's hand to the top of his head. Emily rubs her hand across the top of his head vigorously. "What a good boy."

Emily turns her attention to Jorge. "Let me show you the backyard." The two of them walk through the house to the back-yard. Ace sprints into the backyard and runs the length of the fenced yard back and forth. "Ace sure seems excited," exclaims Emily.

"Hum, maybe he's excited because of the new environment. Our yard at home isn't big enough for him to stretch his legs."

Jorge bends down and unlatches his briefcase and pulls out the folder with Emily's name neatly printed on the front. Jorge prepares to give his customer an estimate on her project. He proudly stands and opens the folder and shows the blueprint to Emily they walk through the designs explaining where each flow-er and shrub will be planted. The project is small, but Jorge needs the work. His wife Luna is due any day with their third child. It doesn't matter, large or small, he needs the work.

Meanwhile across the street, Angela and Cheyanne ring Emma's doorbell once again waiting on a response. As they turn to walk off the porch a faint voice behind the other side of the door yells, "coming." The footsteps grow louder as the person on the other end nears the door.

Emma opens the door but keeps the screen door locked.

"Hi, I am Detective Hall, and this is Detective Winters, and we are with Charlotte Mecklenburg Police." Both detectives show their badges to Emma.

"How can I help you?"

"We are here investigating a missing person's case. Susan Burke reported her husband Jim missing. Have you met either Jim or Susan Burke?"

"I met Susan yesterday. She was looking for her husband Jim. She said she flew down from New York to join her husband, who purchased the house across the street. I told her that there weren't any houses for sale in the community."

"Which house did Susan think her husband purchased?" Angela asks, even though she knew the answer.

"The one across the street." Emma points to Kyndall's house.

Angela asks Emma the same question but more direct. "Did you meet Jim Burke?"

"No, I've never met him," says Emma with a straight face.

Suddenly screams are heard from across the street, the direction of Kyndall's house. The second scream comes from a strong male voice. All three ladies turn and look across the street, and Angela and Cheyanne take flight. Emma snatches her keys from the glass sofa table and quickly locks the door behind her. Much older than Angela and Cheyanne, she struts across the street at a much slower pace.

By the time Angela, Cheyanne, and Emma join Jorge and Emily, Ace has dug a hole in the backyard. He is holding through clenched teeth a femur and sitting beside his owner, proud of his accomplishment. He wags his tail. Emily is swaying from side to side, cradling the cordless phone, explaining the human bone that was found by her landscaper's dog to the 911 operator.

Emma, a little winded, grabs her chest and manages words. "Emily, is everything okay? We heard screams from my house."

Emily covers the mouthpiece of the phone with her hand to shield her conversation from the 911 operator. "I'm okay but a but shaken."

"You can hang up; these two ladies are detectives," says Emma.

Emily removes her hand from the mouthpiece and speaks directly into the handset. "Sorry to bother you; we have two detectives here already."

Angela speaks with the operator and gives her badge number along with her first and last name. She hangs up and hands Emily the cordless phone with her left hand and extends her right hand for a proper introduction. "Hi, I'm Angela Hall and over there is Cheyanne Winters. We were here earlier to speak with Emma about a missing person by the name of Jim Burke. His wife Susan reported him missing yesterday. We heard the screams and ran straight over. The most important question is, are you okay?"

"Yeah, a bit shaken."

"Are you the homeowner? What's your name?"

"No, I'm Emily Graham. My mother-in-law owns the home, Kyndall Graham. I just moved in yesterday. I haven't met Susan or her husband Jim. This is so tragic. What do you think happened to Jim? And who does the bone belong to?"

"We aren't sure at this point of anything. Do you know how long your mother-in-law, Kyndall, owned the house?"

"Actually, Detective, I didn't know she owned the home until recently when she offered it as a place for me to get away."

"There is a report that Jim wanted to purchase the house from the owner; now we are finding out the house wasn't for sale and you are staying in the house. Do you understand why this is confusing to us?"

"No, I totally agree—this entire situation is confusing."

"Emily, what happened here today? Is that your dog?"

"No, Ace belongs to Jorge, my landscaper. Ace started going crazy running up and down the yard and spinning around in circles. He feverishly started digging and came up with that bone. When we looked a little closer it appears it was a human remain and that's when I called the police. Ace dug the hole to my right first and then he moved to the hole over there." Emily points to the far end of the yard. "That's where we found the decomposing body."

"Emily I will need to speak with the homeowner. Will you get her on the phone?"

"Of course, I will get my cell phone. I haven't memorized a phone number in years." Angela nods in agreement. Emily disappears into the house.

When Angela and Cheyanne enter the yard, Cheyanne, a dog lover, walks over to Ace to investigate the bone between his teeth. She notices the bone isn't an ordinary dog bone but a femur, a human thigh bone. She walks over to one of the two holes Ace dug up and, on the surface, sees a hand sticking out of the ground. "Angela, there's something you need to see," yells Cheyanne.

Angela walks over to the shallow grave Cheyanne is standing over next to Ace guarding. Cheyanne makes a few calls to get a full investigative team on the scene. She needs the forensic anthropologist and in a hurry. Cheyanne knows that what she is witnessing is only the beginning.

Angela takes careful notes; she needs to be able to report back to her father everything that happened.

Once the police arrive, they scatter around the front and back of the house. Captain Montgomery calls Angela's cell phone, and he scans the crowd for her. The sound of Angela's phone ringing prompts him to cancel the call. He walks up to her. "Hey, Angela. I was just calling you."

"What's up, Captain?"

"I wanted to assign this case to you. Did you get the call over the radio?"

"No, Cheyanne and I were having dinner last night and met back up at the station. Susan Burke, the wife of the missing husband, came to the precinct to report him missing. While interviewing her my father called, and I was telling him about Susan's story, which didn't seem credible until I told my father the name of the homeowner, Kyndall Graham, the mother of the senator of the State of Pennsylvania, Brendon Graham. My father was investigating a case in DC and Brendon was staying at the hotel where the murder took place."

"So, was Brendon a person of interest in your father's case?"

"Yes, the circumstances surrounding the reason Emily, his wife, came into town was a lie. He wasn't able to dig further into the case because my mother and his partner, Dakota Rose, died in an explosion."

"Is there a connection between your father's case and what you have uncovered."

"Just by me being here for an hour or so, I will say yes. Emily Graham moved into the house yesterday; Kyndall owns the house and a dead body is found in the backyard. Not saying that Emily had anything to do with the dead body, but something surrounding the Graham family doesn't sit well with me. On top of that Susan's husband is missing and they were supposed to purchase a home that was never on the market, according to Emma, the lady who lives across the street."

"Angela, I knew it was a great decision to bring you on my team. The case officially belongs to you and Cheyanne. Let me know what I can do to support you and Cheyanne. We need to close this case ASAP, especially if we have a senator and the wife of the attorney general involved."

"Angela, you need to see this," yells Cheyanne over the noise of the crowd. "Matthew, the forensic anthropologist, just told us that the bone in the dog's mouth isn't the bone from this corpse."

All heads snap in Matthew's direction for an explanation. "The bone in the dog's mouth belongs to a female. The corpse in the shallow grave looks about a week old."

Anthony, the crime scene investigator, agrees with Matthew. "The bugs and larvae indicate that the body is a week and a day old."

"Okay, call the K-9 unit; we need to canvas the entire yard to find who these bones belong to."

Jorge stands next to Ace, who is guarding the hole he just dug. He growls at Cheyanne, who moves her hand toward his mouth. Cheyanne takes two steps back. "Cut it out, Ace," shouts Jorge. Ace cowers, whimpers, his head cocked to the side but still keeping an eye on Cheyanne, the bone thief.

Cheyanne turns her attention toward Jorge. "I am Detective Cheyanne Winters. What's your name?"

"My name is Jorge Guzman."

"What were you doing here today?"

"Emily called me to do some landscaping, just a small job. I was going to plant seasonal flowers around the back and a few around the mailbox. I would have been able to complete the job in a day."

"What time did you arrive?"

"Ace and I got here about 8:00 a.m. He goes everywhere with me."

"Did you notice anything out of the ordinary when you arrived?"

"No, Emily let me in, and we talked briefly and walked through the house to the backyard. She was showing me around when Ace darted off and started digging. Emily and I both screamed, and you and your partner came over."

Jorge is finally able to pull the bone out of Ace's grip. "Can I go now?" he asks.

"That should be all for now; we may have additional questions for you. If you think of anything else, please give me a call." Cheyanne extends a business card to Jorge.

"Yeah, okay. Give me a call if you need to. I just can't stay another minute in this yard with the dead bodies." Jorge jogs around to the front of the house with Ace at his side. Jorge opens the passenger door and Ace jumps in on cue, wagging his tail. Ace leans in and rests his head on his owner's shoulder. He knows he has done a good job by giving his owner the treasure he found in the backyard.

As Jorge backs out of the driveway, the K-9 Unit arrives with Max and his handler Isaac and parks in front of Emma's house. Isaac leads Max across the street and up the sloped driveway and walks to the backyard. Once in the backyard Isaac unleashes Max and whispers, "Go, boy." Max takes off running to the already revealed corpse. He dances in a circle. Isaac catches up with him and the CSI manager hands Isaac the female femur with his gloved hand. Isaac places the bone under Max's nose, and he takes off again, running in circles near a spot near the back of the lot. A team of CSI members start to dig. Max runs to the opposite end of the yard and sits, not moving. "Come here, Max," yells Isaac. Max sits there wagging his tail. "I think we have another location," yells Isaac. Isaac goes up to Max and rubs his head. "Good boy." Max takes off again to the front left side of the yard and runs in circles. Isaac runs toward Max and shouts, "We have another body!"

Angela and Cheyanne are looking at four teams digging to uncover bodies. "Holy crap!" says Angela to no one in particular. She runs her hands through her long, black wavy hair.

"Cheyanne, let's talk." Angela and Cheyanne move from one side of the yard with the teams of police officers doing their jobs.

"Did you think the innocent conversation between Susan and Khan would lead to this mess?"

"My dad says there is more to the Grahams' story than on the surface, so I think we need to question Emily even though she said she moved in the day before. There are four dead bodies in the backyard. My gut tells me she didn't commit the murders, but we should look around."

"Agreed."

Angela and Cheyanne scan the crowd and find Emily near the back door. "Emily, Cheyanne and I were wondering if we can look around inside the house."

"By all means you can look around. I will cooperate with the police. As I stated to you earlier, I am not the homeowner and just moved in yesterday."

Angela and Cheyanne move the search to the interior of the home. Cheyanne searches downstairs. Angela goes upstairs and moves from room to room. She finds her way to the master bedroom and runs her hands across the clothing on the bottom row, thinking of the day she meets that special guy she can settle down with, get married, and have children. She stops the dreamy thoughts when the hangers stick together to expose the gray box tucked away; only the movement of the hangers allows her to view the hiding place. Angela retrieves the box and places it on the cabinet and picks up each piece of jewelry one at a time. She reads the engraving.

Cheyanne walks up the stairs. "Angela, where are you?"

"I am in the closet. I think I may have something."

Cheyanne follows the sound of Angela's voice. "I am glad one of us got something but there isn't anything downstairs."

"I found this interesting box hidden with jewelry pushed in the far back of the closet."

"People place jewelry in boxes all the time."

"Well, this is a little different. It seems as though this is a collection of jewelry from different people because they are all engraved with different names."

"What?"

"Well, I am not sure if this watch belongs to Susan's husband Jim, but it is engraved to someone with the same name."

"Khan, the guy who drove Susan to the airport, says his sister, Lily, went missing; she used to work in the model, which is this house."

"We need Susan and Khan to examine the contents if they don't belong to Emily." Angela and Cheyanne walk downstairs to find Emily in the kitchen.

"Emily, do the contents in this box belong to you?" asks Angela.

Emily glances up from her sandwich, looks in Angela's direction, and says, "I have never seen that box before."

"How do you know? You haven't looked at the contents."

"I don't have to look inside. I don't own gray boxes. I use more cream colors, like the other ones in my closet."

Angela did remember the other boxes were cream. She takes into consideration Emily's point, but she still has to get the perspective of Susan and Khan. "Emily, do you mind if we take the box and review the contents at the station."

"I don't have anything to hide. Take the box."

"Do you have plans to leave town, go back to Pennsylvania?"

"No, not now. As I mentioned to you, I arrived yesterday. However, I do plan to pick up my son, Ian, on Saturday in Columbia, South Carolina, and bring him back here."

"How long do you plan to stay?"

"Not long—just enough time to drive down and bring him back to Charlotte."

"Please write down the address in Columbia." Angela extends both the pen and paper to Emily.

Emily without a care in the world scribbles the address on the paper. "Is there anything else I can help you with?"

"Thank you for your cooperation."

Angela and Cheyanne oversee the investigation in the backyard. Angela steps to a quiet place in the yard out of earshot and places a call to both Susan and Khan. She asks them to come to the precinct to identify personal effects.

Chapter 63

$\mathscr{E}$mily's scream echoes through the neighborhood, and the neighbors scramble toward the sound. Scotty's cab, careful not to hit the pedestrians as they hurriedly run to Kyndall's house, the exact same place Scotty's cab stops. Scotty searches her wallet for her credit card to pay the driver, but he exits the car and runs to Kyndall's backyard. Khan anxiously wants to know what all the commotion is about. He is hoping to find answers about his missing sister Lily. Khan elbows his way to the front of the crowd.

Scotty scribbles her name and number on a piece of paper requesting he call for payment she always pays for service. She jumps out of the car and makes her way to the backyard. In disbelief, her eyes follow the cadaver dog from one hole to the other.

Kelsey and Paige enter the backyard. Kelsey leads Paige by the hand to stand beside Emma. They greet the older woman with a hug. Scotty's instincts as a reporter take over, no longer a bystander but someone seeking answers. Scotty inches closer to the three women until she is directly behind them, close enough to overhear their conversation. Scotty observes the brunette with shoulder-length hair, known as Kelsey, ask, "Is our secret exposed?"

The older woman responds, "I'm afraid so."

Paige, the redhead, face drained of all color, is ghostlike. Just listening to the short conversation Scotty knows the leader of the group and the weakest link. Scotty spots her cab driver shaking his head in dismay. What is his connection to Kyndall? Scotty's attention is diverted once again to the conversation of the group in front of her.

"I can't believe they did this," Paige repeats several times.

Kelsey squeezes Paige's upper arm and whispers, "Shut up, snap out of it!"

Paige, a complicit accomplice in the dirty deeds of the community. Each hole represents a loss of life. A life valued by their loved ones. A means to an end to the wizard behind the mask of the Sweetbriar community.

Kelsey, needing to get confirmation Paige that understood her warning, snatches Paige's arm and swings her body around to face her, the two nose to nose. Paige's body trembles, her eyes avoids contact with Kelsey. Through clenched teeth, barely moving her lips not to draw attention to herself, Kelsey warns, "Look at me, do you want to be next?"

Paige takes a deep breath, shakes her head. She forcefully removes Kelsey's hands from her body. "They all will burn in hell for what they did." Paige turns, runs through the small crowd to her home. Scotty leaves the backyard to follow Paige.

Angela, speaking with Emily, draws her attention to the two women arguing; they must have entered the yard when she and Cheyanne were staring into the shallow graves. Her father always told her to pay attention to the onlookers; the person committing the crime always comes back to admire their work.

Paige turns and runs up the street toward her home. Angela, needing answers, rushes over to Kelsey. "Excuse me, what's your name?"

"My name is Kelsey."

"Who just left the yard?"

"Oh, her name is Paige."

"Why are you here disrupting my crime scene?"

"We didn't mean any harm; we heard the screaming and wanted to help."

"How did you plan to help? Do you know anything that the police should be aware of?"

"Oh, no. I just came over to give my emotional support."

"Do you know your new neighbor?"

"No."

"Why would you give emotional support when you don't know your new neighbor."

"Detective, I was just trying to help."

"You haven't convinced me how you plan to do so."

"Well, I will be leaving."

"Before you go, I need your full name, address, and phone number."

Kelsey rolls her eyes; she just created a situation that puts her in the direct line of fire when she only wanted to know what happened. She is the person everyone goes to stay in the know.

As Kelsey leaves the backyard, she reaches in her back pocket and pulls out her cell phone. Nervously she looks around, not wanting the hard-nosed detective hearing her conversation.

<hr />

"Hey, what's up," says Chip.

"Are you home?"

"Yes, why do you ask?"

"Do you not see the police in front of your driveway and the holes in your neighbor's yard?"

Chip takes his earbuds out of his ear and walks to his bedroom and to the bathroom that faces Kyndall's house.

"When did all this happen?"

"Is that all you can say? We are in big trouble. There are four holes in the backyard. I only know about two buried bodies."

"Well, the third body is Jim."

"Who the hell is Jim?"

"Long story. I will have to tell you later."

"Okay, so that's three bodies; who does the fourth body belong to?"

"That I am not sure, but I know someone who does. I will pay her a visit." Chip walks to the closet and slips on his sneakers.

"We have another problem. Paige is losing her cool and needs to be reminded of where her loyalty lies. She is guilty through association. She may be remorseful now, but she isn't blameless. We need to go over and have a conversation with her now."

"I agree we need to talk to her, but we should wait until after the dust settles with the mess next door."

Chip shakes his head. The situation could have been avoided if June would have a conversation with Emily about outside renovations, especially the house where Emily was living. The house had been vacant, and she knew that they just buried Jim's body. These types of missed details, especially actions that create negative publicity, could hamper their chances to grow the housing concept across the country. The development concept is to create family values, trust, loyalty, and a sense of community. If June wasn't acting like a schoolgirl with Jim, she would have been ahead of the situation.

June will have to be dealt with.

Chapter 64

Paige fumbles with her house keys to enter the front door, but they fall onto the ground. She closes her eyes and takes a deep breath to gain her composure. Scotty bends down and picks up Paige's keys. "Here you go."

"Thank you."

"Are you okay? You seem a little rattled."

"I'm sorry—who are you?" asks Paige, puzzled why this stranger is so interested in her.

"I'm Scotty Richards." Scotty extends her hand.

"Nice to meet you." Paige shakes Scotty's hand to reciprocate the friendly gesture.

Scotty reaches in her purse for her network credentials. She flashes her ID to Paige for verification. Paige reaches for the identification, looks at Scotty, then the picture, then Scotty again. "What do you want with me?"

"I'm investigating a murder in Philadelphia with a connection to Kyndall Graham. I'm wanting to find additional information on June Carter for a story I'm writing as well." Scotty gives her half the truth; she is investigating the death of Doris Massey, which has led to Kyndall and now to June, so she didn't lie. "Can I come inside to speak with you?"

In the meanwhile, Chip drives up the street slowly in front of Paige's house. The two lock eyes. Scotty turns her head in the direction of Paige's distraction. Chip revs his engine to exit the community.

"No, there isn't anything I can tell you."

"You don't know what I want to ask you."

Paige rubs her right arm, which aches from the altercation with Kelsey. She bites her lower lip.

"I'm here following up a lead from my mother. Her best friend died, and she thinks Kyndall Graham is somehow caught up in the murder. My mother saw Kyndall go into the house. I came here and pulled up to Kyndall's home and there are dead bodies throughout the backyard. At first, I wanted to think this was all a coincidence, but now I believe something fishy is going on. I promised my mother I would find answers. If you don't want to help, that's fine but I will uncover the truth."

Paige starts to cry and in a soft whisper murmurs, "Okay, but we can't talk here."

Khan tries to speak with Angela, but she says she will call him later when she has something to report. He walks back to his cab with his head down and hands in his pocket. Now, back at his car, he realizes he didn't collect payment from his fare. He opens the door and finds the note. He smiles—there is decency and kindness in the world after all. He decides not to call. He cranks the engine, pulls off up the street, and slows when he sees his fare. Scotty looks over her shoulder and waves her arms to flag Khan. He pulls up in front of Paige's house. Scotty walks down the steps to the porch; Paige follows and they both enter Khan's cab.

"Where to, ma'am?"

"Take me to the nearest mall. I need a change of clothes."

Paige chuckles. "You literally came all this way to follow a lead."

Khan watches the two women in his rearview mirror while obeying the rules of the road.

"Yes, like I told you, I promised my mother I would find answers to her friend's death, and my investigation brought me here."

Scotty and Paige are both quiet, Khan puts on his turn signal to switch lanes. Scotty remembers the cab driver abandoning his car to find out the commotion earlier.

"Excuse me?"

"Yes, ma'am."

"Do you know the owner of the house you dropped me at before?"

"No, I don't know the owner, but I was hopeful to find answers to the disappearance of my sister, Lily."

"Why would you think she would be buried at the house of Kyndall Graham?"

"I don't know Kyndall Graham, but my sister was the agent showing houses to expand the community."

"Did you go to the police?"

"Yes, the detectives we reported were at the scene."

"Who is we?"

"I met another young lady, Susan Burke; her husband went missing as well. They were moving from New York to North Carolina to buy the house where the bodies were found."

"I think the owner of the home is connected to a murder in Philadelphia."

Khan safely pulls in front of the main entrance to the mall. He places the car in park and turns his entire body around. "Can you help me find my sister?"

"Yes," Scotty eagerly agrees. "Can you get in contact with Susan and we can all talk?"

"Yes, I can make it happen."

"I need to pick up a few items here. Paige and I will meet you back at the hotel in an hour and a half."

Khan checks his watch. "Okay, see you at four thirty."

Scotty offers to pay both fares but Khan refuses. Scotty smiles as she and Paige exit the car and rush into the mall to do some much-needed shopping.

Chapter 65

Scotty and Paige determine they can find everything Scotty needs as far as clothing in the department store; the toiletries she can find at the mainstream general on the other side of the mall, where she grabs two bottles of wine. They scurry around finding what they need, and Scotty calls a taxi to take her and Paige to her hotel. They make it back with twenty minutes to spare. Scotty orders two pizzas, one with cheese, the other vegetables. She jumps in the shower, washes her hair, and scrubs the two-day-old stench of wearing the same clothing off her body. She feels clean, like a different person.

Paige sits in the chair next to the window biting her nails and bouncing her crossed leg. The knock on the door startles both of them, and they jump, turning their attention toward the door.

Scotty looks through the peephole and sees Khan, a familiar face—the woman unknown. It must be Susan, she thinks. Scotty opens the door with a warm smile. "Hi, welcome, come in." She steps aside to allow her two guests to enter.

"Khan, you remember Paige from earlier today."

"Hello."

"Susan, this is Paige and my name is Scotty. I'm a journalist and anchor for *Meeting of the Minds*."

"I've seen your show. It's so nice to meet you," says Susan, encasing her hands around Scotty's. "Khan told me he met you and you were willing to help. I just didn't know what to say." Susan gestures with her right hand to her heart.

Another knock on the door startles everyone in the room. Scotty eases everyone's suspicions by informing them she ordered pizza. Even though Scotty is expecting pizza delivery, she still takes precautions by looking out the peephole. Scotty grabs her wallet, searches for thirty dollars, and opens the door. The delivery driver opens both pizza boxes for Scotty to inspect. Scotty, satisfied with the appearance, pays the pimple-faced delivery driver with a generous tip.

Scotty closes the door. No more distractions—she can focus on what each person has to say. Scotty places the hot pizza on the desk, chews the top off the wine bottle, and pours herself a hearty cup. She is drinking out of the plastic clear cups—nothing fancy, just a cup to hold her liquid joy.

Susan starts with the disappearance of her husband, and Scotty suppresses the urge to call him an SOB. He is still a missing person.

Khan begins to tell the story of his sister and her disappearance from the open house in Sweetbriar. Paige fidgets in the chair, and Scotty notices. "Paige, how long have you lived in the community?"

"My husband and I moved when we graduated from college. Our parents gave us a generous down payment for the home." Paige, feeling as though everyone in the room is judging her, defends her last statement. "We paid them back, every cent of it..." Her voice trails off. "I should have never pushed him to move to Sweetbriar. He wanted to move across town, but I was pursued by June and the future plans. We were expected to double our investment with the extensive amenities and the homeownership advantages." Paige picks at her chapped lower lip.

"Paige, what homeownership advantages other than your home value increases."

"This community was supposed to be the only one of its kind, very exclusive in who was brought in."

Scotty stands. "Exclusive? You mean discriminating against certain groups of people."

"No, I don't mean like that. We only want certain people."

Khan, a Muslim, experiences discrimination on a daily basis. He places his slice on the lid of the pizza box. "What people do you want in your housing community? Do you want all white people?"

"No, of course not. Emma and Harold live in the community and they are African-American."

"Oh," says Khan as he picks up his pizza, disinterested in the conversation.

"Then what kind of people do you want in the community?"

"Swingers, we are all swingers!" screams Paige.

"I knew you all were up to no good. Certain times a year you have parties and people would do and say strange things in my cab. I can hear everything you people say."

"What is a swinger?" says Susan innocently, chomping on a piece of crust.

"Technically we call ourselves a lifestyle group; we don't use the term swinging," explains Paige.

"Let's focus on how the bodies ended up in the backyard of Kyndall's home." Scotty's statement isn't directed at anyone, but Paige is the only person who can explain the mystery.

"All I know is when someone finds out what the community is all about and they want to leave, or they want to report what they discover in the HOA, we never see them again. One night

I was up late and saw June and Chip digging a hole in Kyndall's backyard. I never saw Lily again. The open house sign in front of Kyndall's house was taken down and the prospect of Phase II disappeared."

Khan runs to the bathroom bawling his eyes out; they can hear him with the door closed. Susan throws her uneaten slice into the trash. Her Jim is probably dead as well. Susan weeps for her husband.

"You have to go to the police and tell them what you know," Scotty says.

"I can't put my husband and I in danger. We could be next."

"You don't think Khan, Susan, and who the hell else is suffering? Whatever you know or think can bring the murderer to justice."

Paige shakes her head. "No, no, I can't take that chance."

With all the yelling the group doesn't notice Khan standing across the room with his arms folded, listening to Paige agree to do nothing. Susan wipes her nose with the napkin from the pizza takeout. "I have an idea."

"You are a selfish, privileged yuppie!" shouts Khan.

"Stop shouting! I have an idea! Damn it!" Susan commands the room; the room grows quiet, all eyes on Susan. She hasn't been the center of attention in years; Jim stopped listening to her months after they married.

"Scotty, why don't you do it?"

"Why don't I do what?"

"Why don't you tell the story as a journalist? Expose the community. The police can't deny there weren't dead bodies found this afternoon, and it will force them to give Khan and me answers."

Scotty walks the length of the room thinking about her options. She would have to tell her boss what she has been up to while on vacation. She closes her eyes and remembers the last time she was in Kyndall's crosshairs. She lost her job. She has to be right; she could lose everything. The image of her and her mother forces her to take a chance. Scotty slowly turns to face the group. "Okay, I'll do it, but I have to get it cleared with my boss."

Paige, knowing her world is about to blow up, says, "Is there more wine?" She might as well get some liquid courage to get her through the evening.

Susan picks up the empty bottle. "No, it's all gone."

"I can get a bottle. What kind of wine do you want?" says Khan, the only person with transportation.

In unison Scotty and Paige say, "Cabernet."

"I'll go with you," says Paige. "I need more than one bottle." Paige and Khan leave the room, placing the latch to hold the door open so they can freely enter upon their return.

Scotty gives Susan direction to write the statement she had given the police and rehearse it. She needs to sound credible in front of the camera. "You know your boss will give you the authority to work the story."

"I'm sure as hell gonna give it a try! I'll be back. I will give him a call from the lobby. If he says no, I'm going to do it anyway. I'm just giving him the courtesy of being aware." Scotty winks at Susan as she exits the hotel room for a quiet place to place the call to her boss.

Chapter 66

Angela and Cheyanne are the last to leave the crime scene after the coroner takes away the last of the four corpses at the scene, all in various forms or decomposition. Angela and Cheyanne are both in agreement they have a serial killer on their hands. Angela, the lead detective, barely sits in her chair before she is summoned to the captain's office. No pleasantries, he weighs in with "What's going on with the case?"

Angela flips through her notepad and tells him every interaction and situation of the day. She smiles, confident of how she handled the events. "Everything is under control!"

"Hall, can you explain this shit!"

The captain points his television remote toward the flat-screen in his office. He turns up the volume; anyone on the next floor up or down could hear the television. The room spins, Angela has an out-of-body experience, and her face turns red. A reporter, Scotty Richards, is reporting what she witnessed at the crime scene. Angela closes her eyes. Where was she in the crowd? Angela panics.

She missed it; she missed a reporter at the crime scene. She shrinks in the chair.

The captain turns the sound down, throws the remote on the desk. "Do you call this under control?"

Angela blinks hard and fast to suppress the tears. She can't show weakness by crying. She already has an uphill battle; first she is a new detective, and this is her first case, and she is a female trying to make it through the ranks to captain.

"Give me a few days to review the evidence collected tonight. There were four corpses; our team needs to be able to identify the victims' cause of death and any connection to the homeowner or the current occupant. I know for publicity's sake you want to make this case go away, but I believe in building solid evidence before I make a move."

The captain's shoulders relax. "You have one week to figure out all the details. If I get any heat from anyone, you will be thrown off the case and a more senior detective will be placed as a lead."

"Yes, sir. I understand." Angela excuses herself and walks back to her desk. She spends the next hour typing her official report, checks for mechanical and grammatical errors, and hits submit. Angela reaches in her drawer for her purse and slams the cabinet shut. The cross-body purse in position, she leaves the station and walks to her car. In the car, she cries, defeated from the rebuke from the captain. Angela starts to doubt her new job and her ability to solve the case. Angela calls the only person who lifts her spirits in defeat.

"Hello."

"Hey, Daddy."

Angela starts to cry on the phone with the only person she can be vulnerable with. "Daddy, I need your help with the case I'm working." Angela tells her father everything that happened since their last discussion, even the rebuke from the captain. "Daddy, I need your help. I don't want to fail."

"I will help on one condition."

"What's that?"

"If you help me with the case I'm working, the death of Sophia and Dakota." Angela's heart sinks to hear the names of her family. Sophia, her mother, but Dakota her father's partner will always be family in her mind. "Of course."

The two work out the details of the arrangement. Oliver books his flight for the next morning for Charlotte, North Carolina.

In the meanwhile, Scotty sends Sebastian the news clip of her in action through text. Sebastian beams watching Scotty in action. The thought of the deaths of so many consumes him. Doris, Artie, who's next? An old school fellow, he picks up the phone and dials her number. On the first ring, Scotty answers. "Hello."

"Hi there."

"You've been busy. I liked your investigative piece on Sweetbriar."

"I got one person who lives in the neighborhood to talk. There are two others who are missing loved ones who want answers. I'm trying to decide where to go from here. I don't have a good feeling they are going to find their family alive. There were four bodies in the backyard."

Sebastian plays with his tie, not saying a word. A couple of minutes goes by with silence between them.

"Is Mother okay?" she asks.

"Yes, yes. Why? I feel as though the two of us have a connection. I know when something's wrong. What aren't you telling me?"

"Have you done a body count yet? You have four in Charlotte, there's two in Philly and two in New York. That's a total of eight bodies that we know about, and there could be others."

The room starts to spin as Sebastian breaks down the body count with both cases connected.

"Sebastian, who's next; me? You? Mother?"

"Don't worry about me and your mother. I will make sure she is fine. I'm more concerned about you. I need you to promise me you will be safe."

"I promise. I will talk to you soon."

"Of course, you will. Good night." They both hang up the phone.

Chapter 67

After June leaves the Loews, Brendon decides to start out bright and early the next day to meet his wife in Charlotte. He needs time to reflect on his life, marriage, future, the White House, plus his mother and best friend told him to leave town. He needs to start making his own decisions about his life and start thinking about his family. The fresh air and the wind blowing through his hair relaxes him. He misses his wife and needs to spend time with her. They need to talk about if the White House is what they want. He has his reservations. His life isn't squeaky clean, but he can overcome his challenges; he just isn't sure if he wants his dirty laundry aired for the public and his wife to scrutinize. Emily is aware of some of his indiscretions but not all. She would leave him if she knew how many women he was with throughout their marriage.

Brendon receives a call from Emily as she leaves the car rental area at the airport. "Hey, honey. I knew you are driving. Where are you?"

Brendon takes his eyes away from the road to look at his GPS.

"I am on I-85, two hours and thirty minutes away from Charlotte, so I am another hour and a half from Charlotte to Columbia."

"Okay, just meet Ian and me at the house in Charlotte. The drive from Columbia to Charlotte will give Ian and me time to get to know one another. I only plan to stay long enough to pick him up."

"Why are you calling him Ian? That's the name we gave him. Dave and Julia call him Stanley."

"It's a long story. As to the reason I am picking him up, Ian found out he was adopted and wanted to change his name permanently to Ian, which set Dave off."

"You are doing the right thing by giving Dave and Ian space." There is silence on the phone; the one wants to ask the other the same question but is too afraid. The two start to speak at the same time. "Honey, you go first," says Brendon.

"What will your mother say if she knows Ian is at the house? Do you want me to tell her or will you tell her?"

Brendon thinks for a few minutes back to the conversation he had with her earlier asking him to leave town. "Let's wait before we tell Mother. She is dealing with so much for this election."

"Okay, if you think it's best. Honey, I will see you in a couple of hours."

"I'm going to stop, gas up, and find something to eat so I may be a little longer. I love you. I'll see you soon."

"I love you too."

Brendon's thoughts take him back to the day he and Emily placed Ian in the arms of the social worker. This was the most difficult decision of his life, the day he lost all hope. He turned to destructive devices, escorts, booze, and drugs to give him peace for just a moment in time. His heart aches every day for the son he gave up.

A tear rolls down his cheek, and he wipes it away with his thumb while keeping his other hand steering the car. Maybe his life would have been different if he raised Ian, the hurt he over-comes with escorts and drugs. The start of his decline began when he handed the social worker his sweet baby boy, his firstborn. He went loose in the evil pleasures of society; the drugs weren't enough. He moved to alcohol and the mixture clouded his judg-ment and he went to escorts. The sex never meant anything to him. He loves Emily and cannot live his life without her. He needs to be better, to do better.

After Brendon hangs up with Emily, he takes the next exit ahead for a rest area. Brendon cranes his neck for a parking place, the rest area is busy, people entering and exiting, walking their dogs, not a care in the world. Ah, just his luck, a space in front of the building. He pulls into the space and takes the key out of his rented Ford Explorer, replaying the conversation with his wife in his head. His heart flutters thinking of seeing her soon. A short, scruffy guy walks in front of the SUV and catches Brendon's eye. The stranger's right hand is in his pocket and short steps match his five-foot-four stature; he uses his thumb to unconsciously flick his nostril while anxiously looking over his left shoulder. Brendon knows his kind.

Brendon exits his rental and follows the young man into the bathroom. The stranger is already at the urinal taking care of busi-ness. Brendon takes the urinal next to the stranger, both avoid-ing eye contact. They wash their hands in the sink next to one another, Brendon the first to speak. "Hey, do you have something to ease my headache?"

The stranger cuts his eye toward Brendon, probably reviewing his expensive haircut, Jos. A. Banks suit, and fancy shoes.

"Do I look like a pharmacy?" The man ignores Brendon, now concentrating on the option of air blowing his hands dry or using paper towels. He begins to air blow his hands dry. Brendon towel dries his hands.

"Sorry, man, I just asked for something for my headache."

Brendon dries his hands and throws the paper towel in the trash.

"I may have something to take the edge off. Do you want a pill, powder, or rock?"

Brendon, with his back to the man, smiles and turns to face him. "You know, I was talking to my wife earlier and just wanted to *smack* her."

The dealer reaches in his pocket and shows Brendon the product. Eagerly, Brendon peels two C-notes from his wallet and hands the stranger the money in exchange for the product. He places the drugs in the inside breast pocket of his suit. Quickly, Brendon exits the bathroom, his head down, bumping into a stranger entering the bathroom.

<hr>

The dealer, Bruce, needing another sale or two to make up for the loss of inventory, decides to hang out in the bathroom a little longer to push more product.

The stranger notices Bruce's odd behavior—standing in a bathroom, watching the door. "Hey, man," yells the stranger. "I need a quick fix. Whatcha got?"

Bruce follows his protocol; this is happening too quick and he decides he can't take the risk. "No, man." The stranger air dries his hands, turns to exit. "What do you need?"

The DEA agent smiles and reaches in his wallet for two hundred dollars, flashes the money to Bruce, and they make the exchange. The officer with drugs in hand places the tiny zip bag in his back pocket, pulls out his handcuffs, and wraps them around Bruce's wrists. He calls for backup.

<hr>

Meanwhile, in his Ford Explorer, Brendon opens the tiny plastic bag, licks his index finger, places it in the bag, and rubs the contents of the smack across his front teeth. His lips close in on his finger. He closes his eyes as the euphoric drug releases throughout his body. Brendon licks his lips. The sound of police sirens and blue lights blinking on either side of the SUV bring him back to reality. The senator for the State of Pennsylvania can't be arrested for buying drugs. Brendon hastily seals the plastic bag with the drugs, throws it in the armrest. Sweat rolls down his back and from on his upper lip. He uses the back of his right hand to wipe his forehead. The excitement of the police blows his high, so he cranks the engine of his rental, puts the car in gear, and carefully backs out of the parking space. The rest area now in his rearview mirror, he sees the stranger who sold him the drugs in handcuffs being escorted in the backseat of the police car. Brendon's suit sticks to his body, but he can't stop. He wants to get as far away from the horror that could have ended his career as a senator. He merges onto the highway. Brendon picks up the phone, needing to speak with the one person who can give him comfort.

———))•((———

The phone rings several times. Kyndall, on the phone with her sister, darts her attention to the incoming call. Kyndall was an only child, but Glenda came to live with her family when she was ten years old, when her mother's sister Eunice died from breast cancer. Glenda and Kyndall, two years apart, were inseparable. They dressed as if they were twins wanting to wear the same outfit. The family only had enough money to purchase a few outfits, so one had to wear the other's hand-me-downs. By the time Kyndall graduated from high school and went off to Temple, Glenda had gotten pregnant. She was embarrassed to tell anyone, so she went to the spiritual leader around the corner.

Most would classify Agnes as a witch doctor. On Tuesdays and Thursdays, she performed abortions out of the basement of her healing house. Glenda went home after the abortion and bled for two weeks straight. She passed out in the bathroom at work and was rushed to the hospital. The doctors performed emergency surgery on Glenda to save her life but informed her she could never have children. Glenda worked for a few weeks and saved up enough money for a bus ticket to Upstate New York. After living there for about a year, she moved to Canada.

"Glenda, I have a call from Brendon coming in. I have to go."

"What you are doing isn't right. Mitchell said he has been calling you and you haven't returned any of his phone calls."

Kyndall takes a deep breath. "I can't deal with him right now. He is being an ass about the entire situation. I have too much going on to have this conversation with him again. Sissy, I love you but tell him to stop calling. I'm not going to change my mind. Bye, I have to go."

Kyndall takes a deep breath. The past should stay in the past, she believes. She accepts Brendon's call. "Hello."

"Hi, Mother, how are you?" Kyndall is drained after the conversation with Glenda. "Mother, are you there?"

"Yeah, Brendon. What happened this time?" she snaps, breaking her thoughts from Mitchell to Brendon.

"I want to let you know I am on the road to Charlotte, North Carolina, to be with Emily for a few days, maybe a week. I want us to discuss our future."

"What about *your* future?" says Kyndall as she twists the cap off her bottled water.

Brendon says, "I am not sure I want the White House."

The water bottle slips from Kyndall's hand at the sound of her dream to win the White House fading, just like the water spattering on the floor and the cabinets, escaping her fingertips. She wasn't prepared for that response. "Why? What has changed?"

"Mother, nothing has changed. This drive has cleared my head. I messed up so many times and I am not sure Emily wants all the attention or the fallout."

"Has she said she doesn't want you to run?"

"Mother, to be honest no one has ever asked her what she thought. For that matter, you never asked me what I want. You always told me what you want from me or for us. And by us, I mean you. I just need to go to Charlotte and talk to my wife. I miss her and need to gather my thoughts. And by the way Emily is on her way to Columbia to pick up our child Ian."

"Brendon, you are making a big mistake; you are going to bail on me when we are this close to your seeking the nomination. No, this isn't your turn yet, but the vice presidency would be good for us, for you. We can get you allies on the Hill, people in your corner to get you in the White House the next election cycle. Son, we are almost there."

"Mother, give me time to think about it. I will be with Emily and Ian for a few days; let me run this by Emily. I want my family back, my entire family, including Ian. If I had to give you an answer today, it would be no."

"Okay, take some time to think about the family legacy and what you are doing to destroy it." Kyndall hangs the phone up without saying good-bye to her son.

Chapter 68

*C*hip strolls down the hallway of the nursing home toward his mother's room with half a dozen yellow tulips in his hand. He flashes Joy, the unit secretary on duty, a wide grin. He takes a deep breath before entering his mother's room, and the smile turns to pursed lips. Chip never felt close to his mother. He always brings her a gift, mostly flowers, to win her over, but to his dismay nothing seems to work. Her blonde hair is faded with more silver than blonde. Hands on her lap. Chip still in the doorway announces himself. "Hi Mother. I mean Megan."

⸻ ⁙ ⸻

The sound of Chip's voice makes her skin crawl, and she shudders. Chip is a reminder of her husband's infidelity each time he is in her presence. And on top of that she was forced to care for the bastard child that her husband brought home. Chip has not earned the right to let the word "mother" flow from his lips. For the last several years Megan refused to speak when he visited, always sitting in the rocking chair facing the window. Chip does all the talking; she just stares out the window waiting for him to leave.

Chip looks around the room for a place for the flowers, and he finds the dead flowers he brought two weeks ago. He carefully takes them out of the vase, not dropping any dead leaves on the floor, to the trash can on the other side of the room. He fills the vase with water and uses a towel to dry any water on the outside of the vase, careful not to damage his mother's dresser with a water stain. "Here you go, Megan. Aren't the flowers beautiful?" Megan cuts her eyes in Chip's direction. Chip follows the same ritual each visit; he opens the nightstand, retrieves the pen and yellow notepad, and places it on his mother's lap in case she wants to communicate with him. The doctors told him there isn't anything medically wrong with her; she just doesn't want to speak. Megan takes the notepad and pen and throws them both across the room. She lowers her head and closes her eyes—her ritual when she wants him to leave. He hasn't been there ten minutes and she wants him gone but he refuses to leave. "Megan, I saw another one of those images again. I don't know, something triggers inside me the image of the person who killed my father and appears on the face of the person who is making me angry." Chip swallows his next words he wants to speak. "I get angry and kill them." This is a secret for both him and June and not his mother. He isn't quite sure he can trust her, but she is his mother after all. She is playing games by not talking and he isn't sure why. "The image of my father's killer was very faint, almost blurry. The second was the outline of a woman's face with blonde hair." Chip paces back and forth, his mother's back to him, never seeing her face. His mother grunts. Chip stops talking and walks over to her. "Megan, do you need anything?"

That is when it occurs to him, staring Megan in the face, the image he has been seeing is Megan's face. No, this can't be. Could the woman who raised him be the person who killed his father?

Chip was a young boy when his father died. Chase, his father, had just turned the lights off in his room after he read to him. Chase read the book five times and after each time Chip would say, "One more time, Daddy." And on the fifth time, Chase demanded that Chip close his eyes and go to sleep. Chase turned off the lights; the only light in the room was the nightlight plugged in the wall. "Good night, son. See you in the morning." Chase closed the door behind him.

"Night, Daddy."

Chip, wanting to look at his favorite book one last time, picked the book up from the nightstand with his hand on the switch to the lamp and jumped when he heard the argument in the other room. Chip, a curious boy, dropped the book on the floor and raced to the door. He turned the knob to the right and slowly opened the door. He got down on all fours and crawled toward his parents' bedroom. He saw Megan stab his father; blood flooded the sheets. Megan, covered with blood, shook Chase. "Honey, honey, say something. Oh, no. I can't believe what I have done."

Chip witnessed Megan speaking to their neighbor Mr. Harold. Not wanting to get into trouble for not being in his room, he walked back to his room and closed the door. He climbed in the bed and started crying and shaking. The warm liquid was released from his body into the bed. Chip had been going to the bathroom on his own for about a year. Chip urinated on himself for months after the death of his father until he suppressed the image. It wasn't until now the images of his father have reemerged.

Chip realizes the image he sees is his mother, and he puts the pieces together. "Megan, I know it was you." Her eyes are sad, and tears flood her face and down her cheeks. The guilt and pain of that night overcome Megan emotionally; she cries and holds Chip's hand. Chip gets her a box of tissues from the nightstand. Megan opens her mouth to speak, but nothing comes out. In a low whisper, "I am so sorry. I did kill your father, but I couldn't handle what he did. We argued all the time." She takes several tissues from the box and dabs her eyes.

"Why did you argue that night?"

"Your father had an affair and you were the result."

Chip stumbles back on the bed. He always knew Megan never was very motherly toward him. "Who is my mother?" says Chip with a quivering lip.

Megan has held on to Chase's secret way too long and blurts the name without reservation. "Emma."

Chip sits in silence and thinks back to the night he killed Jim; she was worried about him as a mother would worry about a child. His heart warms. She is still looking after him, but he fumes that she gave him up. "Why did you have me?"

"I killed your father and Emma didn't want Harold to find out she and his best friend had an affair."

"Mother, how did you get the body out of the house? You are too petite to have removed the body by yourself. Who helped you?"

"Harold."

"He knew about the affair?"

"Not at first because he was away on business, but when he was around more often, he found out. I had known for years."

Chip stares at the back of his mother's head. He doesn't want to judge her, so he doesn't ask any more questions. The two sit in silence for an hour, when the dietary department brings her dinner tray.

————)((●)) ————

Felicia, a registered nurse standing at the door with Megan's medication, overhears the entire conversation. She knows Megan is a woman with secrets; she often keep to herself, never giving much information about her family. Josh, the activities supervisor, walks up behind Felicia. "Whatcha doing?"

Felicia jumps, clears her throat, giving her time to figure out a reason for standing outside Megan's door. "You startled me! You should know better than to sneak up behind someone." Felicia doesn't feel she needs to give Josh an explanation. She turns toward the door and pops into the room. "Here you go, Megan! I have your medication."

While Megan is preoccupied, Chip briskly walks out of Megan's room, and once outside the exit door, he vomits. Chip wipes his mouth with the back of his hand and drives back home not sure of what to do next.

Chapter 69

The hour-and-a-half drive to Columbia seems as though it was a five-hour trip. Emily bites her cuticles, thinking the house she is living in has four dead bodies in the backyard. She checks her GPS and pulls into the driveway. Dave pulls into the driveway behind Emily's car.

They both exit their cars at the same time.

"Hey, Emily."

"Hello, Dave."

"I know you are here for Stanley, but I can't let him go with you. He should be with his mother. If anyone should go with you, it should be me." Dave walks closer to Emily and rubs her arm.

"Dave, stop, you disgust me."

"Emily, I love you. Why don't you want me in your life? I am willing to leave all of this for you." He spreads his arms out to show what he would be giving up.

"Dave, I don't want you. I never did. Just leave me alone."

Dave blocks Emily from moving.

Ian walking down the street with his baseball bat in his hand runs into the yard, taking Dave from behind, swings the bat, hitting Dave on his shoulder. Dave grabs his left shoulder and stumbles to the side, then falls to the ground. "Don't you mess with my mother!" shouts Ian.

Emily screams. Julia immediately runs to the front door and onto the porch. Ian approaches Dave to swing the bat across Dave's head. Dave grabs Ian by the leg and pulls his legs out from under him. Ian falls on his butt; then his head hit the ground. The bat hits the sidewalk hard and falls near Dave. Dave quickly grabs the bat and pokes Ian with it, taunting him. "What were you going to do with this, kill your old man?" Poke. "After all, I am old, feeble, and slow, but I can beat your ass every time."

"Stop it!" yells Ian.

"Yeah, Dave, stop. He made a mistake. Leave him alone," says Julia.

"Stop it," repeats Ian.

"What's wrong? You mad you pissed yourself the other day? You didn't think I noticed." Ian starts to cry. "Big baby." Dave slams the bat on the ground. He hobbles up the steps to the porch. Emily runs toward Ian and helps him up. "Are you okay?"

Julia takes one step off the porch toward Ian.

"Julia, where are you going? Come inside; I need you."

Julia looks in Ian's direction; his mother is taking care of him, but Dave has no one. Julia walks in the house to comfort Dave, her husband.

Emily helps steady Ian and looks him over to ensure he doesn't have any visible injuries. "How's your head?"

"I'm okay."

"You stay here, I will get your bag."

"Okay." He smiles at his mother doting over him. He wishes he could stay with her forever. Emily walks briskly to the porch and yanks open the screen door.

She yells, "Julia, Julia. Where is Ian's suitcase?"

Julia appears out of nowhere. "Hey, Emily, you are looking well."

Emily searches the living room for any sign of Ian's belongings.

Nervously Julia rambles, "Dave is going to be okay. I was looking at his shoulder."

"I don't care about Dave and his arm, shoulder, or whatever. Where is Ian's suitcase? We are leaving."

"Why don't you stay for a while, have dinner? It would be nice to catch up."

"No. There is too much tension between Dave and Ian."

"I don't know what has gotten into Dave lately. Dave and Ian have been at each other for months, but it hasn't always been like this between them." Julia wiggles her toes. She can see the impression through her soft leather shoes.

Emily notices Julia for the first time, really noticing her. Julia was the confident one in college; now she looks fragile. I can imagine living with Dave can do that to any woman. Emily walks toward Julia grabs her arm whispers in her ear, "You really need to take care of yourself. Is he abusing you too?" Julia embarrassed shakes her head no. She can imagine how things look to Emily, she can't control her husband or her son. Dave leaves the kitchen and into the hall where Emily and Julia are standing.

"Am I interrupting something?"

Julia turns her head away from Dave, uses her sleeve to dry the tears from both her cheeks.

"No," says Emily as she backs away from Julia.

"I was just getting Ian's suitcase." Julia races upstairs, leaving Emily downstairs with Dave.

"Have you changed your mind about us?"

"Dave, stop it," shouts Emily. "There is no us." Emily fixes her eyes on her crisscross body purse as she adjusts the straps.

"Give me a kiss. You know you want me." Dave puckers his lips and leans in.

"What are you doing, Dave?" yells Julia, witnessing the interaction between the two of them from the top of the stairs.

"Trying to kiss Emily."

"Dave, what has gotten into you? Leave Emily alone."

Dave turns and walks back to the kitchen. He stops, turns around. "Emily, let me know when you want to be with a real man." He winks.

Chapter 70

Once Oliver arrives in Charlotte, he texts Angela telling her not to bother picking him up from the airport; he will rent a car. He knows how it is being a newly promoted detective and needing to focus on work, plus he doesn't want someone babying him. He can drive himself wherever he needs to go, including to his daughter's house across town.

Oliver drives down Angela's street, pulling into her driveway. He lifts his Samsonite Hardside Grey Spinner out of the trunk, places his carry-on on his shoulder, and closes the trunk. He wheels the luggage to the front door, going through his keys to unlock the front door. He steps into the house and closes the door, leaving his luggage in the foyer; he walks into the kitchen and surveys the disarray. The dishes from breakfast and the night before sit in the sink. On second thought maybe dishes from a *week* ago sit in the sink and on the countertop. Oliver takes off his blazer and drapes it around the counter stool and unbuttons the sleeves on his white shirt at the wrist. He rolls the sleeves up and begins to wash the dishes.

It takes him thirty minutes to clean the kitchen, wash all the dishes, wipe the counter and table, and sweep the floor. He takes a step back and smiles at the sparkling kitchen. Enough physical labor. Oliver opens the refrigerator for something to snack on until he can figure dinner out. There's a bag of limes, bottled water, and Dos Equis in the fridge. Oliver shakes his head; his daughter bought groceries just as he would have, nothing other than what he currently was interested in to eat or in this case to drink. He smiles. Oliver pulls out several drawers in the kitchen and finds delivery menus. He orders one large cheese pizza and one pepperoni pizza. While waiting for the pizza, Oliver unzips his carry-on and uses Angela's living room as a staging area to lay out the homicide he is working on. Oliver picks up a picture of Alina. It looks like an older picture, however, still relevant to depict her beauty. He shakes his head at the thought of Alina's family not knowing how their daughter died. Someone needs to find justice for this young lady; she was an escort but someone's daughter.

Oliver, deep in thought, doesn't hear Angela opening the door. The sound of her voice startles him and he jumps.

"Hey, Daddy." Angela gives her father a bear hug.

"Hey, beautiful. How are you?" Oliver kisses her on the cheek.

"I am doing well."

"It is so good to see you."

"You too, Daddy. Wait, you look different. Did you lose weight?"

"No, I just decided to be healthy." Oliver can't bear to tell his daughter he almost lost his job because he couldn't get a handle on his drinking.

Angela takes her father's statement with a grain of salt, not reading anything into his response. She walks into the kitchen. "Dad, do you want a water… Oh dear!" Angela hurries out of the kitchen. "You didn't have to clean my house for me. I would have washed the dishes."

"Yeah, okay," says Oliver, analyzing a photo from his case.

Angela chuckles. "What do you want for dinner? I haven't gone to the grocery store in weeks."

"Sweetheart. I took care of dinner tonight. I ordered pizza and you're not going to the grocery isn't entirely true."

"What do you mean? I don't have any food."

"Correct. You don't have any food, but you sure have plenty of Dos Equis and limes." They both laugh hard.

Angela walks back to the kitchen, opens the case of Dos Equis, and retrieves two bottles, places one under her arm and with her free hand pulls a lime out of its bag. She bumps the refrigerator door shut with her hip She rinses the lime, dries it, and with a sharp knife cuts the lime lengthwise and then in quarters. Angela opens the beer. She puts the lime in each of the bottles and walks back to the living room.

"Here you go, Dad."

Oliver reaches for the beer. "Thank you, sweetheart."

Simultaneously, they squeeze the lime into their beer, tilt their heads back, and take a long drag in silence. Oliver's eyes sad, he frowns as he looks at all the pieces of evidences in front of him but nothing connecting all the pieces. Angela speaks first. "What is all this, Dad?"

"This case is the reason I went on leave. I couldn't shake not finding out what happened to Sophia and Dakota. Alina was the intended victim, but because I was investigating the case, Sophia and Dakota's deaths were a clear message sent directly to me."

"Tell me what I can do to help."

"I came here to help you, not for you to worry about me and my case. All detectives have one or two cases they carry the heavy burden of solving after they turn cold. This is my problem, not yours."

"Dad, we are a team. I help you and you help me."

Oliver beams. He knew he raised his daughter to be someone

who put the needs of others in front of theirs. Oliver's chest rises and falls as he takes in a deep breath. "This half of the evidence is of Alina, the escort found dead at the Loews in DC. The other half is evidence of the blast where Sophia and Dakota were killed." Angela takes off her jacket and lays it across the tobacco brown leather chair. She walks over to the matching leather sofa where her father was sitting.

"As you know the medical examiner identified Sophia's remains in the explosion."

"Right. Why do you have a picture of a uniformed officer?"

"His name is Dennis Jones, a detective with the Philadelphia Police Department. Dakota and I paid him a visit, and days later Dakota and Sophia end up dead."

"You don't have authority in Philadelphia. Why were you there?"

"I had a question about the Grahams, Brendon Graham and his wife Emily. They were at the hotel in DC where Alina's body was found. The alibi for Emily didn't check out. I went to his police department to find out if they were called to the house or knew any helpful information. I talked to this guy, Detective Dennis Jones."

"What do you think his connection is to the case, maybe family friends?"

"Well, Brendon is the state senator and the family is well connected. His father, Wellington Graham, is the attorney general and his mother, Kyndall, has made a reputation for herself to be a bulldog when it comes to her son's career."

"Wait a minute, did you say Kyndall and Emily Graham?"

"Yes, the mother and wife of Brendon."

"The case that I am working on—the house where there were four dead bodies belongs to Kyndall, she is the owner, but she isn't in Charlotte. Emily is using the house to get away, as she put it."

"What is going on with this family and why are there dead bodies surrounding them?"

"Let me get the evidence in my case and we can compare notes." Angela jumps up and runs upstairs to her bedroom, then totes a large corkboard down the stairs with crime scene photos attached.

"Oh, good, we have shown and tell." Angela smiles as she props the board against the wall.

Ding dong. Oliver looks toward the door. "The pizza is here."

"Oh good. I'm starved." Oliver walks toward the door. He looks through the peephole and finds a pimple-faced young boy squeezing one of the zits on his face with his left hand while holding the insulated pizza carrier. He stands there waiting for the door to open. He moves to another pimple on his face. Pop. The red blood bubble on top of the bump and white pus mixes with the blood, creating a lighter shade.

"Hey, the pizza is $25.40." Oliver's eyes fixate on the bloody spot on his face. "Sir, I got two other deliveries. You owe me $25.40 for the pizza." Oliver shakes his head from side to side. "Okay, suit yourself." The boy turns to leave porch. Oliver can't take his attention away from the delivery boy's acne, but once his back is to Oliver, he realizes he didn't pay him for the pizza. "Son, where are you going? I need to pay you for the pizza."

"I asked you if you wanted it and you shook your head no."

"Sorry about that." Oliver reaches for his wallet in his back pocket and peels off $30.00. He hands the money to the delivery boy. "Keep the change."

———◈———

Tom unzips his stay-warm carrier and hands Oliver one pizza at a time.

"Thank you."

"Yeah, whatever," says Tom as he walks off the porch toward his BMW. He unlocks the doors and throws the pizza carrier in the backseat. He looks up at the door closing behind his customer. One more month to go of working this stupid job. His parents are trying to teach him a lesson about hard work and that money doesn't grow on trees, which was their response when he hit the neighbor's mailbox when he was drinking beer with his friends. His parents told him that he was going to pay for the damage to the car and replace the mailbox and stand. He is counting down the days to pay his parents back. He backs out of the driveway and heads to his next delivery.

Chapter 71

*O*liver closes the door and places both pizza boxes on the kitchen counter. "Dad, what took you so long," Angela yells from the living room.

"Oh, it was nothing." Oliver piles two slices of pizza on paper plates and takes them to the living room and doubles back to the kitchen for napkins. While Oliver is serving the pizza, Angela is adding more evidence to her board from a folder she took out of her briefcase. Oliver sits on the sofa and takes a huge bite of his cheese pizza and chews the greasy, gooey slice. "What are you adding to the board?"

"The forensic entomologist gave me a lesson on bugs, which was more than I ever wanted to know about insects, but Dewey was able to tell me information on the approximate time of death just by examining the gross bugs."

Oliver laughs at his daughter. He remembers how petrified she was of spiders growing up.

"So, I was able to put together Dewey's report and what the medical examiner filed as the official report. There were four remains that were uncovered. One male Caucasian, by development of his bones, was about thirty years of age. His body was buried the longest. The gardener's dog, Ace, dug up his femur. The second male was Caucasian as well. He was the most recently buried body. Dewey found the larva of Sarcophaga crassipalpis on the body. Because the larva had not turned into adult flies, which occurs about ten days after pupation starts, the death occurred within nine days of the body being discovered. We identified this victim as Jim Burke. His wife Susan reported him missing eight days before the body was found. We called his wife and she came back here and identified his remains." He was hit multiple times with a slender, elongated object. He took a beating with lacerations on his forehead."

"What caused his death?"

"Well, there were two things. First, blunt force trauma to the head. You can see these lacerations here and here. There was bleeding around the brain; the tissue around the brain was damaged. There was extensive bleeding that would have led to his death. His blood pressure would have dropped and decreased organ flow, which would have led to shock. Jim died because he was buried alive. He died from asphyxiation."

"Wow, that is a cruel way to die. Who would do something like that?"

"That is the million-dollar question."

"What about the other two bodies?"

"They were female and died the same way as Jim. They had the laceration. We did identify one of the female victims as Lily Abdallah. Due to the bone structure we were able to determine the corpse was a female, and with dental records along with the determination when she was found, we are 100 percent sure it is Lily's remains. Her brother came to the police precinct with Susan Burke. Lily is of Muslim descent and was were identified by her family. The beetle that was found was the hide beetle or the Trogidae beetle. Dewey said that this beetle isn't used as much in his line of work because the beetle can show up at different times, either first when a body is charred to eat the skin. But since they eat skin during the mummification stage, they would have shown up in stage five of the decomposition stage. We are still trying to uncover the identity of the other female."

"You probably want to have a conversation with Kyndall, but three of the four deaths occurred after she lived in the house. We need to find out if she knows about the first body."

They both eat the remaining pizza on their plates and down the remaining beer.

"Want more pizza?" Angela asks.

"Sure." Oliver stands and grabs the paper plate from his daughter's hand. He walks back into the kitchen and places one slice of pizza on each of their plates. He walks back into the living room and hands Angela her plate with a slice of pepperoni with extra cheese.

Angela takes a bite. "Pizza was such a good idea. I haven't had pizza in months."

Oliver concentrates on the murders. "Do you know what happened to the developer of the community?"

"Chip owns the community, but his father, Chase, was the original developer."

"Do you think the unidentified male is Chase? Based on the decomposing of the body, this person died over thirty years ago. Are there any records of his death? This would account for the time Kyndall lived in the community. Is she the link?"

"I haven't checked into Chase's death."

Angela rummages through her briefcase and finds a pad and pen. She needs to find out what happened to Chase. Next note on the list: talk with Kyndall Graham. "Dad, do you have Kyndall Graham's phone number?"

Oliver searches his files and rattles the number off to her. Angela dials the number.

"Hi, is this Kyndall Graham?"

"Yes, it is. Who may I ask is calling?"

"My name is Angela Hall. I am a homicide detective in Charlotte, North Carolina. I wanted to ask you some questions about the home you own here in Charlotte."

"Yes, Emily told me you would be calling. How are you?"

"I am well. Four bodies were found in the yard of the home you own. When was the last time you were in Charlotte?"

"I haven't been to Charlotte since I moved out of the house over thirty years ago."

"When did you leave your home?"

"I met and married my husband Wellington and moved to Philadelphia, where he was from. I am sorry I don't have any new information for you."

"Do you know Chase, the developer of Sweetbriar?"

"Chase and I went to college together. I supported and believed in him and purchased the home when he started the community."

"Does he have any living relatives besides Chip, his son?"

"The only person I know is Megan, his wife at the time; all three of us went to college together. Megan and I were in the same sorority."

"Does Megan still live in Sweetbriar?"

"No, Megan lives in an assisted living facility not far from the community. I forget the name."

Angela closes her eyes, visualizing the nearby facilities, and blurts, "Sunrise."

"Yes, the facility name is the Sunrise House."

Angela takes notes. "Kyndall, if I have additional questions may I give you a call back?"

"Of course, I always support law enforcement."

Oliver takes a long swig of his beer, pleased at the end of the conversation he heard. His daughter asked all the right questions. He didn't want to put her on the defensive, but Angela asked enough information to follow up on leads on her end before going back to Kyndall with additional questions.

"Ok, Daddy, let's talk this through." Angela starts to place pictures on the board. She scribbles Kyndall's name on a piece of paper, folds it, and places it in the center of the board. She places Brendon's name above Kyndall's, then Sophia, next Dakota. Alina's name goes on the board along with the DC madame. Both Oliver and Angela work in silence as they lay out Oliver's case. Angela places the links to her case on the floor. Emily at the center, the names of the victims in the backyard, Jim the most recent, Lily, and Chase and the unidentified young lady.

"Daddy, look at this. I know Emily said she just moved in, but the timing of Jim's death is close to the time Emily moved in. Look at the report."

Oliver uses his hand to speed-read through the report. "Okay, I will agree with you, but she isn't connected to the other murders. But that doesn't clear her from Jim's death."

Angela creates a list of people to talk to and unanswered questions. "Dad, we need to speak with Megan."

Oliver takes a sip of his beer. "Right." He takes a bite of his pizza.

Angela looks at her father board "Daddy, maybe Lily, Jim, and the unidentified young lady were caught up in the swinging stuff and were killed."

Oliver laughs at his daughter. "Swinging stuff?"

Angela laughs at herself. "You know what I mean. I do think that is another angle, the swinging community." Angela thinks for another moment, looks at the board again. "What is the connection with Alina?"

"Alina worked for Stella and she died the same night Brendon, Kyndall's son, was staying at the Loews Hotel."

"Okay, so Stella is supplying escorts to the senator and she ends up dead. You turn up the heat and start investigating the family, and Mom and Dakota die. Okay, Dad, my head is spinning. It sounds like there is a DC, Philadelphia, and Charlotte connection."

Oliver stands, reviews his board, and looks down at the papers on the floor for the Charlotte investigation. "Angela, I have an idea. Let's go and speak with Megan, Chase's widow. Perhaps she can give us some information on how her husband died and if Chase's remains ended up in Kyndall's backyard."

"We need to hurry. I am not sure of visiting hours for non-family, especially the police." Angela grabs her keys and a slice of pizza and the two head over to Sunrise Assisted Living to speak with Megan.

They arrive at 7:15 pm and walk to the receptionist desk, where Josh is posting the activity schedule for the next day on the board.

"Excuse me, my name is Angela Hall, and this is Oliver Hall; we are detectives." Angela leaves out the part that her father isn't a detective in North Carolina. They both flash their badges.

Felicia, leaving for the evening, sees law enforcement talking to Josh they are the only ones who flash badges. Curious, she lingers around the desk. "We are here to speak with Megan Carter."

Josh is the only supervisor on shift. "You have to come back tomorrow. Visiting hours are over."

"We just want a quick word with her," says Oliver.

Angela out of the corner of her eyes sees Felicia listening, her purse over her shoulder, holding empty plastic containers in a plastic bag. "Do you have a ladies' room?" she asks Josh, who points down the hall. Angela makes eye contact with Felicia and proceeds down the hall to the ladies' room. Felicia disappears and follows Angela to the ladies' room where they can talk in private. Angela stands at the sink reapplying lipstick. Felicia pushes each of the stall doors ensuring they were alone.

"I know Josh is being a hard ass, but he just want to protect the residents." Felicia places her plastic bag on the sink and moves closer to Angela. "I was bothered all afternoon when I heard Megan confuse to killing her husband, Chase."

Angela careful not to interrupt the flow of information, just listens. "Megan never speaks but today was different when her son, Chip went in to visit with her. She didn't use the pen and paper; I heard her confess to a murder."

Angela looks directly in the mirror examining how shaken Felicia is about what she heard. Angela turns around. "What's your name?"

"Felicia, Felicia Green."

"Felicia, may I record your statement?" She shakes her head, her hand trembles.

Angela not wanting the moment to get away from her ask Felicia to repeat her statement as she records. Towards the end of the recording Angela asks for her name, phone number and address. "What time do you work tomorrow?"

"I'm off."

"I will type your statement. Will you come down to the station around ten to sign the official statement?" Angela extends her card to Felicia.

"Yes, see you tomorrow." Felicia takes the card and picks up her plastic bag and heads home.

Angela waits a few minutes and leaves the ladies' room finding her dad waiting at the exit door. Angela fills her dad in on the conversation with Felicia. Oliver stops dead in his tracks on the way to the car. He beams, then he starts to bark orders. "You need an arrest warrant for Emily and Megan based on the body count in the backyard and the engraved trinkets with the names of the victims."

"You need an arrest warrant for Stella. I am sure your DA can make a strong case. I am sure her daughter knows where her mother is hiding. Dad, this can be huge for us to connect both cases." Excuse me Angela before I get ahead of myself, I need to place a call to my supervisor. He walks to the other side of the parking lot to place the call to Zachary, his boss. Oliver tells him all the details on his investigation of his deceased wife and partner and what his daughter is undergoing with her case in Charlotte with the same cast of characters, the Graham clan. Zachary agrees there is a connection based on the conversation and knows Oliver is trying to gain his reputation back based on his hard work in being a solid detective. He is sober when he comes to work, and he closes cases just as he did when he was in his heyday.

Zachary adds, "New York is upset their witness is gone in the wind. I can convince them to add pressure on their end as well."

"Captain, we need all guns blazing for this family."

Zachary makes a case to the DA to issue a warrant on the home on Stella, the madame of DC, for Monday. He then calls New York to find out the status of their case.

Oliver makes flight arrangements to leave Charlotte on Sunday afternoon, to be in position to witness the execution of the search warrant for Stella. Angela called her captain with her father on speaker, explaining how all the cases are intertwined. Angela insists the DA issues a warrant for the arrest of Emily Graham to sort out the details of the corpses in the backyard. If they arrest Emily perhaps, she can give them information on the mother-in-law. The captain agrees. He will work with the DA in Charlotte to give his support on executing the arrest warrants. Both Angela and Oliver are smug that they were able to connect separate cases with the same suspects who cross several states to commit crime.

Angela smiles. "Dad, when all this is over maybe we should start a detective agency. We can call it Hall & Hall or A & O Detective Agency."

"You are feeling the high of us possibly solving both cases. That's a crazy idea." Oliver chuckles. Both are silent on the drive back to Angela's house. Once inside Angela takes a long drag of her beer and eats a slice of cold pizza. Oliver scratches his head. "You know, starting our own detective agency isn't a bad idea."

Angela turns to her father and says, "What state will we start the agency?"

Oliver contemplates the years on the job; he is closer to retirement than Angela, plus the cost of living is higher up north. "I will move to Charlotte."

Angela leans over toward her father and wraps her arms around his shoulders. "I love you, Daddy. We will make an awesome team."

Oliver smiles. He can leave the department knowing he solved his wife's and partner's murders. Change will do him good. He wonders if CeCe would want to move to Charlotte to be with the daughter she helped raise. Oliver smiles at the thought. The rest of the night the two enjoy father and daughter time.

Chapter 72

$\mathcal{M}$orrison has his plan in motion with New York, and Sebastian encourages the captain to call the bait into the office to monitor his moves. Dennis sashays in. "Good morning, Captain." He takes it upon himself to take a seat without an invitation. "What's up?"

"Good morning," murmurers the captain, not a morning person. "The NYPD detectives have decided to question Emily as a person of interest in the death of Catherine and Samantha, the two escorts linked to her husband, Brandon Graham."

"Why, what changed?" Dennis leans forward, his elbows piercing his thighs. Dennis already knew the witness changed his story, but something seems different about the captain's demeanor. Dennis read people but this time the captain is holding out on information he needs to protect himself and Kyndall.

"The witness changed his story."

Dennis sits back in a more relaxed position, uninterested in the conversation because everything on Team Kyndall is handled by Gregory, who conveniently helped the witness to change his story. Dennis picks at the hangnail on his thumb. "Oh" He successfully pulls the piece of skin from the fingernail flicks it in the air, and watches as it lands on his pants. He brushes it off on the floor.

"Moore and Miller called the witness, and he recanted his statement. They went to his house to convince him to cooperate, but he had left town with his girlfriend and baby, leaving his wife behind. They are working with his wife on possible places where he could have gone, but they don't have anything now. So, they are pausing on Brendon but going after his wife. They seem to think the wife could have killed the two escorts out of rage. She was humiliated her husband was cheating and followed Samantha from her place of employment to her home. La Perla is a high-scale lingerie store, and there is a receipt of Brendon purchasing items from the store. They think Brendon purchased lingerie for his wife, she found out about Samantha, went to the store, and followed her home where Catherine was sleep.

"Moore and Miller are headed to Charlotte to speak with the senator's wife. It appears she is connected to another murder in Charlotte. She moved into a house where the gardener found bodies in the backyard. There are so many unanswered questions—we all just want to bring Emily in to sort out the details. It seems she is the connection to what could be a mastered minded crime she on her own or someone is framing her, we don't know. But she will be arrested within hours.

Dennis, never looking up from his finger, starts to perspire; his armpits soak his shirt. Dennis sharply looks up at his boss. "How are they going to pin random unsolved murders on the senator's wife? If you ask me Moore and Miller sound like amateurs. They are going to make fools of themselves and go back to New York with egg on their face."

"Well, I don't have all the evidence the detectives have, and I have to trust they will do a thorough investigation just as I have the same trust in my team." The captain squints in Dennis's direction as if wondering about his loyalty.

"How did the detectives in New York hear about Emily again?" Dennis isn't finding the connection. "If Moore and Miller don't have a witness to charge Brendon, how did they make the jump to the wife—because the jealous wife angle won't get a warrant?"

"Detective Miller's wife Maria is a therapist who is the counselor for Jim and Susan Burke. Jim went to Charlotte to purchase a house not for sale and has turned up missing. Susan went to Charlotte to find Jim and couldn't, so she called Maria from the airport. Maria gave Susan the address, and Jim's dead body is found."

Dennis throws his hands up in the air in disgust—all the pieces are random. "Captain, really."

The captain ignores him. "Get this. Kyndall Graham, Brendon Graham's mother, owns a home in North Carolina."

Dennis sits up tall when he hears Kyndall's name. He was unaware she owned a home in North Carolina. In the pit of his stomach he feels the story will get worse; for a moment he holds his breath, waiting for the other shoe to drop.

"There were four bodies found in the backyard of her house." Dennis exhales with a sigh loud enough for the captain to hear. "Kyndall isn't living in the home, but the daughter-in-law is Emily Graham, the same lead in the New York case. The detectives are flying to Charlotte as we speak to ask a few questions of Emily. The case in Charlotte may be a stronger case, so all the jurisdictions are working to put the pieces together. They may be able to close the New York and Charlotte case. It seems as though Emily may be a serial killer."

Dennis heavy shoulders weigh his body down. His body is lifeless. How will he tell Kyndall Emily may go to prison for murder? This will break her heart.

The captain's secretary, knocks on the door. "Come in."

"Excuse me, Captain." She diverts her attention to Dennis. "There is a homicide investigation they need you at."

The secretary's talking is a blur; he is still in a daze.

Not sure how he made it out of the building, he places a call to the person he loathes the most.

"Tell Kyndall I love her."

Dennis drives in the opposite direction of the crime scene to his home.

"I'm not sending love messages between the two of you. You can tell her yourself." Gregory asks curious, "What happened?"

"I fucked up really bad. The New York detectives are working with Charlotte police to pick Emily up as a person of interest in their case. I have been a detective for a long time, and it only starts there. If there are any other questions about Emily and Brendon's marriage and dead bodies, which we know there are, she can go to jail for life."

"Man, it's going to be all right. Where are you now?"

"I'm going home. I'm thinking about turning myself in."

"Okay, man, good luck with that."

Dennis places another call to the other person he loathes equally as much as Gregory.

"Hello."

"Meet me at my house in an hour."

"Sure."

"Do I need to give you the address? I suspect you already have the address. You know everything."

"Yes, I know where you live."

"How long have you been investigating me?"

"For weeks."

"I see." Dennis grows silent as he drives down his street, pulls into his driveway, and opens the garage door. He pulls his luxury car into the garage. Dennis holds the phone to his ear in silence as he wanders through the house to his office.

Sebastian puts Dennis on hold and places an officer distress call to dispatch before switching back to Dennis. He hears him respond, "I knew this day would come. I called it the day I pulled up in front of Doris's house how I needed to walk away."

"Walk away from what? What are you involved in?"

Dennis settles in his office chair, placing his gun and badge on the desk. He tries to unlock his personal revolver from the bottom drawer, but it doesn't open. He turns the key to the left, then to the right, then back to the left, and the drawer opens. Dennis is puzzled. Was the drawer open when he initially tried to unlock it?

Dennis takes his revolver out of the drawer and places it on the desk. He walks to the bar and pours himself a drink, Wild Turkey Master's Keep Decades bourbon whiskey. He takes a long swig, then drains the glass with the next taste. He pours another drink, downs the entire glass as soon as he pours it. The third glass he sips. He needs to calm his nerves. Feeling a little tipsy Dennis carries the glass to the desk, holding on to steady his balance to his seat. He sits at the desk and swirls his chair, his back toward the door. He takes a long swig of the drink.

A gloved hand reaches across Dennis's mouth; the index and thumb pinch his nose. The killer counts to 300, which means Dennis doesn't have an airway for five minutes.

Gregory counts, making sure his nemesis is dead. Gently he lays Dennis's head back and funnels the liquor to his mouth to resemble overdose by alcohol poisoning. He takes Dennis's phone out of his hands and puts it on speaker. The caller on the other end of the phone says, "Dennis, don't do anything stupid. I am ten minutes away." Gregory places the suicide note on the desk and ends the call between Dennis and Sebastian. He takes Dennis's pulse, faint but still alive. Gregory sighs. He didn't like the cat, but he needs to ensure Dennis is dead. He grabs Dennis's personal revolver off the desk and places it in Dennis's limp hand, Gregory's finger guiding his hand. The blast of the gun exposes a hole in Dennis's head. Gregory, knowing he only has minutes to escape, races through the back door, across the lawn, over the neighbor's fence to his car as Sebastian rings the doorbell.

———— ►«(◐)»◄ ————

Sebastian rings the door a second time. He dials Dennis's phone; the call goes straight to voicemail. Sebastian turns the knob to the door, and it opens. He announces himself, calling out to Dennis while walking through the house. Sebastian dials Dennis's number again and races toward the sound of the ringing phone. He finds Dennis slumped over his desk. He checks his pulse, none. Sebastian calls dispatch to report the incident, and officers are on the scene in minutes, swarming the crime scene. The next call Sebastian makes is to the captain.

"Captain, I have some unfortunate information to report. It looks like Dennis committed suicide tonight. There was a note."

"I thought Dennis would turn up innocent, but with the heat of an investigation on him, he must not have been able to handle the pressure. I am sorry to hear this news. When you are done processing the house, I will need you to report to IA on your finding. We still don't have the answers we need as far as why he withheld information about the case and what he knew."

"Captain, I will finish up here and sleep for a few hours. I haven't slept for twenty-four hours."

"By all means, I do understand. You haven't gotten any sleep since you started your shift. I will see you in the morning."

Sebastian sits in the driver's seat of his car and pounds the steering wheel. He sighs. Picks up his cell phone and gives Eliza a call.

"Hi Eliza, this is Sebastian."

"What's wrong? I can hear the crackle in your voice."

Sebastian hesitates, then proceeds. "Dennis, the detective that interviewed you, is dead."

"Dead!" exclaims Eliza. "What mess did he get himself into? How did he die?"

"He committed suicide."

"I don't believe that for one minute. He is too cocky to kill himself. No, I can't wrap my mind around that. He must have gotten in over his head on this Doris situation."

"There is a suicide note."

"Where is that Sean guy? Have you found him?"

"No, I haven't had any luck in tracking him down."

"Well, if you find him, you find Dennis's killer!" says Eliza adamantly.

Sebastian thinks about Eliza's statement. "I want you to conduct an eyewitness identification through photo."

"Of course, I want to get to the bottom of Doris's death."

"Okay, I need some sleep. I've been up for about twenty-four hours and will give you a call when I wake up. I will pick you up and take you to the office to conduct one part of the identification process." Sebastian can hear Eliza banging pots. "Did you hear me?"

"I heard you I need to go. I have some cooking to start. See you later. Bye." Eliza hangs up the phone on Sebastian with the phone still to his ear.

Sebastian backs out of the driveway and into the direction of his home to get some much-needed sleep.

Chapter 73

ave turns back the covers to his side of the bed, sits, slides his feet out of his slippers. *The house is quiet after that son of a bitch Stanley left with Emily. If he thinks he can run over me he has another think coming.* Dave tosses and turns and settles in a position with his back toward Julia. *What if I married Emily?* The two of them could have raised their son together. Dave drifts off to sleep with a smile on his face. He and Emily have a private ceremony in his parents' backyard. They recite their vows they created, professing their love for each other. "You may kiss the bride," says the minister. Dave leans toward Emily and their lips lock. Dave pulls away from Emily's embrace. He stirs in the bed, moving his position to his other side. He picks back up where the dream left off. "I will always love you."

Julia, who can't sleep, opens her eyes when Dave says the words aloud. "Oh, Dave, I will always love you too." She kisses him on the lips. His face resting on a pillow they now share. Julia kisses him on the lips again. *Dave can be so sweet.*

Dave moves closer to Julia. "I love you too, Emily."

"What?" Julia shouts as she rises from the bed. She turns and slaps Dave.

Dave yells, "What did you do that for?"

"You just said you love Emily."

"What? What are you talking about?" Dave is still in a fog trying to focus on what Julia is saying to them.

"You said 'I love you, Emily.'"

"I don't remember. I was asleep. Go back to bed." He turns over.

Julia picks up the pillow, hitting Dave repeatedly. Dave uses his hands to shield his face. The last blow Dave grabs Julia's arm; she loses her balance and falls off the bed. Dave turns back over. Julia throws the pillow on the bed and gets up off the floor using the edge of the bed for support. She walks over to the light switch and turns on the light.

"Turn off the light. I don't want to talk about this."

"Do you love me?"

"Turn off the light. I am tired."

"Am I your consolation prize because you couldn't have Emily?"

"I had Emily. We have a child together. YOU never had Emily. Turn off the light."

The comments Dave make to his wife sting. Julia starts to cry. She wails.

Dave opens his eyes and sighs. He gives up on trying to go back to sleep.

"Do you even love me?"

"Does it matter, Julia? I am with you and I come home to you every night. Is that not enough for you?"

"You never answered the question. Do you love me?"

"If I say yes will you turn off the light so I can get some sleep?"

"So, after all these years you never loved me. Do you love Emily?"

"Of course, I do."

"Of course, you do, what? Do you love me or Emily?"

"I love you both in a different way."

"What does that mean?"

Dave blows out a deep sigh. This conversation is going nowhere, and he is tired of being grilled. "What do you mean? Do you love me or Emily?"

"I am very fond of you. We are married, and I take care of you. But I love Emily. She is the love of my life. I fantasize about her. I want to hold her close. I dream about her on most nights."

"Get out!"

"Julia, I am not going anywhere. Get back in the bed and turn off the lights. I need to get my beauty rest." Dave closes his eyes.

Julia paces the floor.

"You haven't turned the lights out and you are going to wear a hole in the carpet."

"Dave, I want a divorce and I want you out of the house in the morning. With you out of the house I can bring Ian back."

"His name is Stanley and I am not going anywhere, and you aren't divorcing me because I won't sign the papers. Get back in the bed," says Dave in a drained tone.

Julia walks to her side of the bed and takes her pillow and jerks the blanket off Dave, leaving him under the beige sheet. She slowly walks to the door, wanting Dave to ask her not to go. Dave, not moving, yells to his wife, "Don't forget to turn the lights out on your way out."

"I didn't know you could be so cruel." Julia exits the room as she turns the lights off. She walks down the hall and down the stairs to the sofa in the living room, where she cries herself to sleep.

Chapter 74

The next morning Dave prances down the stairs with his suitcase in this hand. Julia opens her eyes and rubs her eyes. Julia sees Dave with his suitcase. "Where are you going?"

"You don't want to know."

"Yes, I do. You are leaving the house we share together with your suitcase. I ought to know where you are going!"

"If you must know I am going to be with Emily and our son, Stanley."

"Dave, stop this! Stop professing love for someone who never loved you. You raped her and that's why the two of you have a son."

"It sounds like you are jealous that I am going after my true love." Dave looks in the mirror in the foyer and adjusts his bow tie, winks at himself in the mirror. He pulls his comb out of his back pocket, combs his hair while using his hand to smooth any cowlicks.

"Dave, I love Emily too, but I am not giving up our life together to pursue her. She is married. She has moved on from the both of us. She has made her choice."

"She was young when she married Brendon; now she can appreciate a mature man like myself. You really think she can resist all of this?" Dave moves his hands from the top of his head to as far as his arms will allow his hand to easily move. He winks at Julia.

"Go ahead and embarrass yourself. I am going to make myself a cup of coffee."

"So long," says Dave as he does a two-step and walks to the door. He opens the door and disappears on the other side. He drives to the interstate and heads toward Charlotte to be with the love of his life.

Julia throws the covers off her body and slips her feet into pink fuzzy slippers. She walks into the kitchen and stands at the kitchen sink. She places a new K-cup in position and pulls the silver lever down. The needle pierces the cup, she hits the brew button, and the smell of coffee rises to her nose. She closes her eyes and takes in the aroma. She opens her eyes and looks out the window just in time to see her foolish husband backing out of the driveway to follow his love, Emily. A tear rolls down her cheek and chin, disappearing into the hot cup of coffee.

Chapter 15

Brendon pulls into the driveway and parks the car. He uses the key his mother gave him to open the front door. He looks around the house. Emily has done a great job setting the house up. He smiles. Emily is a good woman. He loves her to his core. She has forgiven him for all his indiscretions. He places his keys on the table in the foyer and walks into the kitchen for some water. He walks to the cabinet in search of a wineglass. Brendon pours himself a glass and takes a gulp—the warm wine flows through his body. He takes another drink, this time a sip. He walks back to this car and opens the trunk. He pulls out two suitcases and closes the trunk. He pulls up the handles on each piece of luggage and a Jaguar drives by him slowly. The driver and Brendon make eye contact as she slowly moves past Kyndall's house and slams on the brakes. She backs up in front of Kyndall's house. "Andy, is that you?"

"Hey, June. Fancy meeting you here!"

"Andy is your name or is it Brendon? I wasn't sure, and I left the hotel and came back home."

"You live here?"

"I live next door with my husband, Chip." June's eyes drift to the pavement.

"I am here with my wife, Emily."

"Where is she? I haven't seen her around today."

"She drove to Columbia; she will be home later."

"How late?"

"What do you have in mind?"

"My house is over there." June points to the house the neighbors call the Nest, the place where the swingers meet for parties. "Give me thirty minutes to get rid of Chip."

Brendon grins. "See you soon."

She takes the car out of park, presses the garage door opener on the visor, and pulls into her driveway and into her garage.

Brendon watches June until the garage door closes. He races into the house and up the stairs with his luggage. He takes the stairs back down to the kitchen, where he retrieves his glass of wine along with the bottle. He walks up the stairs to the bathroom and takes a long, hot shower. Brendon dresses in jeans, polo-style shirt, and loafers. He exits the house to find June, his new conquest.

Chapter 16

Emily and Ian pull up in the double driveway and into the garage past Brendon's car. Emily slowly pulls the car into the garage, thinking she is blessed to have a husband so loving to want to work on their relationship; He drove all the way from Philadelphia. She smiles. As soon as Emily places the car in park, Ian jumps out, slamming the door behind. Emily immediately opens the door and yells in Ian's direction, "Where do you think you are going? Help me unpack the car."

Ian stops and looks in Emily's direction. Without another word Emily hands him a couple of the bags in the car. Ian grabs the bags and walks into the unlocked garage door that leads to the hallway. Emily walks behind him and presses the garage door to close it. "You can put the groceries in the kitchen, on the left." Ian obeys Emily and places the bags on the kitchen island next to the opened basket.

"Where will I sleep? I don't want to be any trouble for you. I can sleep on the floor," says Ian head down.

"Oh no. Your bedroom is the first door on the right."

Ian's spirit lifts. His mother does love him. She gave him a room. Emily walks past Ian, and he follows her. Emily turns the light on and steps inside the room. Ian still at the door looks at Emily then into the room. Emily looks around the room admiring her work. The blue accent wall, the smart television with an Xbox and countless games. Ian doesn't notice the gadgets in the room that could keep him occupied for days without allowing the sunlight to touch his face. "What do I call you?"

Emily, not paying much attention, turns around. "Honey, what did you say?"

Ian grins that she called him honey. "What do I call you? I know you gave me up for adoption."

"What would you like to call me?"

"I don't know you that well, but since you are my mother, I probably should call you 'Mother,' but I know it would hurt Julia. She rescued me from foster care and without her I would have still been in the system until I was eighteen."

A tear falls down Emily's cheek. "I am so sorry. I didn't know what to do after the…" Emily starts to cry. "I don't want to talk ill of your father."

Ian snaps, "I know what he did to you. He never should have touched you in that way. He raped you and he isn't nice to Julia."

Emily stops crying, wipes the tears with the palms of her hands. She turns to Ian. "How do you know what happened to me?"

"I overheard a conversation between you and Julia. I was listening in the hall outside her bedroom."

"I am so sorry you had to hear that conversation. I have always loved you even though the pregnancy resulted from a rape. I didn't know what to do. I was too ashamed to report the rape to campus police because I didn't think anyone would believe me. Dave was a college professor and I was a student. He had a prominent counseling career and tenured faculty at Temple University."

"It's not your fault that Dave is a horrible person. I hate him for what he did to you and how he treats Julia. He doesn't love me. He bullies me every chance he gets."

"I know the two of you are fighting. Why?"

"I watch him lurking around when you and Julia are on the phone. He argues with Mother about how he wants you and she can't have you."

Emily wrinkles her brow. "What?"

"Dave wants you back and I am afraid he will hurt you again. Now that I'm here, I can protect you."

"No, no, no. You are confused. Dave and I were never together. He doesn't want me back. We were never together."

"No, I heard him say he wanted you. I don't know what he is capable of. He fights with me all the time. I think he wants to hurt me."

"Dave is all talk; he would never hurt either one of us."

Ian just says, "If you say so. I am not convinced."

Emily hugs Ian and kisses him on the cheek. "Go ahead, get ready for bed. It's late."

"Where is Brendon?"

Emily hasn't seen Brendon, but his car is in the yard. She closes Ian's bedroom door, walks downstairs, and puts the groceries away, looks out the window; Brendon's car is still in the driveway, but he isn't anywhere to be found. She turns off the lights downstairs, walks into the master suite, and gets ready for bed.

Chapter 77

Ian, staring at the ceiling with his right hand behind his head, can't sleep. He closes his eyes, rehearsing in his head that his real mother loves him and never wanted to put him up for adoption. He has so much energy he will never sleep. He gets out of the bed and puts his clothes on, laces up his black boots and makes his way down the stairs and out the front door. He cuts through the yard of a couple of neighbors. Ian climbs a tree and is perched there thinking about what it would be like to live with Emily full time. He glances up in the distance and sees a couple having sex. Ian's eyes are fixated on the couple. He has never had sex before. The window is open, and a man and a woman are grinding on top of each other. The man is on top with the woman's legs over his shoulders.

Ian leans back in the tree and unzips his pants and removes his penis from his Hanes black underwear and massages his penis back and forth. He pleasures himself and explodes in the air from the direction he was holding his penis. The gravity brings the creamy white goo on the front of his shirt and pants in blobs.

Ian wipes his hands on the front of his jeans. He turns his head toward the couple having sex and raises his upper body from the back of the tree. There is a third person on the other side of the room recording *I wonder if they know they are being recorded. Maybe they do.*

Ian zips up his pants and rubs the semen on his clothes with his right hand. The stain disappears into his black pants. He closes his eyes and drifts off to sleep. He hears himself snore and wakes up. He looks across from the yard into the window of the neighbor. The man is dressed and kisses the woman on the lips. He rubs her ass in a lingering kiss. They slowly separate and he walks out of the bedroom, his lover following. Ian becomes uninterested and climbs down the large oak tree. He places his hand in his pocket, slowly enjoying the brisk night air, still cool enough for a long-sleeve shirt. He approaches Emily's house, opens the front door, and locks the door behind him. He opens the refrigerator and scavenges for something to snack on.

Brendon turns the key in the lock and rounds the corner, surprised to see the boy. "Hey," he says as his head jerks backward.

Ian turns around with his eyes closed, anticipating the first official meeting with Emily's husband or one day his father. He could stay with Emily and Brendon and be a happy family. Ian opens his eyes and stumbles backward into the refrigerator. This is the guy he saw with the neighbor. "Hey yourself," says Ian with anger in his voice.

Brendon rushes toward Ian with tears in his eyes, arms open. Brendon embraces Ian, arms wrapped around his firstborn. Ian pushes Brendon off him. "Get off me."

"Son, I have always loved you. I think of you every day."

"Oh, were you thinking of me when you were screwing the neighbor? How dare you say you love me? Do you love Mom?"

"Who, Julia or Emily," says Brendon, confused.

"Emily."

"Of course, I love Emily. She is my world. I could not live without her; she completes me."

"Then why were you having sex with the neighbor. I saw you."

"What do you mean you saw me?"

"I was sitting in a tree and saw you and that lady."

"Why were you in a tree?"

"Collecting my thoughts. Why were you down the street with another woman?"

"It is complicated."

"I'm listening."

"You are too young to understand."

"Don't treat me like a kid. I know things."

"What do you know?"

"While you were having sex with that lady, someone was videotaping the two of you."

Brendon presses Ian for more information. "How do you know someone was videotaping us?"

Bingo! Ian's accusations are confirmed. "There was a beam of light, almost a flash that reflected in the mirror."

"What else can you tell me about who you saw?"

"The reflection I saw was of a man with broad shoulders, really tall, white. He wore a black suit with black tie."

Brendon is quiet for a moment. He leans against the counter, thinking. He reaches into his jacket pocket and pulls out his wallet. He counts out two hundred dollars in cash. Ian uses the back of his hand to slap the money out of Brendon's hand. The money drifts through the air until it reaches the floor. "I don't want your damn money. I can tell she loves you. You should do right by her. I hate you. I will kill you for hurting her like you do." Ian brushes his left shoulder against Brendon's right shoulder, causing Brendon to take a step back not to lose his balance. Ian walks up the stairs to his room and closes the door.

—————•《◍》•—————

Brendon paces back and forth, running his hand through his hair. He reaches into his jacket pocket and finds his cell phone.

"Mother, we have a problem."

"What is it this time?"

"One of the neighbors in Sweetbriar has a video of me having sex. Ian was sitting in a tree and saw it all. He now hates me, wants me dead."

"Oh, now you need my help. I thought you weren't running for public office."

"I'm still not sure if I am going to run."

"So why do you need my help."

"I don't want Emily to find out I was unfaithful. If she ever left me, I wouldn't know what to do."

"Well, that's the price you pay when you can't control your urges. I'm sure it will all work out for you in the end. Good-bye, son."

"Mother, don't hang up."

"I'm listening."

Brendon takes a deep breath; his chest rises and falls.

"You got yourself in this mess, you clean it up. Good night, Brendon."

"Mother, it's too late for me to run."

"Don't worry about it. I have it all figured out. Beau will announce he wants you as his running mate."

"Mother, can you or he do that?"

"Yes, in 1976 prior to the Republican National Convention, Ronald Reagan announced Richard Schweiker would be his running mate."

"Apparently, you have it all figured out."

"I do. Now tell me about this video."

Brendon gives his mother all the details as she takes notes.

"I will have Gregory book you the first flight out of Charlotte for the morning. I drove. Turn your car in at the car rental and get your ass on the plane and I will see you when you get here. Good night." Kyndall hangs up the phone without waiting on a response from Brendon.

Chapter 78

"Hello, Kyndall, this is Marjorie. I'm calling to give you a heads-up. I received a call from my nephew, who clerks for Judge Fitzgerald Scott. The district attorney called the office wanting to find the judge, and Timothy intercepted the call and sent the DA on a wild goose chase. This will buy you a few hours, but the judge is expected to be back in the office in a few hours. He went to his granddaughter's recital. They are wanting the judge to sign an arrest warrant for Emily."

"What is Emily being accused of?"

"Homicide. They want to question her about two murders in New York. The Charlotte Mecklenburg Police want to know about the four bodies found in the backyard of the house you own but Emily was staying. Once the judge signs the warrant, which he will, Emily will be in custody."

"Thanks for the heads-up."

"You're welcome." Marjorie hangs up the phone and Kyndall places a call to Gregory. She explains everything happening. Gregory sends Kyndall the email with the information she requested.

Just as quickly, Kyndall dials Emily's number. "Emily darling, I need to let you know everything will be okay."

"What are you talking about?"

Ding dong. Emily races down the stairs, opens the door without looking through the peephole.

"Hey, Emily, it's good to see you again."

"Dave, why are you here?"

"I thought I would check on you and Stanley."

"Where is Julia?"

"I decided to leave her behind. We didn't need her around to distract us. Emily, who's at the door? I heard the doorbell."

"Come in and close the door behind you." Emily walks a few feet away to have somewhat of a private conversation with Kyndall. "It's Dave."

"Why is he at the house? Where is Brendon?"

"I'm not sure Brendon discussed with you Ian is visiting. Dave decided to follow us back to Charlotte."

"I know Ian is there, Brendon told me. He also told me he isn't sure he wants to be vice president. You know what I mean; he has to do this vice president thing first then I can get us the White House. Never mind all that right now."

Dave places his hands in his front pockets, rocks back and forth from heel to toe. Dave tiptoes behind Emily, closes his eyes, and takes a deep breath, soaking up the smell of coconut shampoo. His warm breath on her skin makes the fine hairs on the back of her neck stand tall. Emily moves to the right.

"Emily, do I have your undivided attention? Are you listening to me?"

"Yes," Emily snaps at Kyndall.

"I've sent a car to pick you and Ian up. It will take you to the airport."

"What about Brendon?" Kyndall closes her text message icon. Gregory has already instructed Brendon to go to the airport.

Dave moves close to her ear. "Tell me the word and I will leave Julia."

Ian, curious about the voice, cracks his bedroom door. Carefully, he watches Dave taunt Emily. The sound of his father's voice churns his stomach.

"Stop, Dave!" shouts Emily, the phone away from her ear.

"Emily, I need you to pack a bag so when the car arrives you can be ready."

"Why am I leaving?"

The doorbell rings again. Kyndall for the first time is relieved Ian is at the house with Emily.

"Hold on, someone's at the door." This trip to the door Emily looks out the peephole.

"Who is it?" says Kyndall anxiously.

Emily opens the door. "Hey, Julia, how are you?" The two embrace, lingering longer than necessary in a hug. "Come in. Dave is here."

Kyndall throws up her hands. "Oh, Jeez! The entire day has been a shit show and I'm playing a starring role. Emily, you have to get them out of the house before the police arrive."

Emily lifts her head toward Ian's room, his head sticking out the door. "Ian, we are taking a trip. Pack your bag. We will be gone for a while, so get what you need for an extended stay." Emily whispers in the phone, "The police? What's going on?" She races to the bedroom, zips up Brendon's bag, and pulls her suitcase from under the bed, haphazardly packing.

"There are police in two different jurisdictions that want to speak with you. The New York Police Department wants to ask you about two murders that occurred in their city. Brendon was the last person seen with them, and they think you had something to do with the murders."

"Me? I wasn't there."

"They think because Brendon was unfaithful that you killed the two women because you were jealous."

Emily starts to cry. "Why does Brendon keep doing this to me?"

Ian, standing at the bedroom door, listens to Emily's conversation. He balls his fists tight, the imprint of his nails on the inside of his hand.

Kyndall knows the promise she made to Doris and she has to keep her word. Kyndall takes charge of the conversation after she collects herself. "Are your bags packed?"

"Yes, the driver should be pulling up any minute."

"Hand the phone to Julia; she seems to have a more level head than Dave."

Emily uses her shirt tail to dry her eyes. She walks back to the living room, extends the phone to Julia. "Kyndall wants to talk to you."

Dave looks at Julia and Emily and snatches the phone out of Emily's hand. "Hello, Kyndall, this is Dave."

"Dave, I specifically asked to speak with Julia. May I speak with her?"

"I speak for the both of us; you can talk to me."

"Dave, stop being a weasel, leave Emily alone, and leave the house. I can't have you there."

"Why? What are you hiding?"

"Dave, I'm only going to ask you once again. Leave the house. I'm not sure if you know who you are dealing with, but I'm not one to play games."

"No, I'm good. I'll visit with Emily for a bit. You know we have history."

While Kyndall tries to reason with Dave, Julia and Emily speak briefly. Kyndall receives a message the car has arrived. She hangs up the phone with Dave. Dave walks to the front porch. Julia retrieves Emily's phone and gives it to her. Emily pulls the door shut but doesn't lock it per Kyndall's directions; she doesn't want the police breaking down the door.

"Where is Emily going with our son?" says Dave. "Emily, where are you going?"

"There are lots of details to work out, but Brendon may be the next vice president. There's an event at Lincoln Financial Field, so I need to go back home. You can visit Ian. I think this will give the distance you want for him and Dave."

Ian smiles at the smug Dave; he finally feels like he has a family. He's with Emily. If Brendon isn't careful, he may find himself out of the picture.

The driver pulls away from the curb.

Dave grabs Julia's arm, pulls her to his car. "Get in. I want Emily back."

Julia stands at the door of the driver's side of the car. Dave cranks the engine and puts the car in reverse. He powers the window down. "Get your ass in the car."

Julia spits, "Dave, go to hell. I don't know why I even drove here. For what, for you to confess your undying love for Emily? I want you to rot in Hell, Dave. I hope you die a lonely man!" Julia storms off to her car and speeds down the street. Dave backs out of the driveway, passing the police as he exits the community.

The sheriff's deputy leads Angela and Cheyanne into the Sweetbriar community. They stop in front of Kyndall's house. Angela nods her head for the sheriff to make his way in the house. He has his ram gear, but his instincts tell him to twist the knob on the door open. He shakes his head. They are working with a cocky SOB to leave the door open. The police and detectives tear the house up. Angela, standing in the living room, is thinking like the detective she wants to be like, her father. The bodies were buried before the house was filled with furniture. Angela places a phone call. "Captain, we arrived with the arrest warrant, but Emily wasn't here. We haven't found anything other than the gray box we took from the house the other day. We are going execute the arrest of Megan Carter." Cheyanne and Angela gets in the car to arrest their next target.

Chapter 19

The front wheels of the Boeing 757 touch the pavement first; then the rear wheels. Mitchell pulls the eye mask to his forehead, stretches. As the plane taxis to the runway he thinks about the last conversation he had with his mother. It wasn't pleasant. She told him she couldn't visit as often because she had pressing matters in the States. Her sister raised him at birth. She could not have any children and his mother gave him to her. She was pregnant with twins and gave one of her boys to her sister. *She always chose him over me.* The flight crew opens the door and the passengers start to stand. Mitchell stands and reaches in the overhead compartment for his luggage. "Excuse me, sir," says the flight attendant. Mitchell turns in her direction and smiles. She points to her forehead and smiles. Mitchell pauses for a moment and touches his forehead and removes the eye mask. "Thank you. I know I look foolish."

"You are welcome, Senator."

"Excuse me?"

"I understand if you want your privacy," she whispers in

his ear, turns and heads toward the left down the aisle to allow Mitchell to pass. Puzzled, his eyes follow her as she stops, turns, and gives Mitchell a wink. Mitchell turns and exits the plane. He walks through the airport and down the escalator to the taxi waiting area. He stands in line with his luggage, checks his watch. The driver in the black SUV, three cars from the front of the line, recognizes him and cuts the line. He walks up to Mitchell. "Senator, why are you waiting in the taxi line? I can drive you. Where are you going?" Mitchell continues to stare ahead, not sure if the stranger is talking to him. "Senator?" The driver touches Mitchell's arm.

Mitchell's eyes move to the man's hand on his arm. "Yes," says Mitchell.

"Did you hear me?"

"I am sorry, what did you say?"

"Do you need a ride?"

"I do, that's why I am standing in the taxi line."

"You can be more comfortable in the SUV. It will give you more privacy."

Mitchell is next in line for the taxi but decides to follow the driver of the SUV. The driver takes Mitchell's luggage and places it in the trunk. Mitchell opens the back door of the SUV and slides into the truck. The driver stands on the running board of the vehicle and swings his legs in the vehicle, straps the seat belt across his chest. "Where are you going today, Senator?"

Mitchell reaches into his jacket and pulls out a tattered post-card of the Philadelphia skyline he had taken from his mother's drawer. The mother who turned out to be his aunt years ago. Mitchell reads the address to the driver. "Okay, the ride to Society Hill will be about twenty minutes. The traffic is picking up this time of day."

Chapter 80

*T*he driver pulls up in front of the house. Mitchell pays him, and the driver gives him a business card. "If you need transportation give me a call."

"Thank you." Mitchell puts the card in his wallet, opens the door, and exits the SUV. He walks across the street, opens the black wrought-iron fence, and uses the heavy lion knocker. He stands away from the door when he hears footsteps approach.

Kyndall looks out the peephole and immediately opens the door. She talks as she picks up her purse from the table in the foyer only looking up at her guest briefly. "Brendon, why didn't you use your key? Wait, I thought you were at the venue."

"Hello, Mother."

Kyndall stops and stares at Mitchell. Her lips purse and eyes squint.

"Surprised to see me?"

"I am and I don't do well with surprises. I have enough of those daily with your brother. So, cut to the chase, why are you here?"

"You stopped visiting so I needed to see you."

"I told you and sissy that I was a little busy with Brendon's campaign and I would visit soon."

"You have always put him first." His eyes narrow to Kyndall's feet.

"Mitchell, don't start. I don't have time for this."

"I will leave if you can answer this one question. Why did you give me up and not HIM?" Mitchell screams while pointing his finger in Kyndall's face. "I was your son that you gave birth to and you chose to give me up. I would have made you proud. Me, not him." Mitchell starts to cry. "I needed you. I need you now."

"Mitchell, stop making yourself upset. I made sure you were taken care of. You had everything you ever wanted. You went to the best schools."

"Mother, I wanted you."

"You had me. You had the best of both worlds, me and sissy."

"She always lived in your shadows. She followed everything you did. She has this memorial of you and the life of Brendon. I knew something wasn't quite right. She praised the ground you walked on. I asked her why she was so obsessed with you. She just told me that she loved her little sister. Then one day I walked outside and heard Miguel and Glenda fighting. He said that he didn't need a woman who was scarred. Someone who couldn't bear children. He walked out the door to his pregnant girlfriend sitting in the car waiting for him. I went inside the house and asked her if I was her son and she told me the truth."

Kyndall stands still, looking at the hurt in her son's face. *Maybe I chose the wrong son.* Mitchell is the one she should have saved, but she didn't know. She had both babies in her arms; she looked to the right and then to the left. Both babies stared at her; when she turned her head toward Brendon, she thought he winked at her. She glared back at him. She got excited when he winked the second time. In a split-second decision, she handed Mitchell to her sister. She was in the delivery room with Kyndall, and Kyndall knew her sister was happy for her but knew she couldn't have any children and wanted them dearly. "Sissy, you take and care for Mitchell. I kept Wellington away from the doctor's visits; he thinks there is a single baby."

"Are you sure?"

"Yes, when they release me, I will give you Mitchell."

"Mother, do you hear me?" The sound of Mitchell's voice brings her back to reality. Kyndall can't bear to go into detail with Mitchell on her decision to help her sister. "I didn't know what to do," she whispers. "I didn't know what to do."

"What are you talking about?"

"Nothing, Mitchell."

"I am tired of being your hidden secret. Tell Brendon and the world who I am or else I will."

"How dare you threaten me?"

Mitchell feels cocky; he has leverage and continues this tone with his mother. Kyndall folds her arms in front of her. "I will expose your secret. How will that look on CNN on the campaign trail? The mother of the vice president nominee gives son up to sister at birth." As he speaks the words, he motions in the air as though the words were being written as he spoke them. "Your perfect world will blow up."

Kyndall's right eye starts to twitch. "Mitchell, stand down, stand down. This isn't the way to get my attention. I know you are upset and that's why you came this long way to surprise me. I get it, but you don't want to go down the road of threatening me."

Mitchell observes his mother's body language and analyzes her tone. "Mother, I am sorry." He reaches toward his mother and wraps his arms around her. Kyndall stands guard with her arms at her side never touching him. Mitchell whispers, "I love you, Mother." Kyndall's phone rings. She steps out of Mitchell's embrace, opens her purse, and pulls out her phone. "Hello."

"Where are you?" says Gregory, sounding agitated. "We are waiting on you. Brendon needs you."

"Okay, I will be there soon. I had something come up. Hold on a minute." She turns to Mitchell and places the phone on mute. "Honey, will you call a car service. I need to take this call in private."

"Where are we going?"

"I have an appointment. I think it's time for you to meet your brother." Mitchell smiles. He turns and looks up and down the street. The driver of the SUV is still parked where he dropped him off.

Mitchell waves his arms back and forth to get the attention of the driver, who turns the car off and steps out of the car. "Yes, sir."

"We need a ride. Are you available for a fare?"

"Sure. Where are you going?"

"Not sure yet."

The door still open, Kyndall walks further down the foyer with her eyes fixed on Mitchell. Kyndall resumes her conversation with Gregory. "I have a problem and I need your help."

"Whatever you need."

Because of the fuck-ups on Gregory's part Kyndall needs to know that he can be counted on. If he wants to keep his position as her right hand, he needs to do this favor for her without hesitation. Without regret. Kyndall takes a deep breath, bites her bottom lip. Gregory on the other end of the phone waits for his boss to give him an assignment.

"I need you to kill Brendon at the event today." Gregory, drinking a soft drink, chokes. "Are you okay?" asks Kyndall.

He ignores the question. "Why do you want to do this?"

"I am tired of his shit, just fed up. This last episode is causing me to wonder."

"Wonder about what?"

"If I chose the right boy to raise."

"What do you mean right boy? Brendon is just as right as any other boy."

Kyndall, knowing that Gregory doesn't have a clue about what she is talking about, snaps, "Just do it."

"Okay. Okay. I will make it happen."

"Thanks, Gregory. I know this assignment is hard for you. I will see you soon." She ends the call, shuts the door behind her, and gives Mitchell a kiss on the cheek as she loops her arm in his. "I love you too, son. You will get what you deserve soon enough." The driver opens the door and heads to the Lincoln Financial Field to hear the speech of the President elect and his nominee, Brendon Graham. "Honey, I will send you a document. I need you to rehearse because you will be on stage in about two hours asking the people of Philadelphia for their vote."

Mitchell smiles. He will gladly take Brendon's place.

Chapter 81

Kyndall and Mitchell arrive at the venue, and the driver, Raoul, opens the door for Kyndall. "Can we pay you a flat rate? We will need a driver after the event."

"So, you want me to wait. How long will you be here? I can leave and come back."

Raoul was entertained with the arguing before but isn't sure he want that type of drama in his life.

"You can but I would prefer not to wait for you."

"Yeah, I would charge you by the hour. Our rate would be $36.00 per hour; $144 for four hours plus tip." He smiles when he mentioned the tip.

"I will pay $500 for four hours, which includes a generous tip. There will be confidential information that may be shared in your presence and I will need for you to not listen to our conversations. Also, you will have to sign a confidentiality agreement since now you work for me."

Raoul eagerly agrees to the agreement, he is trying to build his business.

Chapter 82

The plane lands in Philadelphia, the police escorts Emily off the plane. She turns to Ian and instructs him to go to Lincoln Financial Field to tell Kyndall and Brendon she has been arrested, they will be looking for her. Ian promises.

Ian had another reason for going to Lincoln Financial Field his new boss, Gregory had a job for him. But what Gregory doesn't know Ian has been plotting to kill his dad this entire time for mistreating his mother. Ian exits the plane and finds a taxi to finally destroy his father. He had to hurry he needed to give his first client a gun, she too had retaliation on her mind.

Chapter 83

*G*regory stands, looks over at Brendon, and wants to tell him to run. Gregory wants to run but he can't; if he doesn't kill Brendon, Kyndall will hire someone else to do the job. Gregory picks up the plastic red solo cup and tosses it into the trash near the door. He turns the knob and glances over his shoulder toward Brendon.

"Good luck, Brendon."

Brendon turns his head toward Gregory. "Thank you, man. It means a lot."

Gregory walks through the door knowing that the next time he sees Brendon he will be in the crosshairs of his rifle. He is an excellent marksman, never missing his target. He needs to go to his SUV to put the rifle together. It is broken down into several parts and stored throughout the car for the purpose of hiding it from officials. He needs time to assemble it and measure the wind. Gregory walks to the SUV with purpose to get his gear together.

Chapter 84

Mason walks to the far end of the stadium to the men's bathroom. He and Timothy exchange bags. Mason gives Timothy the cash for the rifle he smuggled into the stadium. Mason isn't sure how Timothy got the gun into the stadium and never asks him. He just knows what he needs—the gun to kill the one man who has made his mother's life a living hell.

Mason yearned for attention and received it from his underground connections, who knew and accepted him as Mason. They were his family, the family he never had. His father had rejected him from the first time he laid eyes on him. He saw the disdain in his face when he looked at him. And let's not talk about how he made his mother cry. It broke his heart to know one man can cause havoc on everything he touches, even a heart. Mason has no regrets; he is going to kill his father. Careful not to rush and draw attention to himself, he walks to the side of the stage left to the highest area of the stadium. He sits and waits for the festivities to start. His father will make an appearance.

Gregory, needing to secure his position, extends his index finger back and forth. He rests his finger on the trigger. A shot echoes. Gregory looks in the scope—a man down. He didn't pull the trigger—his target is down. People scatter as the second gunshot rings. A third *pop pop* adds to the chaos. Gregory uses his scope. He sees two bodies on the ground and the third staggering off the stage. The secret service run in to grab the candidate, Beau, but instead they shield his body. He is on the ground. The EMT team behind the stage rush in to usher the Presidential nominee off the stage.

A voice from the crowd yells, "My husband has been shot. Help me!" Julia knows it is too late for anyone to save him; the red blood trickles from the corner of his mouth and drips into a puddle on the ground, saturating the floor. Dave insisted he sit in the first row to keep the love of his life safe. She had already gone through so much at the police station with the arrest. He wanted to be there for her. The program he holds tightly in his left hand starts to release beside his body. Julia can see the tiny hearts around Emily's name. *He never loved me;* she thinks as the people run past her to safety.

A slender African-American gentleman wearing a white shirt, black pants, with a helluva spit shine to his cowboy boots trips over Dave's lifeless body. "Ma'am, I am so sorry, are you okay? Let me get you some help."

"I'm fine." Julia stands. The taste of vomit rises to her throat and she swallows hard. "How could I have been so stupid?"

"Ma'am, are you okay? You don't look fine."

Julia stares at the body. "He never loved me. He just settled for me. He always loved Emily." Julia shakes her head and starts to cry for the last time. She spits on his body and walks away from Dave, leaving him to fend for himself. Now she knows Emily is open to the possibility of a relationship and she will pursue the one person she loves unconditionally. She leaves Dave behind to start her new life.

In the meantime, Scotty places the small gun in her purse and Brendon feels a sting in his abdomen. Looking down at his bloodstained shirt, he staggers to the edge of the stage and collapses. Scotty stands over Brendon or this imposter, Kyndall did a good job getting a stand in. Secret Service now run in the direction of Brendon after Beau is carried offstage. They shove Scotty to the side, she needed to know if the person bleeding was indeed Brendon. Scotty badgers her way through to gain access to Brendon with her press credentials. She just needed a distraction to pull her gun out; thanks to Mason. This was the second time she needed his service and he came through. Donovan got what he deserved and so will Kyndall when she kills the one thing Kyndall loves the most, Brendon. Her prize possession Brendon was shot, death knocking on his door, she wanted to make sure he was dead. *You ruin me all those years. No, I have the last word.* The secret service turns her away Scotty gives up and blends into the crowd; she exits the arena and gets on a plane to head back to Atlanta. She needs to get back to work. No distractions.

Mason runs into the men's bathroom, where he bumps into his boss, Gregory.

Chapter 85

*G*regory perches inside the stadium; the cross marks Brendon's chest. Gregory's index finger is on the trigger. He stretches it out and bends it. Moves his neck to the right and to the left to release the tension. His right eye back on the scope with Brendon's body in his view.

Mason aims his rifle at the son of a bitch who makes his mother sad, makes his heart hardened. Both Mason and Gregory pull their rifles simultaneously, and their target drops to the floor. The crowd disperses. Gregory and Mason disassemble their rifles in record time. They throw their duffle bags over their shoulders and enter the men's restroom. Gregory already popping the ceiling tile up and storing his bag, Mason rushes into the same men's room. Gregory stops, one hand sliding the tile back in place. He sees Mason. "What are you doing here?"

"I need to hide this bag. I have a lot of heat on me."

"Here, hand it to me."

Mason's armpits sweat, and the back of his shirt is soaked.

Gregory places Mason's bag in the same ceiling tile as his. He jumps down from balancing on the radiator toward the window. "What did you do? What's in the bag?"

Gregory already know an amateur would have thought only one gunshot, but they were within seconds of each other. Gregory knows he fired the first shot and Mason must have fired the second by the looks of his gear. There is a rifle in his bag.

"I shot someone."

"Who?"

"My dad."

"You went through all this trouble to travel to Philadelphia to kill your father? You couldn't have killed him within your state? It would have saved you a lot of time and money."

Mason, new at the assassination business, thinks about what his boss said. Gregory, reading the body language of his employee, knows he is young, younger than he told him. "We need to leave the gear here until things settle. After the police investigate, I will come back and get the gear."

Ian pulls his phone out of his pants pocket and the face of Emily is displayed on the screen. Gregory, still studying Mason, glances at his phone and Emily's picture on Mason's phone. "Who are you?" snaps Gregory, even more suspicious of Mason. Gregory closes in the space between him and Mason. He tugs on his black leather gloves, ensuring they are snug on his hands. Mason starts to back away from Gregory and glances around the room, wanting to find a way to escape.

"I asked you a question."

"Mason. You remember me."

"That's what you told me but who are you?"

"I don't understand the question."

"You seem to be a smart kid. You smuggled a rifle into a public arena and you just said you killed your father. Don't make me ask you again."

Mason stays silent.

Gregory gives Mason another chance to tell him who he really is. "Why do you have a picture of Emily Graham on your phone?"

Quickly Mason responds, "Do you know her?"

"I do but how do you know her?"

"She is my mother. I mean she was my mother before Julia became my mother."

"What are you saying, kid?"

"Emily is my natural mother but gave me up for adoption, and Julia adopted me."

Gregory, shocked, stares at Mason, mouth open. "Are you Ian?" Before Ian answers Gregory now knows why Mason looks so familiar. He looks exactly like Emily. *Oh shit! I hired my best friend's son to be a killer.* Gregory just can't get out of hot water with Kyndall. Her grandchild is training to be a professional killer. Gregory backs down, and Mason's body relaxes. *Ding.* Gregory pulls his phone out of his pocket and reads Kyndall's message. "Thank you. You have solved my problems. I can now be free and clear." That is Gregory's cue to leave the stadium; he doesn't need additional heat from the Secret Service. He texts back, "We have a problem." One thing he knows about Kyndall—to stay in her good graces, stay ahead of the problem and tell her everything. He needs her to know he didn't realize who Ian was; he told him his name was Mason.

Ding. "What now?"

"Long story but I accidentally trained your grandson to be a hired killer. Remember when I needed help. He answered an ad and I asked him to help with a job."

Ding. "I couldn't care less…at least the bastard child has a career to fall back on."

Gregory shakes his head as he reads the message to himself, not wanting Ian to know his grandmother is ruthless. He will find that out on his own. Only time will tell.

"Cool…"

He places the phone in his back pocket. "We need to go. Promise me you will only work with me and not take freelance work from anybody." He wants to keep an eye on Brendon's first-born to ensure he is looked after. This is a hard profession and he wants to steer Mason to put his talents in other directions, like become a physician. Gregory owes it to his best friend to look after all three children but especially Mason. Gregory was instructed to kill. He doesn't need confirmation that he is an excellent sharpshooter. The picture Kyndall sent is of Dave Banks lying dead in a pool of his own blood. Gregory has taught Mason too well—with one shot he killed the one person who made both his mother's miserable. He is gone once and for all, never to cause grief to anyone again.

Chapter 86

*W*hile the event starts, security and the Secret Service monitor the stage. Brendon is sleeping off the Zoloft Kyndall instructed Gregory to give him earlier for his nervousness. Brendon lay down in the far room with a bunched-up jacket made a faux pillow. He sleeps until his mother wakes him. "Brendon, Brendon, it's time to go."

In a daze he responds, "What? Where am I?" He looks around the tiny room. The driver helps Kyndall steady Brendon. "We need to hurry," says Kyndall as she picks up Brendon's jacket off the floor and lays it across her forearm. At the door, she peeks her head out and looks in both directions—the walkway is clear—and they help Brendon get his bearings. The three walk briskly to the driver's car.

"Where to, ma'am?"

"The airport."

"Philadelphia International?"

"Small chartered airspace."

The driver drives in silence to the small airspace. Stops the car near a chartered plane with the engine already started. Kyndall breaks the silence after the SUV comes to a complete stop. "No matter what you hear or who ask you questions, you don't know anything. And in return I will take care of you. Do we understand each other?"

The driver nods. Kyndall, wanting a verbal response, repeats the question. "Do we have an understanding?"

Raoul clears his throat, "Yes, ma'am, I understand."

The driver is excited that he knows someone of power and influence and is glad to be a part of their inner circle.

Kyndall reaches into her purse, searching for his card, looking for his name. She takes out her checkbook and writes a check for $5,000 for the fare and his silence. Raoul knows the type of arrangement he is getting into but yearns for the excitement he saw outside the rich people's house earlier. He always wanted both his parents living in the same house. His father, a migrant worker, found it to be too hard to take care of his seven children and left his mother to take care of the kids by herself. The neighbors took turns caring for him and his siblings. His mother taught him how to be a man. His mother taught him how to tie a necktie. He is drawn to this woman; maybe she reminds him of his own mother, who died twelve years ago walking home on a direct road in El Salvador. Young kids were driving drunk and did not see his mother in the navy blue shirt and khaki skirt and navy shirt, a uniform issued by the hotel, her second job. She was less than a mile from the house when they hit her and left her for dead. The police said if they would have stopped and called for help, she would have survived. The police found who hit and killed his mother, but their parents were influential members of the government.

Raoul gets out and helps Kyndall out of the car. She and her guest have no luggage—just the clothes on their backs—and they enter the charter plane.

The driver watches the plane take off as he sits and thinks about his beautiful mother. No justice, no peace; no peace for him. He pulls out his phone and searches the Darknet; he has a friend who told him to call if he ever wanted to get even with the people who killed his mother. Raoul he never did anything with the information, but now he feels robbed of the life he was supposed to have with his mother. He browses through several profiles but sends a message to Mason. The driver reads his profile and finds that he is a lost soul too. He feels closer to his past through each case he closed related to this killer; but they have so much in common. Raoul pulls off and finds the main road leading out of the airport. He stops the car, reads the email from Mason.

"Job accepted. I will text you the address to meet me on Tuesday @ 6:00 pm to discuss the details of the mark."

www.ingramcontent.com/pod-product-compliance
Lightning Source LLC
Chambersburg PA
CBHW030350030726
47497CB00002B/265